Jeremiah Healy is "one of the best authors writing private-eye fiction today. . . . FOURSOME maintains the level that we have come to know from him. . . . Highly recommended."

—*The Blotter*

"That most sensitive of P.I.s, John Francis Cuddy, is back . . . an intriguing read, the sort of book that proves that the American P.I. novel need not have evolved into pages of senseless bloodletting."

—*Romantic Times*

"If I'm ever wrongly accused of murder, John Francis Cuddy is the private eye I want . . . convincing character studies. . . . Healy is flat-out amusing too."

—*Kate's Mystery Books* Newsletter

". . . excellent . . . By the time the case is solved . . . the reader has been presented with an elegant solution to a complex mystery. . . ."

—*The Toronto Star*

"Healy has created a winner—his most intricate plot to date. . . . What is so remarkable about FOURSOME is its unmistakable authenticity. A keen observer who misses little, Cuddy is a very savvy and likeable character. His witty sense of humor and insightful questions pepper the pages of this book. The reader feels he's there—alongside Cuddy. For a vacation to Maine without catching a plane, FOURSOME is definitely the ticket."

—*New Mystery* Magazine

Other John Cuddy novels by Jeremiah Healy

Blunt Darts
The Staked Goat
So Like Sleep
Swan Dive
Yesterday's News
Right to Die
Shallow Graves
Foursome

Published by POCKET BOOKS

For orders other than by individual consumers, Pocket Books grants a discount on the purchase of **10 or more** copies of single titles for special markets or premium use. For further details, please write to the Vice-President of Special Markets, Pocket Books, 1230 Avenue of the Americas, New York, NY 10020.

For information on how individual consumers can place orders, please write to Mail Order Department, Paramount Publishing, 200 Old Tappan Road, Old Tappan, NJ 07675.

Jeremiah Healy

Foursome

POCKET BOOKS

New York London Toronto Sydney Tokyo Singapore

This book is a work of fiction. Names, characters, places, and incidents either are products of the author's imagination or are used fictitiously. Any resemblance to actual events or locales or persons, living or dead, is entirely coincidental.

POCKET BOOKS, a division of Simon & Schuster Inc.
1230 Avenue of the Americas, New York, NY 10020

ISBN: 0-671-79557-0

First Pocket Books paperback printing May 1994

10 9 8 7 6 5 4 3 2 1

POCKET and colophon are registered trademarks of Simon & Schuster Inc.

Cover art by Punz Wolff

Printed in the U.S.A.

For Everyone Who's Shown Us Maine

Prologue

VIVIAN VANDEMEER STOOD WITH HER PALMS FLAT ON THE railing of the cedar deck and let the late May breeze from the lake riffle the hairs on her arms. Buying a new wardrobe for a cruise or the Caribbean, she'd often wished that she had fewer of those hairs. However, Vivian had to admit that the touch of the wind on them was one of the most sensual experiences she'd ever had alone, and she'd worn only a short-sleeved safari shirt over her slacks and low heels tonight just to feel it. The breeze also had to be thanked for keeping the mosquitoes away. Vivian was always amazed that there were fewer mosquitoes at Steve and Sandy's summer place in the wilds of Maine than on their patios ten miles outside Boston.

As the wind chimes tinkled over an Aerosmith song behind her, Vivian looked up the lake toward the lights of the village. Steve had cut down all the trees in front of his property—which caused a stink with some people, she'd heard. But the lawn and the brook that ran down the slope—especially with those darling little footbridges—made a perfect foreground for one of the most striking views she'd ever seen. The lights winked out as the locals went to bed early, except for the night fishermen, whose small boats moved slowly across the moonlit water, their little green and red bulbs on chrome stalks—her husband, Hale, called them "running lights"—the only indication they were moving at all.

A sound by Steve's boathouse caught her attention. A scratchy, swishing sound, like some creature moving through the underbrush near the side of the property. Using one hand, Vivian shaded her eyes against the floodlights on the deck. She couldn't see anything except the outline of the boathouse itself, holding the Jet Skis, the kayak, the canoe, the aircraft-engine runabout—that wasn't Steve's word for it, but you couldn't keep track of the technical names for his toys. Tomorrow they'd put on those half-wetsuits for water-skiing that Hale had bought for all of them, then climb into the runabout with the word "FOURSOME" stenciled across its back.

Foursome. That really did capture them. Steven and Sandra, Hale and Vivian. Only Steven Shea was "Steve" and Sandra Newberg "Sandy," while Hale Vandemeer would always be just "Hale," and nobody had ever called her "Viv" except her son, Nicky, to be disrespectful.

Vivian shook her head. One of the problems with hitting your late thirties was dwelling on the mistakes you'd made as a parent. Better to dwell on a great weekend at the lake, starting, as always, with Steve having to hop into his new four-wheel-drive toy to bounce over the rutted camp road— why couldn't they just call it a "cottage" road?—to the country store—which should have been the "general" store—for more wine and other things. When he got back, they'd enjoy a late dinner, with more seventies' rock from the CD player and a few—no, more than a few—laughs. Vivian smiled. Not a bad way to spend a couple of days at this stage of life, girl.

Then, thanks to a gap in the music, Vivian heard a noise from inside the house, and the smile turned wistful. The noise was the throaty chuckle Hale used to make when they were first dating. A noise he'd make before—she always thought of it as "copping a cheap feel," but of course never referred to it that way. Now she didn't hear that noise very often, except by overhearing it. When Hale was around Sandy.

Funny. Through the years, Vivian would have bet the mortgage—and a whale of a mortgage it was, too—that, if anything, she herself would someday have an affair with Steve. He had a good body and a great smile and a—hard to abstract it, really, but it was like he was always leaning forward rather than leaning back. Instead, Vivian came to realize that good doctor Hale was now making some unscheduled house calls on Sandy, probably using the guest room queen-sized so Steve wouldn't tumble to it. But Vivian had, and she marveled that her knowledge of the affair hadn't destroyed either marriage or even wrecked the friendship. It . . . amused her, really. Like a soap opera was being filmed, and she was getting to watch it from the wings, objectively removed from what was supposedly being portrayed.

Another sound from the underbrush, closer this time to the steps that led down from the deck to the lawn. Vivian went up on tiptoes, again shading her eyes with one hand. Like an Indian scouting the desert, she thought. Only in the desert you could see for miles, while here the brush covered everything. Steve said he couldn't take that out, or the state environmental people would scream bloody murder at him.

A third sound, and Vivian felt sure a bush trembled in her peripheral vision. She moved toward the corner of the deck, toward the sound. No need to be afraid; what wildlife she'd seen up here—chipmunks, raccoons, even a porcupine—had been more cute than scary, and anything really frightening—like a moose or, God forbid, a bear—couldn't hide very well in three feet of ground cover. Vivian thought it might be that mink they'd seen one afternoon, just scavenging along the lakefront, although what in the world it'd be doing a hundred feet from where the dead fish would be she couldn't—

The impact rocked Vivian onto her heels and over onto her back. For the second or two before her eyes focused, she was back in grade school, the day that Hale's brother had accidentally-on-purpose swung a baseball bat and caught her square in the chest.

Then Vivian lifted her head from the cedar decking and looked down. She saw the gunmetal gray shaft sticking out six inches between her breasts, the black plastic feathers on its end slanting toward her body. She couldn't place where she'd seen it before, then remembered. Hale's surprise toy last year for Steve. Then she felt a terrible sloughing inside her, and Vivian Vandemeer died without saying a word.

In the kitchen, a large wooden fork in his hand, Hale Vandemeer said, "What was that?"

Sandra Newberg said, "I didn't hear anything."

Hale came up behind her and whispered, "Didn't you feel it?," pressing himself against her.

Sandra stopped chopping the lettuce long enough to say, "Hale, this isn't the time or the place."

He nuzzled her ear. "It was, three weeks ago."

She brushed him away, getting a shred of lettuce in her ear and causing her to shake him off to shake it out. "That was when Steve was in L.A. and Vivian took Nicky to New York. This is a *weekend*."

Hale took a breath. As a doctor, you get used to being right, but he had to concede on this point. Vivian was on the deck, only a couple of walls from the kitchen, and Steve would be back in fifteen or twenty minutes.

"Sorry," he said, "but it has been a while."

Sandy sighed as Hale put down the wooden fork and reached for the tomatoes they'd bought at the Shop 'n Save in Augusta on the way up. She had kind of hoped that the rendezvous at the lake might end it gracefully for both of them, before Vivian or Steve found out how stupid she'd been ever to encourage Hale, much less go past that. Instead, it seemed to spur Hale onward and . . . upward.

Sandy made sure Hale had his back toward her, then risked a smile. No problems with the good doctor in that department. But her dissatisfaction with not having a job, and with the way Steve's job had been driving him, was no reason—well, no *excuse*—for what she'd jeopardized among the four of them. Of course, that was nothing compared to what Steve had told her just after her midweek episode with Hale. His little "secret." On the drive up today, Steve had discussed it with her, and they'd decided that they had to tell Vivian and Hale now, before things went any further. "Change for the sake of change," Steve had said. "Great," she'd said, thinking, he's quoting Chairman Mao, like dead commies held all the answers to life. Sandy sighed again. It was just as well to tell the Vandemeers now, so she could break it off with Hale before—

Sandy felt it rather than heard it. Someone on the deck or the steps, but moving heavily.

"Hale?"

He turned to her, the serrated blade of the paring knife dripping seeds from the tomatoes. "Do you think Vivian's doing aerobics out there?"

"Maybe you should check on her."

Hale put the knife down on the counter and moved out

through the swinging door of the kitchen. Sandy finished with the lettuce and switched over to the tomatoes.

Hale Vandemeer couldn't see anything from the living room of the big contemporary, even though there were three sliding-glass doors leading onto the deck and the floods were throwing light in wide cones. What surprised him most was that he couldn't see his wife.

There was no music coming from the CD player. In a conversational tone, Hale said, "Vivian?"

The center set of glass doors was open, just the screened panel across the opening. Hale went up to it and used his left hand to slide the screen to the left. He stepped out onto the deck, looking first to his right as he closed the panel with his right hand.

Another song started inside the living room, so Hale spoke a little louder. "Vivian?"

Turning to his left, he didn't quite understand what he was seeing, his eyes needing to adjust to the difference in lighting. In shadow at the corner of the deck, a body lay flat on its back, the arms out, the legs together, as though crucified horizontally onto the decking. Only the hair was brightly illuminated by the flood, the color unmistakably the one Vivian had chosen at her beauty parlor.

Hale took a step forward before he realized the shadow over his wife's body was moving, ever so slightly. He stopped as the bolt from the crossbow whooshed up and at him, punching him just below the sternum and taking him back through the screen door, tearing it from the frame as he crashed to the floor of the living room. As the last few seconds of consciousness washed over his brain, Hale Vandemeer thought, "Just two inches lower and I'd have a chance to . . ."

The sound of the crash made Sandra Newberg cut her left thumb with the paring knife. She was too startled even

6

to curse at it, just grabbing a paper towel for the blood as she burst through the kitchen door and down the little hall into the dining area and living room.

Hale was splayed on the floor, the mesh that had been the screened panel rolled over his right leg and hip like a partially closed shroud. But the thing that angled into his chest and his open eyes told Sandy that something she didn't understand had happened and was very, very wrong.

Then the figure filled the doorway where the screening had been, and the bow raised up.

Ten feet away Sandra Newberg hoarsely cried "No!" and brought her hands up to protect herself. The bolt pierced the back of her left hand and the paper towel wrapped around the thumb, pinning them to her chest as the arrowhead bit deeply into her heart, rupturing it and dropping her limply onto the polished hardwood floor.

1

THE GUY ON THE RACING BIKE MISSED CLOCKING ME BY ABOUT the width of the dentist's tool he had mounted on his helmet as a rearview mirror. He used fingerless leather gloves to shift through a couple of his eighteen gears, swerving around the abutment holding up its share of an on-ramp to Storrow Drive. Then he turned in his saddle enough to yell, "Fuck you, you fucking joggers."

Gritting my teeth, I mopped the sweat over my eyes with a forearm but didn't break stride. I'd learned that from the first two bicyclists, who pretty clearly thought that 4:00 P.M. on a hot Monday in June was wheel-time-only along the Charles River. Usually I run in the mornings, but I'd just spent two weeks undercover, playing employee for a high-tech company on the Route 128 beltway. The company thought it had a payrolled worm working his or her way through its trade secrets and siphoning them off to a competitor.

I generally don't like going undercover. For one thing, it cuts you off from most everything else a private investigator is supposed to do, like return phone calls and meet with people. For another, your basic mission is to get relatively nice people to like and trust you so that you can bag them or one of their friends. The company did cover my daily rate for seven days, even though they knew I'd be putting in only five, and the worm turned (sorry) out to be a snobby engineer, late of MIT, who decided industrial espionage would be a quicker route to her first Porsche. For me, though, the reverse commute from Boston thirteen miles west every morning didn't leave much time for running, so I'd been missing that endorphin high. And the schmoozing that goes with being undercover didn't leave me with much time for anything else. Including Nancy Meagher.

I'd finished with the high-tech assignment that morning, then spent most of the afternoon in my office opposite the Park Street subway station, catching up on the crapola paperwork that seems to breed in place when you aren't pushing it every day. Nancy was about to start a long conspiracy trial for the Suffolk County District Attorney's office, but she promised me a home-cooked meal at her place in South Boston that night. I figured four miles along the river would vent some of the tension and pressure that had accumulated over the last few weeks. So, I laced up the shoes, pulled on the shorts, and tugged over my head the T-shirt Nancy had given me last Christmas and I'd worn running the Boston marathon two months before. Unfortunately, the bikes turned out to be just the tip of the iceberg.

A Metropolitan District Commission crew was trying to clear a sewer line. They wore surgical masks, like earthquake relief workers excavating collapsed buildings. With both temperature and humidity well past eighty, the cloying stink stayed strong for another hundred yards.

Half a mile after the sewer line, a cluster of Boston University students sat near the river's edge, smashing wine bottles against the rocks. It looked like the collected empties of a four-year career, the kids drinking and cursing and laughing at their cleverness. You think about stopping the party, but there were enough of them that you'd have to hurt a few, and at least one would dimly recall a television bar scene where somebody came after somebody else with the neck of a broken bottle.

A mile farther on, another crew, this time road workers, had traffic backed up on Storrow while they jackhammered about an acre of macadam into rubble. The car horns nearly drowned out the jackhammers. Nearly.

But the worst, that was saved for the last quarter mile. A sour old man in a Kangol cap and hiking staff and cigar broader than the staff let his Doberman off the leash just as I was passing them by a respectful lateral margin. The Doberman's head flashed up, I tried to dodge him, and his jaws snapped shut on the tail of my T-shirt, wrenching it away from me.

I stopped and looked down at what was left of the shirt. The rending went diagonally through the BODY BY NAUTILUS, BRAIN BY MATTEL legend on it.

Then I looked over as his dog dropped the rest of the thing at his owner's feet.

The man snugged down the Kangol cap and brandished the hiking staff like a lance. Around the cigar, he said, "There's worse where that came from, too."

I shook my head and decided to walk the rest of the way home. Slowly.

I parked my old silver Prelude on the nonstreet that backs toward the Massachusetts Turnpike. The Winecellar of Silene is a terrific store next to the University Club on Stuart Street. They cater mainly to an upscale yuppie crowd, but they know a lot about the grapes and enough about me to recommend something for ten bucks that tastes twice as good as something costing three times as much in most restaurants.

Rubén the manager caught my eye as I came through the door. The features around his brown eyes tightened.

"John, you okay?"

I checked my clothes. I'd showered and put on a polo shirt and a pair of khaki pants over old running shoes. The humidity made the shirt cling a little, but on the whole I thought I looked pretty presentable.

Rubén said, "You look kind of . . . keyed up."

"It's been a tough day."

"We can deal with that. Red or white?"

"Both."

Rubén nodded. "Just be sure to drink them on different nights, huh?"

I smiled and nodded back.

When I got out to the car, the orange cardboard under my windshield wiper reminded me that I'd forgotten to feed the meter.

I inched through bumper-to-bumper traffic toward Nancy's neighborhood. Just before the Central Artery, a derelict black man with a paper bag crimped around a bottle of something sat spraddle-legged against the wall of a warehouse. He glanced up as a statuesque black in a bright red dress, high heels, and a shoulder bag strutted past him. The derelict said, "Norman, boy. Is that you?," and cackled as the tall person picked up his or her pace and never looked back.

On the South Boston side of the Artery, Broadway was choked with people double-parked and just leaning into driver's sides, talking, while cars tried to slalom around them. I'd grown up in Southie and understood the community exchange function of basically blue-collar folks who'd been at work when most white-collars are just getting out of bed, but it was the perfect close to a frustrating day.

12

I finally got to Nancy's block off L Street and left the Prelude four doors down from her building. It's a three-decker owned by a Boston Police family, Nancy renting the top floor. They're pleased to see a neighborhood girl doing well as an assistant DA, and she's pleased to have the incremental security the Lynches represent.

The humidity was making me sweat from just carrying the bag Rubén had filled with a Rafanelli zinfandel and a chilled Waterbrook chardonnay. A drop fell off my chin and into the bag as I pressed Nancy's bell. A minute later the door opened, and my thoughts caught for just a beat, the way they always do when I first see her.

I could show you a photograph of Ms. Meagher, and you'd start by saying, "Smart. Professional woman, right?" Then you'd probably notice some specifics: the nicely spaced eyes, the black hair, the wide mouth. If the camera was good enough, you might pick up the blue in her eyes that owed nothing to contact lenses and the smattering of freckles across the bridge of her nose. Eventually, you'd appreciate how the eyes kept your attention, and the hair framed the face, and the teeth seemed so even if an inviting smile happened to spread the mouth even wider.

"John?"

"Sorry, just daydreaming a little."

She pushed up the sleeves of an old flannel shirt and peeked over the edge of the Winecellar bag. "Two bottles on a work night?"

"We can pick one, save the other for another time."

Nancy heard something in my voice and pushed on her sleeves some more. "Sure. Come on up."

She took the bag from me. I followed her rump as it swayed fetchingly under tennis shorts with the hem turned up once. At the second-floor landing, Drew Lynch opened his door and nodded to me. Just making sure Nancy's company was expected.

The third-floor door was open, and Nancy's cat, Renfield, scuttled out to greet us. The little gray tiger had needed an operation on both back legs, which, nearly a month later, were still crooked and healing. However, he didn't seem to be in any pain, just unable to launch himself from a crouch into a jump.

Renfield rubbed against my legs and purred, then butted his head into my shin until I bent down and picked him up. He sensed something and struggled until I set him down gently, front legs first, then rear ones when he seemed steady.

Nancy put the wine on the kitchen table. "Even the cat can tell."

"Tell what?" I said, a little too sharply.

Renfield ran sideways out of the kitchen, his clawless front paws digging hard at the linoleum, his rear legs trying to come alongside like a skidding car on a patch of ice.

I took a breath. "Didn't mean to scare the cat."

"And if you're scaring me?"

Something from the sea was crackling on the stove behind her. I lowered my voice. "Let's open the wine. The white's a chardonnay."

Nancy turned down the gas under a covered pan. "So long as we talk over it."

I popped the cork and poured into a pair of tulip-shaped glasses. We moved to the front of the apartment, taking floor cushions in Nancy's living room. The television was on, the sound off. The screen showed a much-used clip of the troops coming back from Desert Storm being welcomed by a big crowd at an airport. The civilians were cheering and beaming, the soldiers looking as bewildered as the Vietnam vets from my era felt betrayed.

Nancy clicked off the set, then sat cross-legged, elbow on the glass-topped coffee table. I leaned against the wooden half-moon seat built into her small bay window. The undercover job had been outside Nancy's jurisdiction, so I'd been able to tell her some of it and now was able to fill in most of the rest. Then I got to the part I didn't like.

The glass of wine stopped halfway to her lips. "They're not going to prosecute this woman?"

"No. The general counsel said it would be 'too difficult.' "

"Meaning too much bad PR."

"Probably. The head of security out there is going to take early retirement as it is."

"And the company doesn't want the fumes from this to waft back to its customer base."

"That's right," I said.

"So, the engineer can go on to her next job and play Mata Hari again."

"No."

"No?"

"The company had a sit-down with her and her lawyer and me. Very fruitful. The general counsel said he wouldn't pursue any formal remedies, and she gave the company the kind of letter, signed by her and witnessed by her lawyer, that will be trotted out if she ever uses the company as a reference in the future."

Nancy took a sip of wine. "That means she just doesn't use *this* company as a reference."

"It's her first job out of school. Tough to leave it off the résumé."

"She says to the next employer, 'Oh, but with the economy and all, I've just been twiddling my thumbs these last months.' "

I shook my head. "I guess so."

Nancy set down her glass. "But that's not all that's bothering you, is it?"

"No."

"So, let's have it."

I told her how tiresome the high-tech job had been, how badly the run had gone, how aggravating the traffic had been.

Nancy said, "You just need a change of scenery."

She said it lightly, just the trace of a smile at the corners of her lips, as though she were trying to start the evening all over again at her front door.

"What do you mean, Nance?"

"You're just a little burned out, John Francis Cuddy. You don't usually feel that way, because of how your job works. Generally, you get to do different things every day, variety keeping the boredom at bay. The problem is that you're just a little sick of your surroundings. You need to get away."

I tried for the trace of a smile, too. "With you?"

A frown. "No chance. With this conspiracy trial coming up, I've got to work, even the weekend."

"I'm not really up for a solo vacation."

She reached into a pocket of her shorts, producing a pink telephone message slip. "I got a call from a classmate of mine today."

"From New England?"

"Right. After law school, he went up to Maine."

"Why was he calling you?"

"He's got a heavy case, and he needs some investigation work done."

"Pro bono."

"Uh-unh. This client is heeled and facing life in the slam. He'll be happy to double your daily rate for the inconvenience of visiting the hinterlands."

"Nance, I'm not licensed in 'the hinterlands.' "

"Gil said he could take care of that."

"Gil?"

"My classmate. His last name's spelled L-A-C-O-U-T-U-R-E, but he pronounces it 'Luh-*coo*-ter.' "

"Your classmate's a criminal defense lawyer who can get me waived in by whatever board regulates private investigators in Maine?"

"That's what he said. He really needs somebody who's licensed down here more."

I stopped for a minute. "Who's his client?"

The trace smile again. "Steven Shea."

About all I'd had time to do during the undercover assignment was watch broadcast news, and Shea had been on every channel the prior week. "The defendant in The Foursome case."

"It would be a good one for you. Take a few days up on—it's spelled M-A-R-S-E-I-L-L-E-S, but they pronounce it 'Marcel's'—Pond, then spend most of your time down here looking into the two couples, where Gil really needs the help."

"They were neighbors out by Calem, right?"

"Easily accessible via Route 128."

"Not a selling point right now."

Nancy took a little more wine. "John, you could use the change of pace. It'd be like a paid vacation."

I looked at her, message slip in her free hand, the soft sell of the brass ring. Generally, Nancy couldn't help me much with my business without conflicting her own job, which would mean trouble with both her boss and the Board of Bar Overseers that regulates all attorneys in the state. I knew she'd like the fact that she could give me this one. Also, with her on the conspiracy case, we wouldn't be seeing much of each other for a while. And Nancy was probably right about the change of pace. The clean air and easy life of Maine started looking better and better.

I said, "That's only part of the solution."

"Only part?"

"I realized today that not being able to run has left me depleted of endorphins."

"Endorphins. You mean like from exercise?"

"Right."

Nancy finished her wine and knee-walked over to me,

17

having to lean down just a little to touch my forehead with her lips. "Does that mean you want to have dinner before or after we make love?"

I kissed her neck. "How about in between?"

Nancy used the nails of three fingers to tilt my chin up toward her. "Ever the optimist," she said softly.

There are more graveyards in Boston than even the popular tourist trolleys can cover in a month. The most famous is Old Granary, across and down from my office building on Tremont Street. Old Granary, begun in the seventeenth century on the part of the Boston Common used for keeping grain, was originally supposed to be the overflow field for King's Chapel, where they still have black iron fencing around the well used to dispose of newborns when infant mortality was a given condition instead of a debated statistic. Now Old Granary is better known, the final resting place of Samuel Adams, Paul Revere, and many others. But the most important graveyard in Boston sits on a slope of land in Southie, overlooking the harbor. It's green for five months a year, brown for four, and more or less white for the remaining three. It has mothers smothered by dead-end jobs and fathers drowned by alcohol. It has daughters beaten by abusive husbands in squalid tenements and sons dropped by enemy bullets in foreign wars. And it has one wife. Elizabeth Mary Devlin Cuddy.

I laid the roses that morning at an angle to her stone, the blooms toward the head.

Roses. What's the occasion?

"I'm heading north for a while, Beth."

What's north?

"A case Nancy's gotten for me. A guy accused of killing his wife and another couple at a summer place in Maine."

A pause. *And you'll be representing the guy?*

18

"Not exactly. If I take the case, I'll be working for his lawyer."

Why do they think he did it?

"I've only seen the TV coverage, but apparently The Foursome did everything together."

Another pause. *Everything?*

I couldn't stop the smile. "You know how slow I am about that sort of thing, Beth."

And here I always thought you were a child of the sixties, John.

"I was a college student in the sixties. That makes me a child of the fifties. Hell, it was 1983 before I realized that Eleanor Rigby was waiting for Father McKenzie."

Good line. Pity to waste it on me.

"I've wasted a lot of things in life, kid. None of them ever on you."

I looked down at the edge of the water, the sun just high enough to make it look opaquely gray. Two seagulls were trying to take off into the east wind by flapping their wings and running in a slow-motion, flat-footed, "sproing-sproing" way along the rocks, like old kinescopes of pre-Kitty Hawk flyers and their contraptions.

John?

"Yes?"

You may be a child of the fifties, but don't forget you're also a man of the city.

"Meaning?"

Meaning be careful up in Maine. They may do things differently there.

I thought about the crossbow that every news update, however short, managed to work into the voiced-over videotape, sandwiched between the more familiar urban clips of drug drive-bys and serial killers. "Different, Beth, but ever the same."

She didn't need to ask what I meant.

2

I DROVE BACK TO THE CONDO IN BACK BAY I WAS RENTING from a doctor doing a two-year residency in Chicago. Parking the Prelude in its slot behind the brownstone building, I went upstairs and used the number on Nancy's message slip to reach Gil Lacouture's office in Augusta. In clipped but friendly syllables, his secretary told me that her name was Judy, that it was "a real shiny day up here today," and that her boss would be available by the time I got there. She gave me simple directions from the Maine Turnpike, saying it would probably take about three hours if I did the speed limit.

I changed into a suit, then pulled a Samsonite from the closet in my bedroom and packed what I thought I'd need for a couple of days. The last of the deli meat in the refrigerator went into a quasi-brunch that I figured would hold me until dinner.

Back in the Honda, I took Fairfield Street across Beacon between the buildings that back onto the river. I turned right into the alley that's an extension of Bay State Road and parallels Storrow Drive through most of my neighborhood. At Berkeley Street, I got on Storrow eastbound and began to inch my way toward Leverett Circle.

Over the last fifteen years, the major roads around Boston have become as clogged as the cart paths we laughingly call our city streets. The Registry of Motor Vehicles says the main reason for this is the forty percent increase in passenger cars in the metro region, vastly inflating something called the "congestion severity index." There are plans on the drawing boards for widening some of the arteries and building a third harbor tunnel to the airport. I figured the recession would reduce traffic a little, but the opposite seems to have happened, the rush hour now extending virtually from seven A.M. to seven P.M.

I finally made my way onto the ramp for Route 1 north. After ten miles of car dealers, strip malls, and pancake houses comes Interstate 95. The traffic stayed with me but spaced out. I kept the Prelude at fifty-five and didn't pass anybody for thirty miles.

Skirting Newburyport and Salisbury, the Interstate crosses the Merrimack River and then goes through about fourteen miles of New Hampshire, for which privilege you get to pay the Granite State a dollar at an inconvenient tollbooth. Shortly thereafter, I climbed onto the curving bridge over the Piscataqua River and halfway across the span saw a little sign telling me I was entering Maine. Just after the bridge in Kittery is a bigger sign, a small billboard really. In white letters on a royal blue background, it says WELCOME TO MAINE—THE WAY LIFE SHOULD BE.

I hadn't driven to Maine for a while, and even then really only along the ocean, where Beth and I had taken "getaway weekends" out of season at some of the ports like Bailey Island or Boothbay Harbor. After about five miles, I noticed more evergreens and less development. The people drove faster but better. I saw fewer Massachusetts and New Hampshire cars and more Mainers, white license plates

21

with deep blue letters and numbers and a red lobster logo. Even when the road narrowed, the drivers seemed to be able to merge politely and smoothly. I realized that it was a "real shiny day" and put back the moonroof to let the sun into the cabin. Then I kicked the Honda up to sixty-two and sailed along past Portland, staying with the more inland Maine Turnpike instead of the more coastal Route 95.

About ten miles north of Portland, the horizon seemed to expand, the most sky I'd seen east of Montana. In between the patches of blue were darker, humpbacked clouds, as though a sketch artist had used broad strokes with a charcoal stick. Each time the car topped a rise, the clouds gave the illusion of flying over glaciered mountains, endless ranges of them still in front of me.

I found myself taking deep, regular breaths of the warm but not humid air. I even hummed a little, the melody Nancy and I heard before dropping off to sleep the night before.

The last fifty miles seemed to melt away, and I almost regretted the Augusta exit coming up on the right.

"You must be Mr. Cuddy."

The woman that went with the voice of Judy over the phone was in her late twenties, a fresh-scrubbed look to her plainish face over a simple cotton dress. Gil Lacouture shared office space with a real estate broker and an insurance agent in a huge white colonial house with fluted Doric columns and black jalousied shutters.

"Call me John."

Judy shook my hand vigorously and asked if she could get me anything.

"No, thanks."

"You sure? Coffee, tea?"

"No, really."

Judy indicated a burlap couch with matching chairs and low table that formed the waiting area. "You have yourself a seat, then. Gil is just about finished with a client."

I took one of the chairs. On the table, back issues of outdoor magazines like *Field and Stream* and *Sports Afield* mingled with *Woman's Day* and *Good Housekeeping*. Judy sat behind an old wooden desk and began clacking away on an original IBM PC.

A doorway to what felt like a front parlor opened, and a man and a woman came through it, the woman first. She seemed to be in her late teens, with long black hair and makeup verging on warpaint. Her blue jeans were two sizes too small, making little rolls of fat above and below the front pockets. Large breasts pushed against a T-shirt that read YOU CAN'T BE FIRST, BUT YOU CAN BE NEXT.

The man was of medium height and build, with blond hair short enough to make his eyebrows and mustache look bushy, like a British army sergeant. He wore khaki pants, a plaid work shirt, and a solid wool tie that picked up one of the minor colors in the shirt.

The man spoke more to the T-shirt than to the woman. "And maybe just a white blouse for court on Thursday, right?"

The woman noticed me and smiled. Then she turned back to him, flirting an index finger under his chin. "Whatever you say, Gil." I got a brighter smile and a "Sorry to keep you waiting" as she vamped past me and out the door.

The man watched her go, then came over to me. "John Cuddy?"

I stood and shared a handshake with him. "Right."

"Gil Lacouture. Come on in."

Lacouture's office itself was roomy, with big, multipaned windows on two of the four walls and white floor-to-ceiling bookshelves built into the others. The carpeting was beige,

23

allowing the red drapes to draw your attention to the windows and welcome you to a sense of hominess.

I said, "Nice place."

Lacouture dropped into a squeaky leather chair behind a maple desk, motioning me toward one of two black captain's chairs with the sword and scales of New England School of Law on them. "Almost too nice, John, you want to know the truth. When I left the public defenders up here, I bought a retiring lawyer's practice, and this office came along with it. A great place to spend time, but it's kind of hard to get clients to leave it."

"Like Ms. T-shirt?"

"Cinny? Yeah. She got caught practicing hand relief."

"Hand relief?"

"Genital massage."

"You mean prostitution?"

"No. Just hand relief. As long as there was no intercourse, it used to be legal all over the state."

"You're kidding?"

Lacouture shook his head. "Then the massage places started spreading out from Portland, and a lot of communities like Saco and Biddeford got nervous and banned the practice. A town around here decided to jump on the 'banned' wagon, and the cops picked up Cinny."

"Spelled with a 'C,' I hope."

"Spelled . . . ? Oh, 'Cinny,' right." Lacouture laughed silently. "She says to me—this is technically a client confidence, John, but you've got to hear it—she says to me, 'Gil, they want to see I'm responsible, how about I wear these earrings in front of the judge?' And she shows them to me, and they're condoms, John."

"I saw an article about them."

"Well, up here, they don't read those kind of magazines."

"It was in the *New York Times*."

"Like I said."

24

Lacouture grinned, letting me know he was extending the joke. I wasn't so sure I liked a lawyer who revealed one client's secrets to an investigator he'd never met who might end up working for another client.

Lacouture turned in his chair and brought an accordion file to center stage on the desk. "So, Nancy tells me you're a crack private eye back in Boston."

"Nancy's prejudiced."

Lacouture looked up at me. "She told me why. I want this to sound right, John. Especially after joking around about Cinny. I've known Nancy from first year of law school. She's the best, in every way. If Nancy Meagher's with you, you must have a hell of a lot right with you. I'm going to assume that includes your professional competence, unless you give me reason to think otherwise."

It was as though Lacouture had changed personality. In one sentence, he went from locker room to board room.

I said, "I'm listening."

His hand slid the band off the accordion file in an assured way. "I'm going to let you read this at your leisure, but let me give you the condensed version first."

"Before you do, I'm not licensed up here. Nancy said—"

"—that I'd fix that, and I have. There's a clerk waiting for you at the Department of Public Safety Annex in Gardiner. The commissioner and I went to college together at Orono."

Another classmate. "So I'll be licensed in Maine?"

Lacouture said, "Provisionally. Usually it takes about sixty days for your application to be processed, to schedule you for a written test—"

"Test?"

"On the Maine criminal statutes, the private investigator law, and so forth. But we're going to be spared the test so long as we post a fifty-thousand-dollar bond on you, which

25

I've already arranged for, and so long as you agree to one other condition."

"What's that?"

Lacouture paused. "You won't be getting a certificate of firearms proficiency or a permit to carry a concealed weapon."

"What's the difference?"

"With the certificate, you could carry a gun while you were on the job as a licensed private investigator."

"Provisionally licensed."

"Right. With the permit, you could carry a gun any time, even if you weren't exactly working."

I thought about it. "Since I wasn't licensed up here, I didn't expect to be able to carry in Maine anyway."

Lacouture exhaled. "Good. For the rest of this conference today, the district attorney has given me his word that he won't try to go around the attorney-client privilege on the ground that you weren't yet licensed when you might have heard some privileged information."

Lacouture was elevating my opinion of him. "You're satisfied with the prosecutor's word on that."

Another grin. "This is Maine, John. A lawyer's word is still his bond."

I took out a pad. "Go ahead."

Lacouture rifled through the file, more like he was looking for something than that he needed to refresh his memory. "My client Steven Shea and his wife, Sandra—for business purposes, she kept her maiden name of Newberg when they married—drove up to their summer place on Marseilles Pond a week ago Friday."

Lacouture pronounced it "Marcel's," as Nancy had. "Hale and Vivian Vandemeer, friends of theirs from down by you, drove up separately in their car. The Foursome—I'm guessing you've already heard the media people use that—spent a lot of time together, including some weekends on Marseilles. Well, it seems that Steve did a piss-poor job of checking the larder before driving home each time, so there was always something he had to run to the country store in Marseilles to buy. That night, it was some wine and bread and other little stuff. My client drives his camp road to—"

"Camp road?"

"The dirt road going from his camp—his house on Marseilles, hell of a house, actually—to the lake road to the village. Anyway, Steve gets in his four-wheel-drive and heads to the country store. He buys the stuff he needs, comes back, and discovers a fucking massacre."

Lacouture's voice broke a little, and his hands were quivering as he took out some eight-by-ten glossy photos.

I reached across the desk to take them. The photos were in color, but you would have preferred them not to be. Three showed one body each, two women and a man, an arrow lodged pretty squarely in each chest. One of the women had her hand and what looked like a napkin or paper towel nailed to her breastbone by the shaft in her body. The fourth photo showed a crossbow, gunmetal gray with fingerprints enhanced by the dull brown of dried blood.

Lacouture was watching me as I returned the photos to him. He said, "They don't get to you?"

I thought back to Saigon and my time doing death cases with Empire Insurance and other situations since. "They get to me, Gil. After a while, you just learn not to show it."

"Good." Lacouture made a ritual of putting the photos back in the file, as if once they were secured he was safe from them again. "I'd hate to think anybody could look at those things without feeling something."

"What did your client feel?"

The lawyer kept his face passive. "When Steve came back

27

from the store, he walked up the path with a grocery bag in his arms and stumbled over the crossbow. He bent down to pick it up, couldn't figure why it would be out behind the house instead of hanging in the garage where they kept it. Then he saw what happened in the house, bent over the bodies, tried to hold his . . . wife."

I gave him a minute. "So, Shea's prints were on the crossbow, and her blood was all over him."

"Right."

"Any prints on the arrows?"

Lacouture half grinned, then got himself back into lawyer pose and broadened it. "Nancy's judgment about you seems confirmed. Steve's prints on the one that killed his wife, no prints on the rest. And by the way, they're called 'bolts,' not arrows."

"Any other physical evidence?"

"Two shoes with blood on them."

"You'd expect that, wouldn't you?"

"I don't mean the shoes Steve was wearing. These were up in his bedroom closet."

"They belonged to him?"

"Yes. And those shoes made footprints starting at Hale Vandemeer's body and going across the great room, up the stairs, and to Shea's closet."

I thought about it. "Like Shea killed them, then realized he stepped in some blood and went upstairs to change into clean ones?"

"Yes, but it doesn't make sense, does it?"

"For Shea to do that if Shea was the killer."

"Exactly."

Killers tend to make mistakes, especially if they panic. "How about motive?"

"None. Closest of friends."

I remembered Beth's comment. "Maybe closer than that?"

28

Lacouture shook his head. "Not that I know of."

"What did the friends do for a living?"

"Hale Vandemeer, he was a doctor. Also had some kind of business deal with his brother. Vivian Vandemeer was a housewife.'"

"How about Sandra Newberg?"

"She wasn't working."

"I thought you said she kept her name for business reasons."

"She got laid off. Some insurance company down in Boston."

"Which one?"

"Empire, I think."

Small world. "I used to work for them."

"Great. Might save us some time."

He was going a little too fast. "What exactly do you want me to do, Gil?"

Lacouture spread his hands over the file, as though he were blessing it. "I'd like you to look into things up here, get a handle on what happened. Since this isn't a bailable offense, Steve can't be very much help to me. Then I'd like you to dig around down in Massachusetts, see if you can find anything I can use with a jury to get them to see another way this could have happened without my client being involved."

I glanced through the notes I'd taken. "The TV news said Shea was with some defense contractor, right?"

"Steve *is* an executive with Defense Resource Management down by you."

I'd vaguely heard of them as their initials, "DRM." I said, "Is the company standing by him?"

"Absolutely. The general counsel there is the one who brought me into the case."

"Name?"

"Anna-Pia Antonelli."

"She a classmate of yours, too?"

"No. I'd represented Steve when he bought the land on Marseilles. When he was arrested, he called Antonelli."

"He called her, not you?"

Lacouture gave me a strange look. "Yes. She checked me out, found I'd done a stint in the defenders. Steve trusted me from the property deal, and here I am."

"Any way this could be connected to his work?"

"Steve seems to think so, but you'd have to ask him."

I started a new page in the pad. "Any kids in either family?"

"Not for Steve and Sandy. The Vandemeers had one son, Nick."

"How old?"

"Teenager. Still in high school and I guess not exactly a credit to the bloodline."

"Addresses and full names for everybody in your file?"

Lacouture brightened. "Does that mean you're coming on board?"

"I won't be making up my mind until after I meet with your client."

"I can arrange it for tomorrow."

I closed up my pad. "Might be a help for me to see the crime scene beforehand."

The grin. "I thought you might feel that way. Sheriff Willis can run you out there this afternoon."

"The sheriff will take me there?"

"You bet. P. W. Willis was the first cop on the scene that night. Took the state police an hour."

"Where do I meet Willis?"

"Marseilles Pond is two counties over from here, but even so, it's ten miles from the jail. Be easier for you to just go to the inn and wait for the sheriff there."

"The inn."

30

"Marseilles Inn. It's in the village and about the nicest place we could put you up."

"So I'm on expenses till I meet with your client."

"Steve insisted."

"I notice you keep calling him by his first name. Practicing for the jury, Gil?"

Lacouture lost a little of the grin. "No. This is Maine, John. We personalize our clients even when we don't have to."

"Sorry."

"Forget it. But actually, there's another reason, too."

"What's that?"

Lacouture made the grin go sly. "I'd like to tell you that after you've met with Steve, okay?"

"Okay. One more thing."

"Sure."

"Can Judy tell me how I get to the Department of Public Safety?"

I left the department's annex in Gardiner carrying a blown-down white cardboard about the size of a credit card with my photo on it. The words "PRIVATE INVESTIGATOR" and a four-digit license number were printed in red, other relevant information (like height, weight, and eye color) in black. The card stated it was good for only two months from date of issue. While it was being laminated, the clerk told me once that I must be awfully "well regarded," twice that I dare not represent myself as a sworn peace officer, and three times that I was not to carry a concealed weapon.

By the time I drove back to Lacouture's office, he was gone for the day, but he'd left the Shea file with Judy, and told her to let me take it to read over that night. She also gave me a handwritten map to the Marseilles Inn.

I drove west from Augusta on a divided strip like Route

1, then mended roughly northwestward for thirty country miles. At first the topography was drumlin hills and meadows, some with cows, others with swaybacked horses, a few with swaybacked barns, the roofs sagging against the walls. Some hay was still out, for the livestock, I guessed. The Prelude was pretty much the only vehicle going in my direction, and those passing me the other way were mostly pickup trucks or four-wheel-drives, half of the folks waving to me as though we were neighbors passing on a common driveway.

A little farther on, the farms became fewer. The road started to climb more steeply and drop more sharply, signs for lakes and chainsaw repair and canoe refitting cropping up. A logging truck came around a bend in front of me, poaching into my lane with two trailered flatbeds of large hardwood trunks and nearly sending me off the road and down a hundred-foot slope. Other than that, the trip was uneventful and pleasant: a hawk soaring fifty feet overhead, a skunk wending its way across a narrow strip of pavement, robins and blue jays and other songbirds I couldn't identify very audible whenever I passed through stands of trees.

As I reached the point on Judy's map where I thought I had to make a turn, the tarmac crested, then descended gracefully to a long expanse of dark water nestled in a valley with a peak behind it. I could make out a few islands in the middle of the water, and just around another bend was a crossroads consisting of a small stone library, an even smaller red-bricked post office, a concrete-block country store, and a large clapboard building with a MARSEILLES INN sign in burned letters on a weathered background.

The inn was positioned at the intersection so that it stood catercorner from the country store. The inn's backyard ran down to the lakefront and a large, squarish dock with white chairs on it. The roof sported gingerbread shingles and had a gable at either end above a covered porch with spindled bannister and latticework from the floor to the ground. The clapboards were painted a soft peach, the shutters and other trim a deep orange, creating an unusual but attractive color contrast. A cement boat ramp abutted the inn, entering the water at an angle that suggested it continued down to the bottom of the lake.

I pulled the car into a lot on the far side of the inn. Maybe twenty buildings, from rambling houses to small cottages, radiated from the intersection before petering out into small, homemade cabins along the lakefront and just plain trees in every other direction. I carried my suitcase in one hand and the Shea file from Lacouture's office under the other arm.

The porch steps creaked a little, spooking a calico cat with only one eye that bounded off into the bushes at the end of the porch. At the top of the steps, I could hear an old Rolling Stones tune from behind a screened door.

I opened the door. A black portable boom box rested on the reception counter, the music much louder inside the foyer. It took me a moment to place the Stones piece. It was "Gimme Shelter."

"Helluva song for an innkeeper's radio, huh?"

The voice was gruff but friendly, an accent more like the Philadelphia "O" than Judy's choppy Maine rhythms. The man behind it was early forties, barrel-chested and big-boned, with reddish brown hair and a shambling walk. He wore denim coveralls streaked with paint over a blue T-shirt with breast pocket and old hiking boots. He held a paint bucket and brush in his right hand, and the smile on his face nearly reached the sideburns.

I said, "A golden oldie."

"Oldie? You're not a Mainer, right?"

"Right. Boston."

33

"Well, mister, up here you're going to realize something right off. This is current stuff. The Stones, Jimi Hendrix, the Allman Brothers, Cream. The stations are called The Mountain, Ocean, The Blimp—and speaking of blimps? If Led Zeppelin got their act together, they could be the Grateful Dead of Maine, touring one little town after another, from Kittery to Fort Kent, packing them in at every stop, then just heading south and starting all over again."

"Like painting the Brooklyn Bridge."

He looked down at his bucket. "Huh?"

"The crew that paints the Brooklyn Bridge. By the time they finish, it's time to start painting at the beginning again."

He cocked his head but kept the smile. "I think I'm going to like you. I'd shake but—"

"John Cuddy."

"Ralph Paine. You're the one Gil Lacouture's office called about?"

"I am."

"Well, we've got two rooms with a private bath and a telephone both. Gil said be sure to give you one. No problem since we just lost the bugs."

"I'm sorry?"

"The bugs. The black flies. Little bitty things, look like fruit flies with a thyroid condition. They bite you, spit some kind of stuff in the bite, and you bleed a drop like a picture of the Savior on the cross. Then you get yourself a welt the size of a nickel lasts about a week. You still might see one or two if you go into the woods, but we've got stuff for that, you decide to. That's how come we've got the rooms."

"Because the flies are gone?"

"No, no. Because nobody can really predict in advance when they'll arrive or when they leave. See, they arrive sometime in early May, usually, but we don't get rid of them till the darning needles come out."

"The darning needles."

"That's what we called them back in Philly, anyway. Up here, they're dragonflies."

"The dragonflies come out and eat the black flies."

"You bet. Like the Battle of Britain in reverse. Instead of rooting for the little planes against the big planes, you pull for those dragonflies to down about a hundred black flies every minute."

Paine seemed to notice my gear for the first time. "Tell you what you do. You just set those things here, and I'll get into my innkeeper outfit and be right back out. Wife's over watching the store, so I'm kind of on my own for now."

I told Paine not to hurry. I took an old oval-back chair, the next two rock anthems that came over the radio supporting my host's view on music mix.

Paine reappeared in a pair of clean, creased brown pants and a long-sleeved oxford shirt over the blue T. I signed the middle of a page in a leather-bound register, then got led up a wide, carpeted staircase.

Over his shoulder, Paine said, "We'll put you on the second floor. Got some bigger rooms on the third, but they're not really opened up yet, and besides, they're more for families, what with the bunk beds and all."

We turned right and stopped at what I thought would be a rear room.

Paine said, "This one's probably the one you'll want, but there's another I can show you, too."

He opened the door without using a key and ushered me into a broad room with a four-poster mahogany bed and matching dresser and nightstand. An internal doorway previewed a shower-and-vanity bathroom with no tub but lots of towels. At the back of the room was a window overlooking the lake. I could see the square dock and chairs at the water's edge below, just the hint of houses shielded by trees and other foliage across the bay. Three preteen girls were trying to place a blanket on the grass, turning it this way and that like firefighters positioning a net under a potential jumper.

I turned to Paine. "This will be tough to beat."

"Other room's on the street side. Noisier and no . . ." He moved his hand toward the window.

Conscious of Lacouture's client, I said, "Same price?"

"Uh-huh."

"Then this one's fine."

A nod. "Settle yourself in. Gil said I was to call the sheriff for you."

"Right."

"Jail's only a short drive, shouldn't be too long."

"Mr. Paine—"

"Huh, Ralph's more like it."

"Ralph, you know I'm here about the killings at the Shea house?"

He scratched his chin. "No, but I figured you might be. You have a key to Steve's camp?"

"No. I assumed the sheriff would."

"Probably does. If not, Steve keeps a spare on a nail under the third step of the back stairs to his kitchen."

I stared at him. "How many other people knew that?"

"Couldn't say, but probably quite a few. Summer folks have to leave a way for workmen and such to get in when they might not be there."

I filed that. "The night of the killings, I understand Steven Shea came to the country store to buy some things."

Paine seemed to get slower and more careful. "That's what the wife tells me."

"She was working there that night?"

"We both work there every day and every night till nine, Sundays till seven. We own the store and the inn."

"I'd like to speak to her about seeing Shea that night."

"Okay." He turned to go, taking something out of his pocket. "I'll leave you the key to the room. Lock up if you like, but if you're here more than two nights, don't be surprised you start forgetting to."

"Thanks, Ralph."

"I'll let you know when Patsy comes by."

"It can wait."

Paine stopped and turned in the doorway. "Huh?"

"My speaking to your wife about Shea. I can wait till it's convenient for her."

Paine seemed to laugh to himself. "Patsy's not the wife. Ramona's the wife. Patsy, she's the sheriff."

The innkeeper closed my door behind him.

3

"SORRY TO TAKE SO LONG, BUT I HAD TO GAS THE TRUCK."

The big Chevy Blazer bounced over another rock in a rut on the dirt road from Marseilles around the lake. Sheriff P. W. "Patsy" Willis was behind the wheel, swinging it enthusiastically left and right to avoid the worst parts of the road. We'd left the paved section about half a mile from the village.

"Sheriff, how far is it from the village to the Shea house?"

She looked over at me, then back to the driving. "From the country store to his gravel car park, three point four mile."

Gil Lacouture had said that Willis was the first officer on the scene. My guess was that she'd since measured the distance at least twice each way, just to be sure. Her hands on the wheel looked raw and knuckly, but the skin was soft when she shook hands with me outside the inn. About five-foot-seven, Willis was solidly built, with a sandy pony-tail drawn back and worn under her Stetson and inside her brown uniform shirt. The pants were beige with brown piping, the shoes black Corfam, like parade shoes from the

Army. The eyes were hazel and hadn't blinked since we'd started talking.

We passed a paved driveway on the right with a chain across it. Faded orange telltales were tied to the chain, fluttering in the breeze.

I said, "How'd you get into police work?"

"Grew up maybe ten mile from here. Career opportunities for young ladies weren't what you'd call wicked good. Saw a recruitment ad down to Augusta for the Army, thought I might give it a try, ended up in the Military Police."

"Me, too."

Her eyes left the road again. "That right?"

"Fort Gordon."

"Augusta, Georgia. Thought it was some funny at the time, trading one Augusta for another, fifteen hundred mile away. I did my Advanced Individual Training there, let me see . . . fall of 1973."

"I was a little before that."

Her eyes didn't leave the road this time. "Vietnam?"

"One tour."

"One was more than enough for most, way I heard it."

I didn't say anything.

Willis said, "There was a self-defense instructor at Gordon when I was there. Blond. Louisiana boy, I think. We called him—"

"—'Teen Angel.' "

Willis laughed, a genuine "haw-haw" roar. "Damn, he was good. Some of the noncoms still weren't real happy about women coming through, but Teen Angel, he took the three of us in my cycle aside, taught us everything from Jukado that we might be able to use."

Jukado was a mixture of judo, karate, and other disciplines. Teen Angel was an absolutely straight shooter whose only desire was to teach you how to stay alive when somebody else wanted the opposite.

Willis downshifted. "I recall the time he took us out, showed us knife-fighting. Said he wasn't supposed to, but hell, he'd shown the boys going to Nam how to do it, he couldn't see stopping with the girls going into worse places over here."

Jesus, that took me back. To a sawdust pit on the fringes of the fort, Teen Angel and another guy, a black karate expert. Showing us, all male then, how to use the knife.

Willis said, "I still can see him, only my height, maybe an inch taller. He used me as his demonstrator, saying 'All right, Troop, the human body, it's real well protected if the attack's from above. Skull's thick, jaw's strong, and the rib cage, it slants down like Venetian blinds, protecting all the vital organs. What that means, Troop, is that you hold the knife so's the blade's flat to the ground. Then you come up and in, under the slant of the ribs, get you a lung. Then you're in there, you twist that knife to the right—I'm a rightie—hard as you can, Troop, tear up the lung that boy needs to breathe with. He won't give you much more trouble after that. No, Troop, I—"

"—guaran-damn-tee you he won't.' "

Willis haw-hawed again, then checked on me. "Don't bother you to talk about it, does it?"

"It ought to, but it doesn't."

She mulled that a moment.

I said, "Where were you stationed?"

"Did my hitch around New York City. Patrolling the Bayonne docks on the Jersey side, trying to integrate and get some use out of the reservists they'd send down to Fort Hamilton over in Brooklyn, then bus over to us. Waste of the taxpayers' money, putting those folks undercover as longshoremen, trying to catch a stevedore ripping off a shipment bound for Uncle. I finished up down there and come back up here, figuring law enforcement might not be for me. Then I met the husband."

Based on Ralph Paine's usage, I assumed Willis meant her husband.

"Yes, he was a good man. From down to Portland, originally. He went on the state police, come up here. Met him in January, married him in June. Fine man. When his twenty was up, he decided to run for sheriff. Hell, I knew most of the folks in the county, so one thing led to another, and I started working on his campaign and basically got him elected. Two month in office, and he dropped dead of a heart attack. I got appointed to fill out his term. Didn't blow my foot off, so I got nominated to run the next time, surprised some folks, and won. That was two times ago, been in the chair ever since."

I wasn't quite sure what to say, so I didn't say anything.

She slowed the Blazer to climb a hill. "Haven't blown my foot off yet."

I put the heel of my right hand against the dashboard as we bucked down the far side of the slope.

Willis said, "Not much farther now."

We'd passed only the one driveway and no houses since leaving the paved section. I said, "Nobody else lives on this stretch?"

The sheriff let a hand leave the wheel long enough to push back her hat. "Most of the frontage at this end of the pond was owned by Judson Lumber. They put in this dirt part so's they could haul out logs when they cut. Only houses on it are your client, Ma Judson, and Dag Gates."

While I'd been waiting for Willis, I'd read the sheriff's office and state police reports in Lacouture's file. "That's Melba Judson and Donald Gates?"

"That's right, only I'm not sure anybody'd know either of them by their formal names anymore. Ma, she was the first to get to your client. Dag come up just after her in his canoe."

"I'd like to talk to each of them."

Willis slowed down, then slewed onto a gravel track toward the lake. "First things first."

The gravel snaked its way around a couple of huge trees to a broad clearing. At the back or west end of the clearing, a chipmunk scooted up a path that quickly disappeared into the woods at the base of the mountain. The gravel seemed pretty well raked and distributed to create a parking lot for at least ten cars, though it was empty as Willis killed the engine on the Blazer.

She said, "The villa de Shea."

The house, at the east end of the gravel clearing, was monstrous. Some kind of wildly concocted contemporary, it was as though a giant's spiteful kid had dumped a set of blocks on the site. The windows were all shapes and sizes, with a wide deck beginning at the back door on the west or road side of the house, continuing to the north side and apparently getting even wider at the east or lake side of the house.

I got out of the truck, nearly falling because I'd forgotten how high the chassis was off the ground. Willis landed nimbly on her side and met me at the headlights, the gravel crunching under our feet.

I said, "What's it like from the front?"

"Worse. Don't quite see why folks like your client bother coming to Maine."

We walked around the north side of the house on manicured lawn and little flagstone inserts. The structure itself must have been ninety feet wide, and there were no trees whatsoever left between it and the water. Just lawn and what appeared to be an erosion gully with three ornamental footbridges over it, like something from an expensive suburban development. We stopped by the steps that climbed to the deck at the northeast corner of the house, the wind chimes above the doors to the house tinkling merrily in the breeze.

Willis said, "When Shea and his wife built here three year ago, you were allowed to clear-cut thirty foot of width for every hundred foot of frontage. That's not permitted anymore, but . . . what's done is done."

"The bridges are an especially nice touch."

She looked to me, confirming my sarcasm. "Carpentry is fine. Owen Briss, he did most of the finish work here, and he knows what he's doing. But . . ." Willis moved her hand at the bridges like a baseball manager finishing an argument with an umpire.

I pointed to a stone structure at the water's edge partially hidden by brush and trees. "That a boathouse?"

"It is. Tom Judson had an old-timey camp like his sister's on this site before he sold to your client. That boathouse was already there, so it got grandfathered against the new zoning laws."

"Can you orient me on where we are?"

"Sure can. Let's go down by the water."

We walked down the gentle slope. Paralleling the gully, you could see a lot of sand and silt lying in it.

I said, "The erosion from the clear-cutting?"

"Some. The rest is because of runoff from the roof and driveway. There used to be a whole . . . 'buffer' is what the environmental people call it. You can ask Dag about those things, he's up on them. I do know that once you cut and build as much as your client did, you got basically a big sluiceway for the water and not much holding her back from the pond."

At the water's edge, Willis began to point. "Northward now, to our left, the shoreline runs about two point five mile to the village. Bit longer by car, as I said."

"Three point four miles."

"Right. Now, think of the north end by the village as the

43

base of a fiddle, with a lot of little islands kind of dotting the area around where the strings would cross the hole. Then the pond kind of tapers as it runs south toward us, with the far right or south over there the end of the fiddle's handle."

"How long is it, total?"

"Bit over three mile in length, north to south."

"Hell of a 'pond.' "

"Maine defines anything over ten acres a 'Great Pond.' Sometimes a body of water'll be called a lake, but more often we just use 'pond.' "

"How wide is it?"

"Maybe a mile and a half at the north end, tapering down to oh, half a mile right acrost here."

I looked to the opposite shore. It seemed closer than a half mile, but then water's deceiving that way. "How deep?"

"Need a map to be real accurate on that, but she goes from about five to six foot around the shoreline down to about fifty right smartly, and in some channels, down to two hundred."

"Two hundred feet deep?"

"Marseilles's not just a great pond, but a fine one, too."

She gave out a tempered haw-haw noise.

I said, "Where's Ma Judson's house?"

Willis swept her hand to the right. "The handle of that fiddle bends just a mite as it goes southward, but Ma's place is only a little piece down from here."

A narrow, trodden path seemed to follow the lakefront toward the south.

"How about Dag Gates?"

Willis smiled. "Acrost from here."

I brought my head to the east shore. "Where?"

"You're looking right at his place."

"Across the pond?"

44

"Now you've got it."

This time I studied the shoreline on the far side of the "handle." "I can't see anything but trees and rocks."

"Dag done well that way. Give you a hint. See those three rocks right at the water that kind of stand up together just south of the biggest birch?"

"The birch is the white trunk."

"Right."

"Okay, I see the three rocks."

"No, you don't."

"Sheriff—"

"That middle rock, that's Dag's dock. Weathered spruce."

I studied it a little more. Once you knew it, you could see it. Maybe.

Suddenly there was movement in the brush to our right. A little animal appeared, running steadily along the water's edge, stopping once to chitter away at us before continuing into the brush on our left. It looked like an animated fur neckpiece.

"Was that a mink, Sheriff?"

"Fisher. She'll circle the pond twice a day at about that speed, foraging for food along the shoreline."

"Looks like it burns more calories than it finds."

"Guess not, she's still here."

I looked at Willis.

She said, "What else you want to see?"

"How about the boathouse?"

"Fine."

We walked over to the stone structure, a little more imposing when you were right next to it. "We need a key?"

Willis reached up to a wooden eave under the old roof and came up with one that opened the regular-sized door on the side. The interior had a stale smell, dank from dampness, pungent from oil and gas. A cigarette boat with more room devoted to engine than reserved for passengers was lolling in the water. The concrete parapet let me see its stern. FOURSOME.

Willis said, "Ironic, eh?"

The rest of the boathouse was crammed with conspicuous consumption. Water skis, water sleds, Jet Skis. Lounging rafts with drink-holder pockets. Two aluminum canoes, one painted yellow, the other orange. Other paraphernalia I could only guess at.

Something made a clittering noise above my head.

Willis said, "Just a bat. Dormant during the day."

I said, "Can we try the house, walk me through it?"

"Sure can."

The climb back up the slope was a little tougher, but not much, a total of less than a hundred feet from the water's edge. Rather than use one of the cutesy footbridges, Willis walked around the gully, and I did, too. The worst part was looking up at the house. The architectural hand was no more evident here than at the rear. The structure fit its setting like a beer fart at a wine tasting.

I said, "At least the chimes seem right."

Willis grimaced. "Bear scares."

"What?"

"Bear scares. Folks up here rig things to keep the black bears away from the trash and food smells. Most use tin cans with stones in them. Others have a deadfall."

"Deadfall?"

"Like a log or some lumber. It gets tripped, the noise and movement'll send the bear a-packing. Your client, though"—she moved her hand at the house the way she had at the footbridges—"he likes chimes."

The deck was supported by eight-inch square posts that went up twelve feet or so to the joists of the deck itself. Back at the northeast stairs, Willis stopped.

She said, "We figure Shea was somewhere between here

and the brush when he shot the Vandemeer woman on the deck up there."

"How about innocent till proven guilty?"

Willis left her face neutral. "You didn't see the bodies or Shea that night, mister. I did."

"You even have a motive, Sheriff?"

Still neutral. "In this county, we like to leave that to time of trial."

I swung my head from the brush to the deck above us. "You're going by the angle of entry of the bolt into her chest?"

"And body position. Apparently your client didn't try to move her."

"Okay."

Willis climbed the steps. "We figure he got up here before the doctor—the husband Vandemeer—come out."

"Why is that?"

She stopped at the deck itself. "Had to reload. Once the lab boys finished with the crossbow, I tried it. Takes a time." Her arm moved through the air. "The husband got it out on the deck, crashing back through the screen door. Figure he come out because he saw or heard something, closed the screen behind him. Your client must have already been ready with the next shot. Got the husband straight through the heart. Lab found some tomato juice on his hands and a couple of seeds under his nails, and there were tomatoes sliced out in the kitchen, like he was helping Shea's wife make a salad or something."

"Which door?"

Willis walked to the center of three sliding doors. "This is where the doctor went through. We figure your client stepped over his body here, got some blood on the shoes, then went toward the kitchen and caught his wife coming out of it." The sheriff turned to me without looking at me. "You saw the photo of . . . her and the paper towel?"

"Yes."

Willis nodded once, abruptly. "Your client must have noticed he was tracking blood and went upstairs there to his bedroom to change shoes. He drove to the country store as cool as you please to buy his little bag of groceries, then come back and play the horrified husband."

I thought about it. Shea's changing shoes still didn't feel right. "Can we go inside?"

"We can. Let me just go around to one of the doors with an external lock on it, use the key."

"Sheriff?"

"Yes?"

"I understand they kept a key to the house outside it, like they did with the boathouse."

She nodded. "Back stairs, on a nail under the riser for the third step. But like I said, we figure your client come from the front deck and worked his way through the house from there."

Willis walked around the north side of the deck. I heard a key and a door open, then saw her through the sliding glass door coming toward me across the big room at the lake or east side of the house.

She unlatched the glass door and slid it open for me. "Come on in."

A combination living room/dining area with vaulted ceilings, exposed beams, and hardwood floors with some discoloration in dark brown that didn't match the grain around it. Blue leather couch and imitation Eames chairs with ottomans, some kind of dhurrie rug on the floor in front of a walk-in fireplace. Teak entertainment center with television, VCR, stereo amplifier, CD player, the works. Chrome stools around an art deco dining room table that was a foot too high, the stools having seat slings and backrests in the same blue leather. The walls were festooned with modern art, cubes and slashes with no sense of pattern I could see.

A set of bannistered stairs with a beige carpet runner went up to a second floor.

"Can I see the bedroom?"

Willis shrugged. "Mister, you can see the whole damned house."

She led me up the stairs, some more of the dark brown discoloration on the carpet runner. At the top, a corridor branched left and right, double doors in front of us.

Willis opened the double doors inward, and I moved past her.

The room was huge, a king-sized bed occupying barely a quarter of the floor space. A triple window provided a great view of the sheriff's Blazer on the gravel below. The sheets, carpeting, and other furnishings, in yellow and orange, would have been loud in an artist's loft in the SoHo section of New York.

Behind me, Willis said, "Kind of hard on the eyes, eh?"

"Kind of." There were faint discoloration marks near a set of louvered doors. "This the closet?"

"It is."

I opened the doors. Double poles of clothing, both men's and women's. About half and half, as far as I could tell.

"We found the shoes your client was wearing back in that corner to your right."

I knelt down. You could just see a discoloration in the yellow carpeting on the bottom.

"He buried the shoes under a couple of cartons, but one of the state troopers spotted the stain."

I went through the master bath, then the two guest rooms and baths on either side of the master suite. The house looked large from the outside, but it didn't have a lot of living space on the inside. From the window in the southside guest room, I could see a small stone garage. "That where they kept the crossbow?"

"So your client says."

"Can I see it?"

"Crossbow's back in my evidence locker. The garage, sure."

We went back downstairs, Willis leading me out toward the kitchen. "Sheriff, just a second."

She stopped and turned to me.

I said, "This is about where Sandra Newberg was found?"

"About. Ma Judson said when she came in on your client, he was holding his wife and rocking her, so we figure he moved the body some from its original position."

"You also figure he killed them first, went to the store, then came back and made enough noise to bring his neighbors."

"That's about it."

"Then why did he change his shoes?"

"What?"

"Shea checks on his wife when he gets back, sitting with and rocking her body, he's going to get blood all over his shoes. Why change them between 'killing' them and 'finding' them again?"

Willis kept her face neutral. "Because he doesn't want to get any blood in his fancy new four-wheel-drive. It'd wreck his carpeting and his story of just finding them here when he got back."

"But then why go up the stairs with them on? He'd leave tracks here that way. And why not ditch the shoes somewhere other than his closet? Hell, he's got a forest for his backyard and a lake for his front."

She just looked at me. "You want to see the garage or not?"

Outside, Willis said, "I'm going to radio in. Key's just under the third eave there on the left."

She walked up to her vehicle as I went to the garage. It had two old wooden doors painted dark green that would have to be opened outward, one at a time. I found the key the way Willis had the one for the boathouse. Unlocking a door, I pulled it toward me far enough to let in light to see by. The contents were a land version of the boathouse. All-terrain vehicles, fancy mountain bikes, and so on. Under some gardening equipment, I found a target the size of a round cocktail tabletop with concentric rings of yellow, blue, and red around a black bull's-eye. Above the target was a bare ten-penny nail where a crossbow and bolts might have hung.

I was just pulling the target free of a rake and a hoe when a raspy female voice behind me said, "Probably staple you to that, I was to let loose both barrels."

Her cadence was a lot like the sheriff's, but older. Without turning, I said, "I'll put the target down."

"Might tell me what you're doing here, too."

From a ways off, I heard Willis call out. "Ma! Ma, now don't you shoot that man. He's a detective from down to Boston."

"Boston? The hell's he doing here?"

Willis sounded closer. "He might like to talk with you about that."

4

"HOW'RE YOU DOING BACK THERE?"

"Fine, Ms. Judson."

"Christ come to earth, man. Don't be calling me 'Miz' anything. 'Ma' does just fine for folks up here."

I was following Ma Judson along the winding, overgrown path from the edge of the clearing for the Shea house southward toward her place. Sheriff Willis had a call she had to cover, but before leaving in the Blazer she said Ma Judson or Dag Gates could run me back to the inn when I was finished talking with them.

Judson herself was a study in contrasts. A round, rosy face with gray, milky eyes, the kind that a cookie company would cast in the role of grandmother. However, the scent trailing behind her was less sugar and more garlic, and her hat was a man's snap-brim in green felt, what looked like a nip taken out of the back of the brim. The little I could see of her hair was white, thin, and short. She wore an oxford shirt with a tattered collar under a buckskin jacket that never saw the inside of a boutique. Her pants were baggy, olive drab corduroys, the wale wide. I was pretty sure her shoes were L. L. Bean duck-boots, the corduroys bloused into them like an airborne trooper would his or her fatigues. The contrast was capped by the over-and-under shotgun she carried, breech broken as a foolproof safety.

As we walked, the sound of the barking was getting louder.

Judson said, "You're the cause of that, you see."

"Of what?"

"The dogs. A-baying and a-howling some fierce for them. Don't care for the idea of somebody sneaking up on me."

Over the sound of the dogs another noise came from the lake itself. This was more the long and haunting cry of a creature cutting its heart out.

"What the hell is that?"

"Loon. We're blessed with seventeen adults, we are, and four chicks made it through the end of last summer. We'll be doing a formal count this July, but after a while, you get so you can pick them out. That was 'Diver.' "

Another one of the cries, this one sounding briefer than the first.

"You see?"

"See what?"

"That second cry. That was 'Two Hoots,' I call her. She stops after only two—they call them 'yodels' or 'tremolos.' "

Through a gap in the trees I spotted a huge bird hanging low in the water. It looked like a cross between a Canadian goose and a cormorant. "That a loon?"

Judson came back to me, craned her neck. "It is."

"Which one?"

"Can't tell from here. Have to wait till it calls."

We waited. It didn't.

I felt a trickle of sweat working its way down my cheek. "Maybe next time."

"Presumptuous." She looked up at me, then smiled. "I see one of them got you."

"One what?"

Judson reached an index finger toward my face and touched the sweat. Her finger came away bloody. "Black fly. Mostly gone now, but there are still a few on the wing."

I put my hand to my face and felt a lump just under my eye.

"Don't be itching that, now. Welt'll be bad enough without it."

"Why don't they bother you?"

"The garlic. Eat it for six weeks before they hatch, they don't know you're around. Other folks do, though, I expect."

She turned and continued down the trail.

After another fifty yards of hiking, we reached a clearing more subtle than the one around the Shea house. In the clearing stood a rustic cabin made of hewn logs, weathered to the color of shake shingles, the round ends of the logs showing the rings and checking of old wood. The foundation and chimney consisted of mortared fieldstones, laid flat but jutting out irregularly, smooth with age and plastered with moss. Two Cape Ann rockers and a small table, hewn from the same kind of wood as the logs, sat on a shallow porch nobody could mistake for a sundeck. Rusty nails driven halfway into the porch logs supported all sorts of wood-handled tools with crescent metal blades, from logging or farming, I assumed. The window frames were weathered two-by-fours, three joined together to form the vertical jambs, one each for the lintels above and sills below the small windows. Screens were held in place by brads driven into the boards. The roof was covered by large green squares, like somebody had stripped two dozen pool tables of their covers and tacked them down.

To one side was an old, two-door utility vehicle that looked like an International Scout, with a cream metal top and an aquamarine body. The spare was under the side window behind the passenger's seat. The rear bumper was roped onto the chassis, the license plate taped in the rear window. Behind the truck was a garage full of old junk and an outhouse with the elbow of a tree limb for a door handle. The garage and privy formed the corners of a chicken wire run, three big, mongrel dogs in it, each going crazy to be the first one to come through the wire at us.

"That'll do."

At Judson's raspy command, all three dogs stopped making noise and sat down on their side of the wire. Two big-headed, short-haired dogs could have been twins and looked a lot like Old Yeller, tongues out and tails wagging. The third dog drew his gene pool somewhere between a German shepherd and a malamute, and his ghostly blue eyes didn't give any indication he was happy to see me.

"I take it you don't have a problem with burglaries out here."

She smiled, a fresh-batch profile for the cookie commercial. "Leastways no repeat offenders."

I said, "You in law enforcement, too?"

"Christ come to earth, no. No, I just read the papers from time to time about what goes on in the cities. I got Jack and Jill when they was pups from the pound. Littermates somebody left by the side of a quarry back in the country a ways. Runty, I'm just minding him for Dag, till he gets back from fishing."

"He looks pretty big to be called 'Runty.' "

"Dag named him that because on the TV show, they called Rin Tin Tin 'Rinty,' but Dag thought with only some shepherd in him, he ought to be called 'Runty.' You pumping me already?"

The smile was still fresh-batch, but the gray eyes were now as flinty as a country lawyer's.

I said, "It would be a help if you could tell me what you saw and heard that night."

"I can tell you the truth as I know it. I figure that's my duty as a citizen. But I'm not about to let you record anything, and I'm sure not going to sign anything."

"Agreed."

"Come on up to the porch, then. I can scare up some lemonade, but it's just the store-bought kind."

"Thanks, that'll be fine."

I climbed the two wooden steps to the porch and tried one of the rockers while Judson disappeared into the house. With caning for seat and back, the chair was amazingly formfitting and comfortable, at least until I noticed Jack and Jill and Runty, still watching me.

Ma Judson reappeared without the shotgun but with two gas station giveaway glasses of lemonade. I took mine, tasted it, and said it really hit the spot. She gulped two or three ounces of hers and said they never could get it to taste like the real thing, but who wants to carry home ten dollars' worth of lemons to make it right?

Judson set her glass down precariously on the small table. "All right, young man, now that you've softened me up, what do you want to know?"

"I understand you were the first one to reach the house after the killings."

"Second."

"The second?"

"Shea himself was there first."

"Fair enough. What made you go over there?"

"Jack and Jill woke me up."

"Woke you?"

"They sleep with me, back bedroom." Judson seemed to blush a little. "On the floor, of course."

"The police reports say the killings took place around nine P.M."

"Wasn't looking at any clock."

"What I mean is, you were already in bed by then?"

"Young man, I'm seventy-one years old. I get up with the sun and go to bed by it. I try to sleep, too, at least when The Foursome wasn't raising such a ruckus I couldn't. Then I turned to my muffs."

"Earmuffs?"

"That's right. The first ones were invented by Chester Greenwood, over to Farmington, eighteen hundred and seventy-three. Called them 'ear protectors,' and every December, on the first day of winter, they celebrate with the whole town in earmuffs and a running race and parade and all sorts of things. In any case, though, those city folks over there made so much noise when they were up, I used cotton in my ears and muffs over them to get any sleep at all."

"What kind of noise did they make?"

"Oh, that rock music and carrying on drinking strong spirits and what have you. Sound really travels over the water, hits off the east shore and then down to me."

"When they made noise, did it upset your dogs?"

"At first Jack and Jill'd howl all night. I finally got them trained to where they'd just bark a bit when The Foursome turned up their phonograph."

"Did you start calling them that from the news stories?"

"Christ come to earth, no, young man. That was what they had painted across the Queen Mary in their boathouse. 'FOURSOME.' They'd tear around this little cove, hollering and laughing and water-skiing, scaring the loons half to death. Marseilles Pond wasn't meant for such carrying on."

"Back to that night. What did you do after the dogs woke you up?"

"Well, now, I'm some sound sleeper once I can drop off, so it took me a minute to get the muffs off and the cotton out and figure what was bothering them. There was phonograph music coming from over there, but it was on when I went to bed, and wasn't so loud it should have bothered Jack and Jill to waking me. Then I heard him."

"Him?"

"Your client, I guess. Mr. Steven Shea. Screaming his bloody lungs out."

"You heard Shea screaming?"

"I did. Well, I didn't know it was *him* right then, you see. I had to get myself up and thought about starting the Bronco, but it's been a little iffy lately, and—"

"Excuse me, the Bronco?"

"My vehicle. Outside, you saw it."

"I thought it was a Scout."

"Lots do. Ford made it back in nineteen hundred and sixty-seven, it did. Made it to last, too. Standard transmission, none of this automatic nonsense."

"So you decided to walk."

"Well, run's more like it. I took the road instead of the path. Even though the road's a mite longer, it's better lit if you have some moon, and we had some moon that night. Well, I throw a coat on over my nightdress and grab the Weatherby and get myself over there."

"The Weatherby's the shotgun?"

"Yessir. Weatherby Olympian. Twelve gauge she is, better than the day they made her. Six hundred dollars this feller was asking for his in *Uncle Henry's*."

"A gun shop?"

"Beg pardon?"

"Uncle Henry's is a gun shop?"

"Christ come to earth, no. *Uncle Henry's* is . . . well now, it's like a weekly catalogue, I'd guess you'd call it, for swapping or buying. You got something you want to get rid of, you list it in *Uncle Henry's*, and the world'll beat a path to your door. Guns, boats, cars, furniture, you name it."

58

"Okay. Back to that night, as you're going to Shea's place, did the screams continue?"

"No, not like an opera of them. More like one once in a while, some long, some short. Like the loons."

I felt a little cold. "Then what?"

"Well, I got to the parking lot Mr. Shea had himself built, and I see his truck and the fancy roadster I know the other couple has, and the screams when they come are coming from the house. So, I go up on their—what do you call it, that dock they got built against their house?"

"A deck?"

"The deck, right. I get myself up there and come in the kitchen door, account of that's open, let in every bug in creation. And there's your client in the great room, kind of moaning, cradling his wife's head and shoulders in his left arm like she's a little doll."

"Then what?"

"Then I see the crossbow in his right hand and the arrow thing—they don't call it an arrow, I recollect—sticking out from the poor girl's body, so I kick the bow out of his hand and keep the Weatherby on him."

"He was holding the crossbow while he was holding his wife?"

"He was. One in each hand, like I told you. Then I see this other body, a man's, kind of inside one of those fancy sliding doors, but like he took the screen door with it when he fell. And he's got an arrow-thing in his chest, too. That's when I heard something out past the front—deck, you call it?"

"Deck."

"Deck."

"What did you hear?"

"Heard Dag calling out."

"You saw him?"

"No. I heard him. Something wrong with your hearing?"

"You knew it was his voice?"

Judson stopped. "I expect I know a neighbor's voice, young man."

"What was he saying?"

"He was asking if everything was all right, which it wasn't."

"Do you remember exactly what he said?"

"He said, 'Mr. Shea? Mrs.—no, that wasn't it. She kept her maiden name, some Jewish—Mrs. Newberg, that was it. Then he said, 'Everybody all right? I thought . . .' "

Judson stopped again.

I said, "That was it?"

"That's when I yelled for him to get up and help me."

"Help you?"

"Christ come to earth, yes. I didn't want to take a chance using the telephone while I kept my gun on your client."

"So Dag Gates came up the front steps to the deck?"

"He did. Said something profane I cannot repeat to you when he saw the body of the other girl out on that . . . deck."

"You didn't see her body?"

"Not right then. Not from inside the house, I mean. It was off to the side from where you'd notice it through the glass doors."

"So Gates came into the house?"

"He did. Nearly lost his supper when he saw that first body out on the deck wasn't the only one. I managed to get him on to the telephone to call Patsy's office."

"The sheriff."

"How many Patsys you met up here, young man?"

"And how long before the sheriff arrived?"

"Didn't have need to be a clock-watcher. I was paying attention to your client."

"How did he seem to you?"

"Like he was putting on being quietly hysterical."

"Putting on?"

"He had the bow in his hand when I came in on him."

"So you think he did it?"

"You ever hear of 'a smoking gun'? Well, that's what Patsy called it when she arrived. 'A smoking gun' if ever there was one."

"Why didn't Shea run for it before you got there?"

"I don't know. You're his detective. Ask him."

"I mean, if Shea had killed those people with the crossbow, why wait around, screaming, until help arrives, then stay after you got there?"

"Young man, I don't know these things. I only know what I saw and heard. As you told me would be fine."

I didn't want to lose her. "Did you notice anything else in or around the house?"

"No. I wasn't 'around the house,' though, just inside it. After Dag called for Patsy, him and I stayed right there in the great room, watching Mr. Shea."

"Any footprints?"

"Just some bloody ones, running from near the man's body by the glass door across the floor and—well, now. I don't think I actually saw the footprints go up the stairs to the second floor, but I remember Patsy and the state police talking about them."

I pushed back in my chair. Ma Judson was a good enough observer to be able to keep straight what she'd seen from what she'd been told. And with her forthright manner, she'd make a devastating witness however she dressed.

Coming forward again, I said, "How did Dag Gates get here that night?"

"By boat, same as he always does." Judson squinted past me at the lake. "Same as he's doing now."

I turned. Something that looked like a war canoe was coming toward us, maybe a hundred yards out, apparently under motor, though I heard no put-put sound rolling in front of it. One man seemed to be in it near the back, sitting sideways. To run the motor, I guessed.

I turned back to Judson. "Quiet."

"Dag uses only electric."

"Electric?"

"Electric motor. Call them 'trolling motors.' He's a man with some respect for the environment. Gave more than most for it, too."

"How do you mean?"

She crossed her arms. "I reckon that's for him to tell you, he wants to."

Okay. "I understand Steven Shea bought his house from your brother."

The flinty look, and the arms hugged themselves tighter. "Then you heard wrongly, young man. My brother gave away that land, practically. Out of spite."

"Spite for what?"

"I think I've said all I will on that point."

"I can just ask him."

"Your client? You certainly—"

"No, not my client. Your brother."

Judson stood up. "Young man, my brother is dead some years now. And this interview is over."

The old woman clomped down her steps and marched toward the water, where the canoe was coming in.

5

I FOLLOWED MA JUDSON DOWN THE PATH TO HER DOCK, square like the one at the inn but much smaller. There was an old wooden rowboat, stern in the water, bow and midships hauled up onto a second, sunken dock that functioned as a ramp. She was making room on the square dock, moving a folding chair, tackle box, and fishing rod to the side so that the man bringing in the green, square-back canoe could land and get out.

He was about my age, with a black, droopy mustache and scraggly beard. His hair reminded me of Patsy Willis's: It was long, pulled back into a ponytail, and tucked inside the collar of a pale blue shirt with epaulets. The pants were cutoff khaki shorts, splotches of what I hoped was fish blood all over them. His eyes were the color of his shirt and slanted wisely up toward his temples, the smile beneath the mustache toothy and open. All in all, he looked like a biker masquerading as a game warden.

Except for two things. His left arm and right leg were missing, neither stump even visible under shirt and shorts.

Ma Judson said, "Dag."

The man smiled broader. "Ma, you stepping out on us?"

Judson blushed again, as she had about the dogs sleeping in her room. "Oh, you go on now."

His left foot did something to a black pedal on the bottom of his canoe. A buzzing noise I hadn't really noticed suddenly stopped, the pedal's electric cord running to a truck battery under his seat. He used the right hand to put a rope between his teeth, waiting until the canoe nudged the dock to lever himself up from a sitting position in the stern of the canoe to a sitting position on the edge of the dock, like someone coming out of a swimming pool without using the ladder. Then Gates got his left foot under him and stood up in a hopping motion, swaying in a practiced way until he was in front of me and balanced a little to the left of vertical.

He extended his hand. "Dag Gates."

"John Cuddy." His shake felt like the jaws of an alligator, the arm muscles like bunched cords under the skin.

Gates took in my clothes. "What brings you out here, John?"

His voice had more of New York than Maine in it, the words pronounced like a Brooklynite but with the clipped pacing I'd been hearing all day.

Ma Judson said, "Already been through this myself, you don't mind. I'll fetch Runty for you, Dag."

"Thanks, Ma."

As Judson went back up the path, Gates looked to me.

I said, "I'm a private investigator from Boston working on the Shea case."

"The . . ." His face dropped. "You mean the killings, then."

"That's right."

The index finger and thumb worked on the mustache at the right corner of his mouth. The thumbnail was broken and yellowed. "Guess you'll be wanting to talk to me about it."

"If I could."

A reluctant nodding. "Seems right. Let me just get the dog here, and you can come back to my place, sit for a while."

"John, look to your left, now. About ten o'clock off the bow. See that loon dive?"

The water was crystal clear and not so deep you couldn't see the bottom. The big black and white bird went by the canoe, almost under it, using its wings to propel itself through the water. I almost couldn't believe my eyes.

Gates said behind me, "What does that look like to you?"

"Like it's flying underwater."

"That's exactly how I'd describe it. First time I saw that, I rubbed my eyes, thought I must be hallucinating."

"Mr. Gates—"

"Dag, please."

"Okay. But what's 'Dag' short for?"

A pause behind me. Runty, who was between us in the canoe, snuffled twice.

"Actually, John, it's short for 'diagonal.' After I lost my arm and leg, a little boy saw me in the hospital lounge and said to his mother, 'Look, Mom, it's daggonel man,' on account of how my right arm and left leg made me seem. Well, one of the nurses heard it, and of course the mother was real embarrassed, so I said, 'That's fine, son. Call me Dag from now on. It fits.' And so it's been, though 'Donald' was my given name."

Gates steered the canoe in toward the shore. As we had pulled away from Ma Judson's place, I'd looked behind me, and realized that you could see her cabin only if you were directly in front of it and pretty close to shore, when her boat and dock stopped looking like big rocks and took on

65

artifact form. As we approached the east shoreline, the same was true for Gates's property. The white birch Sheriff Willis pointed out to me spread above a simple dock. Unlike Judson's sunken dock, though, there was a ramp for the canoe made of short logs nailed together to form a series of X-shaped ribs, like an inverted picnic bench. After Gates let me and the dog off on his dock, he guided the canoe at a relatively high speed toward the ramp, pulling up a stringer with one good-sized bronzed fish on it from over the gunwale. He slacked off the motor just as the bow hit the first "X," the canoe riding up onto it and its neighbors. Then he climbed out, the stringer in his hand. A long cane fishing pole with a rubber frog on its line stayed in the boat. Gates hopped agilely to the birch, set down the fish, and then played out line from a small hand winch on the birch. Going back to the canoe, he put a metal "S" through an eyelet on the bow and hopped back to the tree, cranking the winch and bringing the canoe all the way up and out of the water.

I said, "Pretty clever."

"Used to teach shop, John. Or 'Industrial Arts,' you want to be formal. Comes in handy to sort of compensate for things." He picked up the fish again. "Okay if I clean him while we talk?"

"Sure."

"Hate not to clean them while they're still fresh. Take that little folding chair from by the dock. I use it to watch the sunset, but it ought to hold you just fine."

I opened the chair with its white and green vinyl strapping and settled into it, Gates showing me his back as he moved to a rough table a few yards in from his dock. There was a spring clamp on the end of it and some lime-sized stones lying on top of it. Gates whacked the fish on the head with the handle of his knife. Runty barked once as Gates used his elbow to open the clamp and his hand to position the fish's tail under the clamp, releasing his elbow to allow the clamp to hold the fish.

Gates smiled at the dog. "Runty, he gets excited when he sees a smallmouth, John. He doesn't bother my chickens, but these bass, they drive him nuts, don't they, Runty?"

A quick yip.

Gates started the knife quickly on the fish. "So, what do you need to know?"

I looked over to the west shore. The Shea house and its lawn stuck out of the surrounding forest like the proverbial sore thumb. "It would help if you could tell me what you saw and heard that night."

"At the house, or before, now?"

"Before."

"Before. Well, I'd left old Runty here in the camp to go out and try some night fishing."

"You fish at night a lot?"

A rueful grin. "When your client and his friends were up, I did."

"Noisy."

"Some. But, hey, it's their summer place, so I figure they're entitled. Besides, night fishing is usually pretty good. Anyway, I'm out in the canoe, toward the north end of the pond and behind one of the islands, when I hear this screaming. Well, when you're on the water, and behind an island, it's tough to tell just where noise is coming from sometimes. So I pull out into the open a bit, and I can tell it's coming from down our end of the pond. I put the electric on ramming speed and get myself down here fast as I can. Now, I was some distance from the house, but I'd guess it was only ten, twelve minutes till I got there. I beached the canoe by the boathouse and headed up the lawn, calling out for people, see if I got an answer. And I didn't, except for Ma."

"What'd she say?"

"She yelled for me to get the hell up there, onto the deck, I mean. So I managed to do that, and—Christ. . . ."

Gates took a deep breath and set down the knife, busying himself with the clamp and turning the fish over to go for the fillet on the other side.

He had the fish repositioned, but didn't pick up the knife right away. "There's this woman, the wife in the other couple, flat on the deck with an arrow through her, eyes open. . . ."

Gates shook his head, finally starting in again with the knife. "Her husband's across the threshold of the center door, feet on the deck, another arrow in him. Then inside, Ma's got her shotgun on Shea, and there's this crossbow, all bloody, at her feet, and Shea's on the floor, like holding his wife, who's also got an arrow—Christ, John, it was like what one of those Indian massacres must have been like, you know?"

"The crossbow was at Ma Judson's feet?"

"Yeah. I heard from Patsy—that's our sheriff?"

"I've met her."

"I heard from Patsy that Shea's fingerprints were all over the bow, but you must know that, right?"

"Right."

"Well, Ma tells me to call the sheriff. So I use the phone in their great room and reach a deputy, and he says he'll radio the sheriff, get her over right away."

"What did you do then?"

"Tried not to throw up. That's what surprised me the most, I suppose. It . . . the whole scene, it got worse the longer I was there. I thought the initial shock of seeing everything would be the worst, but it wasn't. It was waiting there for Patsy to arrive that got to me."

"Did you see anybody else around the house that night?"

Gates stopped with the knife again. "No. It was a nice night, and I watched the sunset from the dock with a beer just before I went out. I don't recall seeing any other boats or anybody else around your client's place. I wasn't out by the island too long when I heard the screaming start."

Gates seemed to finish with the bass. He used his elbow to release the fish's tail from the table, leaving two sizable fillets. Then he stabbed the fish carcass six or seven times before shoving one of the stones through the mouth and down into the gullet. Gates carried the carcass by the lower jaw to the edge of his dock, flinging it out toward the center of the lake.

I said, "Isn't that kind of littering?"

"No." He hopped back up to me. "Punching holes in its innards and stuffing that stone down its throat means it'll sink to the bottom, where the crayfish and other things'll get a good meal. You saw the size of some of the crayfish in this pond, John, you wouldn't wiggle your toes in her. Come on up to the house."

As he gathered the fillets from his table, I followed him up the gentle incline. Gates—or somebody for him—had cut a winding path like Ma Judson's. His house seemed newer by far than hers, however. A small, one-story bunga-low, the wood was a soft, natural yellow that blended into the shade from his tall trees. There was one picture window with a small deck only two feet off the ground in front of it, a screened porch next to it. The porch was more rustic than the bungalow, with logs as posts and beams and lintel above the door, two Adirondack chairs and a small, slatted table between them as furniture.

Gates got up the three deep steps to his deck and held the screen door with a shoulder for me as Runty went off running after something. This close to the house, I could hear the noise of chickens out behind it. Inside the porch was a door leading to a cozy living room. The walls of the living room were lined with books, here and there pewter beer mugs, hunting knives, and driftwood as whatnots on the shelves. A sturdy black wood stove occupied the center of the room, two easy chairs on a sisal rug facing it. Kitchen and bathroom finished the downstairs, a small sleeping loft shoehorned under the peaked roof.

Gates disappeared into the kitchen. I looked at the books. Alpha by author, but a wide range of subjects, from engineering to art history. A more than representative sampling seemed to deal with the environment. A shelf under a side window held a small laptop computer, a straight-back caned chair in front of it. Next to one easy chair was a *New York Times*, three days old.

From the kitchen, Gates said, "You care for a beer, John?"

"I would, thanks."

"Catch."

I turned. From the doorway he tossed a can of Miller's Genuine Draft to me.

Gates hopped out with one for himself. "Hope you don't mind the can."

"It's fine."

"The pop-top is just a lot easier for me than a bottle cap. Let's sit on the porch."

I let him take one Adirondack chair before I took the other. He had an Audubon Society guidebook on birds on the slatted table, some binoculars and a pad next to it. From the lake, you really couldn't see his house. From his house, though, you could see the lake and the Shea house through the trees, the limbs crossing the view in a natural but not obstructing way.

I said, "How can you have this kind of view without cutting down the trees?"

Gates took a swig of beer, licking the foam off his mustache. "Not so hard, really. You just sit where you want the view from, then tell a couple of the boys to climb the trees and take a limb here, a limb there. Bingo, you've got a window through the woods without the people on the water being able to see you."

I studied the trees. "I don't see where they cut the limbs."

"I had the boys put black paint over the wounds. Covers them cosmetically as well as protects the tree from insects and other critters using the wounds to get inside her."

"Pity Steven Shea didn't do that."

Gates rested his can on the arm of his chair. "You've met him, too?"

"Not yet."

"Brace yourself."

"He comes on strong?"

"Kind of . . . single-minded. When he got started on his building, I went over to introduce myself, feel him out a bit on what he planned on doing. I made every suggestion I could think of to help him protect his land and the pond with it. He just nodded and smiled and then clear-cut to his heart's content. All so legal, all so stupid. You've seen the erosion over there?"

"The gully with the little bridges over it?"

A snort. "The damned fool! How he expected his 'lawn' to make up for trees there going on a century is beyond me."

"I thought there already was a house there."

"Was, kind of. Old Tom Judson's camp. He was worse, in his own way, Old Tom."

"How do you mean?"

Gates looked at me. "Nobody told you the story?"

"I guess not."

He sighed and took another swallow of his beer, forgetting to lick the foam this time. "It was seven years ago this month. Old Tom was president of Judson Lumber— his sister, Ma, she never got much involved in the business. Judson Lumber had title to this whole end of the lake, picked it up for a song from a farmer in the 1880s that clear-cut it for meadowland, then went hard broke in some depression. Anyway, the natural timber growth over a hundred years restored itself, as it will, and it was about time for the company to think about logging it again."

"They're allowed to log so close to a lake?"

"Used to be. Well, I was at Rutgers down in New Jersey in the late sixties and went to the first Earth Day, spring of 1970. You remember that at all?"

"I remember the twentieth anniversary stuff a few years ago."

"Well, back in 'seventy, it was a big thing on our campus. What with the war and all. . . ." Gates paused. "You in it?"

"For a while."

He paused again, then nodded. "There were a lot of us who weren't so much against the war as against everything that seemed to be going on. The draft, Nixon, the rape of the environment. So anyway, that first Earth Day, I went to the teach-ins and demonstrations about how to save the planet, and I came away really believing in them. I majored in education, Industrial Arts in particular, and dabbled with ways to make things better, cleaner. I even started vacationing up in Vermont and New Hampshire, but when I saw Maine, John, I knew I was hooked. I tried to figure out how I could get to be here, since there aren't that many jobs around, period. I finally saved some money and moved up, just about making it in Augusta by bagging groceries at the Shaw's, that kind of thing.

"Well, turns out old Tom Judson is going to cut all this timber except for his sister's parcel and his own. So this environmental group I belonged to got wind of it and decided to demonstrate at his lumber mill. We go over there, and Old Tom himself—big, bluff man, looked a little like Ted Kennedy with the boozer's nose, you know?—ordered us all off. We were being a little stupid, John, carrying buckets of scrap iron to kind of screw up the machinery. Well, I barge past him and a couple of his men and into the mill itself. Old Tom catches me just as I'm about to throw my bucketful into the works. Here, now, it depends on who you believe. Tom said I was swinging the bucket at his head. I say I was just trying to keep it away from him. Anyway, he shoves me, hard, and I . . ."

Gates took some more beer, then applied the cold can to his forehead. "I pitch over backwards and into the works myself. Four witnesses said Tom took his sweet time turning off the machinery, even knocking aside one of his men who was trying to get to the switch. By the time the yelling was over, I'd lost the arm and the leg."

I didn't say anything.

Gates set his can down. "Tell you the truth, I was lucky to live. No hope of reattaching the parts, both ground to hamburger. But it gave me a hell of a lawsuit, John, a hell of a lawsuit. We settled it by Old Tom—actually, Judson Lumber itself—deeding me this side of the shoreline, with a chunk of money to build this camp—all cedar, John—and another chunk to keep me set modestly the rest of my days."

"Quite a story."

"It's a tale, I'll warrant that."

"How did Ma Judson feel about all this?"

"She was appalled. By what her brother did to me, I mean. Don't know that they spoke after that."

"Before he died."

"Right."

"How did he die?"

Gates looked over at me, his eyes sad. "Halloween night, maybe three years back, he stepped into a bear trap."

"A what?"

"A big trap, with those saw teeth in them. Old Tom collected that kind of thing. After he sold his camp to your client and his place in town, he moved up the mountain, big house. He got drunk one night and got himself caught in one of his traps and bled to death."

"Halloween, you said?"

"That's right."

"You think it could have been a prank?"

A thoughtful look. "Hard to say, John. Folks up here treat Halloween differently than most places."

"How do you mean?"

"They'll fill big orange trash bags with balled-up newspapers, some rocks to hold her down, then mark on her in black to make huge jack-o'-lanterns. They do almost Nativity scenes with white sheets on the figures, like ghosts instead of shepherds and wise men. You'll even see a dummy of a devil or a witch, hanging from a tree limb by a noosed rope. Halloween is an important holiday in the woods, John."

"Any idea why?"

"Maybe because it's . . . basic? Like any pagan ritual, it's something you don't let loose of because it reflects the way the environment works much better than recent overlays like Judaism or Christianity."

"Do you know who found him?"

"Tom Judson?"

"Yes."

"Sure. It was Owen Briss."

"The carpenter?"

"Carpenter, mechanic, trapper. You name it, Owen's done it. Built those little gully bridges for your client, used to be a logger for Old Tom till he did something to piss him off."

"Do you know what it was?"

"Yeah. The day of that demonstration at the mill?"

"Yes."

"Owen's the guy Old Tom pushed away from the switch."

Gates had managed to control his voice.

I said, "You know how I can find Briss?"

"Yes. He's got a trailer over the other side of the mountain, maybe five miles from the village. They can give you directions from the Marseilles Inn. Ralph and—"

"I'm staying there."

"Fine. If we're finished here, I can run you back."

"You sure? I can walk."

A smile. "Mosquitoes'll start up any time now, John. You walk through the woods, you'll be eaten alive. Besides, it's just twenty minutes across to the inn."

"Thanks."

Gates dropped the smile, seeming to think about something. "John, one more thing?"

"What's that?"

"You go see Owen, he's a touchy boy."

"Touchy."

"Quick to temper. What I'm saying is, you be careful when you deal with folks up here."

"Careful how?"

"They're . . . they're a little like their holidays. Halloween, for example. Mainers like Owen are basic and natural, John, and nature for all her glory can be a damned dangerous thing."

6

DAG GATES BROUGHT ME BACK TO THE VILLAGE IN HIS CANOE, Runty being left home for dinner. As soon as the sun dropped low in the sky, the air got cool, and once in the boat, almost cold. Gates had the foresight to lend me a sweatshirt to wear over my tie and under my suit jacket. It took almost half an hour at the electric motor's cruising speed to reach the Marseilles Inn, but given the condition of the camp road I'd come over with Sheriff Patsy Willis, the canoe ride probably took no longer than a car would have.

I got out at the inn's dock, returning Dag's sweatshirt to him. Swatting at mosquitoes, I began to climb toward the back of the building. A striking woman in her late thirties with frosted hair in a pixie cut and a genuine smile was waiting for me at the screen door to the porch.

She said, "Mr. Cuddy?"

"John, please."

"John, I'm Ramona Paine. Welcome to the inn."

She had a Maine accent rather than her husband's Philadelphia twang. We shook hands, hers a little powdery, a smudge of flour on one of her cheeks.

Ramona said, "Ralph told me you were here on account of Steven Shea."

"That's right."

"I expect you'll be wanting to talk to me. Before or after dinner easier for you?"

"Whichever is easier for you."

A little whoop. "Finally, a guest who understands how to get good service for himself. You go upstairs and freshen up. Dress casual if you've got them, we don't stand on ceremony here. Dinner'll be ready by the time you are."

I made my way through the empty downstairs sitting room. The major furniture consisted of two love seats opposing each other around a fireplace with black andirons and tools. A number of old chairs, plushly upholstered, were stationed at various strategic points near a reading lamp, a brochure stand, and a dry bar in one corner.

I went around to the big staircase by the front entrance. Still no sign of Ralph.

Upstairs, I showered and changed to a clean shirt with tan slacks. The view out my window drew me to it. Three small outboards, fishermen and their rods silhouetted against the water by the sun dying behind the mountain. A couple of water birds, one the size of a pterodactyl, came in low, then wheeled and disappeared. Some insects were chirping loudly enough to come through the closed glass.

When I got back downstairs, Ralph was in a dress shirt with long-point collar, tending the dry bar in the sitting room.

"What'll you have, John?"

"Vodka and orange juice?"

"You got it. Take a seat and feel free to read instead of talk. This place is supposed to be like home."

I walked over to the bar while he mixed my drink. "This place is already more like home than where I live. You been up here long?"

"Oh, not so long myself. Used to be a trucker out of Philly, come up here on and off. Met Ramona when she was managing one of the motels down to Augusta." He stopped, smiled, and handed me the screwdriver. "Hear that?"

"Hear what?"

"Me saying 'down to Augusta' instead of 'down in' or 'over in.' Even when you don't have the accent, you start picking up on the way Mainers say things."

I tried the screwdriver. "That happened to me in the service."

"Did it now?"

"Yeah. I was stationed in Georgia for a while, and I found myself saying 'y'all' and 'preciate it.' Wore off once I got back to Boston."

Paine said, "How's the drink?"

"Almost too good."

"You mix the first one strong, I've found folks don't complain about the rest."

"Expecting many people tonight?"

"Only got a few staying over, and they're still out sightseeing. My guess is you'll be it for an hour or so."

"As long as we're alone, mind if I ask you a few questions?"

Paine looked thoughtful. "Guess not, long as it would help Steven Shea."

"How well did you know him before this happened?"

"You mean before the night of the killings."

"Right."

"He stayed here some nights, usually weekends, when his house was going up. Him and his wife come in for drinks or dinner once in a while. And of course they'd be in to the store for things when they'd be up at their camp."

"Driving here from Augusta, I got the impression you're about it in terms of shopping."

"Coming from Boston—Augusta way—that's right. Only groceries for twelve miles."

"So they pretty much used your store exclusively."

"Couldn't say that. Most of the weekenders, they buy a lot at the Shaw's or the Shop 'n Save down to Augusta, then come to us for whatever. Steven, now, we'd see him about every day."

"Why's that?"

"You met him yet?"

"Probably tomorrow."

"Well, Steven is kind of a classic sales type, no offense to him. Big smile, shake, hand on the shoulder? But he didn't have much concentration, and that wife of his . . ."

Paine stopped, sucked in his lips.

I said, "What about his wife?"

"I'm not what you'd call religious, but I have trouble speaking ill of the dead."

"It won't go any further."

Paine waited a moment, then said, "She wasn't the kind to use first names, you know? A little snooty, I always thought. And she didn't give him much help in the groceries department."

"How do you mean?"

"Well, sometimes she'd come in with him to the store, but mostly never, and never really help when she did. Just kind of stand around with her arms crossed and try not to brush into anything, like everything had been on the shelves too long and would get her dirty."

Paine had a nice eye for detail. "You didn't see Shea at all that night?"

"Nossir. But I think when you talk to Mona, she'll tell you he come in like always, a little tipsy already and looking to buy some more for his foursome."

"That's really how they were known, huh?"

"Yessir. Out on their deck, you could hear them sometimes all the way up here. Laughing and carrying on. I swear, I'd have bet the homestead they were about the least likely people this sort of thing would ever happen to."

I was about to ask about Owen Briss when Ramona Paine's voice behind me said, "Ralph, stop bending this gentleman's ear and let him get to his supper."

I followed her to the dining room, Ralph behind me. She motioned toward the single bench of a small booth in one corner. The bench was of highly polished maple with a green leather seat. The corner had two windows, each facing water.

Ramona said, "Long as you're alone, this little nook is the best spot in the house."

As I slid along the padded bench, the one-eyed calico jumped up onto the outside sill of one window.

Ramona noticed it and said, "You like cats?"

"Not until recently."

"She bothers you, just tap the glass with a fingernail and off she'll go. I took the liberty of making a Rock Cornish game hen for you. That all right?"

"Fine."

"Stuffing's my own, combination of nuts, cranberries, and you don't want to know what else. Salad before, fresh carrots and broccoli with, dessert after."

Lifting the screwdriver, I said, "You have any white wine by the glass?"

"No. But I do have a bottle in our big cooler that was Steven Shea's favorite. He can't enjoy it, you might as well."

I tried to decide if I felt guilty about that, decided I had no reason to yet. "Fine."

"Dressing?"

"How's the house?"

The genuine smile again. "You are a perfect guest."

As Ramona went back to the kitchen, I looked around

the dining room. Six trestle tables with press-back or ladder-back chairs in this room, two more bench-style booths, others in an adjoining one. Ruffled curtains on the windows, polished hardwood floors, china plates and platters standing vertically in wire holders on shelves.

A ripple of relaxation went through me, and I finished the screwdriver.

Shea's wine turned out to be a Sterling sauvignon blanc so austere it was like sipping dry ice. The house dressing was honey mustard, the hen and stuffing heaven, the homemade bread and cherry pie perfect. I ate more in one meal than I usually do in two days.

Ramona asked me if I wanted coffee. When I declined, she brought a mug for herself and an extra ladder-back chair over to my booth. She used her cupped hand like a broom to whisk crumbs from my tablecloth into her other palm, then disappeared for a moment before coming back and sitting down in the chair.

Ramona said, "I can give you ten minutes now or an hour tomorrow during the day."

"Ten minutes might do it."

She had some coffee. "Go ahead."

"Can you tell me everything you remember about that night?"

"Probably not everything, but here goes. We didn't have anybody for dinner that night, so I was over watching the store. Ralph was lying down upstairs, not feeling so hot. Anyway, I saw The Foursome go by in their cars sometime, kind of surprised they didn't stop."

"Why surprised?"

"Well, they almost always stopped in here for something, but it's better to do it on the way into camp than to get all the way in and have to come back out again. It's a good twenty minutes each way over that road."

Made sense. "Go on."

81

"Okay, Steve comes back alone in his truck, this kind of boyish grin on his face."

Steve. "I don't mean to interrupt, but can you tell me exactly what he said to you and you said to him?"

Ramona Paine took another slug of coffee. "He came in and said, 'Guess what, Mona?' "

" 'Mona?' "

A half smile. "Ralph calls me that. Always has. Steve heard him say it once and kind of picked it up. He's like that, Steve."

"Like what?"

"The salesman, always kind of . . . ingratiating himself?"

"Okay."

"So, where—oh, yes. Steve comes in, says 'Guess what, Mona? Not enough grape juice.' That's how Steve calls his wine, grape juice, like it didn't cost twenty dollars American by the bottle. So he's a little loose already, he wanders around the store, picking up this and that because he's not sure what else they might need out there."

"He say anything while he was wandering?"

"Just small talk. 'How's Ralph,' 'How's business,' nothing, well, memorable."

"Anything about his manner seem odd?"

"No. Patsy Willis and the state police detective, they asked me the same thing. It was Steve Shea, the usual."

"Then what?"

"Well, Steve comes over, things kind of"—Ramona Paine made a holding-the-baby gesture—"tumbling out of his arms onto the counter. I had to catch a can of pineapple, I remember. He bought two bottles of that Sterling you had tonight, and some bacon, and a dozen eggs—we carry them fresh here and at the store, thanks to Dag Gates. Probably Steve bought some other things, too, but not . . ."

"Memorable."

Ramona took a little more coffee. "Right."

FOURSOME

"You have any idea why Shea bought his wine by the bottle when it sounds like they drank it by the case?"

"No, no, I don't. I know he used to bring it up here himself from down to Boston for sure, account of I'd never seen such good wine this far north before. Just not enough market for it. Steve said, though, that it was such a pain to have to bring it up with them that he'd appreciate our stocking it for him, and he was a regular enough customer, we were glad to do that."

Just didn't sound right. "Did Shea mention any of the others that night?"

She looked troubled. "I thought about that, long and hard after we heard what happened. I think the only thing he said to me was, 'They're champing at the bit back there, Mona. I got to hurry.' "

Ramona blinked her eyes quickly and got up without finishing her coffee. As her back disappeared into the kitchen, I heard Ralph say behind me, "Whyn't you bring that last glass of wine out to the porch, enjoy the pond?"

I followed him onto the big screened porch. Its long axis was perpendicular to the shore, half a dozen elephant chairs in green wicker bolstered with yellow cushions. There were two wicker coffee tables, magazines and books on top and an oval, braided rug of a hundred colors underneath. Outside the screens, fireflies winked messages at each other in blips of chartreuse neon.

Paine arranged two of the chairs so they faced the night-skied water. I went toward one of them, Ralph drinking from an old-fashioned glass, Scotch, from the whiff of it. His hand was big enough I hadn't seen the glass in it when he'd moved the furniture.

As we sat down, a monstrous beetle with an orange belly and black carapace banged against the outside of a screen, its wings beating furiously on the mesh, a sound like a baseball card clothespinned to the wheel spokes of a 1950s Schwinn.

"What the hell is that?"

Ralph didn't need to look up. "June bug. Good thing God didn't give them teeth, there'd be none of us left." Then he changed tone. "Mona's still pretty upset about what happened down the pond."

"Understandable. You don't have to see dead bodies to feel them."

Paine nodded. "Why do I have the feeling you've seen more than your share?"

"Because you're an observant man, Ralph."

The wicker creaked a little as he resettled himself in it. "You get that way on the road, John. You get so you notice a lot of things, because basically the road never changes much until it reaches out to grab you. That means you have to notice things along it as you drive, make sure you're spotting the changes coming."

"You see changes coming here?"

"Oh, some. Probably not for the better, either. Don't get me wrong, now. I'm not like Ma Judson, or even Dag Gates. Some development's good, and it sure as hell will improve the profit from the store. But it'll take away a little from the inn."

"Take away how?"

"Oh, not from the place itself, that's always been in a village with other things around it. But from the people who'll stay in it, who won't ever get to see Maine the way Mona did or I did or even you did today. Loon and heron, eagle and hawk. They've been forever, but they won't be forever."

Ralph Paine finished his drink and stood slowly, creaking as much as the wicker. "Enjoy that wine, John, and just turn off the lights when you go up to bed."

7

THE SIGN AT THE DRIVEWAY FOR THE COUNTY JAIL BORE THE subtitle DETENTION CENTER. I drove the Prelude into the parking area.

The building itself was a red brick juncture of two quadrangles, like a squared-off hourglass. There was a sprinkling of cars in the lot around me, about enough for a skeleton shift of corrections officers and sheriff's deputies. Loading bays dominated the near end of the building, a chain-link fence enclosing some old picnic tables. There were broad windows looking on to the area, probably made of bulletproof Plexiglas. Mounted about ten feet above the ground were a series of video cameras that I bet had interlocking fields of vision. Sheriff Patsy Willis spent her budget wisely.

I left the car and walked to the double glass doors under a small portico that looked more designed to slow the snow than shade the sun. A woman came out as I got there. Fat and short, she wore a gaudy dress in blues, reds, and yellows, arms puffy above the elbow and jowly beneath it. I got the impression she'd worn the dress to cheer up somebody inside the place, and I held the door for her and gave her a smile I didn't feel as she said thank you.

Beyond the second set of glass doors was a waiting area like a bus station with fixed, plastic chairs. A windowed counter and steel-barred door occupied one wall, wanted posters another, and a row of vending machines the third.

I went up to the counter, a male deputy in brown uniform shirt and pants behind it. His crewcut head lifted in question, and I gave him my Maine identification card under the glass like a bank customer making a deposit. He studied the ID, nodded once, then again, and motioned with his hand toward the steel door. I walked to my side of it while he walked out of sight, then reappeared on his side with a brass key the size of a mallet. He used the key on the old cyclinder dead bolt in the door.

"Deputy Carl Higgs, Mr. Cuddy."

"Deputy."

Higgs locked the door behind me. "The sheriff, she's out right now, but she said you could see Steven Shea whenever you come by. I have to ask you, are you armed?"

"No."

"Anything metallic?"

"Belt buckle, parts of a pen and pad."

"May I see them, please?"

I showed him.

Another nod. "This way, please."

I decided I liked the way Willis or her husband had trained her people.

Higgs opened a twin to the first door, then a triplet beyond it. A simple, two-trap system that would make it nearly impossible for an inmate to get out. Just past the third door was a small rectangular area with linoleum on the floor and glass-walled rooms on each side.

Higgs pointed to the room on the left. "Just make yourself comfortable in there, and I'll have one of the officers bring Shea in to you. The officer'll stay in sight but not earshot. No passing of anything between you and Shea. Any questions?"

"Time limit?"

"Much as you want." A small smile. "This is Maine, Mr. Cuddy."

"Thanks."

As Higgs clanged the doors behind me, I went into the room. Centered there was an oak table that somebody could turn into a showpiece once the chewing gum, pen etchings, and sweatstains were sanded off. Two old secretarial chairs, one missing a wheel, kept company with a low pine bench worn down at both ends. I sat in the chair that was short a wheel, figuring Shea could use the extra comfort. I took out my pad and pen to wait, but it didn't take long.

An older deputy who could have been a young uncle of Carl Higgs came through a trap on the far side of the visiting area with an inmate in front of him. I recognized Steven Shea from the television coverage. He wore a bright orange short-sleeved shirt and orange pants faded a shade lighter. Whether they were stopped or walking, there was always an arm's-length distance between him and the guard. Shea appeared pale and thin from jail light and food, but he started smiling as soon as he saw me, a smile that was supposed to tell the person meeting him that he could sell anything.

Even his story.

The older deputy recited the same concise instructions as Higgs and then left Shea in the room with me, closing the door and moving to the opposite wall outside to stand at parade rest and watch us.

Shea waited until we were alone before extending his hand and pumping mine when I took his. "Boy, am I glad to see you."

"John Cuddy, Mr. Shea."

"Hey, what's with the 'mister' stuff? You're here to save my life, the least we can do is go on a first-name basis, right?"

I looked into his smiling face. Lots of laugh lines at the corners of chocolate brown eyes. Even features, cleft chin, hair that looked dry and lifeless but still retained some of its styled-every-week contours. An employee who'd been out sick and now wanted to reestablish himself with an open manner and some snappy patter.

"Let's sit down, Steve, talk a while."

"Sure, sure." Shea eased into the seat, but looked behind him doing it, as though he were making sure nobody would pull it out from under him. "Just sorry it has to be in here. Gil Lacouture told you they're holding me without bail, right?"

"He told me."

"Yeah, well, at least they're right about that, you know?"

"About what?"

"About denying bail. They let me out, I'd run like a thief, John. I'd run as far and as fast as I could from this nightmare."

His voice cracked a little on the last word, and Shea coughed to cover it. Not to accentuate it for dramatic effect, but to cover it, a genuine emotion.

He suddenly came back with, "Hey, you hear about this busty Brazilian stripper who left the stage to spend her time saving the Amazon rain forest?"

"No. Steve—"

"They call her 'The Lungs of the Earth.' "

His laugh was hollow, and when I didn't join in, it broke off abruptly.

I sat a little straighter in my chair, compensating for the missing wheel. "Since you're not going to be readily available to me, I'm going to ask you a lot of questions. Some answers I may not need now, but they might help me if I'm in Massachusetts and can't get back to you."

Shea grew businesslike. "Right, right."

"Start with the Vandemeers. How did you meet them?"

He clasped his hands in front of him on the table. "Okay, let's go back twelve years. I was working for a computer outfit then—made minicomputers for large, industrial applications—and I hit a few big accounts, like a lot of guys did back then. This builder had three lots on a cul-de-sac in Calem—you know the town?"

"A little."

"Well, each house on the horseshoe was special, built from a different set of plans. An old couple, the Epps, moved in first. He's dead now, but she's still there. Sandy and I bought the lot in the middle, Hale and Vivian the other one. I really felt like I'd made it, you know? This older rich couple on one side, a doctor and his wife on the other."

"You didn't know the Vandemeers till they became your neighbors?"

"No. Sandy was in the insurance business, but not selling it. More like an office manager for a department of Empire."

"You remember which?"

"Accounting, all her time in Boston."

I closed my eyes for a second. Sandra Newberg would have overlapped with me at Empire. I tried to match the crime scene photo with a live employee's face, but Claims dealt with Accounting a lot more than I did in Claims Investigation.

Shea said, "John?"

"Yes."

"You okay?"

"Yes. Fine. You hit it off with the Vandemeers?"

"From day one. It was like back in college, you know?

Freshman year, you meet some guys, it's like you're blood brothers? Well, that's the way it was. 'The Foursome,' we called ourselves."

"Vacation together?"

"Everything together. Dinners at the new restaurants, shows, symphony. Patriot games at Sullivan, Red Sox at Fenway, the Celtics when you could still buy tickets."

"About the vacations—"

"Vacations? Sure. We used to go on cruises, fly to the islands. Anywhere there was a beach, before Hale got religion about getting cancer instead of a tan. In fact, that was one of the reasons I bought the place on Marseilles Pond. With Hale all of a sudden sun-shy and his practice booming, we figured we needed a place we could all get together without reservations or hassles, kind of away from it all. So, when old man Judson heard I was interested in a lake place, he showed me his, and I jumped for it."

"How did you meet Judson?"

"When I was with the computer outfit, I sold him a new mini for his lumber company. He loved it, and he and I got to talking."

"Judson offered you his summer place because he liked the computer you sold him?"

A shrug. "I didn't press him on why, John. It was like love at first sight for me."

"But you tore down his place and built your own."

"Well, sure. I told him I would. You couldn't ask Sandy and Vivian to . . . *live* in the shack he had there. Besides, you could barely see the fucking lake."

I'd already been down that path with Ma Judson and Dag Gates. "Where did the crossbow come from?"

Shea darkened. He moved his tongue around inside his mouth before speaking. "One of Hale's toys. He was always doing that, always trying to pay us back for having him and Vivian up to the lake by bringing something for us to play with."

"He brought it up that weekend?"

"That . . . ? Oh, no. It was last summer . . . August, maybe? He bought it down in Mass someplace, then brought it up with him one weekend. We had some laughs with it, target practice, making the chipmunks kind of . . . scatter, you know?"

Shea grinned, then dropped it when he saw I didn't like that joke, either.

I said, "Where was the thing kept?"

"In the garage. Or shed, is what it is, really. Left over from when old man Judson had his place. Solid fucking thing, too big to move, too strong to dynamite."

Shea was getting jovial, trying to recover from the chipmunk remark. I was beginning not to like him very much.

I said, "Tell me what happened that night."

The jovial look disappeared, replaced by more clasping of hands on the table. "We kind of caravanned up, stopping at the Kennebunk rest stop to pee and then Augusta to food-shop. Everybody was feeling good, like we always did coming up to the lake. When we got to the house, though, I forgot we were low on wine. Should make a fucking list after each weekend, you know? But we hadn't been up on account of the black flies—bloodsucking little vampires—and I just forgot. So I got in the four-wheeler and drove back to Ralph and Ramona's store, got some wine and a couple of other things."

"How long did the drive take you?"

"Up here, you don't time that kind of thing."

"Approximately."

"Fifteen minutes. You've got to go slow over the road."

"How long were you in the store?"

"Left it at nine."

"How do you know that?"

"Ramona mentioned it. Looked at her watch and said it was closing time, she had to get back because Ralph wasn't feeling too well."

"Why did you have the Paines stock your expensive wine?"

Shea darkened again. "What?"

"Why did you have them stock a wine only you'd buy from them instead of getting it yourself by the case back home?"

He swallowed hard. "I . . . I figured, they're a real convenience to have around, but it's a tough life, trying to make it with just an inn and a general store. I figured, why not give them the business? Plus, this way I don't have to worry about keeping a lot of wine in the house up here for guys to be tempted to break in and steal."

Shea could have kept his supply at his house in Calem, and there were certainly other items in his lake house to encourage burglary. His answer didn't just sound wrong, it felt wrong, too.

I said, "Okay. You've got the wine. Then what?"

"I take the bagful of stuff, wine included, and drive back to the house. I get—"

"How long does it take you this time?"

"Jesus, John. I don't know. Probably a little longer, the sun's all the way down, and that road plays tricks on you, you don't respect it, even in a four-wheeler."

"All right, so maybe twenty minutes. That's about fifteen out, ten minutes with Ramona at the store, and twenty minutes back. Forty-five minutes total."

"Sounds right."

"You see anything on the drive back?"

"Anything?"

"Anybody."

"Oh. No. It's just us and Ma Judson on that road, John. Isolated."

"What happened when you got to the house?"

"I pulled the truck up next to Hale's car and got out with the grocery bag. Then I tripped over something on the path. The bag went flying as I caught myself against a tree, and I looked down, and it was the crossbow."

Shea's eyes got wide, his lips narrow. "I swear to you, John, I don't think I even noticed the thing in the garage since last summer, but there it was, lying on a flagstone. I picked it up, then decided I needed a flashlight to gather up the groceries right, so I went to the back door."

"You didn't have a flashlight in the car?"

My question threw him a bit. "Well, yeah. Yeah, I did, but I wanted to ask somebody what the hell the crossbow was doing out there. I mean, I was mad about it, see?"

"Mad that it made you trip and drop the groceries."

"Right." Shea seemed to realize that didn't ring very true, so he repeated, "Right," a little louder this time.

"Then what?"

"The back door was open—I mean, closed but not locked, just the way I'd left it. We don't usually lock things up when we're here. I came into the kitchen, and nobody was there, so I called out. Then—"

"What did you call out?"

"What?"

"Yes. Your exact words."

"Jesus, John, I don't know. Maybe, 'Hey, where is everybody?' "

"Nothing about the crossbow?"

Shea darkened a third time. "What do you mean?"

"I thought you were mad about it?"

"I was. But I figured, nobody's in the kitchen, I need somebody in front of me to get mad at, right?"

"Go ahead."

"So I went out toward the great room, and I . . . I . . ."
Shea put his hand up to his mouth, like a little kid about

to heave. Then he spoke through his fingers. "I saw Sandy. And Hale. They were . . . they had arrows through them. I don't know . . . I think I must have started screaming . . . I just remember dropping down by Sandy, lifting her head up, trying to hold her and tug the fucking arrow out of her, but it made a noise, and she made a noise, but it wasn't like her saying something or groaning, more like a rumble from inside her, and I knew she was dead. She wasn't cold or anything, she was just so . . . still except for that noise, and I knew she was gone. And I held her and cried, and I don't remember what else."

I gave him a moment. Shea took the hand from his mouth and massaged his jaw, as though it had clenched on him.

"Did you move around the room at all?"

"Huh?"

"Did you go over to check on Vandemeer?"

"Oh. No, I didn't. I don't think I did anything but hold Sandy till . . . I remember Ma Judson being there, and Dag Gates from across the cove. Then just cops and . . . John, they're reading me things you hear from the TV shows. They pull me into the station with just my car keys and wallet, not even my address book. They're telling me I get to make one phone call."

"You don't remember going upstairs."

"Upstairs? At the house, you mean?"

"That's what I mean."

"No. Why should I?"

"You know the sheriff's people found shoes in your bedroom closet with blood on them."

"They told me that."

"And?"

"And what?"

"You have an explanation for why they were there?"

"Of course I do. The shoes were planted!"

"Planted."

"By the killer. To set me up. Oh, they planned this out very cute, John, very cute."

"Who's they?"

He looked around, a conspirator about to share the important fact with his companion. The deputy outside the glass just watched us impassively.

Shea came back to me. "When I got the phone call—back here, I mean, when they brought me in, I called Anna-Pia Antonelli. She's our general counsel."

"Where you work now."

"Right, right. At DRM. She—"

"Why'd you call her instead of Gil Lacouture?"

"Huh?"

"Lacouture represented you when you bought Tom Judson's property, right?"

"Right."

"Then why use your call on a lawyer in Massachusetts rather than your lawyer here in Maine?"

"I'm getting to that. Anna-Pia wasn't there—home, I mean—when I called her, so I left a message, and she got back to me up here. She told me not to say a word, said she'd get in touch with our chief of security."

"Who's that?"

"Dwight Schoonmaker. He used to be government, now he like heads up our counterespionage stuff."

Christ. "What do you mean?"

"Our business, it's tough, John. Super tough nowadays, with the feds cutting back all the defense research and procurement programs that go with it. This whole thing—at my house on Marseilles?—this whole thing is a setup, something somebody who doesn't like us is doing to keep us from getting a contract somewhere."

"How?"

"By discrediting us through me! Don't you see it? One

of our potential clients is about to go with us, a competitor cuts us out by doing this to me and scaring the client away from us."

I sat back in my chair, not sure how far or hard I should push him on the James Bond theory. "You talk this over with Antonelli and Schoonmaker?"

"With Anna-Pia, no. With Dwight, yeah, when they came up here."

"Schoonmaker came up here to see you?"

"Yeah. Him and Anna-Pia both. She was off talking with the sheriff when Dwight and I went over the spy stuff."

"Anybody else come up to see you?"

"Just Tyrone Xavier."

"Who's he?"

Shea smirked. "The guy who wants my job. Ivy League and upwardly mobile. You talk to him over the phone, you can't even tell he's black, 'less the name gives him away."

I gave Shea the chipmunk look.

"Look, John, I'm not some racist asshole. I'm just telling you, like I'd describe Anna-Pia to you if her last name didn't tell you she was Italian. You grew up Irish like me, right?"

"Maybe. Anybody else at DRM who could help me?"

Shea seemed a little surprised. "What do you mean?"

"I mean, when I go out to DRM, is there anybody else I should talk with?"

"John, fuck, I don't want you stirring things up out there."

"Steve, you're facing three counts of murder one. Your only theory of who killed those people is some business competitor. I have to find out about that to give Gil something to work with."

"Hey, hey. I understand that. I do. It's just . . . This thing blows over, that's where I have to go back to."

Blows over. "Steve, there're other jobs."

Shea shook his head. "Not after this kind of thing smears you. But DRM, it'll take me back, no sweat. Just don't stir things, okay?"

I looked down at my pad. "You have a secretary there I could talk to?"

"No. My secretary was an airhead and took off a week before this happened. Hitchhiking around Europe."

"Since you've been in jail, has anybody else come to see you?"

"No."

"Nobody from the Vandemeer family?"

A grunted laugh. "The Vandemeer family is now reduced to two, John. There's Hale's brother, Hubbell, and there's Hale and Vivian's son, Nicky."

"How do I reach them?"

"Hubbell has a car dealership out past Calem, where he and Hale and Vivian all grew up."

"How did the Vandemeer brothers get along?"

"Okay, I guess. Hale told me he was helping his brother out, with the fucking recession and all."

"Helping him how?"

Shea rubbed his thumb and index finger together in a money sign.

I said, "How did Vivian get along with her brother-in-law?"

"Okay, I guess." A weak grin. "Sorry, I keep saying that. I never really thought about it, but I think Hub always had kind of a . . . yen for Vivian."

"Jealous of his brother?"

"I just don't know."

"How about the son, Nicky?"

"He's probably still living in the house in Calem." Shea shook something off. "Bad kid."

"How so?"

"Druggie, runs around with this Hispanic girl from the city. I know, I know, but that's how I think about people, John, size them up. I think about their backgrounds, where they're from originally, to help me see where they're coming from now. The only way to sell, John. The only way."

"What's the girlfriend's name?"

"You'd be wasting your time with Nicky and her."

"Her name."

"Oh, fuck, what is it? Bianca—no, that's Jagger's ex—Blanca. That's it, Blanca."

"Last name?"

"No, it's her first name."

"I mean, do you know her last name?"

"I don't think so. No."

I put a question mark after "Blanca." "If I need to see your house in Calem, how can I get into it?"

Shea seized up, as though the smaller, simpler things were giving him the most trouble. "Fuck, Hale and Vivian had a set of our keys, but the sheriff here has mine, and probably"—a faraway look took over his eyes—"probably Sandy's too, I guess."

Quietly, I said, "Alarm system?"

"No."

"Anybody else I should talk to?"

The eyes came back to me. "What do you mean?"

"Anybody you can think of who'd have a reason for doing something like this."

"A reason? Who the fuck could have a reason for doing something like this?"

"How about you, Steve?"

He froze. "Me?"

"Yeah. The sheriff seems awfully confident, but she hasn't said boo about motive. You have one?"

"No."

"You're sure about—"

"I said no!"

I decided to deflect him a little. "How about a guy named Owen Briss?"

"Briss? That pain in the ass. He's supposed to be working on my place, right? I give him enough things to do, it's like I'm supporting him. Me alone. Well, I tell him, I want that bannister to the second floor to look antiquey, right? So I tell him, put spindle pickets in the thing. So he nods his head and gives me an estimate, and I tell him to go ahead like I did with all the other things, but this time he fucks up, get me?"

"How?"

"He puts in the straight pickets, not spindle ones. So they don't look right, and I tell him I want him to pull them out and do it right. And he wants more money. So I tell him to fuck off, he can't get a specification right when he hears it, what good is he?"

"You think he might try something to get revenge?"

Shea shook his head vigorously. "No, no fucking way. He's got the brains of a jackrabbit. Maybe. Oh, he's a great guy with a hammer and saw, but not something this elaborate, John. No fucking way."

The brown eyes suddenly got misty. "I promised that balustrade for Sandy. As a present to her." He turned to me. "You remember that song Laura Brannigan did like ten years back?"

"Which one is that?"

"It's called 'How Am I Supposed to Live Without You?.' That new guy, Michael Bolton, he does it now. I never could picture a guy doing that song, you know that, John? I never could till now."

I folded my pad. "Everything going all right for you in here?"

"Jail, you mean? Oh, yeah. It's not . . . well, you read

and hear things about it being . . . like, homos and all, right? Well, it's not fucking like that here." The grunted laugh again. "Jesus, John, I'm using 'fuck' all the time now. It's because of this bunkie I got last week."

"Cell mate?"

"Yeah. Bad dude named Rick. Tough, but straight. He's wised me up on how to do time without being done myself. Besides, this is a county jail in Maine, not some state prison like Walpole down by us."

I thought about it. About why they'd give an accused multiple-murderer a bunkmate. About Sheriff Patsy Willis mentioning that she surprised people. "Look, don't say anything to Rick, all right?"

"What?"

"Don't talk with Rick about your case."

"Why not?"

"You don't know he isn't a plant."

"A plant?"

"Like the shoes in the closet. Except he can pass on what he hears."

Shea looked incredulous. "Jesus, John. This is Maine, remember? They're not like that up here."

"Steve, let me tell you something. They're like that everywhere."

8

As he let me out the second door of the double-trap, Carl Higgs said, "Sheriff's back. She'd like to see you before you leave."

The deputy led me through the control area and out another barred door into what seemed a less secure corridor with benches and a water fountain. Over the coffee machine were signs like BRING YOUR OWN MUG—STYROFOAM NEVER DEGRADES and a few others. Higgs pointed to a doorway that reminded me of my office: The top half was pebbled glass and had the word "SHERIFF" calligraphed in a quarter-moon arc.

I walked down the corridor, my shoes smacking on the tiles. Up close, the door gave the impression of being saved and brought from an earlier building. I knocked once and heard Patsy Willis say to come on in.

She was behind her desk, feet up on a secretarial pull-tray, fingers interlaced across her stomach. The Stetson was dangling from a coat tree, her hair coarse and streaked with silver as it was pulled back behind her neck, the heavy hanks sagging down toward her ears like the roof of one of the swaybacked barns.

"Have a seat."

"Thanks."

The institutional chairs in front of her desk had gray metal frames and green leatherette seats and backrests. I took one of them.

She said, "I see you've met up with a black fly."

"No contest."

"They are some fierce. Anything else you'll be needing from me?"

"Could I get a look at the murder weapon?"

"You mean the crossbow itself or the bolts?"

"Both."

Willis chewed on that for a minute, then picked up a phone and pushed a button. "Colin? . . . Patsy. . . . Can you go over to the evidence locker and pick up the bow and bolts on the Shea case?"

I said, "Sheriff?"

"Hold on a second, Colin." To me, "Yes?"

"Could I also have Shea's keys?"

"His keys?"

"To the house down in Calem."

Willis chewed on that, too. Into the phone she said, "Colin, bring all the keys we got from Shea, too. . . . Fine, thank you kindly."

She hung up. "Five minutes. Coffee?"

"No, thanks. Maybe a couple other questions, though."

"Shoot."

"I'm still troubled about what you see as a motive for the killings."

"Expect you'll feel that way till the trial, too."

Okay. "I understand the man that Shea bought his property from died kind of violently."

"Kind of."

"Possible for me to get a look at that file?"

"Not much to look at, and it's hard to see where Tom Judson's death fits into what you're doing here."

"Just trying to be thorough."

Willis patted one of the hanks of hair, then shook her head. "No. No, it's one thing to be cooperative on a current murder when you're the investigator for the defense. It's another to let you go fishing through old files on prominent local folks."

Not an unreasonable position to take for a cop who's also a politician. "Can you tell me something about what happened to him?"

She weighed that and nodded. "Outline it for you, anyways. Wasn't my first death on the job, and it sure wasn't the prettiest. Old Tom kept his spare liquor in his garage. He was partial to whiskey, and around here, it's easy to start on it a little early in the day, especially when November reminds you of what lays ahead."

"It happened in November, then?"

"Right—No, no, come to think of it, it was Halloween. Tom was in his big new place up on the mountain, playing around with his collection—bear traps and such—when the autopsy showed he was in no condition to be turning on a television without help. Somehow he primed a trap, then knelt on it or fell into it, and it closed onto his upper leg, severing that femoral artery there. I swear, there was so much blood around his garage, it was like somebody'd used a fire hose to spray it. He must have tried to pry the jaws open with his hands for a while before he passed out from the pain or blood loss."

"So he bled to death in his own garage."

"That's right."

"It was almost November, was his car there, too?"

"Yes. One car in a two-car garage."

"Wouldn't he have tried to drive out, get help?"

"Tom was owning a stick-shift Jeep Cherokee back then.

Tough thing to manage a manual transmission with the clutch leg in a bear trap."

"Telephone?"

"Looked like Tom tried to drag himself back up the three steps from garage into house, but couldn't quite do it before he went unconscious."

"Where exactly was his house?"

"Same place it is now. Or was, last time I checked on it."

"And where is that?"

"On the mountain."

"Which mountain?"

"The one above Marseilles Pond."

"You mean behind Shea's house?"

"That's the one. We passed Old Tom's driveway when I took you along the camp road, though you may not have noticed it."

"The paved stretch behind the chain with the little orange flags?"

She nodded.

I said, "No sign of foul play?"

"Foul play?" Willis gave her haw-haw laugh and shook her head. "Mister, you're gonna kill a man, you don't go laying traps for him in his garage. Besides, Tom wasn't the most loved of men in the community, but he put a lot of folks to work and food on their tables, and that goes for quite a ways around here."

I had a question for her that Dag Gates already had answered. "Who found the body?"

"Was Owen Briss."

"Briss tell you what he was doing up there?"

"Said Old Tom'd stiffed him on a job. Owen reckons a lot of people do that to him."

Just then, there was a knock at the door, and another

deputy came in with a big, flapped box that originally held photocopying paper.

Willis swung her feet down and said, "Thanks, Colin. Just put that right on the desk here, if you would."

Colin set it down. He handed her a set of keys with a form. She used a desk-set pen to scribble something on the paper. Colin took back the form and nodded to me as he left the room, closing the door behind him.

The sheriff tossed me the keys and moved to the box, lifting out a clear plastic bag with an identifying decal pressed onto its side. "This here's the one that got Mrs. Vivian Vandemeer."

I put Shea's keys in my pocket as Willis passed the bag to me. The bolt inside was about a foot long, gunmetal gray with black plastic fletching, the plastic fashioned to look like feathers. The arrowhead was only slightly broader than the shaft, the head and shaft for four inches below it still caked with dried blood.

"Can I see the others?"

She passed two more bags to me. The bolts seemed identical to the first, clearly a set or close to it.

"How about the crossbow itself?"

Willis showed a little flair in lifting the bagged bow clear of the box, maybe rehearsing the drama she'd create at trial when the prosecutor asked her a question like mine. Through the plastic, her strong hand hefted the crossbow at its balance point. The photo Lacouture had shown me didn't do it justice. Gray with yellow bands around the barrel area, its modernistic design had a recurve on the bow end with an assault rifle's stock and trigger area. The blood brown fingerprints still on it, the thing looked hideous, a death-dealer from the movie *Road Warrior*.

I said, "Can you show me how it works?"

Willis thought about that, then opened the bag and took

the crossbow out. "It's been all checked through the lab. Don't suppose it can hurt none 'less I break the string."

She flipped up a stirrup at the business end of the weapon. Lowering the bow to her right foot, she put the toe area of her shoe through the stirrup on the floor. Then she grasped the string with both hands, one on each side of the barrel, pulling the string back toward her waist until it caught on a lever at the top of the barrel to the rear of the trigger guard. Willis leveled the weapon at the far wall and pulled the trigger, the string making a "thwung" noise as it released and vibrated.

"Can I try it?"

Another hesitation. "Don't see why not."

I took the bow, guessing its weight at six or seven pounds, and recocked it the way she had. The pull was no more than fifty or sixty pounds, not enough strength required to automatically eliminate most people. I left the weapon pointed at the floor as I pulled the trigger. No kick, just an almost pleasant strum sensation from wrist to elbow, like the feeling of hitting a solid forehand in tennis.

I gave the crossbow to Willis, who put it back in the plastic. Returning bow and bolts to the box, she asked if there was anything else I needed.

"Just to know that you won't be asking Rick whether my client talks in his sleep."

A philosophical smile. "Law says we can't put an agent in the cell with your man. Nothing says we can't save the county some money by doubling up on accommodations with another accused felon."

"And if the cell mate just happens to learn something useful to the prosecution and wants to demonstrate his value to society?"

"Then it would be up to the prosecutor to decide whether to do some horse trading with the man. Not my barnyard, that sort of thing. I'm just a simple peace officer, Mr. Cuddy."

I'd made my point, and let it go at that.

I drove through the county seat and then back onto country roads that wound for ten miles through Maine carrying spring toward summer. Frogs peeped in trees, thicker in lower-lying portions of road. Some ducks flew overhead, their shadows crossing the road in front of the car. A porcupine waddled from the tree line onto the shoulder and shied away as I honked to keep it from being flattened.

I drove straight through Marseilles, timing how long it took to get to Steven Shea's house on the pond. Twenty-one minutes creeping over the ruts that Sheriff Willis bounced over in her Bronco. Eighteen minutes coming to the village, as I knew where the bad spots were and how fast the Prelude could go over or around them. In a four-wheel-drive with high clearance and given his familiarity with the route, Shea ought to have been able to shave it to fifteen one way, even a little drunk. That squared with his estimates.

I then doubled back to the paved driveway that supposedly led up to Tom Judson's house. The chain with the little flags was padlocked, the hasp looking like it was rusted into the body of the lock. I didn't have a tool to snip the lock, and I didn't fancy a walk in my suit up the mountain, even on pavement.

Back at the Marseilles Inn, I parked in front and went onto the porch. Ralph Paine was just inside the screened door, paint brush in hand.

"John, you were up early this morning."

"I had to do some visiting."

A nod. "Got a note saying you'd be checking out today."

"Just have to bring my bag down from the room."

"Well, since you've missed your breakfast, how's about we throw together a little lunch for you?"

"Ralph, that's not necessary."

"I know. But it's no trouble, and you can enjoy it on the dock. Ham and cheese on home-baked bread with beer and hand-cut potato chips all right?"

"Princely."

"Be just a second. Go on down and make yourself comfortable."

Somewhere on the lake, a loon was crying—or yodeling or whatever—as I walked to the dock and settled into one of the white chairs. It was made from resin and gave in just the right places, a high-tech descendant of Ma Judson's caned rockers. There was a little resin table, too, so I put my legs up on it, calves rather than shoes on the white surface. The breeze off the water was cool, but the sun was warm, and I took off my jacket and rolled up the sleeves of my shirt.

A young girl in a bikini was expertly sailing a small skiff, what looked like real canvas not being allowed to luff except when she came about. Closer to shore, a man in a felt hat like Ma Judson's cast with a fly rod from a big rowboat, the fluorescent line seeming to stand straight above his head on the back cast, then whistle forward smartly before landing lightly on the water. A very large bird with stilty legs like a cartoon stork waded in the shallows by some lily pads, stepping carefully and swinging its head in a scanning way toward the water around it.

A medium-sized fly landed on my arm. I was about to brush it away when I noticed that it had a trunk like an elephant, which it moved from spot to spot on my skin. The thing had a big red head and a shingled back in black and white, and was one of the oddest creatures I'd ever seen. I stayed still so as not to disturb it as the fly moved all over my arm, sounding with its trunk like a frenetic doctor with a stethoscope.

"John?"

I opened my eyes and realized the fly was gone but Ralph was next to me, a plate and mug and napkin in his hands.

"Oh." I swung my legs down off the table. "Sorry, Ralph."

Paine smiled as he laid out the meal for me. "No need to apologize. Something about being up here just slows things down for you. Like"—Paine looked around us, so much like Shea's gesture about industrial espionage that I jumped a little—"like back when I was young and tried marijuana the first time. Just slowed things down so I felt I had all the time in the world to accomplish everything I ever wanted to do. Up here, it's just sort of a natural high. We all get it."

A telephone rang up at the inn. "Damn, I should buy one of those cordless phones. Enjoy your lunch."

The bread was thick-sliced, the ham and chips the same way, and the cheese brought out a rounding taste in the beer. The best lunch I remembered in a while, I ate it at probably half the speed I would have a deli take-out back in Boston.

When I was finished, I put the plate on the dock and used the mug to anchor the used napkin on it. Then I put my feet back up and waited for Paine to return and give me directions to Owen Briss. The loon started in again, the big bird caught a little fish, and the fly or its cousin came back visiting.

I found myself hoping Ralph's call would be a longish one.

The trailer was set back from the road about thirty feet, a couple of old lawn chairs dumped in front of it. There was no vehicle in the driveway, fifty feet of hardened clay and scant gravel. Strewn next to the driveway were a scoop-faced snowplow for a small truck, a refrigerator missing its door, and a crude brick barbecue with a filthy iron grill across it.

Ralph Paine had said getting to Briss's place would be an adventure because the intersections along the dirt road weren't marked. I realized I'd taken one wrong turn when the road ended at a log-barriered access to a small pond. I eventually got smart and followed what seemed to be the tracks of oversized tires. The tracks led me around a boulder like a blister in the roadbed and to the trailer.

Actually, trailers. It looked as though Briss had grafted a turquoise and white one onto the red and silver one that from its foundation of masonry blocks seemed the pioneer on the lot. A clothesline with both male and female items was spliced from a window frame of the trailer out to a tree at an odd angle. I thought about what Shea told me Briss did for a living. If dentists can have false teeth and barbers lousy haircuts, probably it was okay for carpenters to live in metal trailers.

I pulled into the driveway, and an old spotted pointer came out of nowhere to bay at me. His front paws reached my driver's side window ledge, and the snout he stuck into my face seemed more intent on slobbering than biting. As I scratched him under the chin, the door to the red and silver part of the complex opened. A woman, in blue jeans and a shirt knotted at the navel, stepped out. Or vamped out.

Cinny, the "hand relief" woman from Gil Lacouture's office.

I took a breath and got out of my car, the dog jumping up at me.

Cinny said, "Mourner, Mourner, you stop that, hear?"

The dog slumped down, cowed his head, and looked up at me for intercession.

I said, "That's all right. He wasn't bothering me."

"Don't matter. Wouldn't want to see that fine suit all fuzzed up with dog hairs." She swayed over to me. "You could maybe take it off, and I could . . . spruce things up for you?"

Cinny was about twice as close to me as she should have been for courtesy.

"No, thanks. I'd like to talk with Owen Briss, if he's here."

"Owen." She showed disappointment. "I thought maybe you remembered me from Gil's office and decided to come calling."

"Sorry."

"Well, Owen ain't here, and probably won't be back for a good bit. Pity for you to come all the way out here for . . . nothing."

Cinny used an index finger to twirl some of her hair, like spaghetti around a fork. She gave off a subtle but deep odor that didn't come from a perfume bottle.

I said, "Does Owen know what you do to earn spending money?"

She pouted. "Owen don't own me. Truth is, he don't even take care of me too well." More hair twirling. "I mean, it ain't like we're married or nothing. I got no ropes tying me down, Mr. . . . ?"

"Cuddy, John Cuddy."

"John. My daddy's name was John. You might remind me of him if we was to . . . do some things together."

I was thinking that a hand-relief specialist with a father fixation was not what I needed, when a big engine came revving up the dirt road. The engine belonged to a pickup truck with three gallons of primer on it and outlandishly big tires under it. The pickup belonged to a loutish guy

111

with a few strands of blond hair combed across his scalp and sunburned forearms the diameter of normal people's legs.

Cinny said, "Uh-oh, the man of the house."

Briss stopped the pickup so as to hem my car in the driveway, the door to his cab showing a gouge mark running two feet horizontally. He opened the door and landed heavily on the ground. Without closing his door, which might explain the gouge mark, Briss started walking toward me. He was shorter than I'd guessed, only around six feet, but with enough torso under a flannel shirt to bow his legs. As Briss got closer I could see a faint beard and nostrils expanding like he was about to breathe fire through them.

Cinny said, "Owen. Owen! The man didn't do nothing, I swear!"

Owen kept coming. No weapons or even tools that I could see.

Cinny said to me, "Best you make a run for it. I'll try to slow him down some."

She rushed up to him. His right arm lashed out in a backhand way, connecting with her right side and sending her to the ground.

I expected him to throw a punch, probably roundhouse. Instead he just grabbed me by the throat with both hands and started to squeeze.

I dipped slowly, as though he were driving me down, which wasn't much of an act. When he started to lean into me, I joined my hands like a little kid learning to dive and drove up with forearms at a forty-five degree angle to his own, knocking them free. When my hands were at full height, I brought them down hard and fast, edges karate-style, into the muscles between his shoulders and neck. As Briss went to his knees, I drove my elbow into his jaw, rocking him back onto his ankles, then into the dust that should have been his front lawn.

Cinny, on knees and elbows herself, spoke in a hushed voice. "I swear."

I rotated my head and regulated my breathing to avoid hyperventilating. It occurred to me a bit late that I probably should have been watching out for Mourner to join the fight, but when I finally spotted him, he was huddled under the bumper of my car, taking things in calmly from a prudent distance.

Walking toward the house, I picked up one of the lawn chairs and brought it to where Briss was coming around. I sat down about four feet away, enough space to give me time to rise if he wanted more. The way he looked up at me, he didn't.

"My name's John Cuddy, Mr. Briss." I held up my Maine ID, so he could see it, then put it away. "I'm investigating the deaths on Marseilles Pond."

Briss got himself into a sitting position and looked over at my Prelude. "Ain't no cop's car."

"I'm private."

Cinny said, "A private eye?"

I stayed on Briss. "I'd like to ask you a few questions."

"Yeah, well, I ain't answering nothing."

"Why not?"

"Why not? Man comes on my property, and on *to* my woman, he goddamn don't—"

"Owen, I told you. The man didn't try nothing!"

Briss ignored her. "He don't get squat from me."

I said, "I understand you worked for Steven Shea."

"That sonofabitch! He stiffed me!"

Sometimes people say they won't help, then can't help themselves from doing it. "Why?"

"Claimed he told me he wanted spindles. Goddamn, estimate like I give him, no man in's right mind would of thought he was getting spindles."

"You do a lot of work for him on the house?"

"I did. Ain't nobody better'n me on finish stuff. Nobody. He had a big outfit do the shell and some roughing in, but he'd heard the kind of work I do and wanted me."

"Heard from who?"

Briss seemed to realize how much he was talking. "None of your goddamn business."

"I can just ask Shea, or I can show you a couple more tricks. Your choice."

Cinny said, "Was Ralph and Ramona."

Briss said, "You goddamn slut, keep your mouth shut!"

"Owen, this man's from the city, all right? He can take you with one hand, and I don't need you all beat up just to not give him something he's after."

Briss started to look to Cinny, then didn't. He muttered something I couldn't hear.

"What?"

"I said Ralph and Ramona give me a recommendation to him. I done some work for them, lots of work, when they took over the inn and the country store."

"And everything went fine with Shea until the spindle fight?"

" 'Course it did. I do quality work. Ask anybody."

"You know his wife?"

"Shea's?"

"Yes."

"Met her just the once. She was the kind could go from zero to bitch in six point five seconds, like somebody else I could mention."

"Owen, now don't you go starting on me."

"Why not?" he said.

"Because you know I only got mad account of you was supposed to take me to see Anthrax and them down to SeaPAC."

I said, "Anthrax and SeaPAC?"

Cinny twirled some more hair. "Heavy metal. Anthrax

and Poison and a bunch of other bands were gonna be down to the Performing Arts Center."

I went back to Briss. "Shea and his wife didn't oversee your work?"

He shook his head. "They weren't much around when I was over to their camp."

"How come?"

"He made a goddamn big thing about it. That I wasn't never to be there working when he was up with his 'guests.' "

"The Vandemeers?"

"How am I supposed to know? The man paid the money, I did what he wanted. Even the garage—"

Briss stopped.

I said, "What about the garage?"

"Nothing."

"You go into that garage much, Briss?"

He stopped, seemed to think about it. "No way. Always bring my own tools to a job. Wouldn't touch none of his."

"How about the crossbow?"

"What the goddamn you talking about?"

"The crossbow that was used to kill the three people that night. I'm told it was kept in the garage."

"Then talk to the one that told you about it. I ain't never seen no crossbow."

"But you did know where the key to the garage was kept?"

Briss seemed to think again. "Had to."

"Why?"

"Kept some lumber in there when I was working on the house in bad weather."

"But you never saw the crossbow?"

"Never seen it. Never touched it. Don't know nothing about it."

Not likely. "I also understand you didn't exactly get along with Tom Judson."

Briss seemed genuinely thrown. "Judson?"

"Yes."

"The hell does that old bastard have to do with anything?"

"I heard that you went up to his house to have it out about some money he owed you."

"The rich bastards are all the same. You do your work for them, they stiff you."

"And you found him dead."

"Cold as stone." Briss grinned for the first time, showing horsey teeth and not that many of them. "All his money didn't do Judson no good. All it did was let him buy enough drink to bleed himself to death when he caught his leg in that trap. Same with your client, you know? All his money, just made him kill those people."

"Why?"

"Can't rightly say. I never had much money to learn from."

I stood up, Briss flinching until he realized I was done with him.

I said, "I might be back with more questions."

From the ground, Briss said, "Come back here again, you'd best have better'n a crossbow with you."

I walked to the Prelude, got in, and started up. When I saw Mourner reach the rear of the trailer, I put the car into first and drove between Cinny and Briss over his dirt front yard and back onto the road toward Marseilles.

Gil Lacouture's receptionist, Judy, was nowhere in sight. After about twenty seconds in the waiting area, I called out. "Hello?"

Lacouture's head came around his doorjamb, waving me to come in. As I entered his office, he was just replacing the telephone receiver.

"John, good to see you again. Take a seat."

I did, laying the Shea accordion file on his desk. "You want to hear a summary, or you want a written report?"

"Summary."

I gave it to him, everybody I'd seen in the order I'd seen them. Lacouture smiled when I got to Owen Briss and Cinny.

"That girl does keep popping up."

"You don't see any conflict in representing both her and Steven Shea?"

"Conflict? How?"

"This isn't like an accidental death the cops think Shea hoked up. This is cold-blooded triple murder, Gil, and if you can't give the jury somebody other than Shea for it, they'll hand Shea to the hangman."

"Maine doesn't have the death penalty, John. Abolished it in—"

"You know what I mean. You can't go in there without some theory of the case, somebody to finger as the real killer when obviously somebody did it."

"John, first of all, as a lawyer up here, you run into conflicts all the time. You resolve them without losing clients, or you go out of business." Lacouture pursed his lips. "You think Cinny would be a good alternative suspect?"

"No. I don't think even Briss would be. But at least he's somebody who has a motive for getting even with Shea, and that's more than I got from anybody else."

"No, I don't see Briss for this kind of thing. I met him once. Kind of an in-your-face brawler. Not the kind to play Robin of Sherwood Forest."

"Gil?"

"Yes?"

"Robin Hood used a longbow, but if I were you, I'd lose the clever allusions before I got before the jury."

Lacouture straightened just a little. "I've been before

117

plenty of juries, John. You get to know what you can say to them and what you have to say offstage to keep your sanity. I'm looking at a murder scene that makes the Manson family seem like sitcom material, and I'm representing the accused, who has no motive and claims he didn't kill anybody."

"Yeah, well, you're still going to have to give the jury a target if Shea didn't do it."

"If." Lacouture leaned back in his old leather chair, swiveling it just a little from side to side. "Tell me, what did you think of my client?"

"Three things."

"Which are?"

"One, I didn't like him."

Lacouture lips pursed again. "Kind of the air of snake oil around him, isn't there?"

"Two, I don't think he did it."

Lacouture grinned and slammed his palm on his blotter. "God, I'm glad to hear somebody else say that, somebody who's talked with him. I thought I was losing my touch when I first interviewed him, wallowing in all that idealism the defenders tour should have drilled out of me. He's not the greatest or most sympathetic guy in the world, but— remember when you were in here before, I told you there's something else about Steve that I didn't want to tell you? Well, that was it. I don't think he did it, either."

Lacouture continued to grin, then when I didn't say anything, his lips went back to pursed. "All right. That's two things you noticed. What's the—"

"Third, I don't think Shea has a clue who might have done this to his wife and friends, and neither do I."

118

9

IT TOOK ME EXACTLY ONE HUNDRED SIXTY MINUTES TO CRUISE
the one hundred sixty miles from Augusta to Route 128
north of Boston. It took me exactly one hour to crawl the
ten miles from 128 to downtown.

Stuck behind a diesel trailing fumes, I thought about the
calls I'd make back in the city. Other people's schedules
might scramble the sequence, but it seemed simple enough.

Once in downtown, I turned onto Tremont Street, moving more slowly than the pedestrians passing the old buildings. The people were walking past because most of the
buildings were closed, victims of an economy that sput-
tered before the urban renewal that revitalized the financial
district could make its way uphill to the Common.

Five minutes and as many blocks later, I got the Prelude
into its postage stamp parking space behind my office's
building. Stepping over the assorted trash that didn't quite
make the Dempster dumpster, I went around to the front
entrance.

Up two flights, I opened the office door that reminded
me of the sheriff's door and shook my head as I went

119

through the mail that the carrier had shoved through the slot below the pebbled glass. Mostly junk circulars that ranged from Kmart to Ed McMahon. Some business correspondence that I read and set to the side. Calling my answering service, I got two client messages that could wait an hour and one from Nancy Meagher that could but wouldn't.

I tried Nancy at the DA's office. The secretary told me Ms. Meagher was still on trial in the conspiracy case. She also told me that Ms. Meagher had left word that seven-thirty at my place for take-out Szechuan or Thai would be quite acceptable. I thanked the secretary and let her know that seven-thirty sounded fine to me.

Directory Assistance helped me find Defense Resource Management out in the 508 area code. I asked the first voice that answered for the office of the general counsel and the second voice for Anna-Pia Antonelli.

"May I tell Ms. Antonelli who's calling?"

"John Cuddy."

"And will she know what this is regarding?"

"Maybe. If not, tell her it's regarding Steven Shea."

The voice lost a little of its professional resiliency as I was told to please hold. I timed the passage of eight seconds before a firm female voice came across the line.

"Is this Mr. Cuddy?"

"It is."

"Gil Lacouture of Augusta told me you might be contacting us. Have you seen Steven?"

"Yes."

"How is he doing?"

You can never really gauge things over the telephone, but it sounded as though Antonelli was more interested than polite.

I said, "He's holding up well. A little pale, probably lost some weight, but I'd be worried if he hadn't."

A pause. "Thank you for saying that. I take it this call is toward a meeting?"

"The sooner the better."

"Should I come to you, or would you like to come out here?"

"Out there, I think. I'd like to see a couple of other DRM people as well."

Another pause. When the voice came back on, it was carefully bland. "Any ones in particular?"

"Yes. Dwight Schoonmaker and Tyrone Xavier."

"I'll try to set something up for tomorrow afternoon. Mr. Davison won't be back from Houston till then."

"Davison?"

"Keck Davison is our president."

Nice to be in demand. "Office politics aside, I want to spend some real time with Schoonmaker and Xavier."

"Anything we can do to prepare for you?"

"Shea said his secretary was a memory."

"Yes. She's off around the world somewhere."

"Then I guess that's it for now. Can you call me to confirm the time tomorrow?"

"Yes. And I'll give you my direct dial here to save you the trouble of going through insulating layers to reach me."

Antonelli said the last lightly, not arrogantly. We exchanged numbers and rang off.

"Calem Police, Sergeant Dwyer."

"Paul O'Boy in Detectives."

"Wait one."

I heard some electronic burping, then a voice that brought back another case, a case he and I had managed to botch together.

"Detectives, O'Boy speaking."

"This is John Cuddy."

"Cuddy . . . Cuddy?—Oh, shit. Now what?"

"Thought I might come out to see you tomorrow."

"How come?"

"I'm working on a case, like to talk to you about it."

"Don't tell me. Three of our citizens with arrows through them."

"That's the one."

"Cuddy, you ain't exactly *persona grata* around here, you know?"

"That's why I need to talk to you."

Some paper shuffling came over the wire. "Awright, awright. I guess we kinda owe you one."

"How about I buy you breakfast?"

"Next town over, there's a HoJo's on 128."

"I can picture it."

"Eight o'clock okay?"

"See you then, O'Boy."

More paper shuffling. "I'll be counting the hours."

"Claims Investigation, Mullen."

"Harry, John Cuddy."

"John! How you doing?"

"I'm okay. How about you?"

"Jeez, fine, fine. Thanks to you."

I'd had a chance to close a case in a way that saved Harry his job when those around him were losing theirs.

Mullen's voice suddenly grew cautious. "Uh, what can I do for you, John?"

"A little favor."

"Sure, sure." He sounded more "maybe, maybe."

I said, "The name Sandra Newberg mean anything to you?"

"Newberg? You mean—the woman from Accounting who got herself killed up in Canada there?"

"Maine, Harry."

"Maine, Canada, same difference. What's that got to do with you?"

I told him.

Mullen's voice became more cautious. "What do you want from me?"

"A rundown. Very quiet. Anything from her time at Empire that might tell me why what happened happened."

"Jeez, John. I don't know. . . ."

"Harry."

"It's not that I don't want to help you out. It's just, well, it's gonna be awkward. Most everything's getting folded up around here, and most everybody's blown to the four winds."

"Except for you, Harry."

He got my drift. "Gimme a coupla days, okay?"

"The sooner the better."

"Soon as I can, John."

"Thanks. And take care, Harry."

After some other telephone calls, I drove to the condo on Beacon Street. Leaving the Prelude in the parking space that backs onto Fairfield Street, I walked around to the front entrance on Beacon. From the stoop you can just see a pie-wedge of the Charles River and, on the Cambridge side, the academic buildings stolidly constructed by MIT in the forties and the speculative buildings hastily thrown up by developers in the eighties.

At home, Ed McMahon had sent another cheery package, but there was no important mail or message. The sun was coming in through the seven stained-glass windows in the living room, reflecting off the polished oak-front fireplace and the pink Italian tiles someone had lovingly grouted around the hearth a hundred years ago. I suddenly had a pang. When the doctor came back from the Midwest, I was going to miss the place.

I shook it off and climbed out of my business clothes and into my running clothes. Given the weather, just shorts, T-shirt, socks, and shoes. Before going out the door, I set a bottle of chardonnay on its side in the freezer.

I went downstairs and then across the half block of Fairfield with its private parking spaces shadowed by the two buildings flanking it. I used the ramp over Storrow Drive to get onto the river's macadam paths. The BU kids and sewer crew were gone, but the construction and noise and dirt weren't. I began to wish I'd brought my jogging stuff to Maine.

Back at the condo, I changed shirts, moved the chardonnay down to the refrigerator compartment, and went over to the Nautilus club I'd joined. Elie the manager and I hadn't seen each other for a while, him catching me up on his scuba diving and photography, me telling him what I could about what I'd been doing.

I did a full circuit of the machines, double sets on some and triple sets on the stomach one. Elie walked past me during the third set, saying, "Big date tonight, huh," just quietly enough for nobody else to hear it.

About twenty minutes later, Elie let me use the club phone to call The King and I restaurant up the street. Finishing my workout and warm-down, I picked up the food just as it was coming out of the kitchen.

Which gave me all of half an hour to clean up before Nancy arrived.

She said, "Something smells awfully good."

"Spring rolls, honeyed pork with mushrooms, and pad Thai."

I opened the door wide so Nancy could come past me into the condo. She was wearing a gray suit, plain white blouse, black-toned pantyhose, and one-inch black heels. Battle dress.

124

Nancy said, "Somebody try to poke your eye out?"

"Black fly bite. The welt will go away in about a week, I'm told."

Her eyes moved. "Your hair's still wet."

"I just got out of the shower."

She dropped a briefcase onto the rug in the foyer. The case sounded heavily loaded. "Pity I wasn't a few minutes early."

As Nancy reached her arms up for a hug, that faint, sweet pong of perfumed sweat came off her. Didn't hurt the hug, though.

She let go first. "I need a shower, too."

"Already laid out a towel and facecloth for you."

Nancy arched an eyebrow and subtly shot a hip sideways. "Want to join me?"

"Pity you weren't a few minutes early."

She dropped the pose. "Quoted against myself again."

"Tough day?"

"There've been worse."

"I have another bottle of chardonnay in the fridge."

"No more than two glasses for me tonight. I have to be on for tomorrow."

"Come visit in the kitchen when you're finished in the bathroom."

Five minutes later, I pulled the components of our dinner from the microwave and spooned them into serving bowls. Nancy had changed into one of my rugby shirts, which covered her like a short dress, sleeves bunched up to the elbow to free her hands for food. We helped ourselves and carried our plates into the living room, sitting on the floor, backs against the couch, dishes on my landlord's coffee table. I poured us each some wine, and we clinked glasses.

She sniffed hers. "A delicate bouquet with an overlay of oak in the rounded nose."

I doodled with an index finger on her thigh. "I think it's

an impertinent little beauty with just a hint of vanilla and great legs."

"You're making me feel better."

"Want to talk about your day?"

"Not tonight. Other than the insects, how was Maine?"

As we ate, I told her about the case, the way I usually couldn't because of her potential conflict of interest as a prosecutor. I sort of skimmed over Cinny, as part of Lacouture's own conflict, but there was a change in Nancy's expression as soon as I mentioned her.

"This Cinny. She bear any resemblance to Daisy Mae?"

"Just physically."

"Cute."

"Seriously, Nance, you should see this part of Maine. It's so fresh and clean."

"Sounds like a new soap."

"No, really. Animals, wilderness, lakes. It's like you remember it being not so far from here in the old days."

"Maybe your old days, John."

I set my knife and fork on my empty plate. "It's the kind of place, you see it, you want to spend more time in it."

Taking the last of her wine, Nancy looked startled. "What, do you mean like . . . live there?"

"Crossed my mind."

"John, you're a city boy."

"So were the folks in wagon trains."

"You'd be bored to tears in a week!"

"Never know till I tried."

She moved her hand over our dishes. 'You sample any of the restaurants up there?"

"Just the one at the inn, and it was terrific."

"How about Augusta?"

"They had restaurants there."

"Papa Gino's, Burger King . . ."

126

I couldn't keep back a smile. "Kentucky Fried was prominent, too."

"Oh, well. That makes all the difference in the world."

"So, you'd argue against it, huh?"

"In my usual style."

"Which is?"

"Tongue in cheek."

Nancy took both my hands, guiding them up and under the rugby shirt as she leaned in for a kiss.

10

I GOT TO THE HOWARD JOHNSON'S BEFORE PAUL O'BOY. Even at eight A.M. I had my choice of seats. I slid into a booth with fake cowhide the same shade as my waitress's garnet uniform. She looked to be in her mid-thirties, with pouches under the eyes that suggested her day had started a lot earlier than mine. The nametag read DOLLY, a silly little hat bobby-pinned into a wave in her hair. Something about the hat made you think she wore the hair that way only on the job. I ordered iced tea and said I was waiting for somebody else. The information didn't seem to boost her spirits any.

My iced tea arrived at the table as Paul O'Boy came through the door. Stumpy in build, he was wearing a blue polyester sport coat and clashing green slacks, carrying a scuffed briefcase he might have used as a book bag in fifth grade. The face looked roughed over, like the sculptor hadn't liked the first try but didn't have time to finish the second. O'Boy still had a few wisps of hair in the center of his head, though you'd have to see the fringe of red around his ears to be sure of the color. Either way, he'd never be able to wear Dolly's hat.

"Hey, Cuddy, how you doing?"

I shook with him but didn't get up.

Our waitress came over and said, "Coffee?"

O'Boy looked at her, smiled idiotically, and said, "Dolly, you vouch for the decaf?"

She grinned in spite of how tired I thought she felt. "Not even to Saddam Hussein."

"Then bring me regular, black. I'll make it up somewheres today."

"You got it. By the way, sausage looks good this morning."

O'Boy said, "I ate here every day, my doctor'd have my coronary for me."

Dolly laughed. Both of us ordered, and she moved off toward the kitchen as he put his briefcase under the table-top and took the bench seat opposite me.

Thinking how O'Boy had wanted to meet outside his turf, I said, "You know her?"

"Never saw her before in my life."

"She'll remember you."

"You talk to people, use their first names, Cuddy. Something I learned from my partner in uniforms, the guy who broke me in. You use a first name, it defuses a lot."

"What did it defuse here?"

"Dolly there, she's going to remember me as a nice guy, salesman type, not a cop. You she won't remember from Adam."

On our case together, O'Boy had that ability some cops develop to seem dense while not missing a trick. I had a feeling he hadn't missed many lately.

After some more small talk, O'Boy loosened a tie made from the same material as his jacket. "So, what do you need from me?"

"Like I told you on the phone, I'm looking into The Foursome murders up in Maine."

"And you figure that since the people were from Calem, we ran courtesy checks on them for the cops up there."

"I figure more than that."

He crossed his arms, elbows leaning on the Formica. "Like what, for instance?"

"I figure you've run down all the folks from Calem, living and dead, who might be involved in this, avoid a backfire later that looks bad in the papers."

O'Boy started to say something, then stopped as Dolly brought us our food with the widest grin yet. She served him first, O'Boy thanking her for the recommendation on the sausage as soon as he tasted it. She spun on her heel a little as she left us again for the kitchen.

As we started eating, O'Boy said, "You know we got a new chief?"

"No." I pictured the old chief, a thin, crew-cut man who favored unfiltered cigarettes. "Wooten retired?"

"Early."

"Because of our little go-round?"

"Partly. Point is, it's too soon to crystal-ball how the new commander's gonna run the ship, get me?"

"So we go slow and easy, like meeting for breakfast out here."

"Like. And like nothing I tell you getting back to the cops in Maine as coming from me."

We ate for a time before I said, "You going to be able to show me anything in the bag?"

O'Boy used a toast quarter to sop up some egg yolk. "Probably not. Just brought it along to look at, you had a question I couldn't handle off the top of my head."

"Fair enough. Let's start with my client, Steven Shea."

"The accused? He's off limits."

"You can't tell me anything?"

"Get it from the cops in Maine. One thing, though."

"Yes?"

"You want to talk with the people out at DRM, where he worked there."

"I'm planning to. How about his wife, Sandra Newberg?"

"Professional, managed a department for some insurance outfit till they decided to close down their operation up here." O'Boy looked me in the eye, then went back to the eggs. "You used to work for one of those, right?"

"Right."

"Empire?"

"Uh-huh."

"Same as her, then. Maybe you can use your pull there."

"Okay. Anything you heard about her out of the ordinary?"

O'Boy chewed about half of what was in his mouth. "How come I get the feeling you want me to tell you something without you telling me something?"

I had some bacon.

O'Boy said, "We didn't get anything on her from the insurance connection, but afterwards, after she got laid off . . . You're gonna want to talk with the neighbor there, Epps, I think her name is."

"Thanks, I will. I also have a key to Shea's house. All right by you if I use it?"

"Fine by me. Better let Mrs. Epps know you're doing it, though, you don't want a uniform sticking a muzzle in your ear as you come out."

"Okay."

Dolly came back over to see how everything was. O'Boy asked if there was any way he could get a side order of more sausages. She said she'd fix it and spun a little smarter on her heel.

I said, "How about the Vandemeers?"

Reluctantly, O'Boy looked from the departing Dolly back to me. "The doctor and his wife were solid people. Her name was Vivian?"

"Right."

"She was your basic housewife. Lots of shopping, lots of trips with the other couple. The doc seemed to be one of those guys long on technical ability but short on bedside manner with the patients. Nothing about him around his medical group, though."

"Anything from anywhere?"

O'Boy swallowed. "Mrs. Epps."

"Maybe I should be buying her breakfast."

"I met her. She looks like weak tea and a prune Danish, you could stand to watch her eat it."

"Anybody else?"

"The doctor's brother, he runs a car dealership."

"You know exactly where?"

O'Boy described a commercial intersection a couple of towns away.

I said, "What about the brother?"

Dolly appeared with the sausages, setting the little dish down with a flourish before asking if there was anything else. O'Boy said no, thanks.

After she left this time, he said, "You could find her ten years ago, you'd be nuts not to marry her."

I said, "The brother?"

"Oh, yeah. Seems his balls got caught in the vise, recession and all. Seems brother doc was pouring in money, keep him afloat."

"Sounds like a reason to keep the golden goose alive."

"My guess, but it's your case."

"You hear anything about the Vandemeers' son?"

"Nicky, right?"

"So I'm told."

"Not much. Lost his license for an OUI. Blew the kind

132

of score on the Breathalyzer you'd expect from a can of paint thinner. Runs with a girlfriend from the city."

"Boston?"

"Yeah. Little Hispanic broad, she comes out here for school, you can picture that."

"METCO?"

"Naw, Calem never joined that METCO there. Some kind of 'policy disagreements' over eligibility and funding, I remember hearing. So we bus our own inner-city kids out in the morning and bus them back at night. Stupid."

"How so?"

O'Boy fired up. "Aw, all we're doing is showing the poor kids what they can't have, why they can't compete. The system had any brains, we'd make the rich kids bus into the city, see the poor, learn something about life." O'Boy caught himself, sopped up some more yolk. "But, fuck, I'm just a cop. What do I know about education, huh?"

"This girlfriend have a name?"

"Yeah, but I don't remember it." A shrug that conveyed the soul of innocence.

I watched him. "Would it be in the file?"

"Should be. Hold on a second."

O'Boy delved into the briefcase under the tabletop, rummaging around. A little theatrically, I thought.

"Yeah, yeah." He pulled a typed report from the file, zigzagging a finger down it until he said, "Last name Quintana, first name Blanca."

"Address?"

"Just Boston."

I sat back in the bench seat, pushing my plate to the side and resting my hands where it had been. "O'Boy."

He looked up, confused innocence this time. "Yeah?"

"How come I get the feeling you're telling me something without telling me something else?"

"What do you mean?"

"I think you're telling me the truth but using it to mislead me somehow."

O'Boy winced with his whole body. "Hey, Cuddy. C'mon, huh? I'm easily hurt here."

11

FROM THE HOWARD JOHNSON'S IT WAS EASIER TO DRIVE TO the car dealership than The Foursome's former neighborhood. Following Paul O'Boy's directions, I found the place on the southwest corner of the intersection. There were fifty or sixty shiny cars on the lot, all parked nose out except for a utility vehicle parked sideways that had a marquee on its roof reading MODEL OF THE MONTH. Above the front doors of the showroom was a painted image somewhere between a cartoon and a portrait showing a rosy-cheeked man with a store-bought smile bearing some resemblance to the crime scene photo of Hale Vandemeer's bleached-out face. The caption was HUB VANDEMEER— FINE CARS, FAIR PRICES.

I drove past the premises without seeing any activity in the lot or showroom. Making a three-point turn, I came back, this time driving onto the lot and leaving the Prelude in a slot with RESERVED FOR CUSTOMER hand-lettered on a small picket sign. I climbed the two steps to the showroom, an all-glass affair on one level with six vehicles of differing functional appeal gleaming on the all-weather carpeting.

When I opened the door, a soft "bong-bong" sounded deeper in the showroom, and a pert, quick-stepping woman appeared from one of the Dutch window cubbyholes along the back wall. Maneuvering deftly around a sensible four-door sedan, she was about five-three, with two-inch heels, well-defined calves, and the expression of a weasel that hadn't eaten in a week.

"Welcome to Hub Vandemeer's," she said eagerly. "I'm Emily Tollison. How can I help you?"

I didn't introduce myself. "I'd like to see Mr. Vandemeer, if I can."

"Sure, sure." Drawing even with me, her eyes flickered over to where I'd parked my car. Not a bad idea, having the customer spaces where the sales crew could do a windshield appraisal of the old vehicle. "Only, he's not in just yet. Is there something I can help you with?"

"Thanks, but I need to see him personally."

"Sure, I understand. Can I get you some coffee while you wait?"

I don't drink the stuff, but I said, "Yes, thank you. Regular, please." I looked to some squash-colored easy chairs with little poofs of cottony stuffing edging out the seams. "I'll just sit, if that's all right?"

"Sure, sure. You make yourself comfortable, and I'll get your coffee. Hub'll be here shortly."

I took a seat as Tollison went past her cubbyhole and out of sight. Behind her, I could hear the mechanical sounds of a service shop, which must have had a separate entrance off another street. Full-color brochures on the low table in front of me displayed cover photos of the two makes of machines I'd seen on the lot, one American, the other I thought Korean, though it had been a while since I'd been in the new car market.

Tollison came back with the coffee in a Styrofoam cup.

Thanking her, I added in a sincere voice, "How's Hub doing with the loss of his brother?"

A shake of the head, Tollison crossing her arms under her breasts. "It's been such a strain on him. I don't think I even met Hale my first year here, but lately he was coming by, oh, once or twice a week, and he seemed such a nice man."

"I don't know the son, but it must be tough on him as well."

She suddenly hardened, the arms closing on each other. "Yes, well, he has a number of strains on him, Nicky does. I'll just leave you with your coffee, Mr. . . . ?"

"Cuddy, John Cuddy."

"Mr. Cuddy. Let me know if you need anything else."

"Thanks."

I watched her walk away and wondered why my neutral comment about Nicky Vandemeer had set her off.

Waiting, I leafed through one of the brochures. It managed to gush for sixteen pages over features both standard and optional without once mentioning price tag. Returning the brochure to the table, I saw a candy-apple red convertible, white top down, white upholstery visible, pulling onto the lot. If the vehicles in the showroom gleamed, this one blinded. The fantasy car of every teenager turned young adult with a down payment burning a hole through the money market fund. The driver backed and filled until the car was at exactly the angle to catch both the sun from the sky and the eye from the street. I noticed a chrome trailer hitch at the back bumper, which detracted just a bit from the street-car image.

The man who got out from behind the wheel was an older version of the image over the door, the hair scarcer and the cheeks not so rosy and the mouth definitely not smiling. Tall and lanky, he had an effort donning the jacket of a suit whose glen-plaid pattern was just this side of garish. Vandemeer snatched a leather portfolio from the backseat, tilting his head at my car in the customer slot. I got the feeling he'd categorized me as "Honda Prelude, pretty good shape but the old model, probably time for a new car." Before he could have seen me, Vandemeer put on a yearbook smile and bounded up the steps to the showroom as though this were going to be our mutually lucky day.

Inside the door, he spotted me before the "bong-bong" faded and before Tollison was out of her cubbyhole.

Vandemeer said, "Are you being helped, sir?"

"Actually, I was waiting for you, Mr. Vandemeer."

"Terrific." A smile came out that put the polish on the convertible to shame, while his free hand adjusted the knot on a red tie with a beach-girl-and-umbrella design. "And it's 'Hub,' please."

"John Cuddy, Hub."

"Great to meet you, John. Come on back to my office."

Vandemeer waved at Tollison, who waved back in a pleasant but distinctly "nothing much" way that probably captured the dealership's morning pretty well. Vandemeer never broke stride or smile, saying over his shoulder, "More coffee?"

"No, thanks."

He nodded as we entered his office, which was more a giant cubbyhole. One wall gave a view of the showroom. Another had a very soundproofed window onto the service department, men in jumpsuits working with wrenches and other hand tools on vehicles in maybe half the bays. On my side of his desk was a brass plate on a triangular tube of mahogany that read HUBBELL "HUB" VANDEMEER. The rest of the desk was covered by carefully squared stacks of documents that had the look of not being disturbed recently. There were some Little League trophies on the shelf next to his desk. Most of them were from the mid-eighties, none after 1988. The desk chair looked broken down rather than broken in, but he plunked himself into it and said, "Now, what can we do for you?"

I showed him my Massachusetts identification. "I'm here about the killings up in Maine."

The smile weighed down, taking all the energy from his face and voice. "What's your stake in it?"

When you first spring your profession on someone, it's interesting to hear their reaction. In Vandemeer's case, his question about my "stake" led me to believe he must have one, too.

I said, "I'm working for the lawyer representing Steven Shea."

His mouth gaped before he remembered that he should be playing poker. "I thought the police there had things pretty well wrapped up?"

"My job is to find out how tight the ribbon is."

"This happened in Maine, I don't see where I have to talk to you."

"You don't. You wouldn't even if it happened in Massachusetts. But you don't talk to me, I have to talk to other people. Get things indirectly. Usually that's like a game of Telephone."

"Telephone?"

"Yeah, like from when you were little. Everybody sits in a circle, the kid on your left whispers something to you, you whisper what you thought he said to the girl on your right, then she whispers what she thought—"

"Until it all gets fouled up by the time it gets back around."

"Usually."

Vandemeer brought up a hand, rubbing his chin so laboriously that I thought the car dealer's next words would be "Tell you what I'm gonna do." Instead, he said, "So, I talk to you, and you get my story straight."

"That's the idea."

"Okay, fine. I built my reputation here on being honest with my customers, I'll be honest with you. What do you want to know?"

"The authorities in Maine see the crime scene as Shea setting up a triple murder, then losing his cool. If he didn't do it, then somebody else did, and he just reacted predictably when he found the bodies."

Vandemeer nodded without expression.

I said, "Were you close to your brother?"

A pained sigh. "Like best friends."

"You know any reason somebody would want him dead?"

"None."

"How about his wife?"

"Same."

All of a sudden Vandemeer had gone concise on me. It could have been masked emotion over his brother's death, but it didn't feel right.

I said, "The three of you knew each other a long time?"

"Since we were children."

"So, you knew Vivian pretty well, then."

An impatient "Yes."

I said, "Maybe if you explained your relationship with your brother, it would help me on what else to ask you."

Vandemeer seemed to stall a little, maybe thinking we'd already covered that subject. "Like I said, growing up we were best friends, even joked about my name."

"Joked?"

"You know. He was a couple of years older than me, so we joked that instead of 'Hale' and 'Hubbell,' our parents could have named us 'Hale' and 'Hearty.' "

"I see what you mean."

"At least now, I just get people thinking of me when they hear about that telescope that doesn't work right."

I looked down at the brass plate. "I think that's spelled differently."

"Whatever."

"How did you come to be in this line?"

"Cars, you mean?"

"Yes."

"Our parents had some money, they died on the *Andrea Doria* back in the fifties. Remember that?"

"Just the newspapers."

"Yeah, well, it was pretty scary stuff, being eight years old and thinking your folks were in a big tin can at the bottom of the ocean." Vandemeer shivered. "Anyway, we each came into half their money when we hit twenty-one. Hale used his to go to med school, but he was the only scholar in the family. Me, I was a car man, just crazy about them, had this great Ford convertible in high school, aquamarine with power everything, when you used to see just Caddys and Lincolns like that. So when I was a senior, I came to the guy owned this lot then, and he hired me as basically an office boy. Well, I worked my way up, learned everything about how a dealership runs. When he decided to move to Arizona, I took my share of the estate and bought him out. Been here ever since."

I wanted to keep Vandemeer in a talkative move. "How's it been as a life?"

"Aw, I can't complain. Not really. I got into it back in the early seventies, just before the Arab oil thing. It was tough, but the manufacturers adapted and everything was fine. Even did okay during the early eighties. That recession pretty much missed us in New England, at least as far as cars went. Hell, that Prelude of yours—what, an eighty-one?"

"Eighty-two."

"Eighty-two, new it probably went for list, am I right?"

"I don't know. I got it used."

141

"Yeah, well, nothing goes for list anymore. Oh, maybe that convertible I drove in here, they don't make enough of them with this nice June weather we're having now. But most of the serious shoppers, they come in here with computer printouts yet, showing them how much I paid for the car and then expecting me to do no better than five hundred over invoice."

"Which still gives you some profit, right?"

"Five hundred? How am I supposed to—"

"No, I mean the invoice itself. Isn't there part of that you get back from the manufacturer?"

Vandemeer showed me a smile different from the year-book one. "You know something about the trade, huh?"

"Just a little."

"Yeah, well, let me tell you a little more, so you understand my position. I work six days a week now, just Sundays off. On my American cars, I get the dealer 'hold-back' from the invoice, but only at the end of the quarter, after my money's been laid out for eight, maybe twelve weeks. And I've got to finance my inventory on the lot here, point and a half over prime, carry that as part of my nut every month. And it's getting so I can't move my inventory because if I don't have in stock what—and I mean *exactly* what—the customer wants, the customer knows the dealer down the street will order it—*order* it, customized just the way the customer wants it—for maybe three hundred over invoice. You see what I'm saying here?"

"They can get the car they want for less if they're willing to wait for it."

"Exactly. That's exactly right. Then on top of that I got tariffs on my imports that don't hurt the Korean war orphan that makes the cars, they hurt us U.S. dealers. And I got rebates and APR financing offers from my American manufacturer that I have to juggle around what people read last year and expect me to still make good on out of my 'profit margin.' "

"Which margin is tough to have without sales."

"And nearly impossible to have without salesmen. I guess I should say 'salespersons,' because Emily out there was the best of the four people I had on the floor, and she's the only one I can still justify—"

Vandemeer stopped cold, as though someone had slapped him.

I said, "What's the matter?"

He gave me a canny smile. "You ever been in sales, Cuddy?"

"No."

"Cop?"

"Just military."

"Well, I've done it to enough people, I should be able to spot it being done to me."

"What?"

"Warming me up, drawing me out. You came in here, wanting to talk about that horror movie up at the lake, and I wasn't feeling too cooperative, so you got me onto something I did want to talk about, and now you know I'm not in such great financial shape."

"Wouldn't take a genius to figure that out."

"Yeah, well, I said I'd be honest with you, and I will be. Hale was helping me out here. With capital, I mean."

"Bailing you out with cash?"

"He was a doctor, they make a fortune. He needed investments all the time; this was a good one because he knew me and knew the business. Better than throwing three large a month into some mutual fund run by an MBA brat who doesn't return phone calls."

"So your brother was happy to park three thousand a month in your lot."

"Yes," with the impatient edge to it.

"Investment or loan?"

Vandemeer waited, then said, "His lawyer drew up papers. I gave Hale stock, but it was all just on paper. For tax reasons, I think."

Tax reasons. "Did his wife, Vivian, know about that?"

The car man balked. "Vivian? What's she got to do with it?"

"She was killed, too."

Vandemeer studied me, trying to see if there was anything more than the obvious behind my remark. "Vivian, she did fine with the charge card, but I don't think she was much into numbers beyond that."

"How well did you know Shea and his wife?"

"The wife, not much. Met her at a couple of cocktail parties at the house—my brother's house, I mean. She seemed like a nice woman, kind of . . . aloof, maybe."

"And Shea?"

"Steve? I sold him his last two cars, the one his wife drives—sorry, drove. And that new four-wheeler he had up there when . . . it all happened."

"Any problems with him?"

"Utility vehicle was a gem. Same with hers, no complaints."

"Any problems other than with the cars you sold them?"

His hands fidgeted on his desk near one of the perfect stacks. "Steve . . . I got the impression from Hale that Steve was under some kind of pressure."

"What from?"

"Don't know. I think it had to do with his job, though."

"Just general stress, or something more?"

"Like I said, I don't know. Hale just mentioned it to me, I never knew Shea well enough to talk with him about it."

"When was this?"

"When?"

"When your brother mentioned Shea to you."

144

"Oh, Jesus, I don't know. Maybe two—no, I guess it must have been more like four weeks ago."

"Do you remember your brother's exact words?"

"I asked him how he was doing, and he said fine, and I asked about Shea's car—you do that, you know?—and Hale said something like, 'The car's fine, but Steve's tighter than a drum.' "

"His exact words?"

"I'm not sure, except for the 'tighter than a drum,' part. That was one of Hale's favorite expressions."

"And you didn't follow up?"

"Aw, maybe I said, 'How come?,' and Hale said, 'About work' or 'Over work,' something like that. It was just an offhand comment, you know?"

"Was your brother under any stress?"

"Hale? He was the original duck."

"I'm sorry?"

"Duck. Like water off a duck's back. Nothing bothered him."

I thought about Emily Tollison's reaction to my mentioning Nicky Vandemeer. "How about his son?"

"What about him?"

"I understand the boy is something of a handful."

"Yeah, well, we're going to work that out, him and me."

"Nicky and you."

"Right."

"Why is that?"

Vandemeer flared. "Why? Because I'm his uncle and only other kin, that's why. The lawyer Hale used, he did wills for him and Vivian with me as guardian for Nicky."

"How old is he?"

"Nicky? Seventeen."

"So you're guardian only until he hits his next birthday?"

"Well, technically, maybe. But somebody's got to look

after things for him. He's a little . . . wild right now, you know?"

"I understood he's been a little wild for a while."

Vandemeer looked at me. "You mean the driving-under thing."

"Good place to start."

"What can I say? Nicky's a kid. He gets his license and a few beers in him, he does something stupid."

"Anybody hurt?"

"Just the car."

"Which you sold him?"

"Which I gave him. Practically, I mean. Hale covered just my real cost on it."

"But Hale's in no position to cover things anymore."

Vandemeer flared again. "The hell's that supposed to mean?"

"I don't see a probate court judge approving any transfers from the estate to you to cover operating costs anymore."

"Yeah, well, let me tell you something. Hale was a good brother and a generous man, Cuddy. Nicky's just about rich, the way the lawyer explains it to me. But Hale took care of me, too, in that will somewhere, so in a couple of months, I don't need any judge to get my money."

"How much?"

"What?"

"How much is your share?"

Vandemeer didn't reply.

"I can go to the registry and just look it up."

He rubbed his chin some more. "Not to put you to the trouble. It's two hundred thousand."

"Does that about cover what your brother already kicked in here?"

No reply again.

"Even if it does, though, that doesn't mean that you're

even with the board, Hub. If the stock you gave your brother doesn't revert to you somehow, then you might get the two hundred thousand clear from the estate, but you also have your nephew as a partner in the business."

"I can handle it."

"You said before that you work every day but Sunday?"

"That's right."

"Including the weekend your brother was killed?"

"I already told this to the police here."

"I could always 'telephone' them."

Vandemeer started to flare again, then eased off. I thought about Hale's phrase "tighter than a drum" fitting his brother pretty well. The car man said, "I decided to take a couple days for myself."

"Doing what?"

"Just driving around in the convertible, kicking the leaves, you know?"

"Lots of leaves up in Maine, Hub."

Vandemeer said, "Why don't you go find your junkheap and drive it the hell off my lot, huh?"

12

CALEM WAS SOMEWHAT FAMILIAR GROUND FROM THE CASE
Paul O'Boy and I had worked on together. Using the town
center for orientation, I didn't take too long to find the road
I wanted, the cul-de-sac lying just beyond a cross street
perpendicular to it.

I went around the circular dead end, parking at the same
point I'd entered it. Steven Shea had said that the middle
house was his. The house on the left had withered flowers
in beds around the foundation and grass a foot high. The
house on the right had blooming flowers and a groomed
lawn that suggested Mrs. Epps lived there.

I crossed the asphalt toward the house on the right.

Shea also said the builder had used different plans on
each. He was right. My client's place had the same awful,
tumble-down-blocks look as his lake home. The Vandemeer
house was a towering garrison with attached three-car
garage.

Mrs. Epps had a symmetrical ranch, blue and white brick
but with nice touches like geraniums in large ceramic pots
and a woven welcome mat. As I got to the mat, the solid

door inside the screened one opened, enough darkness behind it that I couldn't see into the foyer.

A measured, cultured voice said, "Can I help you?"

"Mrs. Epps?"

"Yes."

"My name's John Cuddy. I'm a private investigator." I
held my identification open to the screen.

The middle finger of an arthritic hand that must once
have been delicate pressed the mesh against the plastic face
of my ID holder, almost tracing it before falling back into
the darkness. The voice said, "So you are."

I felt a little disconcerted, as though I were being interro-
gated from shadows by someone shining a spotlight on me.
"I'd appreciate a few minutes of your time to talk about
your neighbors."

"I wondered whether someone would bother to see me."

The hand didn't reappear; the screened door didn't open.

I said, "May I come in?"

"That probably would be best."

I heard her move away, so I tried the outer door.
Unlocked.

Inside the foyer, my eyes got used to the light. Or lack
of it. Her voice from off to the right said, "Please, follow
me."

We moved through a darkened living room with black-
out drapes, bulky Queen Anne furniture arrayed around
the perimeter. Then we came to a wide shaft of light let in
by French doors to what became a greenhoused Florida
room with a view of trees and brook and Japanese garden
for a backyard.

Mrs. Epps stood as the centerpiece of a set of atrium
furniture in white iron, silk pillows imprinted with blue
flowers. The floor was ceramic tile, mostly blue, laid out in
a three-square pattern like a tic-tac-toe board, the center
square a white tile with a carefully glazed flower design

that to my eye copied the pillows perfectly. Placed aesthetically around the room were white ceramic vases with jug handles on each side of their mouths and swirl patterns in a blue that in turn copied the tiles perfectly. A cat stood and ran out of the room. It looked to be a white Persian with blue eyes. I got the feeling it might have been chosen less for its companionship and more for its color coordination.

Mrs. Epps herself was quite elderly and short but rigidly straight, with chiseled features, snowy hair in a pageboy cut, and a pair of tinted eyeglasses on a silver chain around her neck. She wore one-inch white heels, white stockings, and a string of pearls and matching earrings over a blue dress that copied the combined decor perfectly. I found myself trying mentally to arrange her on the furniture and floor so that she would disappear into it.

"The dimness of the rest of the house is awkward, but the sunshine from the windows wreaks havoc with the upholstery of the better pieces, I'm afraid. I also find that, as I get on, the natural light out here is preferable to the artificial in there."

Her tone carried all the emotion of an elevator that gives you automated instructions. She didn't quite smile and didn't quite frown and didn't seem quite human.

Epps said, "Would you care to sit down?"

"Yes, thank you."

She moved to the settee, leaving me a choice of couch or chair, with couch distanced a little more comfortably for talking. I took it, sinking only an inch into the cushion before feeling the iron underneath me. Epps sat as straight as she'd stood, feet flat on the tiles, knees together like a girl at her first cotillion, waiting to be asked to dance.

I said, "You've guessed I've come on behalf of Steven Shea."

"There's hardly anyone else left, is there?"

Still the elevator voice. Nothing ventured, nothing gained. "You don't seem too upset about losing your neighbors."

"Mr. . . . Cuddy, wasn't it?"

"Yes."

"Mr. Cuddy, I am eighty-six years old. I have buried two husbands, one whom I loved deeply and another who cared for me beautifully. What remains of my circle of contemporaries I'm forced to visit inconveniently by taxi as they babble incontinently in nursing homes and worse. Such experiences give one a sense of balance that is difficult to disrupt."

I found myself disconcerted again. "I wonder if you could tell me what you can about your neighbors?"

Epps blinked. "Have you no more sense of direction than that for your question?"

"You lived near them, I didn't."

"Very well. Feel free to redirect me at any time, then. My second husband—Mr. Epps, naturally—and I committed to purchase this house while it was still under construction. Mr. Epps's deteriorating mobility required a residence all on one floor. This was suitable, and it was, after all, *Cal*em, if you take my meaning."

"A dignified, well-managed town."

"Precisely. No taverns, no 'T-stops' for bus, subway, or train. A protected, livable environment."

"Go on."

"Well, shortly after Mr. Epps and I moved in, construction began across the way." She motioned with her hand like a conductor silencing the string section. "The house seemed suitable, and the Vandemeers perfectly appropriate, if a bit immature to mix with."

"And then?"

"Mr. Cuddy, I suggested you might wish to redirect me. There is no need to prompt me."

"Sorry."

"Nor is there a need to mollify me. I doubt you can insult me, and I've little regard for your opinion of me."

This time I just nodded.

Unnecessarily, Epps smoothed her dress over her thighs. "Your Mr. Shea and Sandra commissioned their home shortly thereafter. I'm sure it met with the zoning and building codes meticulously, because the most nitpicking Boston conveyancer I could find assured me it did. It was, however—and, as you can see, remains—an eyesore, an abomination."

Mrs. Epps's voice rose just a fraction before resuming its electronic tone. "Unfortunately, by then Mr. Epps was quite immobile, and he dearly loved this ranch. Accordingly, I persevered, adding this room to give us a place of peace and a view of serenity not possible from virtually every other part of the house. After he died, I considered moving, but realized I, too, wished to stay. When those you love pass on, you often wish to move. When those who loved you pass on, you often wish to stay."

I thought about Beth and her hillside in Southie.

"Mr. Cuddy?"

"I know what you mean, Mrs. Epps. I take it, then, you didn't get along too well with Shea and Newberg?"

"On the contrary. Perfectly polite, considerate neighbors, after their fashion. Upon our first snow here, your Mr. Shea even offered to shovel our walk, not realizing that of course we'd simply have our landscaper under contract for such eventualities. Sandra I rarely saw."

"Why was that?"

"Until relatively recently—perhaps a year ago—she was employed in downtown Boston, some sort of insurance post, I believe. Often not home until relatively late."

I thought about Epps spotting me before I'd rung her doorbell. "And Steven Shea?"

"The same, only I would say more so. His original job

152

was something to do with computers. More recently with the—is it the 'aerospace' industry?"

"So I'm told."

"Yes. Frequent travel, long meetings. I'm sure that's what sparked it."

" 'It'?"

Epps blinked again. "The affair."

My stomach played ping-pong with the farmhand's breakfast. "Shea was having an affair?"

"No, no. Are inferences completely beyond you, Mr. Cuddy?"

"I've usually hoped otherwise."

"Yes. Yes, it is always reassuring to hope. In any case, as I told our police, the affair was between Dr. Vandemeer and Sandra."

Just what I needed to hear. "How do you know?"

Epps blinked for the third time. "If by your question you're implying that I'd seen them *in flagrante delicto*, the implication is incorrect. If by your question you're wondering if I have inescapable proof, the answer is yes. The doctor would often come home in the middle of the morning or afternoon, when his wife, Vivian, was predictably out shopping—I believe they call them 'malls'?"

"Yes."

"Well, Vivian was rarely home for lunch, but the doctor often was. I would see him park his car in his own driveway, then go into his house only to exit the back door and dart between the houses to his neighbor's back door. When your Mr. Shea was out of town on business, but Sandra was out of work and at home."

I noticed Mrs. Epps referred to males, even her own husband, by title and last name, but women by their first names. "Often enough to be suspicious?"

"Often enough to be conclusive."

"It seems awfully risky."

"I've no reason to believe either adulterer was diseased in any way, traditional or modern."

I felt myself blushing and fought it. "No. No, what I meant was . . . fooling around in their own houses, with a neighbor across the way."

"Perhaps. And perhaps also it appeared the most innocent. Instead of two neighbors caught by a mutual acquaintance exiting a motel inexplicably, they were simply two neighbors at home—at her home—for an hour or two during different days in alternating weeks."

"You don't think that Vivian Vandemeer knew, then?"

"If I were she, I would have known. Or guessed."

"What about the Vandemeers' son?"

The woman's lips curled. "Nicky at least occasionally attends school. Also, on those days when he came home early, he may not have been in any condition to notice his father's car unusually in his own driveway."

I thought about the driving-under conviction. "By 'in no condition' . . ."

"I mean soused. Pickled, potted. And whatever expression appropriately describes being incapacitated by illicit drugs. The boy is a—junker?"

"Junkie, maybe?"

"And his paramour as well."

"His girlfriend?"

"She hardly looks like a girl, Mr. Cuddy. She drives a rather elaborate car and wears rather alluring clothes and the amount of makeup you would have seen in Old Scollay Square if you'd been twenty years older and a visiting sailor."

"Have you met her?"

"I trust you're joking."

"Have you seen her often?"

"Daily, since the killings. Before that, frequently. During some weeks, it was very nearly a carnival across the way,

154

with Dr. Vandemeer arriving only to leave his house to visit Sandra, and the son arriving with his par—*girl*-friend—and disappearing into his parents' house, seemingly oblivious to the fact that his father might catch him doing heaven knows what with her or bottles or needles."

I shook my head, to clear it a little. "Do you think that Nicky knew about his father and Sandra Newberg, then?"

"I simply couldn't say."

I looked at her.

Mrs. Epps returned the look. "Isn't there another question you should have for me?"

"Steven?"

"Precisely. Do I think your Mr. Shea knew about the affair? I simply couldn't say there, either. But that, it seems, is the best question you could have asked."

Mrs. Epps treated me to a smile, probably her first in quite a while.

Outside Mrs. Epps's front door, I looked over to my client's "abomination," fingering his keys in my pocket. Then I walked to the Vandemeer house instead.

Up close, the grass didn't look any lower or the flowers more alive. The rest of the place was in perfect condition, as though an obsessive caretaker had crossed every "t" and dotted every "i." The front door was a broad six-panel in what looked like cherry with a brass mail slot centered two feet off the sill. I rang the bell, got nothing, and rang again. I waited thirty seconds, then pushed in the mail slot, stooping to put my ear to the opening. Still nothing. Straightening up, I really stood on the buzzer, then pounded on one of the door panels, which made a noise like the natives calling Kong to the sacrificial altar. Zip all around.

I turned away from the door and used my hand as a visor to look in the living-room picture window. No lights on, screen of a fifty-one-inch television blank.

Making my way to the garage, I tried to lift the doors. No go and no windows to see through. I moved around the side of the house. Through a window I could make out one car in the three stalls, a two-door sport version of the foreign line Hub Vandemeer carried. Continuing to the back of the house, I saw a nice patio with empty lounge chairs, a putting green centered in the yard.

From the yard, I cut over to the Shea/Newberg house the way Mrs. Epps described Hale Vandemeer doing it, keeping my eye on her house. If she had been at a front window, she could have seen me walking for twenty or thirty feet of distance before the edge of one of Shea's wings would block her view.

Coming around to my client's brown, flat front door, I took out the key and let myself into a boxy, two-story entry hall. Stopping, I breathed in musty air and listened. The drone of a refrigerator, the "ching" of an electronic clock, the wheezing of some air-blowing machinery courtesy of a grilled baseboard duct. There was a tapestry suspended from the upper story of the entry hall's back wall. It showed Steven Shea's face smiling from a Renaissance Italian costume of tights, jacket, and blowsy hat, my client hanging ten while surfing down a high wave. I shook my head, this time not to clear it.

The living room was clean, airy, and awful. The sit-down furniture was rattan, upholstered in faux leopard skins, the theme of the room being a suburban furniture store's vision of *Out of Africa*. The rattan ottomans were shaped like camp stools, the rug a zebra hide fraying at the hooves. Tribal masks, spears, and shields served as wall decorations. I was surprised to see no trophy heads mounted on wooden crests. Compared to this place, the house in Maine was an exercise in understatement.

The sense of taste was unrelieved in the dining room's Ming Dynasty motif. A paper lantern for chandelier, a black, lacquered locker for china hutch. Snarling bronze dragons guarded a lowboy silver cabinet, intricately painted vases on top of it. More black lacquer for table and chairs, the flocked wallpaper red and gold.

The kitchen was Scandinavian, I think, with butcher block counters, fancy cutlery, and copper pots and pans. Occupying one wall was an ancient, iron oven that looked as if it wasn't sure that the adage "any old port in a storm" had been good advice to follow. Everything was still spotless, though, with one exception.

The pizza box in the sink.

I walked over to it, the cardboard starting to stink from both the two pieces of pepperoni and anchovy pizza still on it and the moldering from some standing water at the bottom of the basin itself. I found the trash basket under the sink, but it was clean, a fresh yellow plastic bag carefully tucked around its edges.

Crossing the room, I opened the refrigerator. Plenty of food and drink in it. Almost stuffed, in fact, but for a gap on the wire shelf in front of a six-pack of Michelob cans. The gap was just the right size for a second six-pack.

I found myself listening for movement overhead.

Taking the other exit from the kitchen, I circled around the downstairs, coming next to a huge den done up in red Chippendale leather like a nineteenth-century men's smoking club. I found the staircase to the second floor, taking the steps slowly, staying off the oriental runner at the center and using the edges to minimize the squeaking of the boards. At the top of the stairs, I waited for a count of ten, then twenty. I didn't hear anything.

Staying to the edge of the upstairs corridor, I checked each of the rooms. The three bedrooms and two baths were empty, but comparatively normal. Just simple guest rooms in pastels of green, yellow, and blue, all with linen and comforters arranged just so, the baths in complementary colors.

The master bedroom was another matter. Tufted black chairs and massive black bureaus sitting on lush black carpet, a large black television screen and black VCR in turn sitting on the lowest bureau. The black drapes and black walls contrasted with the white door to a white-tiled bathroom. Then black again for the ceiling over a king-sized, black bed with black sheets and black comforter. Black threads of varying lengths, with white beads on their ends, descended from the ceiling. The beads twinkled and swayed in the air currents, like stars in the heavens doing a hula dance.

Unlike the other bedrooms, the comforter was uneven on the mattress. I walked to the bed and pulled down the comforter and top sheet. The mattress undulated below me. A water bed. There was a darker oval near the center of the bottom sheet. I touched it. The sheet was satin, the oval still damp, as though someone had made love there earlier that morning.

I moved around the foot of the bed and saw the beer cans. Michelobs, they were on their sides on the black carpet, one having gurgled most of its contents into the rug fibers, slicking them down. I ticked the other three cans. Empty before they hit the floor.

I looked in the bathroom, switching on the overhead light. Shower curtain yanked back, water pooled on the tiles underneath it. No bath mat, but two heavy black bath towels were wadded up in a corner like so much toilet paper.

Coming back into the bedroom, I noticed that the little infinity sign on the VCR glowed a neon orange. On Nancy's machine, that meant a tape was still in it. I went up, hit the "Eject" button, and got nothing. Tried the "Power" twice and got the same. I felt a brain flash and went looking for a remote control device. It was mixed up in the comforter. I managed to find the black dot/white dot sign for "Power" and got a welcoming "glump" and orange glows from several more points of the VCR. I touched "Play." No response. I hit "Rewind," let it chug for twenty seconds, then "Stop" and "Play" again. It didn't take twenty seconds for me to know that the title of what I was watching would alliterate like *Debbie Does Dallas*. I pushed "Fast Forward" and, when the tape ended, the power button again, replacing the remote where I found it but leaving the tape in the machine.

Even though it was the Shea/Newberg house, I had the feeling I'd discovered where Nicky Vandemeer and Blanca Quintana enjoyed breakfast in bed.

The rest of my tour was anticlimactic. I went back downstairs and through the den. No threatening letters from the in-box on the desk, no obvious preparations for a massacre in the woods. Next to the den was a staircase to a basement, where the functional guts of the house were walled off in one corner, the rest of the place devoted to a game room with art deco bistro furniture.

Everywhere you looked in the game room, there was a photo of The Foursome, striking different poses in different settings, but each person sending out a respective, surprisingly consistent message. Hale Vandemeer wore a half grin, not showing any teeth. Vivian Vandemeer had her arm around her husband's waist, her free hand waving to the camera. Sandra Newberg looked politely tolerant, as though her thoughts were elsewhere.

And Steven Shea was always flogging his wholesale smile, leaning toward the lens to get that extra edge.

Leaving my client's house, I tried both bell and knock on the Vandemeers' front door. Still no answer, and still no noise from inside.

Back in the Prelude, I wound out of Calem and toward Route 128. After driving about six miles north, I took the exit that eventually would lead me to Defense Resource Management. Along the way, I found myself on a main road that thirty years ago was probably a farmer's cart path through not-too-productive fields. Now the road was forty feet wide and the fields paved over with strip malls and generic eateries of various price ranges, whose menus you could predict without ever being in the places.

A big breakfast, like mine with Paul O'Boy, tends to whet my appetite for lunch, and I anticipated a long afternoon at Shea's employer. About a mile from DRM, I picked a restaurant that had a liquor license to go with its green walls and red-checked vinyl tablecloths. A sign by the hostess desk told me that if I'd been there the day before I could have had my picture taken with Bosco the Clown. Darn the luck.

The hostess, wearing a dress that looked like it came from one of the tablecloths, asked if I'd like a table for one. A man who sounded a little under the weather was booming a raucous speech to a makeshift banquet table of twenty people, so I asked her if I could get food at the bar. She said certainly, but led me to an empty stool anyway, setting the menu on the mahogany surface in front of the too-high brass rail and murmuring that the bartender's name was Dan, as though it were a secret we now shared.

The stool had padded seat, armrest, and back, but it wouldn't swivel without more torque than was comfortable to manage. I could still hear the speech—or more accurately, speeches, since a new voice was booming from the other room. A youngish guy with clean-cut good looks, carroty hair, and a college ring appeared in front of me. He wore a white, billowy shirt and, what do you know, a red-checked vest. He said, "Something to drink, sir?"

"What do you have on tap?"

"Miller, Miller Lite, Bass, Watney's, and Guinness."

"You're kidding?"

"I'm sorry?"

"No. My fault. I just didn't expect such a selection."

The keep smiled. "No offense taken. It's a plastic dive, but I have some say in the draughts, and as long as business points toward beer and ale, I—"

"Dan!"

We both looked down the bar at a waitress who seemed frantic.

Dan said, "Think about what you'll have. I'll be right back."

I liked the way the guy had finessed that, attending to her probably bigger order first without giving me the impression I was being bypassed. I watched him draw half a dozen assorted brews into frosted mugs, while she wicked cocktail napkins onto her tray and used the spritzer hose to do three or four nonalcoholic drinks into iced tea glasses. Within a minute, she was off balancing ten drinks at shoulder height.

Dan came back to me. "Decided?"

"A pint of the Watney's."

"The big ones are just for sodas. Mugs are ten ounces, though."

"That'll be fine."

As he drew the red ale for me, I said, "I wouldn't think Bosco the Clown'd sell a lot of beer."

Dan laughed, using his left hand to position a napkin in front of me, then setting my drink on the napkin. "Only way to make it these days is to appeal to everybody. So we have the clown once a week for the young mommas and kids, the different taps for the business crowd who can nurse a two-dollar beer better than a four-dollar martini. Even started early-bird specials from five to seven for the senior citizens."

I nodded toward a third voice giving a speech. "Business crowd seems kind of concentrated."

Dan clouded a little. "Yeah. An El-Oh party."

"El-Oh?"

"Layoff. Three guys are getting the ax, so the men and women in their section are taking them out for a hoot."

"Seriously?"

"You bet."

"I mean, it happens often enough, you have a nickname for it?"

Dan leaned onto his elbows, lowering his voice even though nobody was close enough to hear us. "Five years ago, when things were rolling, this place'd be packed. There were fifty thousand people in the defense contractors within a three-mile radius of where you're sitting, and that's just the white-collars. Then came the cutbacks. Remember the last election, everybody railing about how Dukakis had turned the Massachusetts Miracle into the Massachusetts Debacle?"

"Tough to miss it."

"Okay, let me tell you, Dukakis wasn't any more responsible for the downside than he was for the up. It wasn't who was governor, it was Reagan Administration deficit spending on defense contractors in Tip O'Neill's home state that made the miracle, and it was the cutoff of federal spending that shitcanned it. Today, there's maybe, *maybe*, twenty, twenty-two thousand of the fifty still in their jobs, and most of them are holding on by their fingernails, praying God that a rich Arab country with more oil wells than generals wants some fancy hardware can bring down their neighbors' missiles like a falcon on a pigeon."

"You sound like you've been tuned into the conversations around you."

Dan clouded some more. "I don't have to eavesdrop." He rapped his ring on the mahogany bar like West Pointers

162

used to do in Vietnam, then made a fist and showed me the inscription. "Tufts Engineering, Class of 'eighty-five. When DRM cut me loose last year, this is where they threw my El-Oh party."

"I see."

I ordered a mushroom burger and fries, biding my time while Dan put the order in and helped the frantic waitress again. When he wasn't looking, I downed most of the Watney's quickly.

When Dan turned back toward me, he saw the depleted mug. "Another?"

"Please."

Fresh napkin, fresh mug.

As he served me, I said, "How's DRM doing these days?"

A shrug. "Depends on who you talk to. Or overhear." A sheepish smile. "Sorry. Still a little touchy on that, I guess."

"Forget it, my stupidity. It's just that DRM isn't one of the companies you tend to mention in the same breath as Raytheon or Teledyne or—"

"Or General Dynamics or Northrup or any of them. It's one of the reasons I went with DRM out of school, tell you the truth. The president is this guy Davison from the South, mega-military contacts. The place was small enough when I started, you actually got to talk with him as part of the interview process. Then things got bigger, people brought on laterally from other companies, and somewhere along the line, it got too big to move quick enough, and like half of us got pink slips. What I hear, they're coming back a little, but not enough."

"Not enough?"

"For me to get asked back."

I nodded, at which point a little binger went off and Dan

said my lunch was ready. He brought it out, disappeared while I ate, and reappeared only to leave my tab.

Stepping off the stool, I said to him, "Wasn't the guy on those murders up in Maine from DRM?"

Dan's face clouded again. It hurt you to see it. "That's right. He was one of the laterals, brought on from some computer outfit where he was a hotshot sales guy. I never met him, far as I know, but it sounds like he's in deeper shit than an El-Oh party lands you."

Agreeing with him, I took the tab and settled it with the hostess, who hoped I'd have a really good day, now.

13

DEFENSE RESOURCE MANAGEMENT WAS A SLATE BUILDING three stories high that looked like the lower half of a capital "H." The parking lot between the two legs was only about one third full. Unless a lot of folks took very late outside lunches, things weren't any better than bartender Dan suggested. I left the car in a "Visitor" space and walked to the main entrance in the middle of the crossbar, the initials of the company emblazoned in a white and yellow starburst just over my head.

The double, glass doors were reinforced with hexagonal chicken wire, like an old elementary school. Just inside the entrance was a cockpit desk with two people as captain and copilot, a battery of video cameras above their heads, sweeping the reception area. The captain was a middle-aged woman in a polka-dot blouse wearing a headset of tiny earphones and mouth mike. The copilot was a young black man in a powder blue security shirt with impressive shoulders and biceps. When the woman asked my name, I gave it, the security guy consulting a sheet in front of him. I felt as though I were voting in the basement of the

Boston Public Library, where an election board volunteer takes your name and a Boston cop checks you off on a registration list.

The copilot found my name. "Can I see some identification, please?"

I showed my Massachusetts private investigator identification holder.

He said, "Something with a photo on it?"

I got out my wallet and gave him the driver's license. I wasn't carrying, so I left my gun permit in the little pocket where most people kept a credit card or two.

The guard noted something in a logbook. "This still your home address?"

"What difference does it make?"

He stopped writing and very deliberately handed back my license. "Stand still for just a moment, please, sir."

I did.

The woman pushed a button, then a part of their cockpit area made noises like an auto shredder for about twenty seconds. She reached a hand over to the far side of the desk, and a photo dropped into her hand. She took the photo and placed it under a pump handle that belonged next to the well on an old farm. After pressing down on the handle, she lifted up and produced a laminated holder with a plastic string around it, like a pendant on a chain. She handed me the thing, a depressingly accurate likeness of me next to some kind of iridescent hologram. The pendant part was still warm.

As the woman pushed another button and spoke quietly into her mike, the guard said to me, "Please wear that badge around your neck at all times, photo out. Please be sure to return the badge to this desk upon exiting the building."

I put the plastic chain over my head, feeling vaguely foolish. "What do I do now?"

He inclined his head to the woman. "Someone will be out shortly, sir. Please have a seat."

There were a couple of comfortable chairs around a Plexiglas table. Two spartan conference rooms with open doors and empty Plexiglas tables were to my left. The only other door was to my right, a heavy, metal affair with a small porthole of glass and wire. I took one of the chairs and looked at the magazines fanned like a canasta hand on the Plexiglas in front of me. Three covers showed fighter planes, some sleek, some plug-ugly, with summaries of the stories inside. One cover had a missile angled at about sixty degrees from the horizontal on a launcher with bulbous truck tires holding it up. Another displayed a submarine breaching through what looked like ice floes.

"Mr. Cuddy?"

I looked up. I hadn't heard the inner door open, but it was just closing in the far wall. The woman standing in front of me was slim, about five-six in a tweed suit and maize blouse. She had green eyes that turned down just a little at the corners, making her appear slightly sad. The eyes took you away from the rest of the face, both nose and chin small and pointy above and below full lips. If she were a fighter plane, she'd have been one of the sleek ones. She also was wearing a pendant, but hers had a nametag on it that read ANNA-PIA ANTONELLI.

I got up, stretching out my hand. "Ms. Antonelli."

"Call me Anna-Pia. Same number of syllables, but it comes out shorter."

Nice smile between the lips. "And I'm John."

"If you'll come with me, John, we can get started."

I followed Antonelli to the heavy door, a click preceding her reaching for the handle. It opened onto a large room, another security guard by himself behind a smaller desk. We walked through a cornfield of computer terminals and drafting boards, maybe half of each occupied by a man or woman lost in thought, staring at screen or drawing. The dress code seemed pretty casual, a lot of jeans on both genders. The security pendants all had name labels.

I said to Antonelli, "How come my badge doesn't have 'John Cuddy' on it?"

She twisted her neck to speak over her shoulder. "If nobody's expecting you, you'd be seen in one of those unsecure conference rooms in the lobby. If you are expected, that person already knows who you are."

We reached the end of the large room, where a bank of three elevators waited for us. Antonelli hit the button for the middle one, causing it to light up and the doors to open. The buttons on the others didn't follow suit.

As we stepped into the mirrored box, I said, "Private elevator?"

"Yes. To Mr. Davison's office suite."

"The president?"

"Yes."

As the doors closed, I looked back toward where we'd come from. "Kind of a hike for him to save a couple of flights."

Antonelli gave me the smile again, one that could grow on you. "Mr. Davison believes he should see the staff every day and they should see him. From his military service, I think. So he walks—"

"The parade ground while the troops are doing calisthenics."

Antonelli didn't quite turn off the smile. "Something like that, I suppose."

The doors opened, a secretarial cluster in front of us, two women, one older, one quite young, bustling around desks for three. Indirect lighting shone on slate-colored carpeting that mimicked the outer walls. Large green plants, their pots on casters, reached skyward.

Antonelli said, "This way, please."

FOURSOME

We turned right and entered a conference room with no interior windows and a view of the parking lot through the exterior ones. There were three men seated in admiral's chairs around an elliptical Plexiglas table on steel trestles. Two rose as we walked in.

One of the risers was a white male in his mid-forties wearing an olive drab poplin suit, white shirt, and rep tie. He had sandy hair cut short and brushed across, even features, and a raccoon look around his eyes and cheekbones, as though he wore aviator sunglasses outdoors and needed no corrective lenses indoors. His jaw seemed to be having spasms back near his ears, and I sensed that he resented me at first sight.

The second riser was a black male in his early thirties wearing a navy blue blazer, gray slacks, a collar-stayed shirt and twill stripe tie. His cropped black hair was thinning, giving his crown a slightly satanic widow's peak. The nose was broad, as were the lips as he smiled and buttoned his blazer, showing what appeared to be a Rolex Oyster beneath the cuff on the left wrist.

The man who stayed seated could have doubled for the actor Glenn Ford in his late fifties. The salt-and-pepper hair was combed forward to a point just onto his forehead. Floppy ears, a jutting chin, and half-moon glasses under hawking eyes. He wore a flannel shirt, tatty blue jeans, white socks, and some kind of moccasins crossed behind one of the trestles supporting the conference table. I saw him nod almost imperceptibly toward Antonelli, acknowledging some silent signal she'd sent him while I was watching the other two men.

Antonelli introduced them in the order I'd thought of them. "John Cuddy, this is Dwight Schoonmaker, our head of security."

Olive drab just lowered his eyelids to me.

"And this is Tyrone Xavier, who's been subbing for Steven."

The blazer leaned forward with a continuing smile and shook my hand.

"And this is Keck Davison, our president."

Davison said, "Cuddy."

I thought, What, the janitor have another commitment? "Good of you all to see me on such short notice."

Schoonmaker and Xavier sat back down as Antonelli touched a seat for me and herself took an empty chair with a legal pad and two sharpened pencils in front of it. Nobody else had anything in front of them except their attitudes.

I moved to the chair she'd designated, which put me in the center of the long axis of the elliptical table, Davison at the head. The effect was I could look at just one person at a time. I decided to pick Keck Davison.

Antonelli said, "We thought that it would be more efficient for you to be able to interview all of us together."

Still watching Davison, I said, "And why is that?"

Antonelli paused for a moment, as though not sure she should stick to the script of her running the meeting. Then she said, "Why, in case one of us doesn't know the answer to a question, perhaps one of the others will."

"That's not the impression I get."

"I beg your pardon?"

"I get the impression somebody's seen Apaches, and you're busy closing the gates."

One corner of Davison's mouth went up.

Antonelli said, "Mr. Cuddy, we really are doing our best to cooperate—"

An aggressive voice from Schoonmaker's direction rode over her. "Cuddy here isn't interested in cooperation. He's interested in firebombs."

The corner of Davison's mouth went down.

Antonelli said, "Dwight, perhaps if we—"

Schoonmaker said, "Cuddy thinks—"

Keck Davison didn't have to ride over him. The president's hand went up in a stop sign, and Schoonmaker's voice quit as though he'd been vaporized.

"Anna-Pia, I wonder if you and the boys could excuse us while Mr. Cuddy and I have a little talk, see how he can help us with our business?"

Davison's accent came out more hillbilly than southern, with "Anna-Pia" sounding like "Aunt Pee-yah," "help" like "hep," and "business" like "bid-ness."

If it weren't for the deadening effect of the carpet, I think all three chairs would have scraped back in unison. They filed out, Antonelli first, Xavier second, Schoonmaker hovering for a stutter step behind me as he joined them and somebody closed the door gently.

14

KECK DAVISON TUGGED ON ONE OF HIS EARLOBES. "NOW JUST *what* am I supposed to make of you, son?"

I didn't say anything.

"You see that brain trust we just shooed out of here? They spent yesterday afternoon and all this morning preparing themselves for this "joint interview," as Anna-Pia called it, and you go and shoot it all to shit in about a minute-five."

I still sat quiet.

Davison grunted what might have been a laugh. "Kind of tough to get a rise out of you, is that it?"

"Mister Dav—"

"Keck, long's we're one-on-one here."

"That short for something?"

"No. I had me a momma, she was long on the letter 'K.' Her daddy had been Klan down in Alabama before she come up to West Virginny, so she figured she'd name each of her boys with a K, get her 'KKK' after a while? So my oldest brother was Kevin, and the next one Kyle, and the third one Kurt; but then my daddy and her didn't stop having fun, but she did run out of names she knew, and so I got 'Keck,' and my littlest brother, he got 'Kemp.' "

"Sorry I asked."

A real laugh this time, a little braying in it. "You never served in the diplomatic corps, am I right?"

"And you never pronounce it 'West Vir-*ginny*' in your head, do you?"

Davison tugged on the other earlobe. "You're seeing through all my defense mechanisms, son."

"Not in this lifetime."

He let go of the ear and squared his shoulders. "All right, Cuddy. In the clear, or at least what I remember about how to talk that way. What do you need?"

Very little of the hills in that last. I said, "Somebody cut down three people very methodically, very cleanly, but with just enough muff around the edges to put Steven Shea in the middle of what looks like a bungled multiple murder. If he is being set up, then somebody with resources probably did the killing."

Davison's eyes got bright. "Go on."

"Now, it's possible that the target was one or more of the people actually killed, the others included to blur things and implicate Shea as a convenient husband-gone-berserk."

"Granted."

"It's also possible that Shea was the real target."

"They're so good at everything else on this, be awful sloppy not to notice he wasn't there when the arrows started flying."

"No, I mean Shea as the one they wanted to get out of the way without it seeming that getting rid of him was the reason for the killings."

One nod. "Which brings you to DRM."

"Right."

Davison blew out a breath. "I just don't see it, but that

don't make it so. I take it you're going to be wanting to see everybody separately, poke and prod some."

"Yes."

"Who do you want to start with, son?"

"You."

Davison never faltered. "Go ahead."

"How did Shea come to be here?"

"You want it short or long?"

"Long would be nice."

The man settled in the chair, his legs straight out under the table, his arms crossed on his chest. "I started this outfit fifteen years ago. Before that I was a project engineer for another company when the father of my roommate from VMI got himself appointed to the right congressional committee. He wanted the opinion of somebody who'd flown in combat on how things the taxpayers bought really worked. One thing led to another, and thanks to me, my old company had the inside track on a prototype the Navy needed built for a missile guidance system. That project got me exposure in the right places, and pretty soon some venture-capital vultures gave me seed money for a project of my own. That played out right handsome at about twenty bucks to the dollar, and ten years ago we moved from an old airplane hangar to here. Early eighties, son, it was like we were printing money instead of diagrams. But I could see the handwriting on the wall, and it was saying somebody was about to shut off the faucet that fed the trough."

"Which meant?"

"Which meant that I had to find a way to open a new market for what we did. Oh, I could have folded the tent completely, those venture fellas got paid back so handsome, they would have kept me on as kind of a poster-boy, but I didn't want that. So it just happened that Steven Shea was trying to sell us one of the computers his company was pushing a few years back, and damn if he didn't impress me as a man could sell a widow a funeral suit for her husband with two pair of pants. So I hired him away and sent him off around the world with some impressive graphics and videos. After banging on doors across three continents, Steve brought one almost home."

"Almost?"

"This country—we don't need to use names, I hope—this country three generations ago was using blunt spears to herd mangy cattle. Now the honchos in its current government decide they would just love to have what we can provide."

"Which is?"

"Let's just say it's classified."

I leaned back in my chair. "Doesn't wash, Keck. You a design firm or an arms dealer?"

Davison took off the granny glasses and gestured with them. "Ordinarily, I wouldn't go any further without Anna-Pia getting you to sign a nondisclosure agreement. But I'll tell you what, son. Let's just talk hypothetically. Say I've got this engineer, he comes up with something. . . . You watched the Desert Storm coverage?"

"Yes."

"All right. Our boys got these tanks can see on a viewer the heat images of the Iraqi vehicles."

"With you so far."

"Well, let's say my engineer comes up with something better than what our tanks use. Only it's simpler and pretty easy to fabricate and then assemble if you add some components available on the open market."

I said, "And it's for planes."

Davison used the glasses to nod for him. "It is. The pilot in our hypothetical case might use our product to track the thermal trail of a vehicle right back to its source."

"The vehicle itself."

"Right."

"So, the country could buy your gadget, attach it to some other gadgets, and then put the finished product in their existing planes."

"Basically."

"Which would give them a pretty nice advantage without replacing their whole air force."

"An advantage which, given their neighbors, they could dearly use. As a defensive weapon that would discourage incursion."

"And Shea brought all this together. . . ."

"Right man, right product, right customer."

"Almost."

Davison blew out another breath. "Almost. This thing from Maine hitting the news, it's made his contact over there very nervous about us. We have competitors who would love to swoop down on this one, persuade our customer that their product is nearly as good as what we could deliver."

"Care to name them?"

"What, the competitors?"

"Yes."

"You're thinking one of them did this?"

"Shea thinks so."

"Well, like I said, others do. And it's not impossible. It's just that . . . , well, our competitors might try to hire away that engineer. Or maybe compromise him. Or plant some drugs or whatever on Steve while he's traveling, get him clapped into some jail out of *Midnight Express*. But killing his wife and the other two? I just don't see another American company thinking this deal of ours could be worth that to them."

"And even if it were, the killings haven't scotched your deal completely."

"No."

176

"Thanks to Tyrone Xavier?"

"Yes. Tyrone, he's been amazing, I have to tell you. Picking up the pieces, holding everything together."

"How is the sales guy compensated in a deal like this?"

Davison lifted the corner of his mouth again. "That kind of gets negotiated."

"What was negotiated with Shea?"

"Well, it's pretty complicated."

"I'll bet it's pretty simple, Keck, we're just talking magnitude of the dollars."

Davison looked off, out the window toward his under-maximized parking lot. "Steve would have made between half a million and one-point-two, depending."

"Quite a magnitude."

Davison's voice got quiet. "Last few years, I've put back some of what I took out, keep the doors open. Oh, I had to lay off some good folks, but I couldn't stand treat for everybody I'd like to have. This project comes in, son, and I can swing the doors wide again, welcome back some good souls and pull my money back to my own accounts."

"Which is really why we 'shooed out' the brain trust a while ago."

Davison raised his voice to the lecturing level. "You go stomping around like a horny bull, our customer could get wind of it, think there's something major wrong not just with Steve but with the way we do business. I cooperate with you, I expect gentler treatment."

"What does Tyrone Xavier expect?"

"Tyrone?"

"What's his negotiated compensation?"

Davison didn't have to look out the window this time. "He steps into Steve's shoes on the work, he steps into Steve's shoes on the deal."

"Half a million to one-point-two."

"Oh, I won't leave Steve out in the cold. But Tyrone will have earned it, and I can't pay it twice."

"Generous of you to give Xavier the same deal."

Davison's voice got hard. "Nothing generous about it. That's what was negotiated."

"After Shea was arrested?"

"That's right."

"In other words, Xavier came in to you and said, you want the sale, I get the commission."

Same hard voice. "In other words."

"How soon after the killings?"

"Monday after."

"First business day after the Friday killings."

Davison said, "I was on a fishing trip. It was my first day back."

"Where was the trip?"

"Maine, way north of Shea's place, though. Hundred, hundred fifty miles."

"How'd you get there?"

Davison bridled. "You're thinking something, say it."

"I already did. How'd you get there?"

Davison gave it five seconds. "I have a seaplane I use from time to time."

"Land on water, take off from it, too?"

"That's right."

"You ever been to Shea's lake place?"

"Once. We all went up for a weekend last August."

"We?"

"Anna-Pia, Dwight, Tyrone, me."

"And Steve?"

"Naturally. And his wife, Sandy, too."

"How about the Vandemeers?"

"Not that time. Met them once at his house in Calem."

"Anybody go fishing with you?"

"The weekend of the killings, you mean?"

178

"Yes."

"No. Just a getaway, relaxing kind of thing."

I thought about what Ralph Paine had told me about black flies. "What about the bugs?"

"Bugs?"

"The black flies?"

"Oh, they're on the wing, all right, but long's you stay out in the middle of the water, they're not so bad."

I stopped for a while, Davison waiting me out, seeing if he needed to stay alert.

I said, "What about Dwight Schoonmaker?"

"What about him?"

"How'd you get him?"

"Dwight used to be in security at my former employer. After I got this operation going strong, he come over to join me."

"Military?"

Davison gave me a chilly smile. "Dwight did some checking on you, son. MP, Saigon, Tet, and then some. You're as good as I think you are, I'd be disappointed if you haven't guessed about old Dwight."

"That he used to work for another 'company' with three initials as its name."

"You've restored my faith in you. Very helpful to have a man like him around."

"And Anna-Pia Antonelli?"

"Shrewd, smart, and a good teacher."

"Teacher?"

"She's taught me how I offend without intending to. But she taught me quietlike, velvet glove."

Davison allowed me time to ask a stupid question if I wanted to. Instead I said, "Any office relationships I should know about before I 'stomp' on them?"

"Well, well. I do believe somebody's taught you how not

to offend, too. That doesn't just restore my faith in you, it increases it."

"About the relationships?"

"None I know of."

Preserving deniability. "Keck, while my stock's so high in your book, let me ask you two more questions."

"Two. Go ahead."

"If Shea didn't commit these killings, who do you think did?"

"My hand on the Bible, I couldn't even guess about it."

I nodded.

"What's your other question, son?"

"In terms of priorities, what do you want to see happen here?"

Davison went back to the earlobe. "I want to see my customer close the deal, and Steve be out of jail to shake on it."

"In that order."

His turn to nod.

15

"MR. CUDDY. C'MON IN."

If the conference room had been bright and airy, Tyrone Xavier's office was more like a reinforced bunker. The feeling of whitewashed cinder blocks was hard to avoid, and the wall decorations managed to bring out the starkness of the background even more. He did have a window two feet high by nine feet long above his Plexiglas desktop, the three-quarter-inch material seeming to be general issue at DRM.

Xavier came from behind his desk to shake hands again. He'd taken off the blue blazer, a well-developed physique on about six feet under the dress shirt.

"Mr. Xavier."

"Please, call me Ty, all right?"

"All right."

Xavier smiled again, too, showing about as many teeth as a case has beer cans. "A lot of people are put off a little when I introduce myself. You know, I say, 'Hi, I'm Tyrone Xavier,' and they keep leaning in, expecting a last name to complete things."

"Why not add one, then?"

Xavier's smile wavered, then came back as he bade me take an admiral's chair, more general issue at DRM. "I kind of like putting them a little off balance at first. Also, the name's memorable the way it is, and a memorable name helps you cut through when you make a callback."

"Calling back a potential customer?"

"Right."

"How do you like sales?"

The smile wavered again, for only half as long. "It's fine, fine. Lots of freedom, lots of chances to meet new people, make contacts that could help later on. Downside is, the travel's not what they say it used to be."

"What do you mean?"

"Well, used to be, everybody for an outfit like this would get to go first-class on the airlines, best hotels. Image, you know? Customers want to deal with the company that looks like it's doing the best, because that's where the best product likely is. Now, though, we've got a 'corporate travel manager.' Coach instead of first-class—which is really torture, you're anything over five-five—caps on your hotel per diem. You still get to go to some great restaurants, because now you impress the customer with food and wine. But you've got to account for everything, and it's kind of a pain."

"Any other downsides?"

Xavier made his smile go coy. "Well, you heard how traveling salesmen do just fine in the lady department? That's still true. Only thing is, you really got to ask yourself, you get my meaning?"

"AIDS?"

"That's it. That's it exactly. I mean, I'm in a bar, some nice hotel. Lady sidles up, looks nice, talks nice, I got to ask myself first, is she a pro? If not, I still got to ask myself, lady's so hot to trot with me, how many other guys she had the last year? You see what I'm saying here?"

"The best you could hope for might be the worst that could happen."

"That's it. Exactly, again." The big smile, again.

I said, "You don't get tired, cozying up to people you might not like?"

"Hey, the price you pay, right? I mean, there's a reason it's pronounced 'suck-cess,' you know?"

"You ever get tired of Steven Shea?"

The smile went back to coy. "I was wondering why we were going all around the mulberry bush. Figured it was part of the ritual, what a private eye has to go through."

"How about you and Shea?"

"Aw, man. Steve, he was—is—an all right guy. I was recruited out of the service to come on board here after Mr. Davison got Steve away from some computer company."

"How were you recruited?"

"I was nearing the end of my hitch. Spent some time up here, kind of liked the area."

"Where'd you spend your time?"

"Harvard."

"The school, not the town."

"That's right."

"Go on."

"Well, like I said, I was short-timing, so I sent for information on companies up here, papered them with résumés, and got a nibble from DRM."

"From who here?"

"Mr. Davison himself."

"Not Shea?"

"No. At least, not initially."

"Then what?"

"Pretty typical, I think. They flew me into an airport conference center—Continental's, down at Newark—and I met Mr. Davison and Steve there."

"Why an airport?"

"Usually they'd do that if there was some hush-hush about things. You know, you're Company A, and you want a guy from Company B, but don't want Company B to wonder why he's all of a sudden going to Boston one day. For me, I remember it was just that Mr. Davison and Steve were flying somewhere, and Newark was a good spot for everybody to meet."

"Sounds kind of noisy."

"No, no. These conference centers, they're like little offices away from home. I use them all the time, now. An airline will have this club you join, a hundred, maybe a hundred-fifty a year for a fee. Then you get to use their center, with phones, faxes, photocopiers, even personal computers. It's a great deal."

"Why were you recruited?"

"Why?"

"If Steve's such an all right guy on his own."

Xavier moved his tongue around inside his mouth, maybe trying to assess how much his boss would have told me about his employees. "Steve has a great touch with a lot of people, but I guess Mr. Davison felt I might be an asset with some of the customers out there."

"Because Shea hadn't been in the military?"

"Partly. But hell, I was a Marine captain, a ground-pounder, not an electronics jock. Mostly it was because DRM was trying to appeal to some countries run by people of color, and I was a nice addition to the team."

After seeing Shea's living room, I could understand that. "You work pretty closely with Shea?"

"You could say that."

"How do you mean?"

"Well—you know much about how our business works?"

"Just a little."

"Okay. Say we've done some presentations here and there around this world of ours. Say I've helped out with some, but not with others. A potential calls in, wants some more facts, but Steve's on a layover or the middle leg of a long trip. I get the request, coordinate with our tech people, try to get the customer back an answer."

"So you've seen Shea in action?"

"Many times."

"Any reason he'd have drawn somebody's anger?"

"Anger? You're saying, like enough to do the thing up in Maine?"

"Right."

"Lord, no. We deal with heads of major government departments, sometimes the brother of the president for some country you never heard of that's the new name for a country you barely heard of. But by the time we're talking to them, they're past the gangster stage, you know what I'm saying?"

"You don't see any of your potential customers doing something like this."

"Absolutely not."

"How about a competitor?"

"You're going to have to talk with Dwight about that."

"How about the names of the competitors?"

"Same."

I sat back a bit. "I don't get it."

"Get what?"

"I can see you guys being tight with the names of your customers. But why the names of your competitors?"

"Because that's the way it is."

"Meaning Mr. Davison's way is the way it is."

A shrug.

I said, "Meaning Schoonmaker isn't going to give me anything on the competitors, either."

"That would be up to him."

I nodded. "You know much about Shea's private life?"

"You mean away from DRM?"

"Right."

"No. We worked together, but we weren't really social buddies. We had a drink, it was for business reasons."

"You ever been up to Shea's lake place?"

Xavier rearranged himself in his desk chair. "Jumping around like this, it works for you?"

"Sometimes, when people don't try to buy themselves time by asking a question back."

The coy smile. "I've been up there. Once. Kind of a company outing."

"Tell me about it."

"Mr. Davison, Dwight, Anna-Pia. Steve and his wife, Sandy. Me. Friday night to Sunday afternoon. Too much booze, too much barbecue, too much forced laughter. But, hey, like I said, that's why it's pronounced that way."

Success. "What kinds of things did you all do up there?"

"Do?"

"Activities."

"Let's see. We swam, went for a ride around the lake in Steve's boat, some water-skiing. I begged off for an hour, took a little canoe paddle, felt good."

When Xavier didn't continue, I said, "You play with the crossbow?"

"Yeah. Saturday afternoon, Steve hauled it out for a while. It got old pretty fast."

"Where'd he keep it?"

The eyes closed. "I'd bet my next commission you already know the answer to that one."

"Everybody give it a try?"

Xavier opened his eyes. "Everybody except Anna-Pia and Sandy. Mr. Davison was good, I wasn't too bad."

"And Schoonmaker?"

"Like he was William Tell. Bull's-eye or close to it, every time. The reason it got old so fast."

"You have any idea why Schoonmaker was so good?"

"He's got certificates in his office on weapons proficiency."

"Suitable for framing?"

"Suitable for flaunting, more like it. They're off to the side of his desk, where you can't help but see them when you're sitting in his visitor's chair."

"You don't think all that much of Schoonmaker."

"Hard to hide it."

"Why don't you like him?"

"I get the feeling he thinks people of color make good Indians but bad chiefs."

"And he sees you as a chief now?"

Xavier started to say something, then kept it back behind the big smile. "You're right, there. The jumping around, it does make a man want to jump back at you. Fact is, Steve got himself in a load of shit. Fact is, that made me kind of indispensable. Fact is, Schoonmaker resented me before and twice as much now."

"Now that you stand to pull down around a million for the deal."

"Your numbers are off."

"How's a range of half a million to one-point-two sound?"

Xavier's smile wavered some more. "Sure, I sat down with Mr. Davison. Told him he wanted me to close for Steve, I get Steve's package. Nothing wrong with that."

"And you figure you're close to closing?"

"That's why I'm here instead of on the road. Waiting for the little phone to ring. Or bleat, which is how they sound now."

"You're sitting where I am, sounds like one hell of a motive."

Xavier dropped any pretense of a smile. "I'll tell you

something. That's exactly what hit me, too, when I saw it on the TV. Then I thought things through, like you're going to. The money, getting Steve's package, that might give me a good reason to kill him, but accidentally, like a car accident or fall, something might not look like murder. This here up in Maine? No way, José. Man like me wants to step into Steve's shoes, he isn't going to massacre most of two families. Too much investigation, too much publicity that might scare off our potential customer. Besides, when we drove up there for the outing, I didn't so much as *see* another brother once I was north of the New Hampshire border. I'd kind of stand out up there, you know what I'm saying?"

"You mentioned hearing about the massacre from television."

"Right."

"Did you mean the night it happened?"

"Yeah. I was home watching the Red Sox, game was over maybe ten-thirty. I switched to the news, and they just had a bulletin about this 'tragedy' in Maine, no details except for some names."

"Where do you live?"

"Haverhill. Condo in a converted mill overlooking the Merrimack."

Haverhill's an hour north of Boston and only about ten miles from Interstate 95 toward Maine. "I don't suppose anybody else was with you that night?"

"Nobody. But I still didn't do it."

"Then who did?"

Xavier eased back in his chair. "Ask Dwight. He's got a theory you might like."

16

IF TYRONE XAVIER'S OFFICE LOOKED LIKE A BUNKER, DWIGHT
Schoonmaker's was a bunker.

Another uniformed security guard met me at the locked,
bank-vault door to SECURITY CONTROL. Inside the door
was a video room, a wall of monitors showing various
points of the building. The monitors were scrutinized by a
female security guard hunched over a communications
panel in front of her. To the right was a wall of gym lockers, probably for the guards to use when changing from
civvies to uniforms and back again. To the left was a glass-
faced cabinet, its contents four AR-15 assault weapons, a
pair of pump shotguns, and a half-dozen Glock 17 semiautomatic handguns with empty slots for a dozen more. Like
the photo ID process, the arsenal seemed like security over-
kill for DRM's type of facility.

In front of me was another door, to the heavy side of
normal, with SCHOONMAKER on a brown plastic plaque
at eye level. My guard knocked and must have heard something that made him nod to himself, because he nodded to
me and opened the door for me.

Schoonmaker was sitting in a gooseneck chair behind another of the Plexiglas desktops, staring down into a red manila file. There were more files stacked on the corner of the desk. He said, "Sit down," without getting up himself.

I took the admiral's chair, reading his many weapons certificates on the wall before changing the chair's original position so that I faced Schoonmaker directly rather than obliquely. He didn't look up from the file, but another spasm in his jaw told me he didn't like people rearranging his furniture.

I gave him till the count of five after that. Then I picked the topmost file off the stack and opened it.

Schoonmaker jumped up. "What the hell do you think you're doing?"

I didn't close the folder. "Killing time, waiting for some asshole with an authority complex to get around to helping me."

His face mottled with red, bringing out the raccoon-eyes contrast even more dramatically.

I let him come to a boil, then simmer down a little. "Dwight, let me make this easier for both of us. This is your turf, I'm the intruder. Fine. I don't want your job, I just want to do mine. That means you cooperate, I'm gone sooner, and Mr. Davison doesn't get to audition me or anybody else to succeed you, he decides you're not up to the task at hand. What do you say?"

With what appeared to be a heroic effort, Schoonmaker sat back down and closed his file, eyes on me the whole time. I closed my folder and put it back where it came from.

He said, "I've checked up on you."

"So I'm told."

"I knew a dozen fuck-ups like you in Nam." He pronounced it to rhyme with 'Ma'am.' "There wasn't one of you kept his pants dry once the shit started coming in."

"I don't have to check up on you, Dwight. I can picture what life was like for you over there. Desk at the embassy or more likely one of the 'import' companies. Little apartment in Saigon, a girl or two on the side, rotated now and then so you didn't get too badly compromised. Using the black market when it suited you, turning them when it didn't. Kibitzing on some National Police interrogations, maybe offering a hint or two on where to attach the wires from the telephone crank box. Oh, you'd go out into the bush from time to time, babysat by a Special Forces team or a Ranger recon, but basically you lived pretty much like a corrupt cop from the thirties."

As I talked, the mottled look came back. I said, "How am I doing?"

Through teeth about a millimeter apart, Schoonmaker said, "Maybe sometime I catch up with you in the outside world, I'll let you know, my way."

"I look forward to it. But meanwhile, how about we deal with the here and now, since that's what Keck wants."

No response.

I said, "You have a file on this I can look at?"

"A file on what?"

"Dwight, Dwight." I shook my head slowly. "A file on the killings."

"No. No paperwork."

"Can you tell me what you've done, then?"

He seemed to ratchet his emotions down a notch. "When I got the call about Steve, I contacted Mr. Davison. He told me—"

"Wait a second. When you got the call from who?"

Schoonmaker didn't answer right away. "From Anna-Pia."

"Shea called Antonelli from jail."

"That's the way I got it."

"Okay. What did you do?"

"I contacted Mr. Davison. He told me to get Anna-Pia and get up there, find out what the hell happened."

"How did you reach him?"

"What?"

"Davison. How did you reach him?"

Schoonmaker thought for a minute. "He was up in the boonies, but he's got this beeper, only for real emergencies. I raised him on it, he got on his plane's radio and got a patch-in to a phone somewhere and called me here."

So Davison could have been anywhere to use his radio. "You were here on a Friday night?"

"No. I was out, I got the call from Anna-Pia on my tape machine."

"Where were you?"

A level voice. "Just out."

Okay. "Antonelli called you at home?"

"Right. Left a message on my tape."

"Was she home, too?"

"That's what she said on the tape."

"Where do you live?"

"Salisbury, near the beach."

Like Xavier, about an hour north of Boston, just off Route 95 toward Maine. "When did you get in?"

"I checked my watch when I played her message. It was twelve-twenty-eight."

Plenty of time for Schoonmaker to have driven back from Maine. "You have a beeper, too?"

"Yes."

"Telephone in your car?"

"Yes," with some acid on it.

"Why didn't Antonelli try to reach you those ways?"

Schoonmaker used the level voice again. "I don't know. Ask her."

"So you get the message Friday night about twelve-thirty—"

192

"Twelve-twenty-eight."

"Twelve-twenty-eight. You call Antonelli back?"

"Yes."

"At her house?"

"Condo. Beacon Hill."

"She lives in the city and commutes out here?"

"That's how I understand it."

"Then you beep Davison."

"I drive out here, then beep him. Right."

"So, about what time?"

"One, a little after."

"When did you hear back from him?"

"Pretty soon after I beeped him."

"What does pretty soon mean?"

"Fifteen, twenty minutes. It takes a while to get a patch, that time of night on a weekend."

"And he tells you to drive up to Maine."

"Right."

"When do you do that?"

"Saturday morning. I drive into Boston at dawn, pick up Anna-Pia at her place, and we're up there by ten, ten-thirty."

"What happened then?"

"Anna-Pia and I saw Steve at the jail. Then she went lawyer shopping, and I went out to the lake place, do a little recon of the scene."

"You took the car?"

"No. Anna-Pia took the car because they're a little light on subways up there." Schoonmaker opened the ration book where he kept his grins and doled one out to me. "She dropped me off at this inn, and I rented a boat."

"Marseilles Inn?"

"Right."

"Why a boat?"

"When we were at the jail, I had a little talk with the sheriff up there, some bull dyke."

I let it pass.

"She told me to stay off the grounds till the staties got through with it."

"So you rented a boat to see it from the lake."

"Right."

"And you didn't go ashore."

Schoonmaker spent another grin. "Right."

I said, "What did you think?"

The grin vanished. "I did some crisscrossing, measuring distances the way Steve told us he found the bodies."

"And?"

"Whoever did it came through the trees or over the water."

"Why?"

Schoonmaker held up his right hand, separating one finger at a time with his left. "First, Steve said he didn't see any other vehicles on the road. Second, the old woman who lives just south of him has dogs that would have gone nuts if anybody approached from her direction or left by it. So the team came down that mountain behind Steve's house or through the woods from the north or in from the lake to the east."

The team. "The timing makes it tricky."

"They had to be on-station or have somebody on-station, gathering intelligence for the operation."

"Because you think they didn't intend to kill Steve, too."

"That's right."

"In that they timed it while he'd be off to the country store."

Just a nod this time.

I said, "So who do you think it was?"

"I'm not prepared to say right now."

"A competitor of DRM?"

194

A judicious pause. "Yes."

"Which one?"

"I'm not prepared—"

"How about a list of them?"

"No way."

"You know, Dwight, I think this competitor angle is nothing but pixie dust."

He just looked at me.

"Nobody will tell me who the competitors are. That makes it a little tough for me to check on them."

"I'm checking on them."

"Ah. So, I do everybody else, and you cover the competitor angle."

"That's right."

"And when we come to trial, and Lacouture looks over at you, what does he get?"

"Huh?"

"What do you give Shea's lawyer by way of evidence when he needs to show the jury a credible alternative to Steve as the killer?"

"Whatever I've got."

"Which won't be diddly, because the competitor theory isn't for the courtroom, it's for your customers."

"You don't know—"

"You and the rest of the brain trust cooked up the competitor theory so you could slip it to your customers, ever so gently, to keep them on the string and away from the other companies. Only problem is, any competent investigation of the other companies, by me or even by you, would pretty quickly turn up nothing. Zero. So you maintain the viability of the theory by a strategy of not looking for evidence to support it rather than allowing anybody to search for evidence, not find any, and blow the theory out of the water."

Schoonmaker didn't say anything.

"Only one problem with the strategy. It's great for business but kind of thin soup for old Stevie at the defense table."

Schoonmaker gave the impression of a man wracking his brain for something that would make the situation better without accidentally making it worse.

"Tell me, Dwight, you're pretty much into security around here. You keep track of office relationships?"

No reply.

"How about family members of employees?"

The same again.

"Okay, a little different question. When you got the call from Anna-Pia, did you contact Tyrone Xavier?"

"That . . . No."

"Why not?"

"Why should I? He was just Steve's assistant."

"Not anybody important enough to involve in the problem."

Schoonmaker worked his jaw a little before saying, "That's the way we all saw it."

"Before, you said the killer had to come from the mountain, the woods, or the lake, right?"

Very slowly, "Right."

"It ever occur to you that a former Marine captain might have a little experience with overland or amphibious operations?"

Schoonmaker swallowed hard.

I said, "Have to be careful of blind spots, Dwight. They can kill you."

17

AS I WALKED THROUGH THE VIDEO ROOM, THE FEMALE SECU-
rity officer said, "Ms. Antonelli would like to see you in
her office."

"Fine. Can you tell me where that is?"

"Third floor. Use the elevator across this hall and turn
left as you leave it."

"Thanks."

The male guard opened the door for me, the corridor
outside Security Control empty. The elevator was the same
one I'd taken down from Tyrone Xavier's office on the second floor. At three, I followed directions and gave my
name to an older woman working at a computer terminal.
She told me to go right on in.

Antonelli was busy sliding documents into a Gucci briefcase with a shoulder strap. A matching garment bag occupied a visitor's chair. The rest of the office was a larger
version of Xavier's, but with cheery prints of art gallery
showings in silver frames on the walls and small pots of
greenery on file cabinets and plant stands.

Antonelli looked up and down again. "Just in time."

Eyeing the garment bag, I said, "Taking a trip?"

"I hope you won't mind. I need a lift into town. I can take a cab to the airport from there, so you won't have to face the tunnel traffic."

"Meaning, it's time for me to take my leave of DRM."

Antonelli stopped what she was doing and looked up a little longer. "Who else did you want to see?"

"Maybe Davison again."

"Mr. Davison left for Colorado a few minutes after you left him."

"But he had somebody else to drive him to the airport."

"Just to Bedford. He likes to fly himself, in his private plane, when he can."

"This the seaplane?"

"No. He has several others. All set?"

"Yes. Can I get one of those?"

The smile that could grow on you. "Maybe the garment bag? It's lighter than the briefcase, believe me."

"Cute car."

I said, "A compromise between sporty and comfortable."

"Like you."

We were riding down 128 in the Prelude with the moon-roof back, not too much traffic yet. I half turned to look at her.

Antonelli laughed. "Sorry. That must have sounded like a come-on."

"A little. I'm flattered, to be honest."

"Flattered, but spoken for."

This time I didn't look at her. "Schoonmaker must be better than I thought."

"I didn't get that from Dwight. Gil Lacouture told me how he found you."

"Through Nancy."

"Is that her name? He just said a classmate that you were seeing."

"Lacouture tell you much else about me?"

"No, but I think that's because he didn't know much else to tell."

"Most of the rest you can get from Schoonmaker's dossier."

Another laugh.

I said, "What's so funny?"

"Dossier. That was how the Polish word for it was translated when I was over there."

"You travel a lot, too?"

"Do I . . . ? Oh, you mean like Steve. No, not as much. This was in the mid-seventies, my family went to stay for a while."

"Unusual back then, wasn't it?"

"Yes. I was the only American girl in our neighborhood there. But my grandmother still lived in Warsaw, and so they let my dad come over, teach English in one of the 'progressive' schools, the kind of place the government would put on the official tour for visiting dignitaries. I was barely into my teens, but I remember how it stood out against the rest of the city."

"Dreary?"

"Oh, you can't imagine. The people were wonderful, they'd give you the shirt off their back. But the buildings were so drab, the air so polluted. The food was all vegetables and starches, the milk came in clear bottles and wasn't homogenized. And there was never any ice in anything, you drank everything warm. I remember when I first got there and asked for an ice cube, my grandmother said, 'You don't want to catch a cold, do you?' "

"How did you get your name?"

"The 'Anna' came from the Polish side, the 'Pia' from

my mother's, who was Italian-American. When my parents divorced, I took my mother's last name. Defiance, I guess."

"They divorced over in Poland?"

"Oh, no. No, divorce was frowned upon. As was birth control, but only partly because of the Catholic Church. Everybody wanted to have big families."

"To impress the state?"

"No. For shopping."

"I don't get you."

"If you had a lot of kids, each could stand in a separate line to get the one or two types of food that each store sold."

I shook my head.

Antonelli said, "A different way of life."

"Seems you've come a long way from it."

"I have."

"You like living on the Hill, commuting out to DRM?"

"It's great, actually. I get the advantages of city living, but I'm commuting against the traffic, so I can always get a seat on the train. And the trains run often enough I don't need a car to get to work or try to park when I get home." A different element came into her voice, almost flirty again. "Are you interviewing me yet?"

"Let's say I'm starting now."

"All right."

"Just one question."

"Just one?"

"Then, depending on your answer, maybe a few more." Antonelli hesitated before saying, "Ask it."

"Your home phone number, is it unlisted?"

Another hesitation. "Yes. Why?"

"I'm wondering how Steven Shea managed to call you at your place that Friday night from jail."

"I don't know. I wasn't home when he called, so he left a pretty urgent message for me. I called him back at the jail up there, was kind of surprised that they put me through so late."

"That's not what I meant."

"It's not?"

"No. What I'm wondering is, how could Shea call your number if it's unlisted?"

A quick answer, very casual. "He probably had his address book."

"No. He said they didn't even let him bring that with him from the house."

"I . . . I guess he must have called DRM, then. Gotten it from Security."

"Maybe."

"And therefore maybe not?"

"I'm thinking that he had it memorized."

"Memorized?"

"Must have called it pretty often, too, to be able to remember it under the kind of pressure he was feeling that night."

"Just what are you getting at, Mr. Cuddy?"

"Whatever happened to 'John'?"

"Your insinuations are what happened to 'John.' What are you really asking me?"

"Let me catch you up on my afternoon, counselor. After old Keck and I shot the shit for a while, he allowed as how he really didn't buy the competitor-caper theory, and Ty said he just didn't have a clue. All that was to persuade me there was no party line on this theory, which Dwight nevertheless did his boy-scout best to sell me without apparent success. That leaves me with trying to help a client whose own business allies are covering the corporate ass rather than his own. That makes me just a little testy, if you get my drift."

"Is your drift always this vulgar?"

"Only for effect."

"It's not working."

"Sure it is. You didn't even try to defend the competitor theory."

Antonelli's voice grew a little softer. "I'm glad you saw through it."

"I take it the idea wasn't yours."

"I can't say anything else about it."

"Client privilege?"

Antonelli nodded.

I eased the Prelude off 128 and toward the cloverleaf ramp to Mass Pike east. At the tollbooth, I gave the attendant a dollar and got back fifty cents.

As I accelerated through the gears, I said, "What do you think happened?"

"I don't know. That's why I made sure Steve got the best lawyer up there."

"Why not a heavy hitter from Boston?"

"That Saturday morning, I called one I knew from school who's at a firm that specializes in white-collar stuff. Woke him up, actually. He told me an out-of-state lawyer wouldn't cut it in rural Maine. He gave me a couple of names in Portland, but the one I could reach—from a rest stop on the Maine Turnpike, by the way—said even an out-of-*town* lawyer was dicey up there. He gave me Lacouture and two others."

I said, "Lacouture's 'out-of-town.' "

"Yes, but I went with Gil because he said the right things when I spoke to him, and Steve already knew him from the real estate deal on Marseilles Pond."

"All those phone calls, you happen to make one to Tyrone Xavier?"

"No."

"Neither Friday night nor Saturday morning?"

"No. Not till everybody got together at DRM the following Monday."

"Any reason?"

"For not contacting Ty?"

"Yes."

"He was Steve's assistant, but I didn't think of him as helping with the mess Steve was in legally."

"That sounds a lot like Schoonmaker's reasoning."

"It might, but it's not. Believe me."

I said, "You don't think Shea's the killer, do you?"

"No. And neither do you."

"Why do you say that?"

"Because of how you handled things back there, with all of us in the conference room. If you thought Steve did it, you'd have just smiled and gone along, stamping the ticket to show you'd made the DRM stop. Maybe even have tried to ingratiate yourself with Dwight or Mr. Davison toward throwing a little business your way in the future."

"And instead?"

"Instead you came on like the terrier that smells a rat. I liked that."

"Any reason why anybody at DRM would have it in for Shea?"

Antonelli took her time. "No."

"Anna-Pia, I think that's a fib."

"Think what you like."

"You and Shea friendly?"

Up front this time. "Yes."

"See each other socially?"

"In a business way."

"What does that mean?"

"It means I'd see him for lunch when we were both in the building. DRM events at hotels or trade shows. Drink after work once in a while."

"Weekend at his place in Maine?"

Frosty now. "Just the one company thing."

"Where everybody played with the crossbow?"

"Not everybody."

"I forgot. Was that the only time you'd met his wife, Sandy?"

"No."

"Where else?"

"In passing here and there, company things."

"Any reason anyone would have for killing her, then covering it with the Vandemeers as camouflage?"

"Not that I know of."

"How about the Vandemeers themselves?"

"Never met them."

"Steve talk about them?"

"Only . . . what does that have to do with anything?"

"I don't know till I ask. They were killed, too. Maybe they were the targets, and Sandra Newberg—and Steve, if he'd been there—the camouflage."

"Then the answer is no. I only knew they were all friends."

"Just friends?"

"What's that supposed to mean?"

"Another insinuation, I guess. Was there anything more than friendship between any of The Foursome?"

Frosty became icy. "How would I know?"

"The police think there was."

"What police?"

"Probably everybody on the investigation up in Maine. It seems Steve's neighbor saw evidence of hanky-panky across the side yards, and she told the Calem cops about it."

Antonelli didn't speak for about half a mile, which even at sixty miles an hour is a longish time. I slowed down for the last toll, tossing the two quarters from the first booth into the wire basket for this one.

Antonelli said, "Did Steve say anything to you about it?"

I upshifted. "Why?"

204

"Never mind."

"Ms. Antonelli—"

"Whatever happened to 'Anna-Pia'?" Frosty had become glacial.

Quietly, I said, "What is it you're not telling me?"

"I don't know what—"

"Steve Shea knew your home number by heart. I think that means he had a habit of calling you there, confiding in you away from work. What did he tell you that he hasn't told me?"

"It's not . . . It's up to him to tell you what he wants."

"More client privilege?"

"If you like."

"What if I tell Lacouture, and he subpoenas you?"

"Even if the process would be effective here, I'd still decline unless Steve releases me from the bond of confidentiality."

"That's crazy."

"That's the law."

"I get the feeling we're not saying different things there."

Antonelli started to reply, then didn't.

I stayed in the quiet tone. "I think I know part of what Steve told you."

"Good for you."

"Yes, but not good for him."

Antonelli turned to me, straining against the shoulder belt. "What do you mean?"

"I just said the neighbor reported hanky-panky to the police, not who the participants were. The neighbor says it was Hale Vandemeer and Sandy Newberg, but you didn't ask me. That makes me think Steve must have told you about his friend and his wife. So far, I believe the cops know only that Hale and Sandy were having an affair. If Steve's knowing about the affair comes through to the authorities in Maine, his motive goes big league."

205

Antonelli turned back to the windshield, crossing her arms. "Just take the Copley exit. I'll grab a taxi at the hotel."

Moving into the right lane, I searched the lawyer's profile for some idea of what she knew, but her eyes were closed. Shuttered, one might even say.

18

AFTER DROPPING ANNA-PIA ANTONELLI AT THE COPLEY PLA-za's cab-stand, I decided against driving back to Calem to see Nicky Vandemeer. I went to the office instead, finishing some paperwork on other cases and trying to reach Nancy. She was closeted with three witnesses toward the continuation of her conspiracy trial the next morning. I spent a quiet night in the condo with take-out Pizzeria Uno and the Red Sox. Roger Clemens delivered on the mound at the same level he disappoints off the field.

By eight A.M. Friday I was parked in front of the Vandemeer house on the cul-de-sac. The grass was a little higher, the flowers a little deader. I looked across the street at Mrs. Epps's windows but couldn't see any curtains moving.

I walked to the Vandemeer front door and got smart. I opened the mail slot and listened first. Stereo blasting what sounded like salsa music, dampened by some walls.

I rang the bell twice, then started on the door. Somebody's feet trod up to the inside, and I heard "Jesus fucking Christ" as the door opened and then "The fuck happened to your key?"

The voice was high and keening, the boy standing in front of me anywhere from fifteen to eighteen. About five-ten and scrawny, he wore a pair of jeans that didn't fit him well and a black U2 sweatshirt with the sleeves shoved up past the elbows. His brown hair was long on top, a lock even looping across his forehead, but almost shaved around the ears and toward the back. The eyes were blinking rapidly, giving his wan face a rabbity effect.

I said, "Nicky Vandemeer?"

"Who the fuck are you?"

I put my foot against the door. "Who were you expecting?"

He started to push. "Hey, like get the fuck out of here!"

Bracing my left palm against the paneled wood, I exerted lateral pressure until the door gave and the boy went backward. I moved into the house. The door was almost silent as I closed it, just a push button on the inside edge plate to lock and unlock it. Not a neighborhood overly concerned about security. The salsa music was coming from somewhere deep inside the house, maybe a basement gameroom like Shea had.

Vandemeer said, "I'll call the cops!"

"Actually, that's why I'm here, Nicky. I thought we might have a little talk about your pajama party in the house next door."

Vandemeer retreated a couple of steps, bringing the biceps of his sleeve up to rub across his nose and sniffle a few times. That plus the blinking eyes told me his idea of recreational drugs didn't stop at alcohol.

"I don't know what you're talking about, dude."

"Why don't you just call me 'Detective,' Nicky, and that way I won't get mad at you."

More sniffles, another pass with the sleeve. "I got permission."

"Permission to break into your neighbors' house?"

"I didn't break in, all right? I . . . They like gave us a key."

I motioned him toward the living room. "Why don't we sit down, talk about it."

His parents had decorated the living room in a colonial style, camelback couch and love seat and easy chairs with a meadow print, burled wood showing along arms and backs. Nicky had redecorated in junk food memorabilia, with stained pizza boxes and greasy chicken buckets and square Styrofoam clamshells on tables and carpet, empty beer bottles like groupies around each container.

I said, "You have a room that doesn't look like the town dump?"

Vandemeer plopped himself into the couch, tried to regain a little ground. "Yeah. The downstairs shithouse."

I picked up one of the bottles, Coors Extra Gold. "You drink all these?"

"What if I did?"

"What if I ram one of these where the moon don't shine?"

Vandemeer straightened on the couch. "The fuck are you talking about, dude?"

"Detective."

A few seconds, then another pass with the sleeve across the nose. "Detective."

I walked over to him with the bottle, trying to remind myself that the kid's parents had been murdered two weeks ago. "That's better. Now we're going to have a nice talk, okay?"

"Hey, I already told you, they like gave—"

"Us a key. I heard you. Now, what were you doing over there?"

"None of your business."

I raised the Coors bottle an inch. "Again."

Vandemeer sniffled, then licked his lips. "It was just me and my babe, having a little fun."

"You usually have sex with your girlfriend in your neighbors' house?"

"No, Detective," laying hard on the word. "Usually I fuck her here."

"Now that your parents are gone."

A sarcastic laugh. "That's really excellent, you know? When Hale and Viv were around, they'd have turned like totally red, anybody knew this, but they let me fuck her here."

"Your parents . . . ?"

"Let me have Blanca up in my room, Detective. I told them, 'Look, dudes, you got a choice. Either I have the babe up here, or I go into the city with her, and then you don't know where I am. Your move.' "

"And they caved."

Vandemeer smiled. Perfect teeth, but somehow not a pretty sight. "They had like these images of me on a mattress, the floor of some tenement, getting seriously stabbed by a crackhead. Awesome, huh?"

The salsa music came to an end, but Vandemeer seemed not to notice.

I took a chair. "So you got along pretty well with your folks."

"Hale and Viv? They were major jerks, but they lived here, too, you know? Had to make allowances."

I nodded, feeling cold. "Allowances."

"Yeah. I mean like . . . take Hale. Here he's this mega-successful doc, but he can't keep his dick out of Sandy's pants."

I didn't feel any warmer. "Your father was having an affair with Sandra Newberg?"

"I don't know what you'd call it, Detective. I just know he was punching her like a speed bag, offing his seven

210

angry inches every time Viv drove over to the mall. They even did it up in Maine once."

"How do you know that?"

"Well, Viv took me to New York, like maybe a month ago. When I got back, Hale had four hundred miles on his car that I didn't hear him tell Viv about, and that's like from here to there and back."

"What made you check his odometer?"

"I used to do that once in a while, maybe get some serious leverage on him, who knows?"

Hale and Sandy, trysting at The Foursome's lakeside retreat, adding insult to injury and one more motive nail to my client's coffin.

Nicky said, "Can't really blame old Hale, though. Sandy was an excellent piece, if not real fresh. I would've jumped her myself, I didn't have better."

It wasn't so much talking to a different generation as a different species. "Do you think Steven Shea suspected anything?"

"Suspected? He like knew."

"How do you—"

"I told him. Hale seriously pissed me off one day, and I see old Steverino getting into his four-wheel-drive pseudo truck, and I fill him in."

"When was this?"

"Like I told the other cops, it was maybe a month ago, too."

Lovely. "What did Shea say?"

"Say? Old Steverino didn't like *say* anything. He kind of looked like a bug hitting the windshield, though. Hey, what does that mean, anyway?"

"What does what mean?"

" 'Steverino.' "

"It was a nickname for a variety show host back in the fifties."

A laugh. "I figured it must have been something fad like that. Jesus fucking Christ, yeah, Steverino was kind of like a host."

"How do you mean?"

"Aw, he was . . ." Vandemeer blinked some more, but not from the light. "Hey, the other cops that talked to me. They already asked me about The Foursome, but not like this. Not like what I thought of people. The fuck does this have to do with me and Blanca going next door?"

"The officers who talked to you first had an idea of who did the killings up in Maine. I'm here to round out the investigation, ask the questions they didn't think they had to. Now, what do you mean about Shea being a host?"

Vandemeer worked on things for a minute. Then, "He was just like, I don't know, always joking around, trying to make everybody happy. You'd go over there for a barbecue, he'd make like you'd have to have the most awesome time of your life or he'd fucked up somehow."

"You ever go up to the lake place?"

"Coupla times, with Hale and Viv. Now that was seriously stupid."

"What do you mean?"

"Well, like he buys this place out in the woods, right? Only, it's not like a cabin or an A-frame or something different. It's like he builds his house down here up there all over again. Totally fucking stupid."

"So you didn't enjoy it up there?"

"Hey, Detective, I like grew out of that phase, going places with my parents."

Given Nicky Vandemeer's attitude so far, I didn't feel badly asking the next question. "You ever see the crossbow?"

"The 'murder weapon,' you mean?"

"That's what I mean."

"Oh, yeah. Like Hale, he couldn't wait to take it out,

show Viv how he was gonna surprise Steve and Sandy with it, next weekend."

"You saw it down here, then?"

"Yeah. Right in my own backyard. Last summer, Steve and Sandy were already up at the lake, taking a vacation week, and Hale and Viv were going up to spend like the second weekend with them. You should have seen him, Detective. Hale the Mega-doc, trying to put an arrow into a piece of paper tied to a tree so he wouldn't mess up the target thing that came with it."

"Your father practiced with the crossbow here?"

"Yeah. He was always into that."

"Into what?"

"Kind of . . . Like pushing Steve to do something a little cooler than the last thing. Like if Steve said 'Let's go water-skiing,' Hale'd say, 'Let's go Jet-Skiing.' He got off on like pushing Steve over the top."

"How did your dad and your uncle get along?"

"My unc—Oh, you mean Hubadub? Hah, let me tell you, I don't think the old King of the Road liked being partners with the King of the Dick."

Evenly, I said, "Why not?"

"Aw, you'd have to know Hub. He's your basic loser persona, the man who could weave straw out of gold. He gets himself in the hole to his manufacturers like seriously big-time, comes around with his hand out. Old Hale gives him some money, but with a coupla strings on it. Those strings start to get tight around the balls."

"Your father was pressing your uncle for repayment?"

"Aw, Detective, I don't know the details. I just know the strings are still there, because old Hub is like sucking up to me, trying to get appointed my fucking guardian, you can believe it. Like I need a guardian."

I looked around the room. "Yeah."

Vandemeer gave me a fuck-off look, but didn't put it into words.

I said, "So what happens now?"

"Now?" The perfect smile again. "Now I get the insurance money from Hale and Viv, plus a partnership with old Hub, who if he thinks he's getting like another dime for his shitcan business, he's fuck out of luck."

"Meaning?"

"Meaning I hired my own lawyer, and he tells me I can call back what old Hub owed Hale because now he owes me."

"That might mean closing down your uncle's dealership."

"So maybe that's not such a bad thing. Cars, they like seriously pollute the earth, you know?"

"How did your uncle and your mother get along?"

"Hub and Viv? No chemistry there, least not from Viv's side. Hub, on the other hand, if he didn't sell cars, he'd be out sniffing the seats on girls' bikes, you know?"

At the same moment, Nicky and I heard a key in the lock on the front door. It opened quietly, and somebody juggled what sounded like a paper bag as the door closed again. A girl moved across the entrance to the living room, then stopped when she saw us.

She was about five-three and drop-dead lovely, with dreamy Hispanic eyes and ruby lips. Long black hair was pulled up on the right side of her head, cascading onto the shoulder so that you almost thought a little animal was perching there. In her left ear she wore a single gold hoop earring. The off-white blouse was wide enough at the neck to show a gold chain necklace and one bra strap, her slacks some kind of glossy pink material, a little pink box at the waist. She wore basketball sneakers on her feet and carried two Dunkin' Donuts bags in her left hand while jingling a key ring in her right.

"Who are you?" she said, a lilting voice with just a slight accent.

Vandemeer gave her a superior smile. "Cop. We were just talking about my seriously dysfunctional family."

I said, "Blanca, nice to meet you."

She looked from me to Vandemeer to me again. "Nicky, you know him from town?"

Vandemeer looked at me, too. "No. He just came like knocking on the door."

Blanca tried to keep the irritation out of her voice. "He show you any ID?"

Smart girl. She saw my old Prelude on the street and didn't think things added up to official status.

Vandemeer said, "Sure he—wait a minute. No. No, he sure as fuck didn't."

Blanca said to me, "Let's see it."

"Fresh out of badges this morning."

At that point, a shrill chirp came from the little pink box at her waist. Blanca looked down at it, using the key hand to silence the chirp. "I gotta go, Nicky. Don't tell this guy anything else."

"You gotta go? What the fuck—what about breakfast?"

Blanca left the bags on the floor and took off toward the front door.

I got up and followed her.

Vandemeer yelled from behind me, "The fuck is like going on here?"

19

As I came out the Vandemeer front door, Blanca was backing down the driveway. In a gold convertible that, except for color and no trailer hitch, was the twin of the one Hub Vandemeer drove up to his dealership. When she reached into the passenger's seat to rearrange a gold warmup jacket, I stepped behind an evergreen a little taller than I am. As Quintana fishtailed into the cul-de-sac, she glanced up toward the door, but gave no indication of seeing me. Then she changed gears and headed away.

I ran to my car and started after her. I caught sight of the convertible just as it reached a major road leading to 128.

Blanca took the beltway south, her left hand on the wheel, the right one pushing buttons down on the console where the radio would be. Her head bobbed as she seemed to sing along with the music. Traffic was light, and she drove conservatively, so it was easy to stay with her from three or four cars back in the flow.

Quintana put on a turn signal for the exit to Route 9 east, staying on 9 until it became Huntington Avenue. She took a right onto Tremont and a left onto Columbus Avenue, staying with that as it became Seaver before another left onto Humboldt. We were getting deep into one of the toughest neighborhoods in Roxbury, the predominantly black and Hispanic geographic center of Boston. Much of the retail space was burned out or boarded up or both. What remained functioning were largely corner groceries, take-out joints, and hair salons. It was a little early for the gang kids to be on the street, but I still found myself sensing the absence of weight a gun adds to the back of my belt.

Blanca suddenly began looking hard into her rearview and sideview mirrors, making me. Without using the turn signal, she wheeled right onto a narrow street. I sped up and did the same.

And got trapped.

Quintana had spun her car sideways, blocking the street. As I hit my brakes, half a dozen girls with gold warm-up jackets and a single gold hoop through the left ear scurried out from behind the parked cars. They surrounded the Prelude, leveling assorted firearms like fire hoses, their eyes unreadable behind dark, Terminator-style sunglasses. The tallest of the girls carried no weapon and wore no sunglasses, but had her hair up like Blanca's and the same dreamy eyes. There the comparison stopped being favorable, given the livid scar that traveled from just off the left eye down almost to her chin and the two teeth missing from her upper jaw as she smiled.

The tall girl leaned down toward my window, a traffic cop about to give a ticket. She said, "My sister Blanca, she been telling us all about you on her car phone there, you know it?"

"So, Mr. Private Eye, how you like our clubhouse, huh?" They'd taken the blindfold off but left both hands tied behind my back. Even though the room was barely lit, it still took a minute for my eyes to adjust. The tall girl was lying on a velveteen BarcaLounger, reclined about halfway, what looked like my wallet in her lap and my ID in her hand. The room had wall-to-wall shag carpeting on which I was sitting and an attractively proportioned dining alcove and kitchen. The only other furniture consisted of a twenty-seven-inch color TV, assorted throw pillows, and a beat-up Formica table. Several of the girls lazed on the pillows indifferently, still wearing the sunglasses, sniffling once in a while. Two others stood, their weapons—an Intratec Tec-9 grease gun and a big black semiautomatic pistol—pointing at my chest from about eight feet away. Blanca also stood, next to her sister on the lounger, one hand resting near her sister's head.

"Hey, Mr. Private Eye, you don't hear so good, maybe we give you another ear, help you out."

The girl with the Tec-9 raised its perforated, five-inch barrel toward my head, giving me a clear view of the thirty-two-round magazine.

I looked at the tall one. "Nice digs."

She laughed, saying something low and guttural in Spanish to Blanca, who laughed uncertainly, apparently being polite. The other girls, who I guessed to be in their early teens, didn't break pose.

The tall one said, "This place, the bank want to make it work, let the people down at City Hall know how much they was doing for the community, you know it? Only thing is, they didn't figure out who the fuck wanna live on this street, they got the money to buy a place like this. So it just stand here. I go down the bank, I tell the man, 'Look, you got this building, it ain't doing shit. You want it still standing, you let us use it. *Las Hermanas*, we protect it, keep it clean.' "

"Las Hermanas?"

The tall one touched the red stitching on her jacket that showed "Las" in script superimposed over a capital "H." "*Las Hermanas* means 'The Sisters' in Spanish. Nigger homeboys, they take their names from the street they live on, maybe the pro team they wish they play for. We different. We live like family, we call us family. Right, Blanca?"

"Right, Lidia."

Plucking the driver's license from my wallet, Lidia looked over at me. "You don't take such a good picture, man, but you look like you was a jock sometime."

"College."

"College man, too, huh? What sport you in, football?"

"Synchronized swimming."

Lidia laughed, putting the license back in my wallet. "You got some balls, I like that. But, Mr. Private Eye from Boston, how come you take your balls out to the nice 'burbs, bothering my sister's fucking boyfriend?"

I watched the two girls holding weapons on me. There are times you cite to the statute on client confidentiality, and times you don't.

Lidia said, "Okay, man. New ear, coming up."

As she started to say something in Spanish to the two guards, I said, "I'm investigating the murder of his father and mother."

Lidia shook her head. "Those people, they got killed up north somewheres, not even the same state."

"I was hired by the defendant's lawyer to look into it."

Another laugh. "The defendants I know, they don't got money for cigarettes." She let her gaze roam around the room. "One of us get busted, we get some fucking CPCS defender, doesn't know her ass from the hole she shits in. Don't matter much, the judge, he don't know what the fuck to do with us, anyways." Lidia grew thoughtful. "So, what, you out at Nicky's place, you think he done his mama and papa?"

I said, "It's been known."

"You think that little shit, he could kill somebody?"

"Kind of a rough way to talk about your sister's boy-friend, isn't it?"

Lidia laughed again. I was making a great impression on her.

She said, "My sister, she do what she got to do."

"She has to date Nicky Vandemeer?"

"No, man. Blanca, she don't have to go to the movies and the pancake house with the little shit. She just got to fuck him, keep him happy."

Blanca cringed a little at that.

I thought about Nicky sniffling, his eyes reacting to the light from his front door. Then I looked at the girls still wearing their shades and sniffling, too. "So you can spread the coke through his circle of friends?"

Lidia shook her head, coming down off the lounger slowly, languidly, like she was climbing out of bed and doing a slow stretch. She sauntered toward me, reaching inside her back pocket and coming out with a switchblade. Kneeling in front of me, the older sister sat back on her haunches. Raising the knife handle to eye level, she thumbed the release, six inches of gleaming steel snicking toward my face. You try not to flinch.

Lidia lifted the point of the blade to her scar, caressing it toward her chin. "You know how I get this?"

"No."

"Our mother, she have this friend, he come over when Blanca and me was still living at her place. He fuck our mother, sometimes leave her food money for us. Then one day, he look at me different than he look before? He wait till our mother and Blanca go out, buy some things. Then he decide he give me a try. I push him off, he come for more. He have this knife, this one here, he hold it against my throat, get me down on the floor. He get my pants down, too, then he stick his business in me. It hurt a lot, and I'm crying, bleeding, but he keep sticking it in me, over and over. Then his face, it get all screwed up, and he drop the knife, grab my hair and pull on it, make it better for him, I guess. Well, Mr. Private Detective, while he sticking his business in me, I get hold of his knife, and I stick it in him, you know it? He's sticking me, and I'm sticking him. And he grab my hand, and he try to break my arm. I let go of his knife, and he pull it out of his gut, and he take a slice at my face, get me like this. Then he get up, and he start to cry, too, because he hurt bad, but he only get to the stairs and then fall down, all the way to the bottom. Neighbors, they find him, call the cops. I'm like twelve years old, so nothing happens. They ask me where the knife is, I tell them, 'I don't know. I don't remember.' And they send me to this counselor, she know less than the fucking lawyers, that's possible. But I don't need no counseling, because I find out a very important thing. When you got trouble, you take care of it yourself, you better off."

Lidia brought the blade from her face to mine, tracing a similar scar line without breaking the skin. "You make trouble for us, maybe my sisters here, they take care of you. Only you kind of good-looking, so maybe I let you stick your business in me, then I stick this in you." Lidia gave me the smile, the gaps from the missing teeth aging her. "Just like old times, you know it?"

"You be smart now, you keep that blindfold on till you count to fifty, huh?"

I nodded my head. From the sound of the door and the feel of the seat, Las Hermanas had put me behind the wheel of the Prelude after walking me back from the clubhouse. I could hear the squelching of their sneakers on the pavement, then nothing except traffic noise from Humboldt behind me.

When about a minute had passed, I reached up and took off the blindfold. After my eyes readjusted, I thought about driving to the Area B police station, but I wasn't sure I knew anybody there who dealt with gangs.

However, I knew somebody who probably did.

20

SOME YEARS AGO, THE MAYOR HAD THE IDEA TO REVIVE OR replace a few of the police substations closed during the prior fiscal crisis. A great idea politically, and five substations have been repainted and beribboned since for grand ceremonies. Given an era of more tight budgeting, however, the problem has been how to staff them. The one on West Broadway in South Boston got the Homicide Unit.

The unit's sign is a small one, white on dark blue fixed to a medium blue door at the end of a corridor with wainscoting partway up the walls and lockers against the wainscoting. Inside the door are pale blue walls. A big corkboard half covers one with photocopies of new statutes, some mug shots, and a small thermometer. The file cabinets are metal, olive drab in color. The phones are black with gray keypads, and instead of bleating they still ring like all phones used to. The desks are old and made of colorless wood, the chairs padded and black.

Half the desks were occupied that day by men in suits and sport coats and one woman in a blazer and skirt. I walked up to the woman, engrossed in reading the file in front of her. She had long brown hair, big brown eyes, and a pencil between her teeth like a soldier about to undergo surgery without anesthesia.

"Cross, how are you?"

"Terrible." She spoke around the pencil, not lifting her head from the paperwork.

"How do you like the new surroundings?"

"Don't."

Okay. "How about Lieutenant Murphy?"

"He likes them less."

"I mean, is he in?"

"Yeah. Shall I announce you, or you want to take your chances?"

"I feel lucky today."

Cross pointed to another door, never once looking up.

I walked to and knocked on the door, got a "Yeah?," and went in.

Robert Murphy was on his knees, a black hand pulling a green volume of *Massachusetts General Laws Annotated* off the last row of tinny bookshelves behind his desk. He wore a short-sleeved white dress shirt, a crimson paisley tie, and the slacks to a gray suit. His head turned partway as he pushed himself up with his free hand, the other holding the book like a grizzly cradling a salmon in the rapids.

"Cuddy, you're a hell of a private eye. We move, and you still find us."

"This just doesn't have the executive feel of the old place, Lieutenant."

"Executive.' Murphy sank into his chair and set the lawbook down on his blotter near the miniature American flag in a penholder. "Mayor wants to have cops where folks can see them, that's fine. Needs to have some desk jobs where the commissioner can put a couple of uniforms on light duty, that's fine, too. But other than acting as scarecrows, there's no godly reason for us to be over here instead of at headquarters on Berkeley. Sit down, sit down."

I did. The population around the substation was all white, and Southie produced some of the worst rock-throwing and name-calling at black kids during the busing crisis in the seventies. "How are you getting along with the neighbors?"

"What, being a 'colored'?"

"That's what I meant."

"First few times I stopped in the coffee shop, I made sure it was with some other guys in the unit, two of them from here originally. Word spread, only took about a week to lose that feeling of sitting at a fifties lunch counter in Mississippi. Now everybody's used to me. Not sure I like that, but what can you do? How's Ms. Meagher?"

"On a conspiracy trial that looks like it'll take her to the end of the century."

"They do drag on. That mean you're watching a lot of TV?"

"Trying not to."

"The network stuff's crap, but the video, now that's something else again. Last two nights the wife and I rented *Parenthood* and *When Harry Met Sally*. Great flicks. Guess who was behind the camera for them?"

"Ron Howard and Rob Reiner."

Murphy closed his eyes to slits. "I'm impressed."

"I don't know, Lieutenant. It may not be such a good omen that two of our best directors used to be called 'Opie' and 'Meathead.'"

A rude noise. "You got something on your mind, how about we get to it? I pulled two new cases this morning."

"I'm working for a lawyer out of state, some Massachusetts connections, but not Boston until about an hour ago."

"When?"

"When I spent some time in a clubhouse over in Rox'."

"Social club?"

"Not exactly."

"Gang."

"Right."

"Which one?"

"Las Hermanas."

"Las—the Hispanic girls, right?"

"You know them."

"Just some reports, nothing solid."

I pictured all the weapons in my face that morning. "Meaning their bark is worse than their bite?"

"Meaning there's been no cooling bodies for us yet. Couple of drive-bys, slugs all over a porch or store but nobody inside at the time or nobody with their eyes on anything but the nails in the floor, trying to figure out how to get under the boards and away from the bullets."

"You know anybody in the Anti-Gang Unit who could elaborate on them?"

Murphy thought a minute. "Any of this going to bounce back at me with shit on it?"

"Hope not, but I don't really have enough information yet to give you odds."

A smile dallied with his lips without ever getting to his teeth. "Cuddy, honest man like you, how'd you ever get this far?"

On Dudley Street, I parked my car as close as possible to the Area B station. Moving toward the building, I saw several black grandmothers pushing their grandchildren in strollers, two little black boys playing catch with hardball and gloves, and three Hispanic girls sitting on a transit authority bench. The middle girl was a dead ringer for one of my guards that morning, but the colors these kids wore consisted of white blouse, blue sweater, blue tartan skirt, white socks, and black shoes. Their knapsacks looked to contain books, and they almost made me believe in the future of the world.

At the desk, I asked for Larry Cosentino or Yolanda King. Waiting, I listened to a black uniformed officer talking to a black youth, maybe fifteen years old. The kid was decked out in a Hammer T-shirt, purple warm-up pants, and Reebok sneakers. A purple baseball cap with nothing on the crown was stuck by its bill in the beltline of his pants.

The officer said, "Stanley, you're an imbecile."

The kid just glared at him.

"Getting caught like that when you know the store prosecutes." The officer shook his head. "But I'll tell you what."

"What?"

"You can spell 'imbecile' for me, I'm gonna let you walk on this one."

A ray of hope on the kid's face. "Say what?"

"You spell the word 'imbecile' for me, and I let you walk."

"Spell it?"

"Uh-huh. Like A, B, C, and so on."

The kid drew his lips in and under his teeth twice, then said, "E-M-B, uh, A-S-E-L, uh, L."

"You're a genius, Stanley. Walk."

"No shit?"

"No shit."

"Thanks, man. You okay."

"Send me a graduation picture."

"Hey, man?"

"Yeah."

"The fuck does 'imbecile' mean?"

"Mr. Cuddy, Yolanda King. This is my partner, Ilario Cosentino."

"Yollie likes to do things formal. Just call me Larry."

"And I'd prefer John."

227

"Fine," said King, motioning me to a chair. "Bob Murphy called me."

I waited for her to continue, but she didn't. King was early thirties, slender and attractive, with a knowing smile, reddish hair, and a complexion like milky coffee. She wore a yellow turtleneck under a brown houndstooth jacket and over a dark brown pleated skirt. She sat on the edge of a desk in front of a high window with sunshine backlighting her like a fashion model.

Cosentino slouched in a chair behind the desk, one shoe off as he kneaded the ball of his foot through a black sock. He was early forties, stocky, and homely as a bullfrog, with a wide mouth, black curly hair, and a five-o'clock shadow that would have made Richard Nixon look powdered by comparison. He wore an awning-striped golf shirt and black jeans over a Turntec running shoe that had seen its share of gutters.

I said, "Murphy tell you what this is about?"

King crossed her legs. "Didn't speak to him directly. Just left me a note, asking me to talk with a John Cuddy." The knowing smile. "The way the message reads, he trusts you."

"I'm working on a case for a lawyer who represents a criminal defendant in another state. I didn't think Boston had anything to do with it until I met a couple of sisters named Quintana this morning."

King lost her smile, and Cosentino let his foot go to the floor.

I said, "You know them, then."

King uncrossed her legs and walked to the window.

Cosentino said, "What was their gear?"

"Sorry?"

"What kind of clothes and stuff they wear?"

"Gold warm-up jackets, gold hoop earring on the left side, one knife, lots of guns."

Cosentino said, "How'd you meet them?"

While I summarized following Blanca in from Calem and getting suckered off Humboldt, Cosentino was attentive, and King looked out the window, crossing her arms this time.

When I finished, King said, 'John, when you came in, you happen to notice some girls sitting on the bench across the street?"

"Catholic school outfits, knapsacks?' '

"Yes. Did you notice how many there were?"

"Three."

No response from King.

I said, "What's the matter?"

Cosentino said, "Las Hermanas doesn't have a hell of a lot going for it yet. Still way more blacks than Hispanics in Rox', and not many other girl gangs to use as role models."

"I didn't realize there were any girl gangs."

King spoke to the window. "You look at the statistics, you'll see more than ten boys for every girl moving through the juvie system, and most of the girls are brought in for simple assault or shoplifting."

Cosentino picked up. "Some of the girls, they're in gangs just to create kind of a herd, so they can score jewelry off a nongang girl or shoplift wearing their gear, make it harder for the store clerk to ID them. But Las Hermanas, now, they're different. They look to boys' gangs like Castlegate or IVP Intervale for what to do, only they feel they gotta do 'em one better, so the boys'll take them seriously."

King said, "Their major asset is brainpower. The older sister, Lidia, is one smart lady. She has the other girls loyal to her as kind of a surrogate mother. Most children—male or female—join a gang for protection and status, maybe make real money selling drugs on a corner instead of chump change wearing a paper hat and dipping baskets of fries. But they also join a gang for a sense of belonging, something they don't often get from their natural families."

"If they have any," added Cosentino.

"So," said King, "Lidia gives them a place to live and money to spend and some basic pride, with the jackets and all, and she's real careful to use the ones still underage to push the drugs."

Cosentino said, "Anti-Gang Unit got organized about two years ago. First eleven months, we made over two thousand arrests. But we really got rolling when the legislature gave us section 32K."

"What's that?"

King said, "Chapter 94C, section 32K of the General Laws makes it a fifteen-year felony for inducing a minor to distribute drugs. A conviction carries a five-year minimum, though there are some loopholes."

"Yeah, but even so, you can get Lidia on that one, right?"

"Easier said than done. Las Hermanas is like any other gang. Black, Asian, Hispanic, doesn't matter. The members don't use the system against each other. It's nearly impossible to get one of the younger kids to turn on a leader, because the younger one knows there isn't a hell of a lot the system is going to do if he or she just stands up and stonewalls it."

Cosentino said, "The assaults, sometimes they're a little easier. There's gonna be witness intimidation, but maybe somebody's cousin or niece gets caught in the crossfire, the community comes out, especially if we skip district court, where the gang can pack the place, and instead go for an indictment in superior court, where the homeboys and homegirls find things aren't so comfy."

I said, "All right. Las Hermanas pushes what, cocaine and crack?"

King said, "Not crack, not anymore. Lidia, she figured

out something a long time before she got into the trade. She figured that suburban white folks might pay a bit more for cocaine than ghetto kids would for crack and be a whole lot less trouble as customers."

Cosentino said, "So Las Hermanas dealt crack only until they got themselves some buy money, then traded up and out."

I said, "To cocaine and the suburbs."

"Right. Where they probably figure they'll find somebody to front for them."

"As in be their cover?"

"Yeah, but I meant more like to front money, working capital, for them. It's nice to have a few deals going at once instead of needing the proceeds from one week for buy money the next."

I thought about that. "They may have found their banker."

King turned from the window to look at me. "Who?"

"A male teenager named Nicky Vandemeer out in Calem."

"How obvious was it to you?"

"Pretty clear. The kid must be snorting like a racehorse to look the way he does."

"Parents?"

"Killed. Two weeks ago in Maine."

Cosentino said, "The Foursome thing?"

"Yes."

He cracked his knuckles. "John, you got any contacts on the Calem force?"

"One guy I know. Why?"

King said, "Calem, that's a strange town. Up till recently, they had this chief, forget his name—"

"Wooten."

She stared at me. "Wooten. That's right. He your contact?"

"He'd like to have been my coroner."

231

King nodded. "Glad to hear that. Man had his head so far up his ass, he could probably see his molars. Anyway, Wooten ran a very closed shop. You know about Blanca, you know about the special student program they sponsor out there?"

"A little."

"Well, we knew most of the kids in Calem's program were straight, but a couple were bent sideways. Calem still took them and didn't want to hear nothing from nothing about them."

"Or share anything back."

Cosentino said, 'Exactly. Political thing, libbies in the country wanted to see a model ghetto kid, believe what they see instead of city cops telling them something more about the book than its cover."

King said, "I'm thinking, you have a contact out in Calem, John, you don't go visiting there without checking things out with him."

I pictured Paul O'Boy at the HoJo's, playing a little of his version of shuck and jive with me over Nicky Vandemeer and his "girlfriend." To King I said, "My contact has a new chief, probably doesn't want to stir up the political waters any more than the old one did."

Cosentino said, "Meaning you went out there and then walked into Lidia's little mousetrap thinking you'd been told what was what."

"But getting less than half of it."

Cosentino cracked his knuckles again. "Sounds like your contact's worse than no contact at all."

"I plan to tell him that. Meanwhile, about Blanca Quintana?"

King said, "I first met that girl back when Lidia killed a man who raped her. Murphy tell you about it?"

"I don't think he made the connection. But I heard Lidia's side of it."

"Well, I had a lot of hope for Blanca. She really does have brains, only not like her sister. Real study brains."

Cosentino said, "Most of these kids, they ever opened a book, it was the *TV Guide*, see what time the reruns of *Miami Vice* were on."

King looked at him. "Larry, that a new line?"

"Yeah, kind of."

"I don't believe it." She looked to me. "Two years I partner with him, I thought I'd heard them all."

Cosentino grinned at me. "We got a beautiful relationship, huh?"

I said to King, "But there's only so much you can do."

"What?"

"As you watch Blanca follow her older sister."

"Oh, right. I tell you, John, I've never heard of a gang member, regardless of what he or she had done, ever committing suicide. You, Larry?"

"Never. Not once."

King said, "But Blanca . . . I don't know. It's like she wants to do things that Lidia would do, put herself in situations where she's going to be in danger. Like intentionally forcing somebody else to kill her, to get her out of the life."

Cosentino broke in, "This Calem thing, it's probably like a stock offering for Las Hermanas, Inc. I see Lidia—and Blanca—doing just about anything to see it go right."

I pushed that around a little. "Ask you something?"

Cosentino said, "Go ahead."

"The killings up in Maine. With the two parents out of the way, this Nicky kid stands to receive a lot of money a few different ways. What do you think the odds are Las Hermanas could have done it as a massacre to deflect interest away from them?"

Cosentino said, "That was a crossbow, right, not guns?"

"Right."

King said, "Lidia probably thinks a crossbow is something a Valley Girl wears in her hair."

Cosentino said, "Yollie's right. It was guns, now, I could see it. Only there'd have to be about a hundred rounds sprayed all over the fucking house, on account of that's what bad shots these kids are. They buy the weapons on the street, but they don't have a fucking clue how to use them beyond lock and load and hold down the trigger."

Cosentino became animated. "We're receiving something like fifty, sixty 'shots fired' calls a month here. I tell you, John, the kids start shooting, they hit more bystanders than anything, because they almost always miss the one they want first time. Most of the people living in Areas B and C are honest and church-going. But we got only thirty percent of the city's population and something like eighty percent of the homicides. And lots of times, it's over nothing. Trivial shit like stepping on somebody's Air Jordans or dissing—disrespecting—somebody's sister. You drive around Rox' today, just go up and down Blue Hill Avenue, you notice something. You notice how many kids are walking with canes or casts or sitting in wheelchairs. Those aren't torn ligaments from a fucked-up lay-up, pal. Those are gunshot wounds from the gangs that couldn't shoot straight."

King said, "Over in East Boston, one of the schools started this program called Music Mobile, trying to keep the kids off the street." Then, more quietly, "It's gotten to the point in New York, they have a chorus of children who lost relatives to the killings."

I said, "They have a what?"

"It's a chorus, or what do they—oh, right. They call it a chorale. The kids in it are the children or brothers and sisters of people who got killed. Down there, it's so many they have a singing group of the survivors."

I shook my head. "So you don't see Las Hermanas using anything but firearms?"

Cosentino, a little subdued, said, "For a thing like you've got, no."

"Besides," said King, "these are homegirls, John. Born and 'brought up,' in some sense of the phrase, within probably five blocks of where they're crashing now. Maine would be like another country to them."

"Another galaxy," said Cosentino.

"They're branching out to Calem all right."

Cosentino said, "You got a point there, but it still don't feel right. Yollie?"

"Same."

"You see, John," said Cosentino, "these're girls like fourteen, fifteen."

"Except for Lidia and Blanca."

"Even so, we're talking about kids who a year ago were peddling eight-balls—that's an eighth of an ounce of coke—to fourth-graders in the park. They see a bust coming, they're hiding the shit under the sod, you can believe it."

"Under the grass, you mean?"

"Yeah. They pick a spot where they tore up the sod and put it back like Arnold Palmer's divot, then when things are going down, they stash the shit under it."

From the window, King said, "Third one's back."

I said, "The third schoolgirl?"

"Yes, only they aren't exactly schoolgirls."

I thought about how familiar one of them looked. "Las Hermanas."

Cosentino said, "They got us under surveillance, you can believe it."

"You can't do anything?"

He shrugged. "It's a public bench. No crime to impersonate somebody who goes to parochial school."

King said, "Lidia believes in communication, John. She plants some of the underage ones out there, keeping track

235

of who comes in and who goes out. They see somebody of interest, one of them goes off to report in."

I said, "I'm surprised they don't have a cellular phone in the knapsack."

Cosentino said, "They tried it. Too much interference."

From his expression, he wasn't kidding. "So, they know I came to see you."

Cosentino cracked his knuckles a third time. "Basically. Lidia, she warn you to stay off her case?"

"She did."

King said, "Then I'd be very careful, John. We'll keep a little extra eye on the girls, but we can't watch all of them all the time, so maybe you keep an eye out, too."

Cosentino said, "Lidia's the kind who'd cut the balls off Santa Claus, she didn't like what he brung her."

King sighed. "Larry, I'm getting a little tired of that one."

21

WHEN I CAME OUT OF THE AREA B STATION, ALL THREE GIRLS in school uniforms were gone. Walking to the Prelude, I saw a piece of paper ripped from a spiral notebook fluttering under the driver's-side windshield wiper. In black magic marker, the note read, YOUR DEAD, MR. P EYE.

I opened the door of the car very deliberately, put the note on the passenger's seat, and drove first to the condo.

An hour later, I parked in the slanting space behind my office building, next to the dumpster with its usual overflow of garbage. Turning off the ignition, I pulled the Smith & Wesson Combat Masterpiece with four-inch barrel from the holster worn cross-draw on my left side. Usually I prefer a two-inch Chief's Special on the belt above my right buttock, but it's tough to get into your hand from there while sitting in a car. Since the two-incher is also a less accurate weapon, it was hanging handle-down from a calf holster under my left pant leg. The belly-gun would be all right there as long as I didn't try jogging.

I sat and listened. Aside from the faint ticking of the

engine after the bumper-to-bumper traffic from the condo, there were only the usual noises from Tremont Street around the corner. Nothing from the other side of the trash bin.

Opening the car door quickly, I dropped to the ground, looking under the Prelude to see if any feet suddenly appeared from behind the dumpster. Nothing after ten seconds.

Straightening up, I brushed myself off and went around the corner and into the main entrance. Upstairs, I walked past my office door twice, but the lights beyond the pebbled glass were off, and from the corridor I didn't hear anything, much less anything unusual.

Inside the office, there was the same desk, the same two windows overlooking the Park Street subway station, and the ever-changing crowd milling near the entrance and exit of the station itself. I watched for three full minutes, but didn't see any gold warm-up jackets or blue tartan skirts.

Then I got on the telephone.

"Claims Investigation, Mullen."

"Harry, John Cuddy."

"Jeez, John, I was just thinking about this thing here. How you doing?"

"Not great, Harry. Anything on Sandra Newberg yet?"

"Just a second, okay?"

I heard the receiver bonk on his desk top. A minute later, he came back on.

"John, you still there?"

"Still here, Harry."

"Good. Just wanted to close the door there."

"What have you got?"

"Not much. Like I told you, it was kind of awkward asking about her over here."

"Right."

"I mean, not only did she leave, but the people who're still onboard got their minds on other things."

"Harry, I'm pretty pressed. Could we do a little fast forward on this?"

"Sure, John, sure. Like I said, I asked around, best I could. Most of the people from her department are long gone, laid off around the same time she was. But from what I hear, Newberg was a saint."

"No problems at all?"

"None. Solid manager, near perfect attendance record, even organized the blood drive. She just happened to be running a department Empire decided to send south."

"Anything on marital stuff?"

"Everybody was shocked the husband's up for it. Most of the people I talked to never met the guy, but not even a whisper of family troubles or anything."

"Harry, nothing at all?"

"Just that after she got laid off, a couple of the other managers—female ones—had lunch with her. Kind of a mini-reunion, you know?"

"Go on."

"Well, one of them told me that Newberg complained about how bored she was, nothing to do out in Calem there and plenty of time to do it, what with nobody hiring department heads like her."

"And that's it?"

"That's it."

At least he'd saved me some time. "Harry, thanks a lot."

"Hey, John. I owe you, I don't forget that."

"Take care, Harry."

"Every day in every way."

"District Attorney's office."

"Nancy Meagher, please."

"Please wait."

I did.

"Ms. Meagher's line."

"John Cuddy calling. Is she there?"

"Please wait."

I did, again.

"I'm sorry, Ms. Meagher is still on trial. Can I take a message?"

Since I had no reason to believe Las Hermanas knew of our relationship, I wasn't about to leave Nancy a note that would scare her without explanation. "Just leave word that I called and will try her again at home tonight."

"At her home?"

"Right."

"Thank you."

"Hub Vandemeer—Fine Cars, Fair Prices."

An eager, woman's voice. What was her—"Ms. Tollison?"

"Yes. This is Emily Tollison." Even more eager. "How can I help you?"

"Ms. Tollison, this is John Francis. I was in earlier this week, talking with Hub about cars."

"Oh, yes, Mr. Francis. I remember you well."

I doubted it, given that she'd known me only as "John Cuddy," but Tollison certainly made me feel valued. "I wonder, could I speak to him?"

"Sure, sure, Mr. Francis. Just hold on for a tiny moment, and I'll transfer."

After a long enough period to let her tell the boss I might be a live one, I heard "Hub Vandemeer, John. Made up your mind about us yet?"

Nice opening for a potential customer he couldn't remember, either. 'Yeah, Hub. Matter of fact I have. I think you consort with known drug dealers."

A pause. Then a cough. "Who the hell is this?"

"John Cuddy, Hub. We talked about your brother and

240

your nephew and just about everything else under the sun yesterday, but I guess in all the excitement you sort of left out how Blanca Quintana, Queen of the Snow Carnival, is driving one of your ragtops."

Another cough. "I don't remember you asking me about Nicky's girlfriend."

"I'm asking now. Remember what we said about the Telephone game?"

"Yes."

"Good. Why don't you tell me straight and true how she's in one of your cars, so that I don't get it all garbled from somebody else."

A tired sound from his side. "Simple enough. Nicky wrecked his car and lost his license. Boy that age needs to be able to get around. So, he introduced me to his girl-friend, and I sold her the car."

"You sold her the car?"

"That's right."

"His parents know that?"

"I assume so."

"You never told them?"

"What was there to tell? Her money was as good as any-body else's."

"How much, Hub?"

"I don't have the sticker in front of me."

"Lame, Hub, very lame. What's the car you're driving going for?"

Another tired sound. "Twenty-six nine."

"She paid all cash, right?"

"So what? No law against legal tender."

"You ever stop to think how a girl that age from her neighborhood might have picked up that cash?"

"Some people think all those Latins are hookers or drug dealers. I don't."

"Noble, Hub. But it just doesn't wash. How will it look,

she gets caught doing deals from that gold convertible with your name on the metal label over the bumper?"

"Look, I just sell them, pal. I don't keep tabs on where they go or what they do. Anything else?"

"I had a talk with Nicky."

"Hope you enjoyed it."

"I did, but I'm not sure his attitude toward guardianship and yours quite mesh."

"He'll come around. Or the judge will make him."

"But only till he's eighteen, Hub. Then everything, including investment decisions, is up to him."

"Good-bye, Mr. Cuddy."

"Calem Police, Sergeant Clay."

Harold Clay had been a solid patrol officer during my last case in Calem. I was glad to hear he'd gotten promoted, but I didn't want to talk with him. "Paul O'Boy, please."

"Wait one."

More like ten seconds.

"Detectives, O'Boy speaking."

"Cuddy here. At least for a little while longer."

"Cuddy! Good to hear from you. What's the matter?"

"Might have been a nice gesture to tip me about Sandy Newberg and Hale Vandemeer."

"Hey, I gave you the neighbor, this Mrs. Epps, right?"

"I've met her. I've also met the Quintana sisters."

"Quintana . . . ?"

"How about we drop the Lieutenant Columbo routine, okay? It doesn't suit you."

Three seconds. "Yeah, but you gotta admit, I play it well, huh?"

"Well enough. What's the idea of sending me out to Nicky Vandemeer without knowing what his girlfriend was into?"

O'Boy lowered his voice. "All right, all right. I told you, we got this new chief, right?"

"Right."

"Well, he's just getting the scoop on a lot of things Wooten didn't exactly . . . focus on."

"Like some of the kids riding buses into Calem aren't what you'd call model citizens."

"For example. But he just gets appointed, he doesn't want to piss in the soup of one of the selectmen voted for him."

"Which selectman is in love with the special student program."

"Selectman's wife, actually."

"So you what, use me as the cat's paw to get the truth about Quintana out into the open?"

I could almost feel O'Boy looking innocent. "I figured— the chief figured—you come up with something that hits the fan, it gives us grounds for going into everything because we kind of have to."

"The killings at the lake and the Maine authorities didn't do that for you?"

"Hell, no. Nothing to tie Quintana to that. Besides, the Mainers, they weren't interested in the son's girlfriend as a part of their case. They just asked us to do a simple check."

"And that wasn't enough to bring to the selectmen."

"Let's say we thought it was close, but not a sure thing."

"Which I might provide if you slipped me a little information on the side, confidential-like."

"Aw, Cuddy, don't go sarcastic on me, huh?"

"I forgot. You're easily hurt, right?"

"Even one harsh word can do it."

"Yeah, well I'm facing a little more than harsh words, O'Boy. You owe me a big one."

"Depends on how you look at things, don't it? I mean, you're the one called me for help on this, right?"

"A big one, O'Boy."

After the last call, I watched out my window for ten minutes. Nobody I recognized, no clutch of Hispanic girls in any kind of clothes loitering around anywhere I could see. I locked the office and went downstairs.

Walking past the parking alley once, I came back to it, slowly. No activity around the car or the dumpster. Given the stench, I didn't think they'd fancy it a good spot to wait. I got into the Prelude and drove out onto Tremont. Acutely aware of my mirrors, I stayed in the lane paralleling Boston Common.

At Boylston, I took a right. Boylston is one of the borders of Back Bay, but the street becomes one way at Charles, forcing the driver to turn onto Charles and in effect circle half the Common. Being roundabout intentionally, I checked the mirrors for anybody who seemed confused behind me. Nothing but single-occupant cars and one Asian family in a white rental sedan whose faces suggested that they knew they had no hope of finding whatever they were looking for in the city.

As the Public Garden ended, I took a left onto Beacon, passing the facade for the *Cheers* bar on my right. At Arlington, I went left again rather than heading straight on, even though my condo building fronts on Beacon itself. Then I turned right onto Commonwealth. Other than the Asian family, nobody had stuck with me, and even they, arguing over an unfolded road map, took a right at Berkeley, leaving me four full blocks before my turn for home.

I continued up Commonwealth, taking the right at Fairfield. Pulling into the space behind the condo building, I congratulated myself that I'd listed in the telephone book only as to office address, office number, and home number, not home address. Then, getting out of the Prelude, I thought about the last time I was asked about my home address. The security desk at DRM, the guard looking at my driver's license. The same driver's license that Lidia Quintana had held in her hand.

Even so, if they'd used a different car, I might not have made it.

Walking on the Fairfield side of my building, I caught the gold convertible's grille and front fender flashing out from a private parking space on the half block of Fairfield that lies in shadow between the two buildings across Beacon. The girl from the bench outside Area B began to stand up in the backseat with her Intratec, while my other guard cleared her semiautomatic pistol over the windowsill on the front passenger's side. Blanca Quintana was at the wheel, everybody's long black hair whipping in the breeze as she entered the intersection, pedal to the metal.

As the car came across Beacon against the light, it got tagged in the left rear end by the Asian family in the white rental, who apparently had made another random turn. The impact sent the Tec-9 girl up and out of the right side of the convertible, the Asians' sedan caroming into the line of parked vehicles on the north side of Beacon. The convertible dribbled a urine line of liquid under the rear wheels as it fishtailed crazily, and Quintana wrenched at the wheel.

That's when Blanca braked, and the girl with the pistol opened up.

I dove behind an old Pontiac with an engine block the size of a small sofa. The block absorbed a full magazine from the girl. Hearing the slide of her weapon jack open, I came up onto my knees, resting the Combat Masterpiece on the hood of the Pontiac. Before I could say anything, the girl struggling with the pistol tossed it into the back seat and raised another one at me.

I fired three times, half the rounds in my weapon.

The first slug snapped the girl's head back, the second striking her in the throat, a grotesque pinkish blossom spurting upward from her collar. I didn't register what happened to my third shot. Quintana accelerated as the girl sagged down, and the car pulled away.

I fired twice into the right front tire, bursting it.

The convertible, still accelerating, now pivoted on the front hub, spinning the car 180 degrees so that it was facing me. Suddenly, there was a sound like hail, peppering the street in front of me.

I dove again, this time under the front bumper of the Pontiac, and looked toward Beacon. The girl with the Intratec was limping up Fairfield toward me, dragging her bloodied right leg. The bloodied right arm hung at her side, the left hand firing in a clumsy way that told me she was right-handed.

From the gutter, I shouted at her twice to stop. She didn't.

As her next string kicked up gravel and tar in front of me, I held the front sight on her waistline and pulled the trigger on my sixth round. The girl staggered backward like a dazed boxer before her torso closed down over her knees, and she pitched onto the asphalt face-first.

To my right I heard the convertible start forward again. I reached under my pant leg and drew the Chief's Special from its calf holster.

As I came back up over the Pontiac's hood, I could see Blanca bleeding badly from a wound in her throat. Maybe my second bullet after it went through her friend, maybe my third. Hacking blood into her side of the windshield, Quintana accelerated toward me parallel with the parked cars on Fairfield, the convertible grinding on the ruined hub of its right front wheel, the metal shooting sparks behind it like Flash Gordon's spaceship.

FOURSOME

I fired three rounds from the Chief's Special into the driver's side windshield.

The convertible swerved right in an arc, never reaching Beacon but instead smashing into a station wagon parked across Fairfield from the Pontiac. I'd taken one step toward Blanca's car when the sparks from the hub or the final collision found some gasoline from the leaking tank. There was a fuse line of fire that raced toward the rear of the convertible, then a tremendous whoosh and boom that threw me back onto the pavement.

The backdraft from the flaming car made the stench from the dumpster behind my office seem like expensive perfume. I took out a handkerchief, soaked it in some spilled gasoline on my side of Fairfield, and held it to my nose and mouth.

22

I SAID, "HOW'S THE ASIAN FAMILY?"

Ilario Cosentino said, "The what?"

"There was an Asian family in a white rental that clipped Quintana on Beacon as she was coming for me. Do you know if they're okay?"

From behind me, Robert Murphy said, "They're fine. I tried to talk to them, but they're Chinese, not much English. One of the kids just got a little conk on the head."

"How about the car?"

"We're gonna call the rental company, get the family off the hook."

I nodded. I was sitting on the steps of the condo building, my hands still shaking a little too much from the adrenaline to hold the mug of tea one of my neighbors in misguided kindness brought down to me. Caffeine doesn't counter adrenaline very well, but I would have liked to fake drinking it for her sake.

Cosentino was standing, his rump against one of the wrought iron railings leading to the front door of the building. Murphy was sitting on the stoop two steps higher than me, a piece of newspaper under him so that the pants to his suit wouldn't get dirty. My weapons rested in separate evidence baggies between Murphy's shoes. I'd already gone through the sequence twice for them.

On the sidewalk, plainclothes cops were scribblings statements from apparent witnesses. A couple of uniforms were fending off broadcast reporters with mikes in their hands and print reporters with tape recorders in theirs who tried to shout questions at the three of us in general and me in particular. At the intersection, there were still three pieces of fire apparatus, red lights revolving, called in for the burning convertible. EMTs from several ambulances were just marking time, waiting for another call once they realized there was nobody left for them from this one. In the middle of Fairfield, a white panel truck was parked the wrong way near two Boston Police cruisers. The blue lettering on the truck spelled OFFICE OF THE CHIEF MEDICAL EXAMINER. If I turned my head to the right, I could just see the yellow tape with POLICE LINE DO NOT CROSS triangulating the body of the Intratec girl, so I didn't turn my head that way.

Murphy's voice got softer. "How you doing, Cuddy?"

"Not great."

Cosentino said, "We told you, they use their guns like they was dusting crops. You did good to walk out of this here."

I said, "Where's your partner?"

"Yollie? She's with the rest of the unit, trying to round up as many Las Hermanas as they can. You're sure it was Blanca behind the wheel?"

I'd already told them twice, but I tried to picture the convertible as I saw it first instead of as I saw it last. "Positive."

"Definitely not Lidia with her?"

I didn't say anything. I'd already answered that one twice, too.

The plastic baggies between Murphy's feet made a crinkling noise. "We have to take in both your guns, you know."

"I know."

His voice got smaller this time. "You got any backups?"

"They're it."

Murphy stopped, maybe looking to Cosentino. "Cuddy, a shoot like this, procedure says I should pull your Permit to Carry."

"Couldn't blame you."

"Only thing is, without it, you carry and get caught, it's a year in the slam."

"I know that, too."

Cosentino blew some air out his lips. "Year in, week in, wouldn't matter. Lidia'd cut a deal with somebody, say a prison gang like the Latin Kings, put your lights out."

Murphy laid his hand on my shoulder, the first time I could ever remember him touching me in any way. "What I'm saying here, Cuddy, you might want to disappear for a while, till Larry and Yollie figure a way to gut Las Hermanas."

Cosentino said, "No promises on that one, either."

I said, "Kind of tough to disappear in my line of work."

Murphy said, "This thing you're working on, got you messed up with these girls. That's in Maine, right?"

"Right."

"Might be you could spend a few days up there, let things run their course some down here."

I wasn't thinking too clearly, but he made sense. "Sounds like that'd be a good thing to try."

Cosentino said, "I was you, I'd try it tonight. Be on the road soon's you can."

Murphy didn't ask me if I was up to a long drive right away, but if I were him, I'd have been thinking it.

I said, "I never checked my car. Did it catch any strays?"

Cosentino said, "Sit tight. I'll cut through the jackals, let you know."

He went down the steps slowly and just kept shaking his head as the reporters swamped him, staying with him to the corner.

Murphy waited a minute, then said, "You know, I never did tell anybody about the shotgun thing you did on that guy last year."

"I didn't figure you ever would."

"Something I'd like to know, though."

"Ask."

"That guy, you set him up, smoked him, account of you knew he was poison. These girls, though, they come after you."

"That's right."

"But doing him, that didn't get to you like this here."

I nodded.

Murphy's voice got both smaller and softer. "How come?"

It had been playing around the edges since I'd held the gassed hankie to my face, me subconsciously trying to put this situation in the right pigeonhole among the other lives I'd taken. "In Saigon, I opened up on a shadow in a doorway during the Tet Offensive. I'd just lost two men to a shooter in the doorway before it. All of us were wound tight, it was the right thing to do. Reflex."

Murphy said, "But?"

"But it turned out to be somebody just hiding, probably terrified. A child, Lieutenant, maybe eight or nine."

"Not much younger than these here."

"Same feeling, anyway."

"Yeah, well, might be the same feeling, but it's not the

251

same situation. These girls, Cuddy, don't matter how old they are, they haven't been children for some time now."

I heard the newspaper rustle as he stood behind me.

Murphy said, "Got to check in." As he came past my step, he rested the hand that wasn't carrying the baggies on my shoulder again. "I hear up in Maine, the gun laws, they're not so strict. A man might want to buy a backup piece, he has the time."

Murphy reached the bottom step. To his back, I said, "What about my Permit to Carry down here?"

"Forgot to ask you for it. Commissioner'll ream my ass, me fucking up like that."

I watched him walk toward the corner, holding his free hand up to ward off reporters, the photographers giving ground as they clicked away at the baggies in his other hand.

"ADA Meagher."

"It's me, Nance."

"Jesus Mary, John, I caught the case just as I was—"

"It's okay. A bad situation, but I'm not hurt."

A sound over the line that came from her throat but wasn't quite a word. Then, quieter, "You're calling to tell me you can't see me for a while."

"You know enough about gangs to know that's a good idea."

A heartbeat. "It's wise. That doesn't mean I think it's a good idea."

"I'll accept the friendly amendment."

"Where will you be?"

"In Maine. I'll call you, probably tomorrow."

"How about tonight?"

"I'm driving up there tonight."

"I meant, how about calling me tonight, let me know you made it all right."

"I'd like to."

"Does that mean you will?"

"Ever the lawyer."

"Ever yours."

"Does that mean I can call collect?"

"Ever the jerk, too," said ADA Meagher, and hung up.

Roses for me twice in a row?

"Mrs. Feeney mixed you a bunch. Three different varieties, she said."

What's the occasion?

I looked down her hillside toward the harbor. A boat that appeared handmade, the cabin too far forward to be proportional, edged its way through the chop, the sun dwindling in the west.

John?

I came back to her headstone. Seeing Nancy at her house three blocks away was a risk, given the methods Las Hermanas had shown me so far. Seeing Beth here was not.

"I had a bad day, kid."

How bad?

I told her.

Oh God, John. I'm sorry.

Nodding, I watched the boat clear the Castle Island point.

But Murphy's right, you know.

I nodded again.

He is, John. You didn't make those girls join that gang and decide to eliminate you as an . . . inconvenience to them.

I got tired of nodding. "I know."

You're heading somewhere, aren't you?

"Good instinct about now."

Where?

"Back up to Maine, try to pick up a few threads, tie them together."

A pause. *Do you have a gun?*

"No, but I packed some ammunition and a couple hundred in cash to maybe get one up there."

When are you going?

"Soon as I leave you."

Another pause. *I never thought I'd say this to you, John, but in that case, please leave now.*

I looked down at her. "Why?"

Because the way you seem, I'd rather not think of you driving the whole way at night.

I felt a smile, one I'd used with her when we were first married. "Because I'm distracted."

And distraction leads to mistakes, John. Don't do anything stupid, okay?

"For your sake."

For Nancy's sake.

I found I wasn't quite as tired of nodding as I'd thought.

23

THE FRIDAY AFTERNOON TRAFFIC ON THE CENTRAL ARTERY was thick and balky, not improving much even though I decided to use Route 93 north instead of Route 1. A nice day weatherwise, the promise of a better weekend up-country filled the lanes with the cars of people not used to commuter driving. I was one of them.

Sudden noises made me jumpy. The sound of a diesel truck venting its stack, the blare of a rap song over some-body's radio, the skittering of a muffler and tail pipe not quite held up by wire twisted around a bumper. I tried to concentrate on my driving, to hum familiar tunes, but then I drew even with an old Chrysler in the breakdown lane, chuffing along with a blown front tire, an elderly man stoic behind the wheel. That grinding noise was a little too close to recent reality.

I let the Chrysler get ahead of me, to the sound of horns from behind me, then edged onto the shoulder and sat for a while, taking deep breaths. It didn't help, so I made a break in the traffic and continued on.

At Route 128, I headed north, the traffic at first worse

255

and then suddenly better. I got on Interstate 95, the pavement widening, the scenery improving a little toward the green side. Then good time until the New Hampshire tollbooth, and better time as I crossed over the bridge to Kittery and saw the billboard with WELCOME TO MAINE— THE WAY LIFE SHOULD BE.

I felt the next deep breath take hold, as though my whole chest were moving independently inside my rib cage, the organs reordering themselves into a more natural alignment. As the miles went by, I realized the jumpiness was dissipating, too, my hands resting steady on the wheel instead of being clamped to it. The next hundred miles of the trip wore less than the first ten.

Just before Augusta, I debated about where to stay, since I hadn't called ahead to the Marseilles Inn. Ralph and Ramona might have a room, and then again they might not. In any case, I wasn't about to impose on them for dinner, and I didn't relish driving in the dark toward them after eating somewhere closer.

I took the Augusta exit and found a nondescript motel that advertised ESPN on cable. The proprietor, a gruff gent in a green and black lumberjack's shirt, allowed as how the Kentucky Fried Chicken might be my best bet for dinner. I thanked him, paid in advance for my room, and walked by the ice machine to get to it. Plastic paneling, two double beds, a bathroom with just a shower and a washbasin, no tub and no vanity. However, the TV worked, ESPN coming in loud and clear and promising a baseball doubleheader, the second game at ten-thirty from the West Coast. I showered, put on some casual clothes from the suitcase, and went back out to the Prelude.

It was just getting dark, and I considered stopping in a bar first for some reliable relaxant. I drove past several in downtown along the river and one on the strip with my motel. None seemed inviting, and there were at least three vehicles outside each that looked enough like the high-wheeled pickup Owen Briss drove that I wasn't dead sure none of them was his. I thought back to the advice about not doing something stupid, and I couldn't remember whether Nancy or Beth had been the source. That did it.

I found a state liquor store in a shopping center and paid seven bucks for a pint of vodka. There was a payphone in sight, so I went over to it and called Nancy. I told her I'd arrived safely and about my plans for the night without asking if she'd inspired them. Then I found a gas station cum convenience store and bought a half gallon of orange juice, a bag of potato chips, and a box of pretzel logs. I stopped at the Colonel's for a bucket of chicken parts, some original recipe, the rest extra crispy.

Driving sedately back to my motel, I put the vodka and the orange juice in the bathroom sink. Then I covered both bottles with ice from the machine outside my door. I tuned in the television, settled into bed, and watched a long inning of baseball over dinner and drinks. I had one screwdriver every inning thereafter until I noticed that the chips and pretzels were gone and that I wasn't sure which team was ahead. That's when I turned off the set, turned out the lights, and turned in for the night, missing the late game with little regret.

I came awake with a start, the sound of a key in the lock rousting me from a deep sleep, the sound of the door coming open making me realize I didn't know where I was. The maid, pushing fifty as well as a laundry cart, jumped back out of the room, mumbling something that might have been an apology. I also realized that I hadn't looked for a DO NOT DISTURB sign the night before.

My watch on the table between the two beds red 11:05. I'd slept for a good twelve hours, but didn't feel any after-effect of the drinking except for that cottony dryness around the tongue. After cleaning up, I checked out by dropping off my key with the same man in the same shirt. I had terrific pancakes in a local spot that was packed with people in all the odd rooms it had accreted over the years. Then I drove toward Gil Lacouture's office.

"Hey, John Cuddy. How about a beer?"

"Thanks, but I just had breakfast."

"How'd you find me?"

I stared at Lacouture, standing over a barrel grill with a white, puffy chef's hat on his head and a long-neck Bud in his left hand. In his right he held a spatula, the butcher's white apron covering a Hawaiian shirt that didn't look as though a stain, no matter what color, would show anyway. Behind him a crowd of seventy or so men and boys of all ages mingled in a picnic ground on the bank of the river that ran through Augusta. Some were reaching for communal mustard and ketchup squeeze bottles, already taking bites from hot dogs and hamburgers on paper plates that wouldn't stay flat for them.

I said, "Judy at your office said you'd be here. I don't want to interrupt anything."

"Don't worry about it. This is just our father-son picnic. Another Lion can mind the store for a while. Hey, Cholly? Cholly!"

A round mound of seersucker shirt and green pants came over and took the spatula but not the hat from Lacouture, who wiped one hand and then the other on his apron, shifting the Bud as needed.

Scanning the crowd, I said, "Which one's yours?"

"Sorry?"

"Which of the boys is yours?"

"Oh." A small smile, maybe shielding some embarrassment. "I just do these for business generation, John. I don't have any kids. Or even a wife, for that matter." He perked a little. "So, what's up?"

I looked at the crowd again. Cholly and at least four others were within earshot of us.

I said, "Can we step away from things a bit?"

"Sure, sure. Let's go toward the falls."

A pretty impressive waterfall was upriver of us, on a line with what I thought would be the end of downtown. The water dropped ten vertical yards onto jagged rocks the size of compact cars.

Lacouture said, "Couple springs ago, the Kennebec went to full flood stage, water rose more than forty feet."

"Forty feet?"

"It ruined a lot of folks, carried away a few others. But that's just the river's way of showing us she's still vital, like the stripers that feed through here."

"Striped bass?"

"Right."

"I thought they were more a saltwater fish."

"They are, but they come up the rivers, too. Even the Hudson down by New York City, you can believe the papers. Of course, the ones down there might not be such good eating. I read about a rat popping out of the entrails of one being cleaned for a tourist who caught him. But anything out of the Kennebec would be mighty fine, I'll tell you." Lacouture eyed me, then took off the chef's hat. "Somehow, though, I don't think you've come all the way back to learn about our fishing."

I said, "You hear about a shooting in Boston yesterday?"

Lacouture frowned. "Just some gang thing over the television. Girls, too, I think it was."

"That was me."

His eyes grew wide. "You?"

"One of the leads I was following down there got me

259

targeted by a gang called Las Hermanas. They tried to kill me."

"Christ." Lacouture looked me up and down. "You all right?"

"Mostly."

The lawyer grew more lawyerly. "Does this mean you don't want to stay on Steve's case?"

"It means I thought you should know about it from me firsthand."

"Because you think this gang figures in with what happened up here."

I shook my head. "I'm pretty sure it doesn't, at least not directly."

"Why not?"

"These were high school kids, even junior high, some of them." I swung my hand toward the picnic. "No older than a lot of the boys back there. I doubt they could have found Shea's house up here, and given the way they dealt with me, they wouldn't have been subtle enough to use a weapon like a crossbow."

Lacouture seemed to process that. "All right, then why'd you say 'not directly'?"

"Because I got onto them through Hale Vandemeer's son and brother, who have pretty good motives for wanting the Vandemeers dead."

Lacouture scuffed at the ground a little with the heel of a shoe. "I don't know, John. Doesn't sound much more promising than the gang possibility. Anything else?"

"Maybe. I also spent some time with the folks at DRM."

"Anna-Pia and them."

"Right."

"And?"

"And they tried to sell me the 'stop-at-nothing competitor' theory."

Lacouture nodded. "Steve's already bought that."

"I don't blame him. From where he's sitting, it's the one thing that explains a nightmare he can't understand."

"Or wake up from." He took a slug of his beer. "Something tells me you don't buy it, though."

"As a theory, it sounds good. As your only argument to the jury on what happened that night, it doesn't hold up too well."

"Bad TV movie."

"What?"

"You know, made-for-TV movies? The star of the month from some stupid series getting his or her dramatic 'big break'? Hell, John, even up here most of the jurors I'm likely to draw learn most of what they know from watching the tube. There's kind of a bedrock sense they'll have of what's good TV and bad TV, and the competitor theory is going to sound like bad TV to them. Unless, of course, we can back it up."

"Not from what I've seen so far. I think DRM would like to have Shea back, but not at the expense of losing a big deal over him. This theory is their way of keeping all options open while committing to none."

Lacouture used a thumbnail to worry a corner of the label on his bottle. "You don't have any evidence on a competitor. Does that mean you think it's impossible?"

"No. And I'm going back up to the lake and try it out on people who might have seen something beforehand. Just don't make it the linchpin of your defense, okay?"

Lacouture looked up from his bottle. "But you still believe Steve's innocent."

A while since I'd thought about it. "Yes. I do."

"I'm glad to hear that. You get deep into a big case, you lose your sense of perspective." Another sip of beer. "So, do you need anything more from me?"

"Maybe. Shea ever tell you he had some kind of . . . secret?"

Lacouture gave me the lawyer look again. "Secret? About what?"

"I don't mean the affair."

Bewilderment that seemed genuine. "The affair?"

"Between Hale Vandemeer and Sandra Newberg."

"No. Oh, no."

"Shea never told you?"

"Not a word. If he had, I would have told you. You sure he knew about it?"

"For motive, you mean?"

"Hell, yes."

"Nicky Vandemeer said he dropped the news on Steve around a month ago. At least one other person—a neighbor down in Calem—was aware of the affair, and both Nicky and the neighbor spoke to the cops about what they know."

More scuffing with the shoe. "John, this is not good news."

"There may be worse."

"What do you mean?"

"Shea ever say anything about any other secret?"

An edge of panic crept into Lacouture's voice. "A-*nother* secret? About what?"

"I don't know. Except it might have something to do with DRM, based on the source that brought it up."

A slow, then emphatic shake of the head. "No. No, John, Steve told me DRM is into a lot of stuff that's 'secret' in the kind of national security sense we used to respect in this country. But he never even implied to me that he had a secret himself. What do you think it is?"

"I'm hoping you can arrange for me to see him again this afternoon so I can ask."

Lacouture made a face as though somebody forgot to ice his beer. "I can do that. But John, go easy on Steve, okay?"

"What do you mean?"

"He's having a little more trouble adjusting to jail."

None of the pickups outside the bars on Friday night belonged to Owen Briss. I know, because the truck parked at a careless angle outside the Marseilles Inn had that distinctive gouge mark on the driver's side door. What looked like half a load of lumber lay in the bed of the pickup, extending past the tailgate with no red flag on the extension. I got out of my car just as Briss, wearing an old chamois shirt and cutoff shorts, stepped through the front door of the inn and onto the porch. The sounds of sixties rock trailed behind him, something from the Byrds, I thought.

The balding head reared liked a horse that had seen a snake. "The goddamn hell do you want?"

"Nothing with you, my friend."

As the carpenter bristled, Ralph Paine came out behind him. "John! Mona said you'd called up from Augusta. How are you?"

"Well, Ralph, thanks. Okay to come in?"

"Okay? Why shouldn't it be?"

Briss moved down the steps before I started to move toward them. "I got a truck needs unloading."

He began sliding two-by-fours forcefully onto one shoulder. Ralph watched him thoughtfully, then came back to me. "John, why don't we get you signed in and all, so Owen can have a free hand with the lumber?"

"Fine by me."

I got my suitcase out of the car, but let Briss go first with his load, stomping up the steps ahead of me.

As the rear end of the wood disappeared down a first-floor hall, Paine turned down the radio and said quietly, "You had a run-in with Owen, then?"

"I did."

"Most do. He's a fine carpenter, but a mite hard to get

along with. He won't bother you long's I'm around."

"Good. I've had enough trouble for a while."

Ralph nodded. "Saw the late TV news last night, tape from Boston. That was you, wasn't it?"

"Yes."

"Sorry for your troubles there. How long can you stay with us?"

"I'm not sure. Couple of days, maybe."

"Well, whatever. Your room's waiting for you."

"Same one's available?"

"We make that effort." A broad grin.

"Terrific."

"Be having dinner with us tonight?"

"I'll be gone most of the afternoon, but I'd love to, if there'll be an empty chair."

"Empty chair? John, that little nook in the corner's just been crying for you." Paine dropped the jovial mood. "The thing in Boston. Sounded like it was kind of tough."

I didn't want to talk about it. "Kind of."

"Tell you what, then. You come back here after whatever you've got to do this afternoon. I'll set something up for you, take your mind off things."

"Ralph, don't go to—"

"Won't be any trouble at all. Just need some clothes you don't mind maybe getting wet."

24

THE PARKING LOT OF THE JAIL COMPLEX WAS A LOT MORE crowded than the first time I'd been there. Saturday figured to be more available for visitors and therefore more popular as well. Inside the main entrance, Deputy Carl Higgs nodded to me from behind the windowed counter.

"Sheriff'd like to see you."

Patsy Willis said, "I don't expect a progress report."

"That's good."

She moved her mouth in a way that wasn't quite a smile. Willis lounged at her desk, feet up on the pull-tray. The Stetson was on its prong of the coat tree, her brown and gray hair parted in the center and drawn back in those over-the-ear waves.

She said, "I expect yesterday wasn't the best time in your life, so I'm sorry to have to ask you this, but long's I'm in this chair, I'll do what the job requires."

I sat down in front of her desk. "Ask it."

"Saw the thing about that gang come over the wire. Actually, I didn't see it, but Carl did, and he showed it to me. This morning early, I called Boston PD, asked for Homicide. Eventually got a woman named Cross. Said she knew you, but didn't exactly like you."

"You got the right person, then."

A minimal nod. "This Cross said the shoot-out with the gang wasn't the first thing you've stepped in that went a little bloody down there."

I let her go.

"Also said the lieutenant in charge of the case took your weapons away from you. I asked her if he got them all and your permit to boot, and she went kind of vague on me. Now why do you suppose that would be?"

"Cross runs hot and cold sometimes."

Less of a nod. "Well, hot and cold, that's something that runs in a lot of jurisdictions, mister. Sometimes without much warning. Seems to me you're working in Maine on good graces, seeing as how you're just provisionally licensed by our glorious state. Also seems to me you might want to cooperate a little more fully with a peace officer up here asks you a reasonable question about what went on down there."

"Your point's well taken, Sheriff."

"Good. Now, let me ask you that reasonable question."

"Go ahead."

"You carrying a hideaway gun around my county?"

"Not this trip."

Willis watched me. "You planning to?"

"Before I head back to Massachusetts, I might pick one up."

"Gun dealer can't sell to you without some kind of picture ID showing a Maine residence on it."

"Thanks. That'll save some time."

Willis watched me a while more. "Your not carrying now mean you don't expect what you stepped in down there to come visiting up here?"

I gave her what was becoming my stock comment on Las Hermanas and their lack of geographic mobility.

"Makes sense." She exhaled hard. "Wouldn't reflect too well on me, we had one of those drive-bys invading the county because of our courtesy to you."

"It would be a tough sell, next election."

"Then we understand each other. I expect you'd like to see your client about now."

"If he's free."

This time Willis did smile. "Try that joke on Shea himself. Might be he could use a belly laugh about now."

He was three years more haggard than he'd been three days earlier.

The guard that looked like Higgs led Steven Shea to the same space we'd used last time. Same room at the inn, same guard, same room at the jail. A tradition throughout the culture.

Shea sank into his seat, the loss of another five pounds showing in his face and beneath his chin.

I said, "You feeling all right?"

"Yeah. Yeah. I'm just fucking ducky."

"What's the matter?"

Shea looked away, toward the guard outside the glass windows. "You were right."

"About what?"

"About Rick."

"Your cell mate?"

"Yeah. I kind of, you know, confronted the fucker about what you said. He fucking laughed, said we could be"— Shea looked farther away—"we could be asshole buddies anyway, I wanted to. I started yelling and didn't stop till I had the fucking cell to myself."

I thought about Shea's remarking on his use of four-letter words and wondered if he still noticed it. "Probably would

267

have happened anyway, so long as you didn't give them anything through him."

Shea came back to me. "John, how the fuck much longer am I going to have to be in here?"

"That's more a question for your lawyer."

"Yeah, well, I'm beginning to think my lawyer doesn't know shit."

"Steve—"

"I mean, Gil comes in to visit me, I tell him what you said about Rick, and he tells me, 'Maybe Cuddy's right, maybe he's wrong. Either way, you play along, the worst thing that happens is you've got a good cell mate, and the prosecution doesn't find out anything bad to use against you.' I ask you, is that what my fucking lawyer's supposed to be telling me?"

Probably. "Look, Steve, Lacouture might know about when the trial's likely to be and all, but from what you told me before about no bail, you're in here till then, at least."

Shea reached an index finger up and started to pick his nose, then realized what he was doing and buried the finger in a crossed-arm gesture. "Shit, excuse me. I . . . I've been in here—what, two weeks now?—and already I'm becoming a barbarian. This jail stuff, John . . . and this is just the county lockup. What happens if Lacouture can't persuade the jury that one of DRM's competitors did this to me, huh? Then I'm in *real* jail, the state pen at Thomaston. Forever. For-fucking-*ev*-er, understand?"

"I understand, Steve."

"I hope so. I really hope you fucking do, John." A brightness came into his eyes, the salesman who desperately needs to close the current deal. "You went to DRM, spoke with Dwight about the competitor?"

"I saw them, Steve."

"Them?"

"Everybody at DRM."

"Anna-Pia, Mr. Davison?"

"Even Tyrone Xavier."

Shea let that pass. "And?"

"And I don't think we're going to fly very far with the competitor theory."

"What?"

"It just doesn't—"

"What the fuck do you mean, you don't think we can fly with it? That's what happened!"

"I doubt it."

"Man, the fuck is going on here? I'm framed for something I didn't do, couldn't ever fucking dream of doing, and first my fucking cell mate and then my fucking lawyer and now my fucking investigator turns against me?"

I didn't want to lose him. "Steve—"

"What do I have to do, fucking break out of here through a tunnel?"

"Steve."

Shea began breathing shallowly, one hand raking through his hair. He was choking back something, something like a sob.

I said his name again.

Shea looked up, but just shook his head.

"Steve, why didn't you tell Lacouture about Hale and Sandy's affair?"

All the animation, however negative, seemed to leave his face at once. "How did you find out about that?"

A way of phrasing the question that said Nicky Vandemeer had told me the truth, giving the state all the motive a prosecutor could ask for.

I said, "They were seen."

"No."

"And Nicky said he told you about it."

"No, no." The hand went back through the hair again. "Does that mean that DRM knows?"

"Steve, it means that the cops know that you knew about the affair. The ones in Calem told the ones up here, which gives you—"

"But does . . . does Mr. Davison . . ."

I couldn't quite follow him. "Does Keck Davison know about your wife's affair?"

Shea suddenly closed down. "Never mind."

"Never mind?"

"Right. Forget it."

"Steve—"

"Just fucking forget it, all right?"

"Steve, what are you holding back about DRM?"

"Nothing."

"You are. You memorized Antonelli's home number, which tells me you'd been confiding in her, and she's the lawyer you called when you first got into trouble up here. I have to know what's going on."

"You don't have to know shit. My fucking lawyer doesn't have to know shit. Even my fucking cell mate doesn't know shit because I don't have one anymore."

Shea laughed nervously, a man on the edge of hysteria, his hands shaking and his face twitching.

"Steve, I'm just trying to help you."

Tears welled behind the twitching. "As long as Sandy was alive, it mattered, but it doesn't anymore, so I can't tell you. It's my last chance, don't you see that?"

"What's your last chance, Steve?"

He stood up. "I'm sorry, I have to go back now."

"Steve, please. Your last chance to do what?"

The nervous laugh. "Today's Saturday. They do box lunches on Saturday, so the inmates can eat in the visitors' area with their families." Looking over to the guard, Shea cranked his head up and down. "With their families, John. I think I'll just eat in my fucking room today, nobody minds."

FOURSOME

I sat for a minute in the little glass-walled space, watching Steven Shea walk unsteadily ahead of the guard back toward his "room."

"You look like you could use a drink."

"I could, Ralph, but I used a lot of them last night, and I used to use a lot more."

Paine scratched his chin. "Well, then, how about that other way to relax?"

"If you tell me and I turn it down, I hope you won't feel bad."

"Not at all. The Marseilles Inn is a full-service *re*-sort, but that doesn't mean you have to do everything you can do."

"So what service are we talking about?"

Paine turned toward the lake, "Easier to show you."

"Do I have to wear the life jacket?"

"No. She's pretty calm this afternoon, John, and still too early in the season for most of the damned water-skiers. Just keep it handy by your seat there, case a warden decides to check you."

"Ralph, I thought it took two people to paddle a canoe."

"Nossir. You been in Dag Gates's square-stern, right?"

"Yeah, but he uses a motor."

"Same difference. I'm just going to put this sandbag up in the bow, centered under the seat like a person was sitting up over it."

"Okay."

"Ballast, you see?"

"I think so."

"The sandbag, that'll keep her nose down, so you can paddle into the wind. You've heard of Murphy's Law."

"Whatever can go wrong will go wrong?"

"Right. Well, Mona has a rule like that for canoeing."

"What is it?"

"The wind is always in your face on the way home."

"Okay, the sandbag keeps me stable that way, but I'll still have to keep switching the paddle over to go in a straight line."

"Nossir. Put your right hand on top of the handle, and your left hand just above the blade. A little further up. Perfect. Now put the blade in the water on the port side of the canoe."

"The left side."

"Right. I mean, correct. The left side."

"Okay?"

"Good. Now just push your top hand down and your bottom hand back, like you were making a straight stroke through the water."

I tried it. "Pushes the front of the canoe all the way over to the right."

"Of course it does. Now do the same stroke, but finish it to the side, like you were making the letter 'J' and sweeping out the curved part at the bottom."

I tried that. "Not as much to the right."

"You'll have to make allowances, depending on the wind, any current, and so on. But use the J-stroke, or the reverse of it on the starboard side, and you'll be able to keep the paddle on one side as long as you have strength for it."

"When should I get back?"

"You start back two hours after you head out."

"Two hours?"

"Seems kind of long? It won't be, believe me. And we'll hold dinner for you, don't worry about that. But you'll want to be in before dusk, otherwise the skeeters'll have you for dessert."

"Any suggestions?"

"Head south, through the islands. See some things you might never have before."

272

"Thanks, Ralph."

"Enjoy. And relax."

The canoe was yellow, with walnut caned seats mounted under the gunwales and the word GAZELLE on the side. Ralph had said the company manufactured the Fiberglas canoes nearby, so he was able to get a good price on them. Aluminum ones were more durable, but they made a hellish racket for a supposedly genteel sport. Mine was surprisingly stable with just me in it, though I didn't try any barrel rolls to test it.

After a couple of hundred feet, I got the hang of the J-stroke, then changed to the right side and worked on my form there as well. The canoe hissed trough the water, the chop only a few inches of crest and trough dappling the surface in the afternoon sun. My paddle blade made little slurping sounds as I lifted it, the twin whirlpools from the stroke boloing backward and outward in a steady pattern. The physical resistance of the water felt good to and through my shoulders, like having an internal massage on muscles that were cramped from too much desk and too much driving and too little of everything else.

I approached the nearest island, a loon moving away from me. It began calling, and at first I thought I was hearing its echo from down the lake. Then I remembered what Ma Judson had said about each bird's call being different, and I listened a little more carefully. After five repetitions by my bird, I was sure the "echo" was another loon returning the call, subtly different in note and tempo. Something, maybe me, spooked the loon. Instead of diving, though, it began to flail its wings to get its lowslung body enough out of the water to start walking across the surface, flailing harder now and actually running on the water, the webbed feet making a slapping sound as it mustered enough speed for a final, struggling takeoff.

At the island, something the size and color of a dark brown cocker spaniel scrambled down a bank and into the pond. As it began swimming, I could see only its head. I thought it might be an otter, or a muskrat, or even a beaver, but I couldn't tell and didn't want to risk scaring it more by chasing it.

After the first island, there was another and another, distributed about a hundred yards apart. Some were pretty sizable, a city block or more in area. Others were tiny, less than half a tennis court. All had trees reaching toward the sky, evergreens mostly. At the top of the tallest tree on one of the smallest islands I saw a big nest silhouetted by the sun. I shaded my eyes and heard a high, squeaky whistle, repeated three times. Swinging my head like an antiaircraft gun, I spotted a gray and white bird, larger than a hawk but not quite an eagle. It swooped past and then wobbled down toward the nest. The bird had a fish about a foot long clasped in its talons and began to use its beak to tear the fish apart, pausing after each head thrust to peer around, maybe making sure everything else was still below it.

In between the islands, I heard no noises, no motors, nothing but the sound of the *Gazelle* and the paddle and almost my own breathing, if I stretched things a bit. A bird I thought was a female mallard flew into a tree, landing on a lower limb and grunting instead of quacking. A couple of other birds, perhaps swallows, strafed the surface after insects. That's when I noticed how long my shadow was on the water. I checked my watch.

I'd been out nearly two hours.

I pushed the envelope a little to go around one more island. Some minnows cleared the water in squadrons of three and four as a large wake followed behind them. On the near shore, two red squirrels ran along single file, the rear one never quite tagging the front one. A sudden hammering opened up above me. When I looked up, it was a woodpecker in a dead tree, only the thing was over a foot tall and had a red crown just like Woody the cartoon character.

Turning the canoe back toward the inn, I thought about that billboard just over the bridge into Maine and realized that I'd forgotten that life could be like this, and that at least a part of life should be. Then I thought about Steven Shea, and how he'd had all this but wasted it with a tasteless house and no regard for the land around it. Then I thought it was looking pretty certain that he'd never again have the chance to see even what he'd contributed to ruining. That he'd . . .

Catching myself, I realized also that a sport like canoeing can do that to you. It gives you time to think.

I picked up my pace and started to sprint just a little, before I thought about some other things the last few hours had helped banish for a while.

"Probably a muskrat, John."

"And the fish hawk?"

"That's an osprey. They're very touchy about people coming near their nests."

"How about the duck?"

"Probably a wood duck, maybe a merganser. Dag could tell you for sure, if you're seeing him tomorrow."

I looked over at Ralph. We were sitting on the inn's screened porch again, dainty insects with schooner wings flitting toward the lights. I swirled a little after-dinner brandy around the bottom of a snifter while he sipped a Scotch on the rocks. His wicker chair rocked, the creaking from the frame a nice counterpoint to the flow of conversation.

I said, "You ever get tired of running an inn, Ralph?"

"Me? No. Oh, there's headaches, sure. You're on call

twenty-four hours a day, seven days a week. City people—no offense—come up here, expect you to be able to fix anything for them right away or call somebody who can. And you got to be able to run the business as well as coordinate the meals and turn down the beds. But hell, John, all the other things I ever did in my life, nothing compares to this."

"I just meant that Ramona told me you were sick in bed the night things went wild at Steve Shea's house."

"Oh, that. Just a headache. A real headache, I mean, from working outside without the hat on. Happens in any job. But inn-keeping? You get to meet people from every state, even a lot of countries. You learn more from them than you ever did from the teachers in school. You're also your own boss, your own planner. *You* decide what color to paint the bedrooms, *you* decide what to put on the menus, *you* decide that maybe you don't tell this guest or that every little thing about the place account of you just don't have a good feeling about them."

"That happen often?"

"Not really."

"Ever happen with Steve Shea?"

Paine stopped rocking. "John, are you trying to . . . interrogate me?"

"Probably just from reflex, Ralph."

The creaking resumed. "Hope so. You're grasping at straws like me, things can't be going too well for you."

"They aren't. Tell me, in the couple of weeks before the killings, did you see anybody out of the ordinary?"

"How do you mean?"

"Somebody walking the road, maybe not dressed for it?"

"Not that I recall."

"Maybe renting a boat from you?"

"No, but then all we got are some canoes, a rowboat, and a little sailboat."

276

I tried to picture Keck Davison's "fishing trip." "How about a seaplane?"

"Seaplane? Well, we do see them from time to time, but I don't recall one this season as yet."

"They pretty hard to miss?"

"Yessir. Those pontoons hit the water, you'd swear a truck was dragging a line of trashcans behind it." Paine looked at me more seriously. "What do you have in mind, John?"

"If somebody other than Shea committed the murders, there had to be timing involved."

"Timing."

"Timing that was the product of planning, and planning that was the product of surveillance or at least a pretty careful survey of the place."

The rocking got slower this time, but didn't stop. "And you figure the somebody walked in or came by boat?"

"It's a possibility."

"Well, now. I guess if I was going to kill those poor people and hoped to pin the thing on Steve, I wouldn't want to be seen or connected with the place in any way."

"Granted."

"That seems to argue for somebody sort of—what, staking the place out, not just walking or cruising past."

"Any suggestions on where that might be?"

Ralph seemed to ponder it. "Just Old Tom Judson's place."

"Ma Judson's brother?"

"Yeah. His new house—well, not so new anymore. In fact, it's kind of gone to ruin since he died. Anyway, Old Tom's place overlooks Shea's house from up on the hillside."

"It does?"

"Oh, not so's to spoil his view. Old Tom's, I mean. No, you can't see Steve's place from Tom's windows, but if you position yourself just so, I believe you could still look down onto Steve's property pretty well."

"How do you know?"

"How? Why, Old Tom pointed it out to me, once when I was up to see him."

"Judson pointed out Shea's place below him?"

"Right."

"What did Judson say?"

"He said something like—mind now, Old Tom was kind of a nasty sort—he said, 'Quite an eyesore, isn't it, Ralph?' "

"And what did you say?"

"I agreed with him."

"And what did Judson say after that?"

"He didn't. Just laughed. Kind of nasty, like I said."

I swirled my brandy a little more. "You also said the house hasn't been kept up."

"Uh-huh."

"Why not?"

A shrug that threw off the rocker's creaking. "Ma didn't care about it."

"Ma Judson owns it now?"

"Sure. She didn't care much for her brother, either, but that didn't stop her from inheriting from him, did it?"

I downed the last of my brandy. "It never does."

Paine inclined his head toward the empty snifter. "Anything else I can get you?"

I thought about the sheriff's gun shop remark. "Yeah. You have a copy of this week's *Uncle Henry's* lying around?"

25

SUNDAY DAWNED BRIGHT AND CLEAR, A LITTLE CHILL IN THE air that Ramona Paine assured me over breakfast would be gone by ten A.M. She also told me the road up the mountain to Tom Judson's house was pretty steep for easy walking. I thanked her, saying I'd try it anyway.

Out in my trunk, I found the old pair of running shoes I kept there just in case. They weren't hiking boots, but they were comfortable and went on over some cotton socks. Wearing rough chinos, and a long-sleeved chambray shirt, I took the plastic water bottle Ramona offered me and started down the road.

I'd seen the village a few times by car, but you learn a lot more about a place walking it than driving it. The housing stock declined in sophistication as I left the village center behind me. Tongue-and-groove clapboard and painted shutters and shingled roofs gave way to peeling plywood and taped plastic and tin roofs. Then came the trailers, some abandoned, two others so dilapidated you'd have thought they were, but for the variety of clothes on nylon ropes between storm-damaged trees.

Finally even the trailers gave way to woods interspersed with patches of meadow and clumps of wildflowers, individually sparse but collectively colorful against green and yellow backgrounds. Birds sang in the branches of now leafy trees, the weather beefing up the foliage since I'd last been there.

Reaching the paved drive for Judson's place, I stepped over the padlocked chain with the orange telltales. The driveway angled left and up, and I started climbing, marveling at the size of the boulders somebody had bulldozed to the sides of the road to make even the one-lane width possible.

There were two switchbacks to the road, each about equal in length by the time my watch said it took to travel them. I got to the top of the second switchback about 10:10. Ramona was right about the chill, the air now flirting with seventy. I stopped to sit on a boulder and drink half my water, saving the rest for the top.

After another fifteen minutes, the driveway broadened onto a plateau, showing a typical split-level in disrepair, a two-car garage partly under the upper level. The condition of what would be the front yard made the Vandemeer place back in Calem look like a candidate for *Better Homes and Gardens*.

I walked up to the house, but the front door was barred by a couple of one-by-sixes nailed in an X-pattern across it. Moving to the garage, I used the palm of my hand to rub the grime and dust off a square, porthole window. Nothing but shadows and old tools and a couple of those jawed animal traps Patsy Willis had described. There was one blotch on the floor that looked awfully big to have been an oil drip. I pulled on the garage handle, but it was locked.

I move around to the rear of the building. Just more high weeds, some little creature I never saw startled enough to flee through them, the stalks swaying from its passage. The back door had a wooden X nailed over it as well.

Finishing my circle of the house, I ended up in front of it again. Except for the obviously suburban structure, I had the impression of visiting an old temple in the jungle being reclaimed by nature, a kind of Elm Street Angkor Wat.

Moving toward the edge of the plateau, I understood what Ralph Paine had meant by view. Someone sitting inside a window of the house would enjoy a vista of surrounding peaks and valleys. However, at the drop-off I could look down and see the gash and slash area of Steven Shea's house and Marseilles Pond itself, about five hundred feet beneath me. The line of sight to the back door of Shea's house and the parking area was unobstructed. Even with the advantage of my elevation, I could barely make out Dag Gates's roof contrasting in shade but not color with the trees around it. Looking south, I couldn't see Ma Judson's place at all. Looking north, I could make out the white, boxy Marseilles Inn clearly, the road running alongside it like a ribbon from a Christmas gift.

I walked the front edge of the clearing until coming upon the path I thought would lead to the back of Shea's property. The trail seemed overgrown, but still followable. Finishing my water, I started down.

Though steeper than the driveway, the path was surprisingly easy, only a few places where I had to turn sideways, the edges of my running shoes acting as cleats to slow my descent. I'm not exactly an Indian scout, but I stopped occasionally to examine the ground and branches and so forth. No bits of torn clothing, but there were some indistinct footprints in flattened areas and a couple of broken-off twigs that indicated someone walked the path, even if not frequently, over the last few years.

When I got to the bottom, I could see Steven Shea's rear door across his graveled parking area. My watch said it had taken me only ten minutes, and that including dawdling over the twigs and other signs.

Going up the steps to the door, I looked back above me. I knew that Judson's driveway and house were there, but I wouldn't have been able to tell that, and I had to bend my neck to the cricking point to see up to where I thought I'd been.

I moved around the deck to the front of the house, listening to the wind chimes and looking downslope toward the waterfront. Some spiky plants were already visible, coming up through Shea's lawn, especially down near the water's edge. Amazing. Nature reclaiming here, too.

Then I went back to thinking about what happened and how.

I want to kill three people, or at least one of them, and blame it on the fourth, Shea. I sit up on Judson's driveway, watching the house below me. I do that for enough weekends, and I get a pretty good sense of Shea's Friday night routine. Or, I already know the routine, and I just wait there that Friday, watching for him to go, then come down.

When do I pick up the crossbow and shoes?

Probably earlier that day, using the keys under the eave and the step, figuring Shea wouldn't check the garage or his bedroom closet before going out for dinner necessaries. That way I don't run a risk of being seen or heard by any of The Foursome before I'm ready.

Assume Willis was right about Hale Vandemeer and Sandra Newberg making a salad together. I'm the killer, and I'm approaching the back door. I hear two people in the kitchen, probably talking to each other over the clattering of cutlery. Because of the time it takes to reload, I need to do them one at a time. So, I move around to the front of the house instead. Slowly, maybe looping down toward the lakefront and using the brush as concealment. I see Vivian Vandemeer on the deck. I maneuver until I have a straight-on shot, or I make a little noise to attract her attention, maybe shaking a bush or two, get her walking over toward me.

Then I aim and fire and bring her down.

Reloading with the stirrup thing, I climb the steps and take Hale Vandemeer, coming out to check on his wife because he heard something. Probably not a scream, since he took the time to close the screen behind him.

Then I reload again and come over Vandemeer's body and take Sandra Newberg coming out of the kitchen.

A cold, cold-blooded sequence.

I leave through the kitchen, laying the crossbow on the path to the gravel car park for Shea to find. Then I climb back up to Judson's house.

No. No, that would leave me kind of trapped. But I can't go out toward Ma Judson's, because it's a dead end, and her dogs would go nuts. Dwight Schoonmaker realized that from one visit. I've been here long enough to stake things out, I'm not going to miss the obvious.

Which leaves the road or the water. All the killer has to do is walk up the road, watching and listening for first Shea, then emergency vehicles, to come down from the village, hiding when they do. Or have a boat somewhere along the waterfront, a little less likely because it's a little more exposed to Dag Gates or anybody else going by in a boat themselves, but still possible.

All in all, simple enough. Awfully subtle, and distant, for Las Hermanas. A good fit for Schoonmaker's evil-competitor theory, if the theory itself made sense. One thing about Schoonmaker's idea did make sense.

Somebody had to have spent some time up here, getting comfortable with the setting and developing the plan. And somebody other than Ralph Paine might have seen a part of that.

* * *

Jack and Jill knew I was coming before Ma Judson did, but I don't think by much.

She was feeding them outside their fenced enclosure, and they suddenly bolted up the road toward me. It was the first time I'd walked the part of the road that went over to her place, having taken the lakeside path the last time I was there. Her section seemed less maintained than Shea's, the ruts deeper and the vegetation encroaching more on the sides and growing in the center of the lane between where tires would roll.

The dogs came to a skidding stop about ten feet in front of me, baying and woofing more than growling. I stood my ground, then did a deep knee bend, resting my butt on my ankles. "Hey, hey, what's the matter?"

The dogs quieted a little, circling each other like excited young skaters practicing figure eights. Down the road, Ma Judson stood with legs apart and fists on hips. The same green felt hat and the same buckskin jacket and, as far as I could see, the same everything else she'd worn five days before.

"Christ come to earth, you back again?"

"Afraid so."

"The bad penny. What is it this time?"

"Same as last time, just some different questions."

A labored sigh. "Well, long's you don't expect me to feed you, too. C'mon up."

She went onto her porch and into the front door of the log house. Jack and Jill ran ahead of me, then ran back, then did their figure eights using me as the center point for the rest of the way. By the time I'd reached the porch steps, Ma Judson was back outside, another bucket of lemonade and two more glasses in her hands.

"Set."

I sat in one of the rough-hewn rocking chairs.

"Say when."

I let her fill it, then drank about half.

Pouring some more for me, she said, "Been spending yourself, have you?"

"Doing some hiking."

"Making the job work for you?"

"Not exactly."

Judson poured herself a glass, then sat on the other chair. "Ask your questions."

I'd given some thought to the order in which I'd bring up the topics. "You're here most of the time, Ma?"

"Most of it."

"In the weeks before the killings at the Shea place, did you see anybody unusual around?"

"Unusual."

"Yes. Anybody you didn't know."

She took a gulp of lemonade, running the back of her hand across her lips, then smacking them. "Can't say I did."

"Seaplane?"

"Seaplane? Not this year."

"No cars, no hikers?"

"Cars by his place, I wouldn't have seen them. Same for hikers. About the only thing I'd see, maybe, is somebody by boat, and the only feller I can think of was after the killings, not before them."

"After."

"That's what I said."

"Can you describe him?"

"I can. He was about your age, probably not as tall. Wore a baseball hat, a jacket like for golfing, not fishing, and he didn't have any tackle in his boat anyway, I could see. Pants looked kind of dressy, too."

So far it could have been Dwight Schoonmaker on his "recon." "Ma, can you describe his features?"

"Didn't get that close to him."

285

"Then how do you know how old he was?"

"The way the man moved. Different people, different ages, move differently."

"How about the boat?"

"What about the boat?"

"Did you recognize it?"

"It was a rowboat with a gas outboard on it."

"Like the one Ralph and Ramona Paine have for rent?"

"Like it. Couldn't swear it was theirs."

Again, the careful observer. "All right. What'd this man do?"

"He come down into our cove here, driving the boat at trolling speed, only he didn't show any tackle, like I said. He made two, maybe three passes back and forth in front of your client's hacienda there, then pulled his boat in."

"Pulled in?"

"Docked it like, by their boathouse. Then walked onto the land."

Dwight, Dwight. "What'd you do?"

"Same as I did with you, young man. Got the Weatherby and went to ask him his business. Only as I'm on the path, I could hear him starting up and moving off. By the time I was onto your client's lawn there, the feller was showing me his back from a quarter mile up the pond."

"So you didn't see if he took anything?"

"No. Can tell you one thing, though."

"What's that?"

" 'Less he knew I was watching him arrive, he didn't bring anything with him that couldn't fit in a pocket."

I looked at her. "Why would he bring anything with him?"

"To plant in the house."

"You mean . . ."

"Incriminating evidence. Christ come to earth, used to

happen every other week on *Perry Mason*, back when I was watching the boob tube."

Then Judson blushed, as she had when she mentioned the dogs sleeping with her. All I could think of as a reason was the word *boob*.

I said, "But nobody before the night of the killings?"

"They pay you more, asking the same question so many times?"

I had to smile over my lemonade. "I went up to your brother's house this morning."

A stiffening. "That's private property."

"I didn't disturb anything. I just walked the land up there and looked down. Pretty good view of Shea's house from the edge of the drop-off."

"Godly view of everything. That's what killed him."

"The view?"

"The attitude he had. That he was God just because he ran the sawmill and could build that house when he had a perfectly good place down to Augusta and the prettiest little camp here you'd ever want to see. He sold them both, then sat up on his mountain like he was Zeus himself, collecting those implements of torture and drinking himself into a stupor. Toasting himself, most likely."

"Have you been up to the house lately?"

"Go up once a week. My duty, as I see it. Check on the place."

"It's in pretty bad shape."

"It's in the shape it deserves to be in, young man. My brother built that house, then was arrogant enough to think the traps couldn't kill him, kill him for what he encouraged people to do to animals by collecting the infernal things in the first place. He sinned this way and that, and the Almighty just caught up to him, is all."

"So you're letting the place go to ruin."

"And why not? I own it, it's my right to do with it as I see fit."

"When you go up there, have you seen any evidence of other people having been there?"

"Better not."

"Why is that?"

Ma Judson looked at me. "Because it's private property. You haven't learned at least that from all the questions you've been asking me, this interview is over, too."

I walked to Dag Gates's place, making enough noise to alert his dog, Runty, well in advance of my getting there. Making noise was easy, the road really deteriorating almost as soon as I left Ma Judson's place at the south end of the cove and began moving along the east shore. It was hard to see how a vehicle could make it over this section in good weather, much less under winter conditions.

I didn't hear any barking, but the chickens started up as I came into view of the back of his house. They flustered around their wire enclosure, probably wanting me to feed them. No dog, though, and no Dag.

I walked through the dust between the coop and his house. Not seeing or hearing anything, I moved toward the lake. The green and white lawn chair was folded and leaning against a tree, but there was no canoe on the ramp. At the tree, I opened the chair and sat down. A loon slid by, beak preening the feathers under its wings. After the loon was a distance away, some fish began rising, making little rings at the surface as they fed on what I assumed was a hatch of insects. A hummingbird zoomed and hovered a foot from my face, whirring like a special effect in search of a Spielberg movie, then zoomed off before I could even register its colors.

About fifteen minutes later, I heard some barking from up the lake. Turning my head, I saw Gates returning in the canoe, hugging the shoreline, Runty up on his forepaws at the bow. One more bark, Dag saying something I couldn't make out, and the dog slid down into the hull.

Gates reached his little dock and turned off the electric motor. Runty jumped onto the weathered planks, staying near Dag rather than coming up to inspect me.

Gates said, "Just in time for lunch."

"Don't go to any trouble."

He raised a metal chain stringer out of the water, Runty yipping at the sizable bass on it. "Brought take-out from my favorite restaurant. Plenty for two, and no trouble past what I'd be doing for myself."

"Then thanks. What can I do?"

"Nothing for now except sit there and tell me what's on your mind."

I watched as Gates repeated his routine of securing the canoe and hopping with the fish to the table with the clamp on it.

He looked back at me over his shoulder. "Go ahead. I can listen, maybe even talk, while I clean this beauty."

I said, "The weeks before the killings, did you see anybody unusual around the Shea place?"

"Unusual?"

"A seaplane, for instance."

"Seaplane. Well, that would be unusual."

"Why?"

"Most folks using seaplanes are fishermen, trying to get into ponds up north you can't access by roads."

"Anything else then?"

"You mean, like somebody who wasn't supposed to be there?"

"Yes."

A shake of the head as the hand did something with the fillet knife. "No. But then, I'm out on the pond a lot, John. You have any particular somebody in mind?"

"If Shea didn't do it, the killer set it up awfully professionally, which would have required some sort of surveillance and planning to get the timing right."

"Time it so the killer got in and out while Steve was down to Ralph and Ramona's."

"That's right."

Gates put a fillet onto the side of the table and played with the clamp again. "Probably two ways of doing that. One's from the water. Just put in a boat over at the public launch in the village, then come down here, making like you're trolling or just sightseeing."

"What's the other?"

Using his knife, he pointed across the pond and up. "Old Tom Judson's place is just about over where Shea's house is, that driveway you see to the right with a chain and orange flags on her as you come onto the camp road off the paved one. You might be able to look down and watch the house from his property."

"I've been up there. You can."

A nod.

I said, "You didn't see anybody suspicious, then?"

"No, but like you said, John, if this person was a real professional, I guess that means I wouldn't have, right?"

Made sense. "How about after the killings?"

Gates crooked his head around to me. "After?"

"Yes. You see anybody then?"

"Anybody suspicious, you mean."

"Right."

"No, aside from all kinds of boats just cruising by the place, like people slowing down in their cars to gawk at a traffic accident. The news up here was full of what happened, and the house is sure easy to spot, you know what you're looking for."

He turned completely around, holding the second fillet

in his hand. "The entrée is ready for frying, but it would be a help if you'd slice up a couple of tomatoes for us."

Ten minutes later, we were sitting in the Adirondack chairs around the camp table on his log-framed porch, a can of Miller's Genuine Draft flanking each plate. The plates contained the fish in breadcrumbs, the tomatoes and dressing, and a couple of hunks of bread. Simple, but another fine country meal. I took a deep breath, felt the diaphragm do a rise and fall, and lifted the beer to my lips.

Around a mouthful of fish, Gates said, "She's getting to you a bit, isn't she?"

"Who?"

He gestured with his fork. "The pond."

I set down the can. "Maybe Maine in general, Dag, or at least this part of it."

"You have that same . . . I don't know, sense about you I remember having back when. I tell you, the people like Shea who come up just for the summers, they don't know what it can be like."

"Being nourishment for the black flies?"

Gates laughed. "Sure, they're a part of it, because everything is. But I mean the folks who see only the daisies in June or the raspberries in July or the blueberries in August, they just miss so much. The leaves start turning the second week in September, yellows and oranges and reds, more than three colors, a dozen varieties of each. Especially the red of the sugar maples, John, like a tall old lady with just one saucy hat. Then the loons band together in October for the flight south, getting themselves into this sickle pattern on the water, fifteen or twenty of them, the way battleships formed up in a newsreel of the South Pacific during WW Two.

"After that, the female black bears begin hibernating, birthing their cubs about a month later. The mother bear, she doesn't leave her den, suckling the cubs without herself urinating or defecating. Some life, huh? She spends half her year half asleep.

"But come November, John? The moon when it rises is . . . different. Here the moon comes up on its side, quartered horizontally, not vertically. The first frost takes care of most of the bugs that bother you, so you can sit out on that dock and watch the sun set and the moon rise. So clear and bright, John, you'd think God's poured fluorescent milk into a glass bowl and suspended it there, just for you, the clouds moving past it so fast in those first winds down from Canada, it's like one of those time-lapse nature films of a night into day."

I'd stopped eating, and Gates suddenly noticed it.

"Sorry," he said. "Sometimes get kind of carried away."

He fumbled his fork, and it flipped over and away from the table. I got up before he could and retrieved it.

"Just give it back here, John."

As Gates cleaned it on the paper towel he used as a napkin, I said, "None of my business, but have you ever tried a prosthesis?"

He smiled. "Tried one. This hook thing. Didn't care for it. And the leg, well, that has what they call phantom sensation."

"That you still feel the leg?"

"More that it still hurts, even though the docs say the injury's all healed. Can't really stand to have the leg thing on. You ever hear about that champion skier, Diana Golden from down by you?"

"No."

"Well, she lost a leg to cancer a while back, so she skis on just one. Clocked her up to sixty-five miles per hour downhill, I heard. She doesn't like to use an artificial leg, even for walking. I'm the same way."

"How about the arm, though? Don't they have these kind of bionic things now?"

A nod. "Call them myo arms—myoelectric, I think is the real word. But I like things simple, John, simple and natural. Besides, getting one of those things repaired, especially if it got wet, wouldn't be so easy up here. You don't rely on it, you don't miss not having it."

I motioned back toward the road. "But how do you get around in winter?"

"I have a phone inside, so I can call Ma. Her old Bronco tracks pretty well so long as you start your driving before the snow has a chance to get too deep. Plus Ralph has a snowmobile, so he can come over the pond to me once a week for what I need and take my eggs back with him."

"What does a snowmobile weigh?"

"Eight, nine hundred pounds, I guess."

"The ice is strong enough for that?"

A laugh. "John, the ice gets thirty, thirty-six inches thick by February. The boys drive *trucks* on her."

"Come on."

"God's truth."

"And they don't go through the ice?"

His face toned down. "Once in a while. Maybe eight, ten a year statewide die doing it."

"That many?"

"Out in Minnesota I hear it's more like thirty a winter. See, what happens is, the ice gets thin over a spring. They call it a rift, because there's like this floe in the center of what looks like solid ice."

"And somebody drives onto it."

"And the floe flips over like my fork did, with the car going down. Not straight down, because the engine is heavier, so it kind of dives at a forty-five-degree angle, away from the rift above."

"And the people inside can't open the doors."

"Right. Hydrostatic pressure, and if the windows are

electric, forget winding them down. That system shorts out as soon as the car's in the water."

"Jesus."

"I talked to a state police scuba guy once. He told me the cold water would seep up through the vents and the undercarriage as the car's going down, gloves and cups and whatever starting to float around your head. Even if you had some air around your face, though, you'd lose lower body function after about three or four minutes on account of the temperature. The victims, he always finds them without their fingernails."

"Their nails?"

"Yeah." Gates stopped a moment. "They always break them off, trying to claw their way through the windows as the water comes up around them."

I thought of Blanca and the other girls from the convertible and set down my fork.

Dag said, "I'm sorry, John. I guess I didn't realize how bad that story sounds."

I took a little beer. "It's not the story, it's me."

"How do you mean?"

I gave him a very short version of the incident outside the condo building.

Gates chewed thoughtfully, then drank from his can. "I can see how the ice story could get to you, John, and I'm sorry for bringing it up. But it seems to me you had plenty of reason to kill those three, and that's all that matters."

"Not quite." I stood up. "But thanks for lunch. It was great."

Dag looked like he was going to ask me to stay, then said, "Can I run you back in the canoe?"

"No, thanks. I think the walk will do me good."

And it did. Some.

26

LYING ON MY BED AT THE MARSEILLES INN THAT SUNDAY AF-
ternoon, I tried to figure out what else I could do. The
answer was, not much from the Maine end. I didn't know
what Steven Shea's "secret" was, and he wasn't about to
tell me. I called DRM, on the off chance that Anna-Pia
Antonelli might be there. She wasn't, and one of Schoonmaker's people manning the switchboard actually laughed
when I asked him for her unlisted home number. He said
to try back again on Monday.

I hung up and called Nancy's home number, but got no
answer. Instead of worrying over that, I dialed the Lynches
downstairs in her building. Drew told me that she was
catching up on some research at the district attorney's office. I was able to reach her at her desk.

"Oh, John, how are you?"

"I'm fine. The case isn't going so well, but I haven't seen
any sign of trouble from Las Hermanas."

"I didn't think you would."

"Neither did I."

Nancy lowered her voice. "I called Area B today. I hope
you don't mind."

295

"I like thinking of you thinking of me."

"A detective named Yolanda King said she'd talked to you."

"What'd she have to say?"

"Apparently the Anti-Gang Unit threw a net and caught everybody but the queen bee."

"I think you're mixing your metaphors, Nance."

"Whatever. Lidia Quintana's dropped out of sight."

"They check with Calem?"

"King said they tried, but other than a car stopping at the house—I think she said of the dead sister's boyfriend?"

"That's right."

"Except for a uniform knocking on the door, nothing from Calem, and no sign of Lidia there or here."

I thought about it. "Then I'm coming back."

"John, she knows where you live."

"If King says the troops are all accounted for, Lidia can't be receiving any information. Either she's in a deep hole with the cover down tight, or she's parked on my doorstep. Whichever it is, I can't live my life hiding from her."

"Well, this Lidia certainly doesn't know about my doorstep."

"Nancy, no."

"John, I've never prosecuted any of her gang, and even if I had, she has no reason to think that I know you, much less that you'd be staying with me."

"Look, my car—"

"So leave it five blocks away and walk to my place. The exercise should do a man your age some good."

"Nance—"

"Or would you rather stay at some cheap motel and have me, an officer of the court, seen lurking around its darkest corners?"

I had to laugh.

Her voice lost the bantering tone. "It's good to hear you laugh, John Francis Cuddy."

"It's better in person, I'm told."

"When can I expect you?"

"About five hours from now."

"Five? I thought it was only a four-hour drive."

"It is, but I have at least one stop to make along the way."

"Mr. Zachary?"

The wiry man set down the heavy maul he'd been holding as the Prelude pulled into his driveway. The house was a small saltbox on some wooded acres, a detached garage half built to the side of the gravel. I'd interrupted Zachary as he was using an old stump to support smaller-diameter log sections for splitting into stove-sized hunks.

Zachary tugged at the brown work pants he wore under a riverboat shirt and over what I'd bet were steel-toed shoes. "You the one called the wife about my ad in *Uncle Henry's?*"

"That's right." I got out of the car and walked toward him. "John Cuddy."

Zachary stropped his hand on the thigh of his pants before shaking mine. He was about thirty-five, dark-haired and clean-cut. "I'm not sure about selling a weapon on the Sabbath."

I looked at the wood. "You need to work on the Sabbath to bring in fuel for the winter. I need to buy a gun on the Sabbath to protect me in my work."

He looked skeptical. "What work would that be?"

I held up the Maine private investigator card, my thumb conveniently over the August expiration date.

Zachary compared the photo on the card with my face. "That's you, all right."

I put the card away and waited.

He made a decision. "Stay right here."

Zachary walked briskly into the house. When he came out a minute later, he was carrying in his palm something wrapped in cloth. Behind him, a woman stood at the front door, watching us.

When the man reached me, he pulled on the string that crossed over the package like a bakery box. Then he delicately unfolded the wrapping.

Zachary said, 'Go ahead, heft her."

It was a Chief's Special Airweight, the aluminum dull, the walnut handle a little nicked. Using the release button on the lefthand side, I swung out the cylinder. Empty.

He said, "I don't have any ammunition for her."

"That's all right. You know how old it is?"

"The wife's father bought her new back in 'sixty-eight, when he moved down to Portland."

I examined the chambers and barrel. "Any idea how many rounds have been through it?"

"No, but I don't think many. He had her for protection in his night table. When he died, we found her there. Too light for my taste, so I've never shot her."

I closed the cylinder. Pointing at the ground, I dry-fired five times. Everything seemed to work right.

I said, "I have some ammunition with me. I'd like to try a few bullets."

Zachary seemed nervous. "On the Sabbath?"

"You wouldn't buy a used car without test-driving it, would you?"

He looked around his yard. "Where?"

I picked up a flat-faced piece of split wood and set it down upright against a big hemlock beside the unfinished part of the garage. I stepped back twenty feet and reached into my pocket. Coming out with three bullets, I opened the cylinder, slipped them into the chambers, and closed the cylinder again.

"Mr. Zachary, could you move back a little, please?"

He did.

I held the gun in a combat stance, pushed the rising memory of Blanca and her friends from my mind, and fired one round single-action, the other two double-action. The piece of wood shuddered three times against the hemlock.

I opened the cylinder and ejected the shells, putting the casings back in my pocket. "I'll give you two hundred for it."

Zachary got indignant. "My ad said two-fifty."

"Two hundred cash. Today, right now."

"Seems low."

"Mr. Zachary, there were two other handguns in *Uncle Henry's* that'd suit me just fine. I called them, too, but I stopped here first because you were the closest. If I have to drive to them, I won't be back."

He wet his lips. "Lumber to finish the garage'll cost near four hundred. That's why we're selling the gun."

"Take my two hundred, and you're halfway there."

Zachary looked at me hard, then turned toward the figure in the doorway. He held up two fingers to her. She nodded vigorously.

Zachary returned to me. "Done."

More than three hours later, I left the car at a parking lot near South Station and waited for the irregular Sunday night bus. I took it a couple of miles down Summer Street to the stop on L Street past Nancy's corner. Then I walked back, a baseball cap down to my ears and an old fatigue shirt over the chambray one, the Airweight like a bulky stone in the side pocket of my chinos.

I made a pretty easy target, but nobody tried me.

After ringing the bell, I heard Nancy loping down the interior stairs. She opened the door for me with a dish towel draped over one arm down past the hand and a blue turtleneck over white tennis shorts as the leisure outfit.

I looked down at the towel, picturing a snub-nosed revolver with a little scored button atop the shrouded hammer. "The Bodyguard."

"Yes." She kept her smile in place. "Despite the fervent hope that I won't have to use it."

As we climbed the steps, Drew Lynch stood outside the second-floor door, a large-caliber revolver in his right hand, the long barrel lying against his right thigh. He nodded to us and went back into his place.

I said, "He's been watching out his window, right?"

"I called him from the office, only to find out you'd already checked on me with him. That was good of you, John."

Nancy opened the door to her apartment, Renfield's back claws clicking on the linoleum as the rear legs churned like the linkage arms on a locomotive.

"He's glad to see you, too, John."

"Wish I could say the same."

"Oh, come on now. You know you love him."

I bent down to tickle Renfield behind the ears. "Anything more on Lidia since this afternoon?"

"It's Sunday, remember? Everybody rests sometime."

I suddenly realized how tired I was, partly from the hiking that morning and the drive that afternoon.

Nancy said, "I have marinated country spareribs in the broiler."

I stood back up. Moving forward, I closed my arms around her. "Can they wait?"

A sly grin toyed with me. "I started the ribs because I thought you'd be too weary."

"I was thinking of a nap, Nance. Just a plain, real nap."

The grin lost its slyness. "Only if I get to tuck you in."

* * *

300

The next morning, I waited until Nancy left for work, watching her walk safely to her car. Then I got on her phone.

A regular receptionist at DRM put me through to Antonelli's office, but her secretary said she was out of the office until noon. I didn't leave a message.

Dead end on Shea's secret, at least until after lunch. "Dead end" reminded me of the cul-de-sac in Calem. When you're blocked off, sometimes it helps to go back out the way you came, maybe see or hear something you missed the first time. I defrosted a couple of English muffins for breakfast, then cleaned up and found a fresh shirt I'd left at Nancy's. Without benefit of disguise, I made my way to the bus stop, rattled with six other people and a surly driver for three miles, and redeemed the Prelude for just under the national debt of Chilé.

I made one pass on the cross street before the cul-de-sac. Everything looked the way it had the prior week except for one thing. Hub Vandemeer's candy-apple convertible sat in his dead brother's driveway, the chrome bulb of the trailer hitch thumbing its nose toward the sidewalk. The kind of hitch you might use for towing a boat, come to think of it.

Parking a block away, I decided to try Mrs. Epps before Nicky and his uncle. It was a good decision.

She answered her door right away, letting me in this time without even asking for the password. The pale blue dress was almost identical to the first one I'd seen her wearing.

The eyes fixed on me. "I trust this is somehow important?"

"It could be. How long has that red convertible been in your neighbor's driveway?"

"I don't keep a journal of such things."

"Ballpark."

"Perhaps since some time on Saturday."

"Saturday."

"Yes. As in two days ago."

"Did you see who drove up in it?"

"No. I have better things—"

"Anyone used it since?"

Epps didn't like being interrupted, and let me know it by taking her time answering my last question.

"Not that I've seen."

"Have you seen anyone else around the house?"

"The Vandemeer house?"

"Yes."

A slight smile. "No."

I looked at her. "What question should I be asking you, Mrs. Epps?"

The smile grew bigger but colder. "There is more than one house within sight."

"My client's place."

Nothing from her.

I said, "Have you seen anyone around the Shea house?"

Epps let the smile take over her face. "Yes, as a matter of fact I have."

"Who?"

"The house-sitter."

"House-sitter?"

"Yes. She introduced herself to me, said Steven Shea had hired her to look after things."

"Can you describe her?"

"Spanish girl, quite tall, in one of those ghastly parochial school uniforms."

Here we go. "She have a scar on the left side of her face?"

"Rather a prominent one."

"All right if I use your phone?"

That terminated the smile. "I trust for only a *local* call."

27

HALF AN HOUR LATER, I WALKED UP THE PATH TO THE VAN-demeer house, just putting one foot in front of the other and keeping myself from glancing at the picture window. Instead of even trying the bell, I started banging on the door. When it opened partway, I bulled through it, my hand lingering on the lock plate before closing the door behind me.

Nicky Vandemeer faced me, empty-handed, in jeans and the U2 sweatshirt. The first time I'd met him he'd seemed cool and confident. Now he looked strung out, his color bad, the hair matted instead of just mussed.

"Hey, man," he said, voice cracking a little from the tension inside him as he raised it, "I would've let you in, no sweat."

"Don't you ever go to school, Nicky?"

He jammed his hands into his jeans pockets like an embarrassed cowboy. "My parents got wasted, remember? It's like an excellent excuse."

Still the raised voice, too loud for the distance between us. I just watched him.

303

Beckoning me to follow him into the living room, he said, "Come on in, man."

Come on in, not "So, what do you want now?"

I followed him. There was no salsa music this time, no sound at all in the house.

Vandemeer tried to plop himself into the colonial-style couch again, but like the voice and the attitude, he couldn't quite pull it off.

Taking one of the matching chairs, I said, "You seem awfully cordial for the boyfriend of a girl I had to kill."

He cocked an ear, which clinched it for me.

Nicky said, "Hey, man. I mean, like what could you do?"

I just watched some more. And listened.

The kid fidgeted in the couch, his sneaker losing traction on the carpet. "So, that it?"

"No, Nicky, it's not. Actually I'm here to talk with your uncle."

The bad color drained to white. "My . . . uncle?"

"Hub. I'd like to have a talk with him."

"He, uh, he ain't here."

I tilted my head toward the picture window. "That's his car in your driveway."

"That?" A failed laugh. "Oh, that's not his. That's—"

"It's his, Nicky. Where is he?"

Her voice came from the dining room threshold. "He's down in the game room, Mr. Private Eye."

I turned my head slowly to look at her. Lidia Quintana was wearing the school outfit, her hair in a braid and no makeup. Another Intratec Tec-9 rested in her right hand, the perforated barrel lazing in a slow circle circumscribing my chair.

I said, "I thought you'd be next door."

Quintana smiled, the gap in the upper teeth like a third eye on me. "I seen you go up to the old lady's house. I figure, you be stopping here next, so I come over first."

Vandemeer said, "Lid', I don't—"

"Shut up." Never breaking the smile. "Nicky, you go over, give our Mr. Private Eye a little frisk, make sure he don't have nothing on him."

The boy wet his lips, clearly not crazy about the suggestion. "Lid', what if he like . . . grabs me or something?"

I said, "Then she'll shoot us both."

Quintana laughed. "You a smart one, all right. Nicky."

He got up awkwardly, quartering his way over to me. With shaking hands he did the front of me, not very comprehensively.

Lidia said, "Okay, Mr. Private Eye. Now you stand up, and Nicky checks the other places."

I rose, slowly. Vandemeer ran his hands quickly and lightly over my back, hips and legs, clearly feeling funny about touching another male at all,

"He doesn't have anything."

Quintana said, "Okay. Come on, Mr. Private Eye. We gonna go down, see the uncle. Nicky, you go first."

He didn't argue with her, which I thought showed some sense on his part. As he drew even with Lidia, she backed away from the line of march, making sure there were always at least eight feet separating her from me. Very professional.

Vandemeer led us into the kitchen and down a half flight of stairs. Despite the differences in the architecture of the houses, the paneled game room resembled the one in Steven Shea's place. The furniture was teal leather rather than art deco, but another wet bar nestled into one corner and duplicate photos of The Foursome in slightly different frames dominated the walls. A relatively happy space in which to be entertained.

Except I doubted the preceding guest thought so.

Hub Vandemeer lay sprawled on a leather lounger that seemed about half reclined. His hands dangled off the armrests, his head lolling at an uncomfortable angle into the light. The uneven eyelids told me the angle and the light weren't having nearly the impact that Lidia's knife had delivered to the center of his chest. The room had a jumbled smell to it, the coolness of the basement retarding but not preventing decomposition and not even retarding the reek of urine and feces.

Nicky put his hand up to his mouth and nose, covering them.

I imitated him at the door upstairs, letting my voice rise and crack. "Hub looks pretty dead."

Quintana said, "Mr. Car-man, he come over Saturday, just after I get here. I have to walk fifteen blocks from the bus, they don't got real good public trans' out here, you know it? Anyways, he don't know I'm up in the bathroom, looking at the blisters I got on my feet from these fucking shoes. Mr. Car-man, he's really on the rag, screaming to Nicky about how one of his cars—like he still owned it?—one of his cars, it gets used in a drive-by, these spic chicks—you like that, Mr. Private Eye? Spic chicks?"

"Not especially."

"Me neither. I come out, I show Mr. Car-man my spic-chick Tec-9 here, he all of a sudden decide he don't like it, either. He start apologizing, but he seen me here, recognize me from the television and all. I say that to him, he say, oh, no, no, he don't gonna tell nobody I'm here. I tell him that's right, we gonna tie you up in the basement for a while, just so I can get away. Mr. Car-man, he wanna believe that, he wanna believe it so much, he probably pee his pants right then, promising me he don't tell nobody, we let him go after that."

I looked over to the body. "Where're the ropes?"

Quintana's scar curled over her cheek. "Poor Mr. Car-man, we don't get that far. I sit him in the chair, I decide I really don't like that spic-chick shit. So I come up behind him, tell him to put his hands behind the chair, and I come down with my knife, both hands, like I'm gonna do myself the way those Jap warriors used to in their own stomachs, but surprise, surprise, his heart get in the way."

She laughed. "For a car dealer, he got a big heart."

I thought I heard Nicky stifle a wretch.

Lidia gestured casually with the Intratec. "How about you sit down in that other chair, Mr. Private Eye."

"I don't know, they look kind of hazardous."

She laughed again. "You got some balls, man. Too bad we don't get a chance to get it on. But I don't know, maybe I shouldn't be thinking about fucking the man killed my sister. What do you think, Nicky?"

The boy didn't know what to do, other than he didn't want to take his hand away from his nose and mouth. So he just shook his head twice.

To me, Quintana said, "Nicky, he fucked my sister enough. She told me about it. But since I'm here, he can't seem to get it up."

She turned to the last living Vandemeer. "Well, tell you what. How about you take a little *venganza* for Blanca, huh? A little revenge for the love of your life, maybe get your business back in business?"

Nicky started to shake his head, but Lidia leveled the Tec-9 at his chest, which froze him. Then she brought the muzzle back to me, walking to him carefully, using her free hand to bring his right one up to receive the pistol. She kissed him on the right ear, her tongue outlining the cartilage.

Releasing the weapon to him, Quintana said, "All you got to do is pull the trigger." Nicky's eyes stared at me hollowly above the hand he still had held to his face.

As Lidia stepped behind him, her eyes lit up, the scar on her face doing a snake dance of pleasure.

In the rising voice, I said, "O'Boy."

Boots and shoes seemed to tumble down the basement steps. Nicky was a touch slow turning his head and body, dropping the weapon as he saw the boots came with black pants and black Kevlar vests, M-16s pointing at him under the steady eyes of Sergeant Harold Clay and another cop I didn't know. Paul O'Boy was behind and between them, his snub-nosed thirty-eight on Lidia, not Nicky.

Even Quintana seemed thrown off by the noise. Then she inched a step toward the weapon on the floor, her right hand flexing.

O'Boy said, "Go ahead, you can make it."

The tone a father might use to coax a kindergartener onto her first two-wheeler.

Lidia weighed something. Then, crossing her arms, she said, "Fuck you."

And that part was over.

308

28

"YOU SAY THE UNCLE WAS DUE BACK AT WORK TODAY? THE kids were pretty stupid not to hide his car."

I said, "I doubt they were thinking that far ahead."

O'Boy nodded. We were sitting in the front seat of his unmarked sedan, engine off and windows down. The flurry of official activity around the cul-de-sac and the Vandemeer house reminded me enough of the scene outside my condo building that I was trying not to pay attention to it.

O'Boy said, "Still, it was good of you to go in first and rig the door for us, case the guy was still alive."

I looked at him. "He deserved the chance."

Another nod.

I said, "Can I have my gun back now?"

He passed it to me, handle first, cylinder out and empty. The bullets trickled like nuggets from his other hand into mine.

Reloading, I looked toward Mrs. Epps's ranch. I couldn't see her, but I imagined she was having a field day through one of the windows. "You never checked the Shea house?"

O'Boy shrugged. "Got the word from Boston about the

drive-by with you and the girls there. Had a uniform stop at the Vandemeer house once Friday, another time Saturday, talking to the kid Nicky as kind of a pretext for watching for this Lidia. A real sweetheart she turns out to be."

"The uniform didn't call in the convertible?"

"He did. We ran the plate, came back registered to the uncle's dealership. Seemed righteous enough to be in the kid's driveway, uncle visiting the orphan, you know?"

O'Boy said the last in his innocent voice.

I ignored the lead-in. "But you never checked the Shea house?"

Another shrug. "Who knew? Besides, I kind of figured that was your territory."

This time I picked up on him. "Because of me investigating the killings up in Maine."

"That's right." O'Boy fiddled with the turn signal. "So, you figure this here cleans that up for you?"

"No."

"How come?"

I explained why the gang theory didn't wash.

He mulled it over. "I don't know, Cuddy. I was you, I'd really think about trying to hand your jury this Lidia on a platter. No harm done, seeing she's gonna be a guest of the Commonwealth for the rest of her natural life, and she's a nice place for Shea to lay off the killings up there."

"The jury might buy it, but I don't."

"So what do you do next?"

I looked at him, thinking about how he'd used me as a cat's paw for his new chief. "I think Lidia summed it up pretty well."

"Huh?"

"When she said, 'Fuck you.' "

O'Boy shook his head. "Harsh words. They're never a help, Cuddy."

* * *

When I gave my name to the receptionist at DRM, her security guard companion called Dwight Schoonmaker. I waited until he came through the door, trying very hard to give the impression he hadn't been running.

"What do you want?"

I said, "I need to talk to Anna-Pia Antonelli."

Schoonmaker's shoulders moved around inside his suit, a tan poplin today. "She's been away. She's probably pretty busy."

"I'd like to see her anyway."

He seemed to make up his mind as though the decision already had been dictated to him. "Come on."

"No security badge this time, Dwight?"

He looked at me, then his guard, before saying to the receptionist, "Do it."

Thirty seconds later, I followed Schoonmaker through the heavy door, into the big room with lots of employees, and to the special elevator.

I said, "Antonelli's with Keck Davison?"

The doors opened. The chief of security stepped in and said, "Come on," stressing the last word this time.

Inside, I waited until the doors closed. "You know, you really shouldn't have gone against the sheriff's orders."

Schoonmaker's jaw rippled. "What orders?"

"About not going onto Steve Shea's property up in Maine."

"I don't know what you're talking about."

"You were seen, Dwight baby."

Without having to, he pushed the button for "3" again.

Tyrone Xavier was waiting for the elevator as it opened on Davison's office suite. Xavier wore a blue suit instead of the blazer, converging wrinkles behind the knees of his pants. He seemed surprised to see me, but not particularly startled.

"Mr. Cuddy, right?"

"Good memory."

"For the things that matter."

In a clipped voice, Schoonmaker said to him, "Mr. Davison available?"

Xavier never shifted his eyes from my face. "You'll have to ask one of the secretaries, Dwight."

Schoonmaker bit something back, then walked to the nearest woman behind a desk.

Xavier said, "How's Steve doing?"

"Getting by."

"That bad, huh?"

I kept my voice neutral. "How's business?"

The smile of a Marine who's set the perfect ambush and knows it. "About to be booming."

"I'm glad for you."

"I earned it."

"Maybe that's why I'm glad."

Xavier's smile wavered as he raised his wrist. "I've got a meeting in the city. You be needing to see me about anything?"

"If I do, I'll leave word with Keck. By the way, is that really a Rolex?

"No, but it will be." His smile dissolved. "Take care, Mr. Cuddy."

"You, too."

As Xavier went by me and into the elevator, Schoonmaker's voice said, "Hey, Cuddy, let's go."

Today Davison had on a suede sweatshirt with horizontal bands of burgundy, ivory, and kelly green over the blue jeans. His office looked more out of *Star Trek* than a wardroom. A modernistic, contoured swivel chair in turquoise leather and matching visitors' chairs complemented the thickest piece of Plexiglas I'd seen in the building. A black halogen lamp like an oil derrick rose from one edge of the desktop.

Davison watched me over the half-glasses from the swivel chair as I took one of its sisters across from him. When Schoonmaker started to sit as well, the boss said, "Dwight, I believe I can handle Mr. Cuddy on my own."

Schoonmaker bit back something else. Another day like this, he'd have no tongue left.

As the door closed, Davison came forward a little in his chair, hands folded prayer style on the Plexiglas. "You come to tell me something?"

"No. I'm here to see Anna-Pia Antonelli, but I'm guessing you told Dwight to let you know if I came back, and he told his watchdogs to let him know."

Davison regarded me for a moment. "I seem to keep forgetting, I can't very well play the bumpkin with you, son. I don't like to find myself forgetting things like that."

"I don't think you forgot, Keck. I think you just try each part of your game plan each time. Most of them have worked in the past, you never know when one might work again in the future."

He settled back in the chair, wiggling his nose to reposition the grannies a little. "I wonder, can we drop the sparring and get down to it?"

"We already have."

The nose stopped wiggling. "Anna-Pia."

Aunt Pee-yah. "That's right."

"Why?"

"Between her and me."

"What if I say no?"

"Then I wait outside her place on Beacon Hill and catch her coming from or going to work."

Davison considered something, maybe whether I'd been to Antonelli's condo. He decided not to find out. "What if that might cost her this nice job she's got here?"

"That would be your choice and probably her lawsuit."

A grin. "You know, I thought about that before I hired her. I really did. A woman, good-looking like she is. What if there's trouble, what if she causes an uproar, how'm I supposed to deal with a sexual harassment claim if it's brought by the company's own goddamned lawyer?"

"But you hired her anyway."

"Because she was the best available. Not just the best woman. The best. You build a business by working hard, son. You keep a business by bringing in people who can keep it going. Anna-Pia's one of those people."

"And Steven Shea another?"

"Or Tyrone. Like we said last time."

"I saw Xavier on the way in. Seemed pretty buoyant."

"There's reason to be. Looks like that sale is going to close."

"Despite Shea's situation?"

"Because of Tyrone's intervention. He's done a fine job."

"Xavier is good. Antonelli is good. Even Schoonmaker's good, at least in doing what you tell him."

"No vice in obedience, son."

"Where does that leave Shea?"

"Welcomed back if he's found innocent."

"And if he's not?"

Davison grinned again. "When I was in college, they used to say sociology was the restatement of the obvious. I never liked sociology."

"Then let me see Anna-Pia, or you'll be living with the obvious for a long time to come."

He came forward more, reaching up and taking off the glasses at their bridge. "You think Steve didn't do those killings."

"That's right."

Davison's eyes engaged me directly. "I want an honest answer to this next one, son, or I swear I'll crucify you. You figure I got a skunk in my woodpile here?"

"I don't know, and I won't unless Antonelli answers some things for me."

The man tossed his glasses to the side of the desk, hard enough to release some steam but not hard enough to break them. Then he pushed a button on a panel. I heard the bleating noise that Xavier had described.

When Antonelli's voice came on, Davison said, "Anna-Pia, Mr. Cuddy's going to be there to see you in about two minutes. You tell him whatever he wants to know."

Without giving his general counsel a chance to reply, Davison pushed the button again and looked up at me. "You gonna let me in on what you find out?"

"Probably not."

"Thought so."

"It's not his privilege to waive, John."

We sat in her office, the plants providing a nice counterpoint to the austerity of the DRM standardization and her gray business suit. The Gucci garment bag occupied a corner on the window wall, the briefcase lying against it.

I said, "How was your trip?"

Antonelli tapped a pencil on her blotter. "Difficult. The meetings in Atlanta went poorly, and then we were dragged to an oldies disco where the waitresses jumped up on the bar to shimmy, and some of the female patrons sat on steps, doing chorus-line leg kicks to Frank Sinatra's "New York, New York." The one hour I had to myself at the pool was shattered by some crazy guy in a jogging suit who race-walked around and around the atrium, headphones on and a book held up to his face."

"We?"

"I'm sorry?"

"You said, 'We were dragged to the disco.' "

"Yes, Tyrone and me."

I pictured the wrinkles in his pants, the kind you get

from sitting through a long flight. "He didn't mention he'd gone with you."

"Why would he?"

She had a point. "Let's back up a step. Why isn't it Davison's privilege to waive? He's the president of your client, right?"

Antonelli seemed more comfortable returning to lawyerly ground. "The attorney-client privilege belongs to the client, but here DRM isn't the client. Steve came to me for personal legal advice."

"Which you can't tell me about."

"Right."

"Because his telling you is protected."

"Not even a court could make me reveal what he said."

"Even if it involved a future crime?"

She suddenly seemed less comfortable. "You've been talking to a lawyer about this?"

"Not yet. I had a year of law school a long time ago."

"Well, if you talk to Gil Lacouture, he'll tell you the same thing."

I thought back to Nancy and her concern about conflicts. "Actually, I wasn't so much thinking of seeing Steve's lawyers in Maine as the Board of Bar Overseers down here."

"The Board . . . ?"

"Right. The people who license you and who might want to hear about any conflict of interest that jeopardizes one or both of your current clients."

Antonelli tapped the pencil harder, then realized it and stopped. "I don't know what you mean."

"I think you do. I think Shea told you something that strains his relationship with DRM, something you maybe didn't see coming until the cat was out of the bag, and what you'd heard put you into a conflict of interest between him and the company. I think that's eating you up because of the mess Steve's in, otherwise you wouldn't have raised it with me the first time I met you."

She said, "It's still Steve's privilege to waive."

"He won't talk about it. I don't understand why, but he won't. And if it could help me get him off, your refusing to reveal what Steve told you is like sealing the death warrant he's already signed."

Echoing Lacouture, she said, "Maine doesn't have the death penalty."

"You saw Shea a few days ago, you might have some doubt about that."

Antonelli blanched. "He's . . . all right, isn't he?"

"He's going out of his mind, seeing the frame close in around him and not being able, or willing, to clear himself by telling me whatever the hell you and he talked about."

"I don't see . . . I don't see how what he told me could help him in this."

"Let me, or Lacouture, be the judge of that."

"I can't even tell Gil unless Steve allows it."

"Look, counselor. I'm at an impasse here. Three people are dead in Maine, four more down here. I've been bouncing around, not finding much that will help Shea. If you've got—"

"But don't you see, the information . . . What he told me can only hurt him, not help him."

"Why?"

"Because it gives him . . . It could be construed as a motive for his wanting to kill . . . some of the people who died."

"Let me guess. We're back to the affair between his wife and Hale Vandemeer, right?"

Antonelli's hand shook with the pencil in it. "I can't tell you—"

"And you're afraid that if Steve's knowing about the affair came out, he'd be seen to have a pretty good reason for killing Sandy and Hale and probably Vivian as well to make it look like some roving psychotic had wasted the whole house."

"You don't—"

"Well, let me remind you, counselor, that little dose of extramarital poison isn't exactly a secret anymore. Half the law enforcement personnel in two states know about it, so the only thing you can do is maybe give me some kind of antidote for it. Why did Shea talk with you about the affair?"

Antonelli put down the pencil. Standing, she went to the window and looked out. I was about to start again when she said, "Steve found out about the affair from the Vandemeers' son, but he didn't tell Sandy he knew. He really didn't even blame her, he understood how all his traveling and her losing her job could send Sandy off a bit. Steve was just sorry he hadn't seen the affair coming, especially since they were all such good friends."

"What was Shea going to do about it?"

"He had an idea for maybe saving the marriage, but he wanted to pass it by a woman and a lawyer, and I was the only person he knew who was both. With the glory of hindsight, I think he kind of wanted to put me in a conflict. He's like that, you know?"

"Always wanting to have an edge."

"Yes." She exhaled. "Yes, like putting me in a bind that I think he sensed without his maybe being able to explain it technically."

"So?"

"So he told me his idea, which conflicted me because he obviously didn't want anybody else at DRM to know about it, especially with his big deal coming down. Which is the only way he'd be able to afford to do it, anyway."

"Afford to do what?"

29

"YOU MUST BE WICKED IN LOVE WITH HIGHWAY DRIVING, MR. Cuddy."

"Sheriff, I'm not exactly thrilled about being up here again. And I wouldn't have to be, if you'd put me through to Shea when I called from Massachusetts."

Feet on the typing tray, Willis patted the sagging hank of hair on one side of her head. "Wasn't me. Was your client."

"My client?"

"Shea didn't want to take the call. Not even sure he'll see you in person."

"I'd appreciate a shot at it."

She patted the hank on the other side. "Well, you kept your promise about that gang stuff not coming up here." A stern look. "You aren't carrying a concealed weapon around my county?"

"Locked in the trunk of my car."

"That where it'll stay?"

"I hope so."

Willis kept the stern look.

I said, "How about Shea?"

She dropped the look and reached for her phone. "Long's you're here, I suppose it doesn't cost anything to try."

He shuffled ahead of the same guard. If I weren't expecting my client, I'm not sure I would have recognized him.

There was a stain on the orange uniform shirt, and his pants drooped. He hadn't shaved, probably not since I'd seen him Saturday, two days before. The eyes were bloodshot and vacant. A man losing a shaky grip on what he used to call his life.

Shea didn't even wait for the guard to close the door to the room before saying, "What the fuck do you want now?"

"Steve, I need to ask you something."

He stayed standing. "What?"

"Sit down."

"Why?"

"Please?"

Shea dropped into the other chair as though he'd never be able to make it back up. "If you can't get me out of here, why don't you at least leave me the fuck alone?"

I didn't have too much time before he'd walk on me. "I spoke to Anna-Pia Antonelli this morning."

"So what?"

"She told me about your conversation with her, about your plan with Sandy."

It turned out Shea did have the strength to get up. "That bitch! That fucking two-faced cunt! What the hell right did she have?"

He was looming over me in a menacing way. I kept my

320

seat, waving through the glass that I was okay. The guard stopped coming forward, but didn't go back to his station against the wall.

Shea's eyes were blazing, then he slumped down into the chair again. "Christ knew about betrayal. Now I do, too."

I gave him a minute. Then, "Steve?"

Nothing.

"Steve."

"What the fuck more do you have to hit me with?"

"I think that your plan to save the marriage was a good idea."

Shea lifted his chin an inch. "You do?"

"I do. It takes a pretty big man to get whacked with his wife's affair, then try to save things without telling her what he knew."

Tears glistened at the corners of his eyes. "I only wanted . . ." Closing the eyes, he lowered and shook his head.

I said, "To be willing to sacrifice your career, move up to Maine year-round to spend real time together. That took a lot of courage."

Shea just kept shaking his head.

"Steve, why didn't you tell me about this before?"

The head stayed down. "When Sandy was . . . alive, the plan made sense. Then when . . . everybody got killed, I realized the plan implied I knew about the affair, and that seemed . . . I don't know, so *damning* somehow. Also, if I did beat this thing—" The head jerked up, the eyes blazing again. "And I am innocent. I didn't do this!"

"I believe you."

Shea looked at me, but I couldn't tell what he was seeing. "When I did beat this thing, I wanted to be able to go back to DRM, start my life again. I couldn't very well do that if they . . . if DRM knew about what I was going to do. Keck

Davison wouldn't welcome back somebody who'd been ready to jump ship."

It made sense. At least to a man in Shea's mental and emotional condition.

He shook his head some more. "Besides, I didn't see any . . . point to it. I mean, what difference does it make that I was going to quit DRM and move up here?"

"That might depend on who knew about it."

"Nobody."

"Anna-Pia did."

"Yeah, but she wasn't supposed to tell anybody."

"Getting your conversation out of her was like pulling teeth. I don't think she told anybody else."

"Then I don't know."

I remembered something that had bothered me. "The wine."

"What?"

"You asked Ralph and Ramona to stock your favorite wine."

"Oh, right. I wanted to see if they could get things like that for when we were up here year-round."

"Could they have known about your plans?"

"Not unless Sandy told them."

I stopped. "Your wife knew?"

Shea's turn to stop. "Yes. I mean, I kind of . . . broached it to her a few weeks ago—no, a few weeks before . . . that night, to see what her reaction would be. It was more positive than I thought. She looked at it as maybe an experiment she could help manage, kind of a 'Yeah, let's give it a try,' you know?"

I nodded to keep him going. "Could she have told somebody?"

"No. No, we were going to start by telling Hale and Vivian about it at dinner that . . . that Friday. But there'd be no reason for anybody else—"

Shea stopped cold, though I hadn't interrupted him. "What is it, Steve?"

He shook his head. "I . . . I just remembered. As we were driving up that Friday, Sandy said . . . We were talking about raising the idea with Hale and Vivian, and I was being real careful about my words, because I didn't want her to know I knew she was . . . the affair thing. And Sandy said, 'Oh, I called Owen Briss last week about the plowing.' "

"The plowing?"

"The snowplowing. If we were going to be up here all winter, I'd need to have the road plowed, and sure as hell Ma Judson wasn't going to spring for it."

I pictured the plow on Briss's property. "Why would your wife have spoken to Briss, though?"

"He mentioned to us once, when he first came to the house, that he did all kinds of other stuff, like chopping firewood, plowing in the winter, if we ever needed anything like that."

"Yeah, but didn't Sandy know you'd had a dispute with him?"

"No. No, I just told her that the guy had ordered the wrong things, and we'd have to do them differently. You see, I didn't want to tell Sandy anything that might make her leery of moving."

Like having an angry workman living a few miles away. "What did Briss say to her?"

"Something like, 'You want your road plowed, call somebody who can do it right.' He's a blunt sort of asshole."

"How did you leave it with your wife?"

"Just that I was going to straighten things out with him. But I . . ." Shea ran down. "I never got the chance to."

I thought about it.

My client shunted his head until I looked at him.

He said, "I still don't see the point, John. What the hell

difference does it make if Briss knew we were thinking of moving up here?"

"I don't know, Steve."

The sun was a ways from going down, but the shade thrown by the dense trees kept me from seeing the big rock pushing through the top of the dirt road. I felt the Prelude bottom out on it, but fortunately the car kept jouncing along. As I pulled into sight of the mated trailers, Owen Briss was standing on the dirt that passed for a front yard, holding a beer can in one hand and straddling something beneath and between his legs.

The something was Cinny, her body drawn into the fetal position, the fists up, covering her face.

Never an easy day, I thought.

Briss looked over as the Prelude came to a stop, dust wafting up around me as I got out of it. He crushed the beer can, spraying himself a little with what he hadn't drunk. I began walking toward them, no sign of Mourner, the spotted pointer. "Evening, folks."

"Get off my property."

I kept going. "Not till I get a few answers."

"Man your age oughta know better than to talk like that."

"Man my age was able to talk like that last week. Let her up."

As I got closer, Briss backed off from Cinny. He threw the crushed can at me, missing by a mile. "What do you know about it?"

I didn't think he'd need much goading. "To meet you is to know you, Briss."

That got a roar and a charge. I moved to the side and used the edge of my shoe to scrape his right shin from knee to instep. He went down, more whining than roaring.

"Mother of Christmas! You broke my goddamn leg. You broke it!"

"Not likely."

Cinny had uncurled and was sitting up, smiling demurely like a 1940s bathing beauty at the beach. The impression was spoiled by the jeans and torn blouse and bulges over the belt and pocket lines.

She said, "You saved my life."

"I don't think that's possible."

Cinny's smile was unaffected. Briss had stopped writhing long enough to pull up a pant leg to check on his shin.

I said to him. "I want simple answers to simple questions. You feed me a line, and I think Cinny will know it, and she's going to tell me so."

"Damned right," said Cinny.

I stepped toward Briss. "First, when did Sandra Newberg ask you about snowplowing the road to their house?"

He looked up from his leg. "What?"

"When did she call you about the snowplowing?"

"Christ, I don't know. Week, two weeks before the killings, maybe."

"What'd she say?"

"Said her husband and her were gonna move up here full-time. Said they'd need their camp road plowed, and was I interested in being the one to do it."

"What'd you tell her?"

"I told her to find somebody else."

"Why weren't you interested in doing the job?"

"Because her goddamn husband already stiffed me on the bannister work. What do you think I am, stupid?"

"We'll come back to that. What did you do about it?"

"Do? I didn't do nothing."

I said, "Cinny?"

"I don't know," she said, twirling some hair around an index finger. "He's a mean fucking nail-driver, he gets himself going."

The carpenter glared at her.

I said, "What did you do about it, Briss?"

Sullen glance at me. "I told you, nothing." He rallied a little. "You don't have no badge. I can call—"

I decided to try a bluff. "I think whoever knew about their moving killed those people."

The sullen look got lost. "What?"

"You heard me."

"What are you saying? I wouldn't plow for them, I'm gonna kill them?"

"You tell anybody about their plans?"

"No."

"Nobody?"

Briss tended to his shinbone. "Well, I maybe mentioned it, is all."

"Mentioned it."

"Yeah."

"Who to?"

Eagerly, Cinny said, "I know."

The sign at the Marseilles Inn was flapping a little on the breeze coming off the lake. Walking toward the screened front door of the inn, I didn't hear either sixties music or the noise of dishes and silverware.

Ralph Paine's face came out before I got to the entrance. "John Cuddy! Didn't think we'd be seeing you again so soon."

"Neither did I, Ralph."

His voice was light, but mine wasn't, and he could tell. "What's the matter, John?" His eyes drifted to my car. "Oh, I see."

When I didn't turn around, Paine came out the door and ambled toward me. I sidestepped carefully, but he just moved by me to the Prelude. As he knelt beside the left rear tire, I saw what he'd meant.

FOURSOME

Paine touched his index finger to the puddle of brownish liquid growing on the ground under the wheel well. He brought the finger near his nose, then held it up for me to see.

"Afraid it's clutch fluid, John. You must have cracked the case."

The rock on Briss's road. "Can it be fixed?"

"Yeah." A grunt as he got to his feet. "But not by me. We can call the garage in the morning."

"Ramona around?"

"On the porch. Mondays we don't serve dinner. Not much call for it." His brows knitted a bit. "Why?"

"I'd like to speak to both of you, if I could."

"Sure." Not so sure, then a little more oomph in it. "Sure, sure. Come on."

I let him go ahead of me.

Opening the screened door, Paine called out. "Mona? Mona!"

Her voice carried in from the porch. "Yes, Ralph?"

"Mona, it's John Cuddy. He's back."

"Well, bring the man out here and then fetch him a drink."

Ralph smiled and gestured I should go to the porch. "Screwdriver?"

"No, thanks."

I waited until he processed that, then waited some more. He went in front of me to the porch.

Ramona was sitting in one of the elephant chairs, looking out at the lake, some sort of needlework in her lap and overflowing onto the wicker armrests. "Sorry I can't get up, John, but if I do, I'll send a million things to the floor."

"That's all right."

Ralph said, "Have a seat, John."

I shook my head.

Ramona looked at her husband and then back at me. "What's the matter?"

"I just had a talk with Owen Briss."

Ralph shifted his weight a little and leaned against the wall between the porch and the inn. "He was over here today."

Ramona said, "Doing some finish work in one of the rooms. We're having a little love seat built under one of the bay windows on the second floor."

"I talked with Cinny, too."

Ralph said, "Cinny? What about?"

Ramona looked at her husband and back to me a second time. "What's the problem, John?"

"A week or so before the killings, Sandra Newberg let Owen Briss know they might need snowplowing done, starting this winter."

Ralph and Ramona exchanged confused looks.

I said, "Cinny said that Briss told you two about it the next day."

Ralph scratched his chin. "I believe he did."

Ramona said, "We were kind of surprised, but . . . what difference does it make?"

I watched them. It was possible that a married couple could improvise a George Burns and Gracie Allen routine this well, but I doubted it.

I said, "Just surprised?"

Ramona frowned. "Well, Steve never said anything to us, so we didn't pay much attention to it."

Ralph said, "Mona, that's not quite right."

She looked at her husband. "What do you mean?"

"I remember hearing you talk about it in the kitchen that next morning."

"You . . . remember?"

"Sure do." Ralph looked to me. "I figured, Steve and his wife want to move up here full-time, that's their business.

328

But Mona, she was rushing around, trying to put breakfast on for a couple of guests, and she just sort of blurted it out."

"To one of your guests?"

Ramona said, "Oh, I remember now, Ralph."

He scratched his chin again. "Thought you might."

30

"GIVEN UP ON MOTOR VEHICLES, JOHN?"

"My car broke down over by the inn, so I borrowed a canoe from Ralph."

Dag Gates nodded amiably through the screen. He was sitting in one of the Adirondack chairs on his porch, Runty lying against his master's hiking boot, ears up, watching me with his ghost eyes. Gates himself had a can of Miller's on the small camp table to his right, a series of rope sections over the arm of the chair next to his right hand. No weapons in sight or within reach. Unless you counted Runty.

"Come on inside."

I opened the screen door and stepped across the threshold, just far enough into the porch so the door wouldn't slap me in the rump.

Gates said, "Have a seat?"

"No, I think I'd rather stand."

"Suit yourself, John, but the signs are good for one spectacular sunset tonight. We could share a beer, watch her together in about half an hour."

"I don't expect to be here that long."

He nodded again, thoughtfully this time, and reached for his beer. "What's on your mind?"

"I figured it out, Dag."

"Did you, now?"

"Yes. From the beginning, I couldn't really put a finger on it. Some of the people back in Massachusetts had a motive for killing one or more of those three people and wanting Shea out of the way, but the thing required a lot of local familiarity and planning, which made it hard to believe somebody from down there was the one."

Another nod.

"But I couldn't see any motive up here. Why go after the seasonal goose that lays some golden eggs in a poorish area, even if a goose like Shea does kind of get on people's nerves a little? It didn't make sense, till I found out that the goose decided to stop migrating."

Gates took a healthy swig of beer.

I said, "Or, more to the point, you found out about it, delivering eggs to the inn one morning."

He set down the can, deliberately. "Well, you got half of it."

"Tom Judson being the other half?"

Gates lowered his hand to scruffle Runty between the shoulders. "Old Tom did this to me, John, and I made him pay for it with the piece of land you're standing on. Only thing is, it ate him up to think of me across the cove from him, on *his* land. So he found Shea and sold out, moving up atop the mountain to look down on me looking over at Shea and wincing, John, wincing every time I saw what he was doing to the land."

"It was legal at the time, I'm told."

"Legal and right, those are two separate concepts, John. Completely separate. Anyway, after I watch Shea's construction crew strip the land and build his house and lay his 'lawn' all the way down to the waterfront, into what should have been a buffer zone for runoff, I couldn't take it. Halloween night, I got on my old leg prosthesis and hoofed it up to Judson's new place."

"Hell of a climb."

"Used his driveway. Took me a time, but I was all fired up. Old Tom, he was sitting in the living room, drinking and watching his television. All the natural beauty around him, John, and the man ossifies himself in front of the tube. Well, he listens to me for about ten minutes, then starts to laughing and pushing me out, out through the door in the kitchen to the garage, the 'servant's entrance,' he called it. Then he went back inside, locking the door on me. I stood there, seething with frustration about him, what he'd let happen, and I see the cases of his liquor in one corner and all his traps hanging from hooks on the wall. So I figure where Old Tom'd walk to get to his car or his booze, and I use my hand and foot to open a trap and set her down in his path. Like a trick or treat, see? I figured, he'd sold out to Shea and let the land be ravaged, I couldn't maybe do much about that. But he'd also done this to me, I'd show him what it was like a little."

Gates stopped petting the dog. "But then I'm walking back home here, I figure maybe I shouldn't have done that. Wasn't right for him to do it to me, maybe it isn't right for me to do it to him. So I get in the door, and I dial Old Tom's number, only I don't get any answer. I try three more times that night. Nothing. I'm not up to climbing all that way again, the stump's killing me from the prosthesis. I decide I'll try him again in the morning. Well, I guess Old Tom, he was running out of whiskey, and he went out to his garage to get some more. He tripped and went down into that trap on his knee, and what should have been a broken ankle or lower leg ended up getting him killed, bleeding to death, wiping off all my fingerprints as he thrashed around."

Gates looked hard at me. "I had some bad nights after that, John. Bad nights. Not worrying so much about getting caught, no. More about what I'd done. But after a while, guess what?"

"The guilt started to wear off."

A nod and a little smile. "I thought you'd understand, especially after you telling me about those gang girls you had to shoot. I got away with Old Tom, and pretty soon it started feeling like it was the right thing to do."

"Like it was right to do The Foursome?"

He looked as if he wanted to spit. "They had no respect for the land, John. Or the sense of the pond, the things they did. The parties, the Jet-Skiing and the water-skiing, the music blaring out across the cove so's you couldn't hear the loons over it. The noise that was bearable a couple weeks a year, six, eight weekends, that would not be bearable all year, every year."

"Why kill them in May, then? Why not wait till they were up here in the fall or winter?"

Gates dug little furrows in his forehead. "Wasn't sure I'd be able to pull it off first time I tried. Maybe Steve wouldn't need to go to the store for once. Maybe they'd stay bunched together all night, so I couldn't get them one at a time and be able to reload. And besides, why should I waste another whole summer with them, John? Why wait another three or four months to start restoring things to the way they could be and should be? The trees, now, all the trees they destroyed? Takes five minutes to cut one down, but fifty years to grow one back. I likely won't be around for that. But I've already been over there a couple times at night, planting some low shrubs and bushes."

I thought about the new growth I'd seen from the deck the prior weekend.

He said, "Those'll take hold and spread out, with the rain and the birds helping them along. They'll re-establish that buffer zone, John. Slow the runoff and stop the silt before it gets into the pond."

I shook my head. "Won't change the house, Dag. Somebody else will just move in, maybe bring back the lawn and be noisier than The Foursome ever were."

A grin that stopped just this side of madness. "I get wind of that, a little prudential lightning just might have to strike the place. She'll burn down fast, before any fire equipment can get in to her. Shea won't rebuild, he'll need the insurance money for that fancy defense you're helping him prepare. Pretty soon, the whole area'll look like Old Tom's place must now. Restored, returned to nature."

"What if Shea gets off?"

"Not likely, John, not likely. Patsy Willis has a pretty strong case, and what's more, she believes in it. Folks around here know her and trust her. Jury'll hear Patsy telling it and believe her. All you've got is a pipe dream of how some poor crip gimped his way to your client's house and somehow shot three people in cold blood with a crossbow. Doesn't hold up, John."

"Doesn't have to, Dag."

More little furrows. "The hell does that mean?"

"I don't have to convict you. All I have to do is give Lacouture enough ammunition to create a reasonable doubt in the jurors' minds about Shea doing it. He gets off, maybe you stay free, but he's still going to be across the lake from you, and after the testimony at his trial from me, you'll never dare try anything on him again. You'll be back where you started, only with three more killings on your conscience."

The next smile crossed the line into madness. "Conscience. I'll tell you something about conscience, John, though I bet it's something you already know about yourself. After that first one, after Old Tom, I was troubled something fierce, like I told you before. But after these last three? Not a sleepless night, not a wink did I lose over them. They despoiled their surroundings, Shea and his friends, turning this little piece of heaven into . . . into New Jersey, for God's sake. They deserved to die for that, and he deserves to spend the rest of his days in a prison, staring at the human despoiling he's going to see all around him. He could have had this, John. What I had. Instead he raped the earth, and he'll reap that harvest."

"Not if I testify, Dag."

An exasperated sigh. "I thought you might be different, John. I knew you were from a city, too, but I thought you could see the beauty of this place, feel for yourself what I did when I first saw her, appreciate why I had to do what I did."

"You didn't have to do it, Dag."

He shook his head slowly. "You're a smart man, John. But not smart enough for your own good. Runty!"

The dog was up and snarling, screwing its haunches into the porch floor and about to spring. I reached into my pocket for the Airweight, hoping not to have to use it. My eyes on Runty, I took a step backward toward the door-frame, just catching Gates yanking one of the rope ends on the arm of his chair.

Something like a battering ram hit me in the back and sent me sprawling toward his foot, my hands reflexively out and down to break my fall, Dag's boot already arcing in a nifty soccer kick that turned out the fading sunlight.

The cramping in my right thigh brought me most of the way out of it, the low quizzical clucking of the chickens helping a bit. Some wooziness welled inside my head under the gag in my mouth and over the pain in my cheek. I opened one lid, then the other. Lying on my back in shadow rather than darkness, I hadn't been out long, but when I tried to move my left wrist from under me to check my watch, I got only a clinking noise from a plastic-covered chain that constricted the cramp in my thigh even more.

I was on the ground in the rear yard, my right lower leg doubled up under the back of my thigh, some of Dag's stringer wrapped around the thigh where it joins the hip and the ankle above my shoe, like a Hollywood harness to fake an amputation at the knee. The rest of the stringer was around my left wrist somewhere behind me, tying lower right limb to upper left limb in a . . . diagonal.

"Good to see you're awake, John."

I turned my head. Gates and Runty sat on a log, watching me. Halfway between us, two hunting knives from his bookshelves were sticking in the ground, most of both blades still showing.

"Ralph helped me do that section of log over the door as a deadfall, to scare away the bears. I saw you coming down the pond, I figured you might just have figured out what happened. Seemed like a good idea for me to get her ready to greet you, in case reason didn't work. Which, I'm sad to say, it didn't."

I rocked until I could roll onto my side. The dog whoofed softly, like a mock cheer at a ballgame.

Dag said, "Don't think you'll be able to do too much with that gag, only one hand. Slipknot, bitch of a thing to undo even with ten fingers working on it. And once you get to that knife, I won't be giving you time to use it on anything but me. If you can."

I tried to estimate the distance to the knives. Maybe eight feet for each of us, with Gates a strong favorite to get there first even if he didn't know when I'd move.

Dag shook his head slowly, like he had on the porch. "Sorry to haul you out here, but the ground'll soak up blood a lot faster and better than those floorboards."

I felt the dirt of the yard. A full inch of dry powder from

being pounded by his foot every day back and forth to the chickens. He was right about the blood.

"Of course, I thought about just towing you out behind the canoe and sinking you once we were in good deep water, but I'd still have to kill you first. To be sure you weren't going to come to and thrash around like Old Tom must have when he felt the teeth of that trap chomping through the femoral."

A warped smile. "No, I'd have to poke some holes through your lungs anyway, might as well be here and in a fair fight, let you go out like a man should." The smile turned wise. "Now, I know what you're thinking. You're thinking they'll be on to me no matter what, finding your body and checking for rope marks or knife wounds or whatever. Well, I have to tell you, John. This time of year, the little beasties on the bottom are all feeling that surge in the appetite brought on by the spawning spirit. I weight you down right, maybe using that popgun of yours to help, my guess is the crayfish alone'll pick you clean before Patsy and the state boys think to start dragging the pond for one missing private investigator. Besides, I leave Ralph's *Gazelle* back by the northern islands, everybody'll start looking over there, especially after I tell folks you must have had a problem on your way back because you sure left here safe and sound and chipper as a munk."

I shook my head as slowly as he had his.

"Come on now, John. I got away with Old Tom without even any planning aforehand. I grant you I worked on doing Shea and his friends for almost two weeks. Just before I heard from Ramona about Shea's moving up year-round, I saw his wife and the guy in the other couple, saw them through my binoculars, loving each other up in the middle of the week when their spouses didn't seem to be around and they didn't think anybody was watching. Well, I was watching, and thinking, too. Thinking about what a good motive that'd give your Mr. Shea for killing them. So I started using the spare keys to get into the garage and house, practicing with that crossbow till I could split a twig at fifteen yards, picking the spot on their shoreline where I could beach the canoe nice and quiet behind the underbrush. Then that day, using the keys again to get the shoes and the crossbow, toodling along that night in the canoe, the binoculars letting me spot Steve starting up his four-wheeler and leaving for the country store. Easing on over there, crawling through the brush, and taking those despoilers, one by one as they came to me. Even left Patsy a little help, wearing my prosthesis and Shea's shoes to make them bloody. I thought that was a nice touch, John, a one-legged man managing to make both shoes bloody, instead of just one. I left the bow itself where Steve'd find it and scoop it up, getting his prints all back over it."

The warped smile again. "But, at worst your situation here falls somewhere between the two extremes, so to speak. I've had a little time to plan it, and besides, my on-the-job training in these matters should stand me in good stead. What do you think?"

I was thinking what Teen Angel had taught Sheriff Willis and me years apart a long time ago. Blade parallel to the ground, come up and in under the ribs. Twist hard to the strong side of the major hand, do as much damage as possible.

Gates hopped up, Runty slipping to the ground. "Oh, I know. You're thinking this isn't really going to be all that fair a fight, what with me having a good deal more experience in being shy the relevant limbs. Well, I apologize for that, John, I truly do. But I can't see any other way."

He gestured to the knives and then to me. "Probably your best chance is to kind of scrabble on your hand and knees over to take one of them, then hope you can get me as I come down at you with the other. But I guess you have to go with your own sound judgment on this sort of thing, eh?"

I got onto one hand and two knees and began moving toward the knives, learning pretty quickly that I could pick up only one support at a time if I didn't want to collapse in the dust. Gates gave me a head start of three or four lurching steps before bounding nimbly as a kangaroo over to the knives and snatching one of them before bounding back. I grabbed a fistful of dirt as he hefted his weapon in the palm of the right hand.

"Just had a flash of me letting you get to the knives first only to see you throw one into the woods and come after me and Runty with the other."

I nodded. He smiled.

Then I rose to a full kneeling position and threw my fistful as hard as I could at his face.

Gates's forearm came up, but not quickly enough to keep all the dirt from his eyes. He troweled the forearm back and forth across them as I used my right hand to get upright onto my left leg and come forward for the other knife.

That's when Runty charged me.

I dropped down again and used my open hand to shovel a sandstorm at him.

The dog yelped and veered, yowling as his paws worked furiously at his closed eyes. Gates got one of his own eyes cleared, rubbing at the other as he tried to shush his dog. Instead Runty kept yowling, bucking around the yard in circles, his snout dowsing toward the ground.

Two more stutter steps and a lunge by me, and I had the other knife. Dag noticed and feinted toward me once clumsily, the closed eye hampering his depth perception. I rolled and braced with my hand and got up on the left leg as the dog crashed through the underbrush and out of sight but not hearing, its cries piteous.

Gates said, "You're going to go a little more slowly on account of Runty, John."

As I tested my hopping, Dag worked on clearing his other eye, getting to where it just blinked rapidly, the tears running down his face with some pink to them from burst blood vessels somewhere in the white. My weight canted a little to the left of vertical, I found I could do pretty well, as long as I didn't hit a soft spot in the dirt.

Gates now began to adjust to his worse eye, hopping forward in a bracketing way, shepherding me toward the log he'd been sitting on. I wanted no more part of that than a fighter wants to be backed into a corner of the ring, so I tried to sidle left and away. He cut me off, his left leg a pogo stick, mine a faulty crutch. The Jukado from the service gave me some balance, the jogging and Nautilus some muscle strength, but against Dag I had no hope of winning an endurance test.

He seemed to sense what I was thinking. "Not as easy as it looks, eh, John? Those tendons and ligaments around the knee, you got to do lots of leg lifts, some with the foot out to the side, to build up and support the joint for this sort of thing. Why don't you try and end it quick, either way? Come for me, John. Come and kill me."

No, it was still my best bet to make him come to me first. He kept the left-right/in-out bracketing going, edging closer after each series of movements. Runty's yowling had calmed down, as the dog seemed to be going hoarse.

Then Gates feinted wide right before leaping left. In a smooth movement he spun around, slashing at me with his knife. I instinctively shifted my weight and, without a right leg under me, went down heavily.

"Sorry, John," he said above me, "Looks like this'll have to be it."

"That'll do, Dag."

Gates and I both looked over to the rutted, weedy road

mouth. Ma Judson stood there, left foot in front of right, green felt hat at a determined angle, the old Weatherby at her hip and holding a little north of Dag's belt buckle from thirty feet away.

"Ma, what're you doing?"

"Might ask you the same. Heard Runty raising a ruckus, and I come over to find you trying to skewer a man."

While Gates hopped a few steps toward her, I slid the knife carefully between my neck and the gag and began sawing away on the cloth.

Dag tried a smile. "Cuddy here, he went just plain crazy, Ma. Tried to kill Runty with one of my knives."

"That why you trussed him up like that?"

"Well, yeah. I had to—"

"That why you got him gagged, too?"

Gates seemed confounded by that one.

Judson said, "What's the matter, you afraid he'd *bite* Runty?"

Dag tried a laugh that didn't work.

The sound of my knife ripping through the last fibers of the cloth brought his attention back over to me.

Watching Gates, I said, "He killed your brother, Ma. And the three people across the cove."

"Don't listen to him, Ma."

Judson said, "Why not? Listened to you first, didn't I?"

I said, "Dag found out that Shea and his wife were going to move up here year-round. He couldn't stand that idea, so he set up Shea by killing the others."

"Shut up, Cuddy!"

Judson lowered the muzzle a little. "Dag?"

He changed tacks. "They were going to ruin it for us, Ma. Ruin things all the year through instead of just for a little of the summer. I couldn't abide that, and neither could you."

The old woman gnawed her lower lip.

Gates said, "But he's the only one who knows, Ma."

I said, "No, I'm not."

"He came here alone. We get rid of him, we'll be all right. The pond'll be all right. We'll get everything back to normal again."

Judson said, "Dag, what that Mr. Shea did to his property was wrong, but what you did was wronger. This here, this killing of another innocent, that'd be wrongest of all."

I saw Runty coming back cautiously through the woods behind her.

Gates saw him, too. "But Ma, Cuddy'll just spoil it for all of us!"

"No, Dag. He'll just spoil it for you, account of what you've done already."

"But—"

Judson said, "Put down the knife, Dag."

I said, "Ma, Runty is coming up behind you."

She didn't look back. "Don't matter. He won't bite a hand that feeds him, no matter what Dag here might tell him." A breath. "Dogs are a lot better that way than people, oftimes."

Gates looked at his dog, then at Ma, then at me. I was no more than two bounds away from him.

He said, "I don't believe you'd shoot me, Ma."

Judson brought the muzzle back up to serious. "Be a bad thing to count on, Dag."

Gates executed a turn to me on the ball of his foot, like a member of a precision drill team. Raising my knife, I got to my knees.

Judson said, "Dag, don't."

He gave me the madness smile with the half of his face she couldn't see. Dr. Sardonicus. "Don't believe you'd shoot a neighbor, Ma. Not over Old Tom and those despoilers."

"Wouldn't be over them, because I can't bring them back. I can save Cuddy here, though, and I will."

"Ma—"

She brought the stock to her shoulder. "It's wrong, Dag, wrong, wrong all over wrong. And if you can't see that, my not pulling this trigger can't never save you."

The madness smile spread wide, and his torso dipped a little, putting the coil into his spring. Gates left the ground and was still on the rise when a barrel from the old gun spewed flame and thunder. A sickening sound filled the air, the whumping noise a broom makes hitting a rug over a clothesline. Dag lofted left and capsized, losing the knife and landing on his back.

Runty was to him first, yipping and pushing his nose at what used to be the left side of his master's chest. Ma Judson moved quickly, almost beating me. Gates's eyes were open, the right one fluttery, maybe from the residual dirt, but I doubted it. Every time he breathed, there was a gurgling sound in his throat, and little bubbles of blood came up through several of the red-rimmed holes in his shirt.

Judson took one look and said, "I'll get the Bronco."

Something like Dag's voice said, "Ma, hospital's . . . twenty miles."

"We'll still try."

"Ma, I wouldn't make it . . . to the end of the camp road."

Judson's voice quavered. "Well, we can't leave you in the dirt to die, Dag."

He looked toward the west. "Sun's setting. Be mighty fine . . . to sit in that lawn chair a while."

Judson got me untied from the chain stringer. I went to the waterfront as she took off her buckskin jacket and pressed down on as many of his wounds as she could. Between us we managed to get Gates up and into the chair at the side of the house, the far ridge across the pond visible between a couple of tree trunks and over a low, needled pine branch.

The sun touched the ridge tangentially with its rounded bottom, firing the underbellies of the clouds above it like bricquets. The shoulders of the clouds blushed toward lavender and then deep purple before the pale blue background of the sky. The part at the horizon finally hazed toward pink as all the clouds darkened and scudded slowly southward.

Dag Gates got to see most of it.